"If this is to go any further, ma'am, You must come here and be kissed."

"We are still virtual strangers, my lord."

"Even so."

Judith had taken the impression that the earl was young and overcivilized, unlikely to assert his will. She was learning her error. She slowly turned and stood in front of him.

He took her hands in his, capturing her with those intense eyes. "I understand that you loved your husband dearly. In fact, his hold on your affections is one of your greatest recommendations. But if we are to be married, I expect you to be able to accept my kisses and attentions in bed without shrinking. If you cannot, tell me now."

There was always a price to pay, but marital duties would not be an unbearable burden. She just didn't much like to be kissed on the lips. It was such a sloppy business. "I will do my duty."

He nodded. "There is another condition. I insist that you leave off mourning entirely."

Judith thought how strange, and pleasant, it would be to be out of black, then remembered she must not let that pleasure show. "Very well."

She waited tensely for his kiss, but he hesitated thoughtfully then drew her toward a chair, sat, and pulled her onto his lap.

"My lord! What are you doing?"

"Forgive me for being forceful," he said while holding her with quite remarkable strength, "but I need to be sure we are physically compatible."

Dear Reader,

I hope you'll enjoy *Christmas Angel*. I particularly enjoyed writing this novel because it's a Christmas story, and also an older woman/younger man story, both storylines that I enjoy, and both potentially stressful, especially in a new relationship. The children made it more so, of course.

Apparently, it's theater lore to avoid child characters because they don't always do what they're supposed to. In books they can be very useful, however, because they can be relied upon to not always do what they're supposed to and thus upset adult plans one way or another.

I loosely based the structure of Leander's house on Bodiam Castle in Sussex. If you have access to the internet, you can read about it here: www.wikipedia.org/wiki/Bodiam_Castle

In case you're wondering, I wrote Sebastian Rossiter's poetry myself, which is why it's not very good, despite its popularity at the time!

Christmas Angel is the third book in my Company of Rogues series, following *An Arranged Marriage* (Nicholas and Eleanor) and *An Unwilling Bride* (Lucien and Beth). Both those books dealt with edgy topics, and I remember my editor at the time saying, "Jo, remember: this will be a Christmas book." I got the message, but truly, I enjoy writing books in which the problems are ordinary misunderstandings, lifestyle differences, and a boy's pet rat.

An Arranged Marriage was the first book I ever wrote, and I finished it in 1977—a decade before I was published, so I've known these guys a long, long time. I wrote the last Rogues story, *To Rescue a Rogue*, six years ago. You can find the complete list on my web site: www.jobev.com/reghist.html

There you'll see another book after *To Rescue a Rogue*. Though I've completed the stories of the Rogues themselves, there are spinoffs and there will be more because the Rogues' world is my Regency world. They're simply there, and so are their friends and families. Readers have asked for stories involving the families of the two Rogues who died in the war before my stories begin. They also want the story of a smuggling earl.

So now it's the Rogues' world, and there will be more stories in time in which Rogues will play a part. I, too, enjoy catching up on their lives and their families. Some, like Beth and Lucien, are still working the kinks out of their relationship. Others are completely happy, and probably hiding from me in case I do anything to disturb that!

You can see my recent books at www.jobev.com/recent.html and also sign up there for my occasional newsletter.

Happy reading always,
Jo

CHRISTMAS ANGEL

JO BEVERLEY

ZEBRA BOOKS
KENSINGTON PUBLISHING CORP.

http://www.kensingtonbooks.com

ZEBRA BOOKS are published by

Kensington Publishing Corp.
119 West 40th Street
New York, NY 10018

All Kensington titles, imprints, and distributed lines are available at special quantity discounts for bulk purchases for sales promotion, premiums, fund-raising, educational, or institutional use.

Special book excerpts or customized printings can also be created to fit specific needs. For details, write or phone the office of the Kensington Special Sales Manager: Attn.: Special Sales Department. Kensington Publishing Corp., 119 West 40th Street, New York, NY 10018. Phone: 1-800-221-2647.

Zebra and the Z logo Reg. U.S. Pat. & TM Off.

ISBN-13: 978-1-4201-3114-7
ISBN-10: 1-4201-3114-1

First Printing: November 1992

20 19 18 17 16 15 14 13 12 11 10

Printed in the United States of America

Chapter One

"If only they wouldn't keep falling in love with me."

Leander Knollis, Earl of Charrington, leaned his head against the high back of his chair and soberly contemplated the shadowed ceiling. It was late on a November night. Only a crackling fire and one branch of candles provided illumination in the small drawing room of Hartwell, the Marquess of Arden's charming cottage in Surrey.

Despite Leander's lugubrious tone, the said marquess did not seem inclined to tears of sympathy. In fact Lucien de Vaux burst out laughing and even his wife, Beth, hid a smile.

"What else can a handsome war hero expect?" asked Lucien.

"Good God, man. War heroes are two a penny within months of Waterloo."

"I did say *handsome* war hero. Stop smiling at the young hopefuls at Almack's. You know the power of your smiles."

Leander flashed him a humorously bitter look. "I do ration 'em, Luce. But I can hardly go a-wooing with a scowl on my face."

The three of them were comfortably informal. Leander and Lucien had shed their cravats and let their shirts stand open at the neck. Beth was in a loose cloth gown with a large Norwich shawl around her shoulders. She sat on a footstool by her husband's chair, resting contentedly against his knee, his hand a warm, familiar presence against her neck.

"I don't know," she said thoughtfully, studying Leander with a twinkle in her eye. "There's something so irresistible about a tortured soul. I think we ladies all think we're the only one able to provide the needed solace. No woman can resist such a challenge."

"I don't present a challenge," protested Leander. "I've been a very paragon these past weeks. I dance with the wallflowers, I'm polite to the chaperones, and I'm not too obvious in my search for a bride."

"Then," Lucien said, "I suggest that you choose a bride with all speed. I can vouch for the fact that marriage makes life more comfortable in a vast number of ways." His fingers played a secret message among the curls at Beth's nape, and she looked up at him with a smile.

They were still newlyweds, at least in their own opinion. The wedding had been in June but their marriage had not truly started for some weeks after that, and a number of other events had conspired to keep them from this delayed honeymoon until September.

And now, after only six weeks of blissful privacy, an uninvited guest had arrived at the door.

Leander Knollis, Earl of Charrington, lately of the Guards, had only been a name to Beth before this evening. He was one of the Company of Rogues, however, and so she had not been surprised when Lucien unhesitatingly made him free of their rural retreat.

The Company of Rogues had been formed in his

first days at Harrow by the enterprising Nicholas Delaney. He had gathered twelve carefully selected boys together, and formed them into a protective association. During their school years they had defended each other against injustice and bullying. In the years since they had largely been a social group, coming together when occasion permitted, but it was understood that the bond still held. Any of them could call on the others at need.

Beth was familiar with seven of the Rogues and three were dead, killed in the wars against Napoleon Bonaparte. The remaining two were Simon St. Bride, who held an administrative position in Canada, and Leander Knollis. All she knew of him was that he had abandoned a promising diplomatic career to join the army; had survived Vittoria, Toulouse, and Waterloo; and was now apparently seeking a bride and being balked by the fact that all the young ladies were falling in love with him.

Fleeing London and the Little Season he had, of course, headed for the nearest Rogue—Lucien.

"I would be happy to choose a bride," Leander said somewhat sharply. "I thought the world was full of females who only cared about money and title. Here I am, prepared to lay both at the feet of a suitable lady without reservation, if only she won't fall in love with me."

"And they all do?" queried Beth skeptically. In her opinion, Leander Knollis was a little too high-flown in his manner to be taken seriously.

Leander looked at her. "You seem a sensible woman. You wouldn't fall in love with me, would you?"

Beth looked at him, really looked at him, for the first time. She found she wasn't sure of the answer.

At her hesitation he groaned and leapt to his feet. He dragged Lucien up to stand beside him. "Look at us! I am *not* a particularly handsome man!"

Beth studied them. It was hardly a fair comparison for Lucien was quite ridiculously good looking, and that wasn't just her wifely partiality. Even when she had first seen him, when she'd feared and hated him, she'd compared him in her mind to a Greek god. He was over six foot, with clean-cut features, guinea-gold curls, and beautiful eyes and lashes she coveted for their as yet unconceived children.

Lord Charrington was a head shorter. Though he was well made and graceful, there was nothing remarkable about him except a slightly foreign air. That was not surprising, for he had been born and raised abroad. Beth was not sure what created the Continental impression, for his clothes, speech, and manners were all impeccably English. Perhaps it was the occasional eloquent gesture, the number of words he wrapped around a simple statement, or the quick-silver expressions which could flicker over his lean features.

The average English gentleman was much less *mobile*.

Apart from these mannerisms he was quite ordinary. His hair was as plain a brown as her own, though he wore it in a wavy, rather long style which was appealing in its very carelessness.

But then there were the eyes.

Whereas Beth's eyes were a simple blue, his were a strange, pale color, perhaps a light hazel; it was hard to tell in the candlelight. Slightly sunken and heavy-lidded, they still had a bright intensity which caught the attention and, quite likely, the heart. They shone and yet they contained shadows suggesting hidden pains. Doubtless it was just a trick of their deep setting but, along with that Continental flavor, it was an intriguing combination.

He looked both *different*, and *wounded* and, she added to her surprise, *dangerous*.

Not particularly physically dangerous, as Lucien was, but formidable in his secrets and his will.

She shook off her thoughts, surely products of the late hour and the port she'd drunk. "No, you're not particularly handsome," she said, "but I can see that a woman might easily lose her heart . . ."

"Enough," interrupted Lucien. "Do I have to throw him out?"

Beth smiled at him. "I was about to add—if that heart is free." She turned to the earl. "Tell me, my lord, why do you object to a young lady you are wooing falling in love with you? It would seem to be highly desirable."

"Perhaps, if I'd settled on one yet."

"Only perhaps?"

He resumed his seat with a sigh and she thought he would not answer. He was clearly uncomfortable with discussing his feelings. But then he said, "I seem to lack the capacity for romantic love. I have never experienced it and so I doubt I ever will." He shrugged. "I can imagine nothing worse than to be bound for life to a woman who dotes on me, when I care rather less for her than I do for my favorite horse."

It was shockingly blunt and Beth was silenced. She instinctively reached for Lucien's hand.

It was Lucien who said, "I don't recollect that you have a reputation for celibacy."

Leander looked up coolly. "What has that to say to anything?"

"And did all these women fall in love with you?"

Leander glanced at Beth. "I think we may wish to save this discussion for later."

After a blank moment Lucien laughed. "For fear of offending my lady's delicate ears? She'd have your balls!"

Leander looked shocked.

"Lucien!" Beth exclaimed, "just because I am a

follower of Mary Wollstonecraft does *not* mean I will tolerate vulgarity.''

He met her eyes with a hint of challenge. "I've told you—I'll treat you as an equal, or a lady on a pedestal. Your choice.''

Beth let the matter drop. These difficult questions were still not entirely settled between them, and perhaps never would be. They managed. She smiled at the earl. "In truth, my lord, I would resent being protected, especially from such common matters as a gentleman's amatory adventures.''

His brows rose but he said, "I assure you, there has been nothing common about mine. . . . However, if I am to let you into my bedroom, I insist that you cease to be so formal. My name, as you know, is Leander. My friends call me Lee.''

"And mine is Elizabeth. My friends call me Beth. So, Lee, tell us why your past lovers never fell in love with you.''

He took a thoughtful sip from his glass. "To be truthful, Beth, I'm not entirely sure they didn't, which makes me uneasy. I don't like to think myself a cruel or thoughtless man.'' He shrugged. "But it's the way of the world. An unmarried man takes married women or whores to his bed. He does not expect them to fall in love with him. It would be a singularly pointless thing to do.''

"Do you think then that love is under human control?''

He met her eyes. "Yes, I do, at least as far as avoiding foolish love. However, I fear it is not possible to force oneself into love. If it were, I would be happily at the feet of Diana Rolleston-Stowe who is well-bred, intelligent, healthy, and possessed of thirty thousand pounds.''

"And one of the doting ladies, I gather. But if love is so easily restrained, why is Diana in love with you? All she has achieved is to have driven you away.''

He caught the satiric edge to her comment and smiled without mirth. "Ah, but that is the fault of our romantic modern ways. Time was, a marriage could be arranged without much attention being paid to feelings. Very civilized. In these degenerate times girls think they should fall in love with their husbands, so as soon as an eligible *parti* pays one particular attentions she sets her heart free. I have not yet devised a way to show even a guarded marital interest without triggering this response."

Lucien entered the debate. "You should pretend you're marrying for money."

"I tried that with Miss Rolleston-Stowe. It failed to make a difference. Of course, being the owner of a large fortune and Temple Knollis hardly helps my attempt to pass myself off as a fortune hunter." His features expressed self-derision, emphasized by spread hands. "I am a rich earl, recently freed from the wars, and only twenty-five. Who would believe I would single out a young lady for reasons other than impulses of the heart?"

Beth was interested to note that Lord Charrington became more flowery the closer they came to the nub of the problem. She left the obvious question to Lucien.

"So, why are you singling them out?"

The earl's expression became flat and Beth knew he would lie, or at least evade. "I am an only child. I have evidence from battle that life is a chancy thing. I think I should marry."

"On the other hand," countered Lucien blandly, "you have, I believe, a fair clutch of cousins."

If possible, the earl's expression grew even blanker. "Yes, my uncle has sired eleven children, ten living, eight boys. The name and title are assuredly in little danger."

"So, my advice is to put aside any matter of marriage for a while. No good comes of rushing these things. If you give yourself time you will encounter a female who does stir warmer feelings."

"But I wish to marry now."

"Why, for God's sake!"

He gestured apologetically. "I'm sorry. I'm hardly being fair, am I? I barge in here seeking help, but then become obstructive. I have my reasons, Luce, but they do not affect the issue. It is a simple need to marry and settle down." A rueful smile lit up his face in an extraordinary way. Even Beth, armored by her love for Lucien, felt her heart do a little flip. "I shouldn't have intruded on you like this because of a mere attack of funk." He rose.

Lucien also stood. "You can't go anywhere at this hour of night."

"Of course I can. It's a full moon."

Lucien put down his glass. "You leave this house over my dead body."

Leander's eyes lit up. "A mill?"

Beth leapt to her feet. She knew the Rogues. "Start a fight and you're both out on your ears. Lee, it's past ten. You will assuredly sleep here. Tomorrow, if you wish, I will give you safe escort to the stables. But you are welcome to stay. Truly."

He studied her for a moment, and a sweetness in his expression truly did steal a tiny corner of her heart. It was boyish and endearing, but behind it were the shadows, and that hint of danger. No wonder the blooms at Almack's had been lying wilted at his feet. He took her hand with a distinctly foreign flair and pressed a warm-velvet kiss on her knuckles. "You are a jewel, Beth. Why can't I find a woman like you?"

"Lucien found me in a school not a ballroom," she pointed out sternly, trying to dissipate the effect he was having on her. "Perhaps you should look there. And don't overestimate my sanity, sir. If you'd come courting, I suspect even I would have melted just like all the rest."

Lucien pulled her out of the earl's grasp. "I've changed my mind, Lee. You may leave as soon as you wish."

Later, when their guest was settled and they were in their own bedroom, Lucien looked at Beth. "Could you have fallen in love with him?"

Beth hid a smile. It still astonished her how jealous he could be when he was one of the most handsome, most desirable men in England, and she was the most ordinary of women. "I was hardly in a mood for love back in my teaching days, but yes, I think I could."

He frowned. "Why? You were devilish reluctant to fall in love with me, and I am not lacking essential charms."

Beth slipped off her satin wrap. "But you were my oppressor. It's hard to love a conqueror, no matter how handsome. I began to love you when I saw that you, too, were a victim."

He caught her by the shoulders, eyes flashing with anger. "Are you saying it's *pity*?"

Beth laughed aloud. "Lucien. Even at your lowest you were hardly an object of pity except for being entangled with me." She slid her arms up around his neck. "But I began to see you needed me. It's good to be needed."

He wrapped her in a warm embrace. "Then where's Lee's magic? He's always been devilish self-contained, needing nothing and no one—like a cat. A very high-bred, sleek, Persian cat. And these days he has the world in his hands."

Beth rested comfortably against his shoulder. "So it would seem, love. But there is great need in him. I don't know what it is but it's like a gaping hole. I think that's what is melting all the females at Almack's. They just want to fill that hole."

Lucien chuckled. "Don't you have that switched around, sweetheart?"

Beth blushed, something that surprised her after months of marriage. "You are a very wicked man." She wriggled out of his arms and flashed him a naughty grin. She slipped off the shoulders of her satin nightgown so it fell to the waist. "Are you going to prove again that a wicked man's the only kind worth having?"

He pulled her into his arms, swayed back so she was presented to his mouth. "For ever and ever," he murmured against her breast.

"Amen," breathed Beth.

They never made it to the bed.

When Beth stirred her hot sticky body she was looking down into her husband's dark, sated eyes. They had even rolled off the carpet onto the oak floor under the window. He was on the floor. She was on top.

She brushed his damp hair off his brow. "You'll have plank marks on your back."

"Merely proves that gallantry is not dead." He put his hands behind her head and kissed her with stunning thoroughness. "When did I last tell you I love you?"

"Hours ago."

"I'm a neglectful swine. Perhaps we should help poor old Lee. Marriage is a wonderful invention."

"Help him to a marriage without love? That would be no kindness." Beth traced Lucien's beautiful features. "When did I last tell you I love you?"

"Hours ago."

"I love you."

"I love you."

They kissed. They somehow progressed to their bed. They made love again.

Three-quarters asleep, Beth muttered, "The Weeping Widow."

"What?"

She stirred herself enough to make sense. "If Lee really wants a marriage without love he should marry the Weeping Widow. Anyone who adored her first husband as devotedly as Judith Rossiter did, will be able to resist even Leander Knollis."

"Don't be a gaby," said Lucien, drifting off to sleep himself. "It's just some bee he has in his bonnet. He'll come to his senses."

But the earl did not appear to change his views.

After being pressed, he agreed to stay for a few days and proved to be an unexceptionable guest. He was polite, charming, and thoughtful, and knew when to make himself scarce. Beth began to doubt those shadows she had sensed on the first night.

And Lucien had been right about his self-sufficiency. No man is an island, said Donne, but Leander Knollis came close. He moved through the days like a skillful courtier—charming, and with the most exquisite manners, but unentangled.

She was not surprised to learn that his first career had been that of diplomat, following in his father's footsteps. The late Earl of Charrington had been famous for his ability to pour oil on troubled waters, and had devoted his life to the work. Leander had clearly inherited the gift, and been trained to the life. He had been born in Istanbul and raised everywhere. He had not even visited England until he was eight.

His next visit to England after that had been when he was twelve and en route to Harrow.

"And," he confessed to Beth one day in the rose garden, "I'm not sure I would have survived if it hadn't been for Nicholas and the Rogues. I don't know why he picked me, but I'm eternally grateful. I could handle kings and princes of every nationality, but I had no idea how to rub along with other boys, and was woefully unfamiliar with all kinds of English customs.''

It was a beautiful sunny day for November, and Beth was poaching on the gardener's preserves by snipping the last dead leaves off the roses. "It seems a little thoughtless of your parents to have sent you to Harrow so unprepared.''

"Oh, I had the best tutors. I speak eight languages.''

She looked up sharply. That wasn't an answer to her implied question at all. It seemed to Beth that whenever Leander's parents entered a conversation, that conversation took an adroit turn. He was good at it, very very good, but she noticed. She decided to probe.

"When did your father die?'' she asked.

"A year ago in Sweden.''

"And your mother?''

"Three years earlier in Saint Petersburg.''

He was not evading her questions but there was a distinct restraint in his manner. Did he think of his life solely in terms of geography? Perhaps it lacked any other fixed point.

Beth left the basket of dead leaves for the gardener to dispose of and led the way back to the house, stripping off her gloves. "I suppose you didn't see much of them at all during your school years. Where did you spend the holidays? At Temple Knollis?''

He held open one of the French doors for her. "No. My maternal grandfather had a London house, and an estate in Sussex. I also spent some time with one or other of the Rogues. There was never any problem. I was always a welcome guest.''

A professional guest, in fact. But, thought Beth, where was your *home?* She had grown up as somewhat of a waif herself in Miss Mallory's School for Ladies in Cheltenham, but it had become a home because it was permanent, and because of the genuine affection between herself and Miss Mallory. Had Leander Knollis ever had a home of any kind at all?

Suspecting she would be wiser to talk about the weather, she said, "I suppose it would have been a long journey into the West Country, but you must have been sorry not to be able to spend time at Temple Knollis. It is said to be one of the most beautiful houses in England."

He stopped and she saw his eyes had that flat expression. The silence stretched too long and almost became an embarrassment before he said, "My father hated the Temple and he raised me to feel the same—that it was a foolish, wasteful folly, and dangerous. I never visited it until earlier this year, when I returned to England." He raised his chin slightly and she suspected that for once he had said more than he intended.

There was something here and it needed to be exposed.

"And do you think it beautiful?" she asked, simply fishing for a reaction.

He met her eyes but all the barriers were well in place. "Oh yes," he said. "It is undoubtedly very beautiful. Excuse me."

With no further explanation he was gone.

Beth went thoughtfully in search of Lucien and found him in the stables. "What do you know of Temple Knollis?" she asked him.

He didn't look up from a poking inspection of a hoof. He was in shirtsleeves and very grubby. Beth still found it remarkable how gentlemen loved to play the groom.

"The Temple? That's how Lee always referred to it. I gather his father didn't like the place so they never went there. They were hardly ever in England anyway and the first earl—Lee's grandfather—didn't die till eighteen-ten or thereabouts, so it wasn't even their home.''

"But Lee was obviously going to inherit one day. You'd think everyone would have wanted him to learn about the place.''

"I gather his grandfather tried quite hard to get him down there.'' Lucien finished his task and straightened. "Why the interest?''

"He just told me he was raised to hate it.''

Lucien nodded. "That could be. He's always been uncommunicative about his family, and I wasn't one to push him. My relationship with my father wasn't remarkable for its warmth.'' He looked at her quizzically. "Do you know what? I think you're turning meddlesome. Clearly some Greek lessons are called for to raise your mind to a higher plane.''

Though Beth was proficient in Latin she had never learned Greek, and so Lucien was somewhat lackadaisically teaching her. For the moment, however, she had no interest in academics. "I hope my mind will never be above the welfare of my fellow man. Your friend is troubled.''

Lucien sobered. "It does seem so. But I doubt there is anything we can do other than be here if he needs us.''

"Why is it that men always take that line? There are any number of things we could do. For example, we could tell him about the Weeping Widow.''

Lucien went over to wash his hands in a bucket. "Not that again. He hasn't mentioned marriage since that first night, and if he was still insistent on it, Mrs. Rossiter would hardly be a candidate. She has two young children, she's still draped in black long after her husband's death, and she must be years older than he.''

"Surely not.''

Lucien turned, wiping his hands on a cloth. "How old do you think she is, then?''

Beth thought. "She looks younger than I. . . ."

"That's because she has those big eyes, but think. Her son is turned eleven."

"Heavens. So she must be close to thirty." Beth sighed. "And I had quite decided it would be the answer to everyone's prayers. Though she's too proud to admit it, she must be dreadfully short of money. If that dreamy poet of hers left her with a guinea I'd be astonished. Though she's very reserved, I think I could like her if she would cease seeing me as the local Grande Dame. And if Lee truly wants a loveless marriage she would be ideal."

"Who would?"

Beth turned around guiltily, to see their guest at the stable door.

"Sorry if I was eavesdropping," he said, "but no one can resist the sound of their own name. Do I gather you have a candidate for my hand?"

It was all very light but Beth sensed a serious interest. Whatever was motivating Leander Knollis it was not a whim soon to be forgotten. She purposefully didn't look at Lucien. "I thought so, but Lucien has pointed out that she's ineligible on all counts."

Leander picked a straw out of a bale and twirled it. "Not on all counts, surely. You are far too clever to have scored a duck, Beth. What makes her eligible?"

Beth shrugged. "She's highly unlikely to fall in love with you. It's the local melodrama. She was married to Sebastian Rossiter, a poet who rented Mayfield House in the village. He died before I married Lucien, so I never met him, but at the drop of a hat any of the locals will tell you the affecting story."

"It'll affect you to nausea," Lucien interjected, shrugging into his jacket. "Sebastian Rossiter was a strip of dreamy wind with long flaxen ringlets—I'll swear he put them in curling papers—and long, limp white hands. I'm surprised he managed to beget two children."

"He was very beautiful," countered Beth firmly, "or so the local ladies say. He was also gentle, kind, generous, and utterly devoted to his wife. They were madly in love, never apart. He wrote nearly all his poems about her, or to her. I believe one had a minor success—'My Angel Bride.'"

Lucien emotively quoted, *"Though Angels throng the Heavens high,/ And bend to soothe each human sigh,/ Mere man's bereft on this bleak earth/Lacking an Angel by his hearth."* Though he declaimed it satirically, even he could not entirely blight the beauty of the sentiment. "There's more. Let's see . . ." he said reflectively. *"My Judith sits in God's pure light/ And holds our child to bosom white./ And dew that pearls the gleaming grass/ Shows Angels' envy as they pass."*

"I certainly couldn't compete with that when courting."

Lucien shook his head. "I'd disown you if you were to try."

"So," said Leander, "what are the impediments to the match?"

"Two children," said Beth.

"How old?"

"A boy of eleven and a girl of six."

Lee considered and said, "I don't see any problem there. The boy is old enough not to become confused about our own children and the inheritance. In fact," he said with a sudden inexplicable gleam in his eye, "I'd quite like a ready-made family."

Beth shared a look with Lucien.

"Lee," said Lucien, "think how old that makes her."

Lee considered. "Over thirty?"

"Not quite that, I suppose, but you're only twenty-five."

"Why the heat? Nearly all my lovers have been older than I. In fact my father's firm advice was to have nothing to do with a woman younger than myself until I was at least thirty. I should have listened. If I'd gone bride-hunting among the older set from the start I'd have been far more likely to find a woman of sense, one too wise to make a fool of herself over me."

He nodded contentedly. "Marriages of practicality are still common on the Continent, you know. I'm not uneasy at the notion. As long as this widow's still likely to bear me a few children, I don't care about her age. However, I see no reason why the lady would consider me if she still grieves as much as you say."

Beth was succinct. "Money."

"Poetry not lucrative?"

"One gathers not, though 'My Angel Bride' was on every sentimental schoolgirl's lips a few years back. Not everyone can be a Byron, I suppose. When Mister Rossiter died the widow had to leave Mayfield House and take a cottage in the village. I gather she is one of a large family of a curate and can expect little help from that quarter. Her son is coming to an age to need schooling and a start in life. It's possible that she has been able to put money aside for her children's future, but I doubt it."

Lee leaned against the edge of a stall and stroked a horse's nose. "I have to confess, it seems a situation cut to my requirements." He looked at Lucien. "What bothers you?"

"Go to hell in a handcart if you wish," said Lucien shortly. "But," he added, putting a hand on Beth's shoulder, "love in marriage is not a thing lightly to dismiss."

Chapter Two

Judith Rossiter straightened up from the washing tub with a hiss as her back complained. She hated washing day. She had the sheets and underclothes boiling in one corner of the small kitchen, and was wringing out the colored garments. Her hands were red and the room was heavy with sour steam.

She was nearly finished with this task, but it seemed that the work was never, ever, done. Now she had scraped together the money to buy more dried fruit, she had to chop it for the Christmas mincemeat. That meant there were raisins to be stoned, another job she disliked.

Perhaps she should look on the bright side; poverty had reduced the number of raisins to be stoned.

She sighed over it. If she put in lots of apples maybe no one would notice the lack of imported dried fruits. She was determined, one way or another, to give her children a proper Christmas.

She threw the last item into the tub and called Rosie to help her to peg out. She hauled the tub onto her hip, and went out into the garden.

She was assailed by delicious, fresh, cool air, and stole a moment to relish it.

It was a lovely late autumn day. The air was crisp, the sky clear blue, and the leaves on the trees were russet and gold. As she watched, some drifted down to join the gilded carpet on the ground.

When Sebastian was alive they would walk out on days like this, across fields and through woods. The children would run about and explore, while Sebastian thought up elegant phrases and noted them in his book. Judith would just drink in the sights, the sounds, and the aromas, and be content.

There had been money then. Not a lot, but enough with careful management for a cook, two maids, a gardener, and leisure.

Time and security, the two things she missed most.

Six-year-old Rosie, a pretty girl with her father's fly away pale blond hair and her mother's big blue eyes, came running to help. She passed the pegs and supported trailing ends as Judith fixed the laundry to the rope.

By the time they'd come to the bottom of the tub, Bastian, as her second Sebastian was always called, came out. "Can I help you with the prop, Mama?"

Judith smiled. "Thank you, dear. That would be wonderful."

The two children fixed the forked end of the long stick under the line then pushed up, settling the other end securely in the earth. They checked the laundry was raised well away from ground and bushes and that the prop was secure then turned, well satisfied with themselves.

Judith gave them both a hug. She was blessed with wonderful children. They didn't complain at their simple life, and they did their best to help with the work. They were her greatest joy, but also her greatest concern. She noted that Bastian's head was up to her shoulder now. Her first babe was growing fast, too fast.

Keeping him in clothes was a strain on her purse, and she had no idea how to provide for his future.

She knew her own family would always give her and the children a roof over their heads, but more than that was impossible.

Sebastian's family were not particularly wealthy either, but they had provided a small but adequate annuity for him when he decided to set up as a poet. It had continued even after their deaths, and been sufficient. Judith had not known that income would die with Sebastian.

That blow, on top of his sudden death, had almost undone her. She had written to his brother and received help. Thank heavens for Timothy Rossiter. If it wasn't for that small quarterly allowance, she didn't know what she would do. From his letters, she feared Timothy could ill afford it, but she could not refuse to take it.

If only Sebastian's poems had made money, even a little, but instead he had actually paid to have them printed—on vellum, bound in Cordovan leather—and then given the handsome copies away. It had seemed a harmless indulgence when the money had been available, but now she grudged every glossy leather volume.

He had kept one copy of each work. They sat in a row in the front room of the cottage—eight slim volumes full of poetry about her. Her sole inheritance.

She was occasionally visited by the traitorous thought that real devotion would have been more provident.

She had just enough money for this austere life, but there was nothing to spare. Even the fee for an apprenticeship in some skill would be a perilous expenditure, and Bastian was entitled to more than that.

"Mama." Bastian's voice was a welcome interruption to depressing thoughts. "You know Georgie's rat?"

Judith shuddered. She knew Wellington all too well. Georgie was Bastian's closest friend, and Wellington was Georgie's inseparable companion. The creature was well behaved and even seemed clean, but she still had an urge to beat it with a broom.

Bastian took the shudder as answer. He sighed. "I don't suppose you'd let me have one . . ."

"No!"

"But it wouldn't eat much, and Georgie's found another clutch of babies. He's taking one for himself, because Wellington's getting old—"

"No, Bastian. I'm sorry, but I could not tolerate a rat in the house. Off you go now, both of you and finish your work." Impulsively, she decided the raisins could wait. "When I finish the whites," she promised, "we'll walk down to the river."

They hurried back into the house, and Judith sighed. Really, they asked for so little, and got even less. . . . But a rat! The Hubbles' cat had just had kittens. Perhaps she should take one, and that would do as well . . .

Judith went back to the laundry, popping into the front room of the cottage to check that the children were doing their work correctly, and praising them. They were both so bright and good. They deserved a chance in life. Was she to see them end as servants?

As she began to haul the steaming whites out of the boiler and into the rinse water, she thought bitterly that a more useful woman would be able to earn some money—be able to write novels or paint pictures. Something with a marketable value. The only thing of excellence she could create was elderberry wine. She looked at the rows of newly bottled wine, her hope of some small increment to their income, and sighed.

They would make no impression at all on her desperate situation.

Leander sat on his gray, Nubarron, and considered Judith Rossiter's cottage. It was one of a row that lined a lane winding off the main street of Mayfield. It, like all the rest, was small and thatched—could do with rethatching, in fact—but it had the distinction of rose vines around the door. They were bare of blooms now, but he supposed they would pretty the place up in season.

He also supposed the cottage to be damp and cramped. He knew such houses, and they were rarely as appealing to live in as to look at. He'd checked out Mayfield House on his way here; this was quite a comedown for the Weeping Widow.

In truth, he was put off by that description, for though he didn't want a doting wife, a sorrowful one would be little better. A pale-faced creature in dripping black could become wearing very quickly. In fact, he decided, if he did offer marriage to this woman he'd insist she stop mourning entirely. That could hardly be considered an unreasonable request.

He thought he heard voices at the back of the cottage and looked for a way around. There was a path at the end of the row and so he trotted down and followed it. As he hoped, it took him to a spot overlooking the narrow back gardens.

The widow's garden was clearly devoted to vegetable production and was mostly turned and bare, though a few plants remained. He had no idea what they were producing; such matters had been no part of his education. Three people stood talking on a path. They had just finished putting out laundry; three small dresses, and one larger black one, flapped in the wind. The figures were a blond girl in pale muslin and shawl, a dark-haired boy in nankeen trousers and jacket, and the widow in black.

Her hair was as dark as her dress. She wore it in a knot on her head, but strands were coming loose and flying about her face in curly tendrils. Every now and then she would push them back. She was turned away from him so he could not see her features but her figure appeared good, and there was an impression of energy and supple strength. He did not find it unattractive. Certainly not a drooping, weary type.

He suddenly felt self-conscious about sitting here assessing the lady's parts, as if she were a mare he proposed to buy. He pulled the gray's head around, and returned to the lane onto which the cottages fronted. He knew, however, that he was definitely interested in pursuing this matter of marriage to the Weeping Widow. He considered carefully how to go about it.

He could simply ride up and put the matter bluntly. There were various arguments against this. In the first place, without the briefest meeting, he could not be sure she would do. Though his requirements for a bride were minimal, he didn't think he could bear an inane chatterer, or a particularly shrill voice. There were doubtless other characteristics which would make a lifetime in her company impossible.

In the second place, no matter how businesslike the whole affair, experience had led him to believe that people, and women in particular, preferred even business wrapped up in spangles and lace. If he was too blunt he could be refused as a matter of principle. On the other hand, he had golden-tongued diplomacy in his blood, or so he was told, and should be able to sail through this assignment.

So how to meet the Weeping Widow?

He rode slowly back to the main street of the village

aware of curious glances from the people of May-field. They'd stare even more if they could read his thoughts. He himself wondered occasionally if he were crazed, but without great concern. Some of the most interesting people he had met had not been quite as most people were.

He wanted to settle in England and put down roots, and would go about it in the most direct and expeditious manner possible.

Still, he sometimes wondered if he should have accepted Lord Castlereagh's offer of a post in Vienna. The man had as good as told him it was his duty to put his skills to work for his country, but Leander had had his fill of a wandering life.

He stopped Nubarron in front of the Dog and Partridge under the interested stare of a couple of ancients soaking up the afternoon sun. He gave his horse to a stable lad, and went in for a jar of ale.

He told the publican that he was a guest of the Marquess of Arden and soon had the beefy man chatting. It was a natural skill of his to put all kinds of people at their ease.

"And I hear you had a famous poet in these parts?" he asked at one point.

"Aye, sir. Mister Rossiter. He could spin a lovely verse, he could. Had 'em printed up in Lunnon."

"Died, I hear."

"Aye, over a year back." The man shook his head. "Took a chill and it settled. Never did have the look of a hearty man, if you know what I mean. Once or twice I said to him, 'You ought to take to drinking stout, Mister Rossiter,' I said. But he mostly drank tea and water, and never a barley brew. And look what come of it."

Leander took a deep draught of his ale to prove he wasn't so foolish. "Indeed, but perhaps it's the poetic temperament. So many of them seem to die young. Did he have family hereabouts?"

"Came from Lunnon, as I hear tell, sir. But he married a Hunstead girl. His wife and children still live in the village. If you know of him, you'll know of her. Wrote nearly all his poems to his Judith."

"Ah yes." Leander put on a sentimental expression. " 'My Angel Bride.' "

"That's right, sir!" declared the man with a pleased smile. "Can't say I go for that sort of rhyme misself, but the womenfolk love it."

"It was a very affecting piece. Does the lady live nearby? I would like to gain a glimpse of her."

The innkeeper gave him a narrow look then shrugged. "She seems to be quite famous. I've been asked afore." He gave directions to the cottage. "You might care to visit Mister Rossiter's grave, sir. A very touching monument his widow raised, I must say." He leant forward confidentially. "Round here they call her the Weeping Widow, took it so hard she did."

Well, why not? A wise soldier scouts the territory before going into action. Leander paid for his ale, checked on his horse, and strolled off toward the village church and graveyard.

The church was ancient—he thought he saw Saxon work—and the churchyard was graced with mighty spreading trees and old, tilted stones covered with moss. Beyond the ranks of stones the land sloped away down to the same river that wound along the edge of the gardens at Hartwell.

He wandered through the churchyard looking for the poet's grave. It was easy to find because of its newness and grandeur. In fact, it looked very out-of-place. An angel drooped on a pedestal, weeping, two cherubs at its—her?—knee.

He read the inscription.

In loving memory of
Sebastian Arthur Rossiter,
Poet

Jo Beverley

Born May 12, 1770. Died October 3, 1814.
Sadly mourned by his wife Judith
and his two children, Bastian and Rosie.

He had been a good deal older than his wife, then. Leander had gained the impression that he was a young man. There was a verse engraved below.

When I am gone to rest be sure, my dear
That I will watch and treasure every tear.
On high, forever faithful, I will wait
Longing to greet my angel at the gate.

Presumably the poet had composed his own epitaph. Leander thought it distastefully morbid and possessive but noted there were fresh flowers on the grave. He questioned his plan. Would there be a ghost in the marriage bed?

Pondering this, he continued through the graves and down the slope to the river's edge to idly toss stones into the shallow water.

He wondered whether Judith Rossiter really did long to join her dead husband; what it felt like to feel such grief. He hadn't mourned his parents, for his father had been too wrapped up in his work to engender fondness, and his mother had been too wrapped up in his father. He'd grieved for the death of a number of brothers-in-arms, but he'd felt damn-all desire to share their fate.

If this miserable clinging was the consequence of love he was better off without it.

But then he found himself thinking of Lucien and Beth. They'd made him welcome and not at all uncomfortable, and yet he sensed the power of the bond between them. They fought—which wasn't surprising in view of Lucien's blue-blooded arrogance and Beth's egalitarian principles—but they were bound together in a way no petty disagreement could touch.

That, he supposed, was love. But he couldn't imagine, if either Beth or Lucien should die, them wanting the survivor to hurry to meet them.

It would be hell to be married to a woman who thought only of joining her first mate in the grave. He laughed at his situation. It appeared his choice was either a wife who drooped over him from excessive devotion, or one who did the same from excessive grief.

Really, Vienna would be a far more sensible choice. . . .

He heard the laughter of children and turned just as they ran into view between the gravestones and headed down the hill. He thought they were the Rossiter children. They paused momentarily but then came on—startled by a stranger but unafraid.

They seemed unsure, however, as to whether to speak or not, and so he did. "Good day. Do you live around here?"

The boy gave a little bow. "Yes, sir. In the village." He was handsome, with dark curls and an attractive confidence in his manner.

"I'm staying with the Marquess of Arden," Leander offered as credentials. "He has a place farther along the river, as you doubtless know. My name's Charrington, Lord Charrington."

The boy bowed again. "Pleased to meet you, my lord. I'm Bastian Rossiter, and this is my sister, Rosie."

It was them indeed. Was this an augury from the gods?

The girl, who had bewitching deep blue eyes and flaxen hair like silk on her shoulders, drew herself up. "Rosetta," she said firmly.

Her brother groaned, but Leander gave her a very proper bow. "Delighted to make your acquaintance, Miss Rosetta Rossiter."

With a grin that showed two charming dimples she returned the honor with a curtsy.

Leander looked up to find their mother had come up behind, a neutral expression on her face, but wariness in her eyes—large blue eyes, just like her daughter's, but made even finer by thick dark lashes. She didn't look lugubrious, thank God. In fact she looked sound as a ripe peach. He glanced meaningfully at Bastian and the boy took the hint.

"Mama, may I present Lord Charrington? He's staying at Hartwell. Sir, this is my mother, Mrs. Rossiter. "Then he looked between them anxiously. "Did I do that right?"

"Perfectly," said Leander, and was rewarded by a touch of warmth in the widow's expression. She held out a black-gloved hand. "My lord."

He took it, making rapid inventory. She was above average height so her lovely eyes were almost on a level with his own. Her dark hair was now firmly tamed under a plain black bonnet. Other than those eyes, her face was unremarkable except for a hint of roundness in the cheeks. He suspected there'd be dimples if she ever smiled. The roundness and the eyes gave an impression of youth that most women would envy.

Perhaps that illusion of youth was what suddenly made him feel protective, or like a knight errant come to rescue the lady in the tower. He was drawn to her. He wouldn't at all mind taking her to wife. Should he seize the moment?

To achieve anything, he needed to keep her in conversation. Presumably the easiest opening would be the dear departed. "If I may be so bold," he said, "I assume you to be related to Mister Rossiter, the poet."

"That is so," she said without particular warmth, most of her attention on her children, who were walking ahead. "I am his widow."

"A sad loss. Please accept my condolences."

"Thank you."

She was clearly not thrilled by this conversation. The children had run off to investigate the shallows of the river, and she moved to follow them.

Leander went along. It was refreshing that she wasn't blushing and simpering at first acquaintance, but he found that for once in his life he was struggling for something to say. "This is a beautiful churchyard in which to take his final rest."

She glanced at him. "It is indeed a charming spot, my lord, though I can see no reason, sentimental or spiritual, why the dead should be supposed to care."

As she walked on, Leander realized he was making a fool of himself. Clearly, no matter how deep her grief, the widow was not to be reached by the sentimental route. For a moment he was annoyed by the absurd situation in which he found himself, but then he smiled and adjusted the tilt of his elegant beaver.

By her cool behavior the lady had passed the last test. There was nothing about her he found objectionable.

The wisest course now would be to seek some conventional way of courting her, but that could be difficult. Beth had told him the widow took no part in county life, and had little free time. He wanted all this settled so he could get on with his plans. He couldn't spend months hanging around Surrey.

Why shouldn't he just press his suit? He was, after all, the one who had managed to pacify the Duke of Brunswick after he had been insulted by one of the minor Bourbons, and was flirting with the idea of throwing his state behind Napoleon. Persuading a penniless widow to become a countess should be child's play.

Still, he hesitated.

He hesitated, he realized, because he cared about the outcome. There was something about this composed woman which made him want to know her better, and ease her way in life. He was attracted to her children.

Good God, he actually *wanted* to marry her!

She stopped her stroll and glanced back at him, clearly wondering about his actions. A slight smile tugged at her lips. "Should I apologize, my lord? I fear I shocked you."

There was the faintest hint of dimples.

She was referring to her comment about the dead. He walked to join her. "No," he said, "but I fear I am about to shock you."

A flicker of wariness passed over her face and she glanced once at her children, made a move toward them.

"Please," he said quickly, "I'm not going to do anything you wouldn't like. . . . Good heavens! Would you believe I was reputed to have a golden future as a diplomat?"

She relaxed slightly, and her lips twitched. Those dimples flickered once again. He conceived a strong desire to see them in all their glory.

"Not at this moment, no," she said. "Is there some way I can help you, my lord?"

He pulled himself together and gave her one of his best smiles. "Yes, in fact there is. I would like to talk to you about it. I see a stone over there well shaped for sitting, if it would not be too cold."

After the briefest hesitation she walked toward it. "Not at all. I usually do sit here while the children play. They call it my throne."

She sat on the lump of granite, gathering her black bombazine skirts neatly together. With permission he sat beside her. There was not a lot of room but she made no silly protest about them sitting so close. He liked her more by the moment.

She turned to look at him with polite expectation.

"You are going to find this a little strange . . ."

"And even shocking," she added quizzically.

A sense of humor as well. "I hope not too much so." He still could not quite see how to open the subject.

There was distinct amusement in her eyes. "I'm likely to be so overwhelmed with curiosity, my lord, that I'll take a fit of the vapors, and scare you to death. Have pity, please."

He laughed. "One of the first lessons a fledgling diplomat learns, Mrs. Rossiter, is how to handle a lady with the vapors." Even so, he couldn't imagine this woman in a state of collapse. For a moment he wondered if he had the wrong lady and was about to propose to the vicar's wife or such. But then he remembered that she had admitted to being the poet's widow.

He braced himself. "Despite my diplomatic background, Mrs. Rossiter, I can see no fancy way to dress this up that would serve any purpose at all." He summoned up an expression of sober worthiness. "The simple truth is that I would like to marry you."

She paled. In a second she was up and standing, looking away "Oh, good heavens," she said. The tone was pure exasperation.

It was not a response he had expected. He rose to his feet, too. "It may be precipitate," he said sharply, "but it is an honest offer, ma'am."

She turned back, eyes snapping. "Honest! When you don't know anything about the woman you are proposing to take to wife?"

"I know enough."

"Do you indeed? I can't imagine how. Well, so do I know enough. The answer, sir, is *no.*"

She was marching away. Leander hurried after, feeling more like a green boy than he had since he was sixteen, when he'd tried to kiss a daughter of the Duke de Ferrugino and had his face soundly slapped. If the Rogues ever heard of this they'd die laughing.

He caught up to her. "Mrs. Rossiter. Please listen to me! I can offer you all kinds of advantages."

She whirled around in a swirl of black skirts to face him almost nose to nose. "Name one. And no, I do *not* need any more odes to my eyes!"

He stared at her. Those eyes were so magnificently filled with rage that he was tempted to try. But he said, "That's as well. I wouldn't know where to start."

She took a step back. "You are not a poet?"

He extended his hands. "Diplomat. Linguist. Soldier. Earl. No odes on any subject, I give you my word."

"Earl?" she asked dazedly.

He bowed, thinking that at last they were making progress. "Leander Knollis, at your service, ma'am. Earl of Charrington, of Temple Knollis in Somerset."

"Temple Knollis?" she queried faintly, showing the awe with which he was all too familiar. At the moment, however, he'd take any advantage he could get.

"Yes. There's a London house, too, and a hunting box. An estate in Sussex, and a place in Cumberland I've never seen." Good lord, he thought. I sound like the veriest mushroom listing off my properties like this.

Perhaps she thought the same. Color flushed her cheeks. "I don't know what game you are playing, sir, but I think it unconscionable of you to amuse yourself at my expense. Bastian! Rosie!" she called out. "Come along. We must leave."

The children ran over. Bastian took one look at his mother and turned on Leander pugnaciously.

Leander backed off. "Don't fight me, lad. I'd have to let you win or your mother will never marry me."

The children stared at them both wide-eyed.

Judith Rossiter, however, glared at him as if she'd like a mill herself. He saw her hands were clenched into serviceable fists. "Good-day!" she snapped and stormed off up the hill, her children running behind.

She was like a ship of the line with a pair of pinnaces in tow. He could quite imagine that at any moment she would turn and broadside him into oblivion.

Leander watched them go, wondering ruefully what had possessed him to so mishandle matters.

Chapter Three

By the time Leander arrived back at Hartwell, he had reluctantly decided he would have to tell Lucien and Beth all about it. He needed help.

After dinner he related the incident. Despite all their efforts his hosts burst out laughing at his description of the scene.

"Gads!" said Lucien. "And you were always the one with the winning ways. The one we'd send to turn cook up sweet. Lost your talents, Lee?"

"They certainly seem to have deserted me in my hour of need. What do I do now?"

Lucien frowned. "You mean you want to go through with it? Why?"

There was a distinct withdrawal. "Rather an impertinent question, ain't it?"

"Probably," said Lucien, unmoved. "When have we ever bothered about such things?"

Leander abandoned his momentary hauteur, wondering why he felt so prickly about the matter. "I like the woman. She has spirit, and strength, and good humor. I like her children, too, which is helpful itself, and argues to her advantage. I think she'll be a good mother to mine. And she needs me as much as I need her." He fiddled idly with his signet ring. "I think that is the most attractive feature, to be needed. It all seems to add up to a sound basis for a practical marriage."

Lucien grimaced. "I still don't understand why *you* need *her.*"

Leander was tired of ducking this very obvious question. "I have come back to England to stay. I decided a few years ago that my parents' rootless life did not appeal, but it was at Waterloo, I think, that I made the firm decision." He glanced up at them. "I almost died, you know. I was trapped under my horse, and if I hadn't fallen into a dip I'd have been crushed. My men managed to get me out just before the French swept over that spot. Strange as it may seem, through the years of the war I'd never really thought of my own mortality. Then I did. Life suddenly became very precious. And life, at that moment, came to mean a home. A permanent place. In England."

His hosts looked at him. Lucien said, "You have a home. More than one, in fact."

"I have properties," said Leander. "I want a home. I intend to make Temple Knollis my home but I don't think I can do that alone."

Lucien shrugged. "I can't see there's much to it. A home is a home."

"Think, Luce," said Leander impatiently. "This isn't your true home. Belcraven is. You've lived there all your life. You know that land with your heart and soul. You know the people. You *understand* the people. On a larger scale, you know and understand England. I don't." He made a gesture of frustration. "I understand Saint Petersburg and the Vatican, the intricacies of the German states, and the bloody entanglements of the army. I don't understand my own country."

"You think a wife will help?"

"I hope an Englishwoman will help, yes. But I also

need a companion. What am I supposed to do? Go down to Temple Knollis and rattle around there alone?''

"You have a large family down there somewhere, don't you?''

Leander's face tightened. "I have a large family living at Temple Knollis. The trouble is that I don't think they will approve of my plans for the place. They'll have to go."

"What plans?'' asked Beth. "I understand it's perfect, a jewel of a place.''

"Indeed it is. A precious jewel. Too precious by far. As far as I can tell, the building of the Temple drained the land around, and the other estates of the earldom. I intend to correct the balance. I'll sell off the treasures if necessary. We all know the end of the war is bringing hardship. It's our job to help where we can. I can't imagine my Uncle Charles approving, though, after he's spent his life bringing the Temple to such a high shine.''

"But does this really necessitate a hasty marriage?'' Lucien asked skeptically.

"I think so. How would you feel, walking into an estate in Russia and taking charge?''

"I'd hire good advisers. Mrs. Rossiter can know little of estate management.''

Leander sighed. "I knew it wouldn't make sense to you. I find it hard to make it make sense to me. I think it comes of that moment at Waterloo. It created an urgency to put down roots. And as I said, I am more comfortable with marriages of practicality than I am with ones based on fancy. Judith Rossiter understands England, and she will be a helpmeet, a companion, of a sort I could never hire. That she brings a ready-made family is an unexpected bonus.''

Lucien slid back in his chair and glanced at Beth. She shrugged. "I like Judith Rossiter very much, and her children are delightful. I think Lee could do a lot worse if he's set on it." She looked at Leander with a smile. "And I do like the fact that you seem to appreciate her important qualities—her strength, and her spirit. A lesser man could have been distracted by a fine figure, and stunning eyes."

"Could he?" Leander drawled. "But the master of the Temple would never be so crass, would he?" All the same, he'd been impressed by those eyes, and hadn't failed to note the figure.

"Perhaps she wanted you to write a sonnet to her eyes," Lucien suggested, "and that's why she got in such a tiff."

"I didn't have that impression."

Beth spoke up. "Perhaps she thought you would and that upset her, remembering her husband."

"More likely. Which reminds me," said Leander with a frown, "have you seen that monument, and that epitaph."

Beth shuddered. "Yes. It would make me feel his ghost was hanging over me, watching my every move. But most people find it touching. I suppose Judith must or she wouldn't have had it put there."

"Consider," warned Lucien, "that if you marry her you'll doubtless have old Sebastian as a third in your marriage bed."

With a slightly wary glance at Beth, Leander said, "Then I'll have to make sure he sees something worth his effort, won't I?"

Lucien burst out laughing. "I must admit, you and Rossiter wouldn't seem to be in the same style in such matters, and she is a fine figure of a woman."

Beth cleared her throat. "Is it my turn to be jealous?"

"But my dear," said Lucien with a glint, "you know I love you for your mind alone."

Diplomatic instincts clamoring, Leander interrupted this. "So," he said, "how do I mend matters?"

Beth grinned at him. "Afraid of an outbreak of war?"

He grinned back. "Old habits die hard."

"It seems to me," Beth said, "that Mrs. Rossiter decided you were either an impostor, or were playing some kind of trick. After all, if this match comes about it will be a stunning one for her from a worldly point of view, one normally considered out of her reach. She is connected to the aristocracy, but only insofar as her father is the fourth son of a viscount. She must find it most improbable that an earl pop out of the ground with an offer. Tomorrow I'll go to her and explain that you are at least in earnest. Perhaps then she will give you a fair hearing."

Leander smiled. "Thank you, Beth. Plead my case sweetly?"

Beth was again aware of his charms. "I'll pave the way, that's all. You, my lord, are well able to plead for yourself."

Judith had been in a fury all the way home, but it was a suppressed fury for she was trying to pretend to the children that nothing in particular had happened. It was not easy.

"But Lord Charrington said he wanted to marry you, Mama," said Bastian with a frown. "Do you not like him?"

"I don't know him," she said as calmly as she could. "And I very much doubt that he is lord anything."

"Why would he lie?" asked Rosie, tears threatening in her eyes. "I thought he was ever so kind."

Judith rested a hand on her daughter's shoulder. "Sometimes people pretend to be kind, dearest. The gentleman was merely teasing. Put it out of your head for we'll see no more of him."

In the end to distract them, she stopped at the Hubbles' cottage to look at the kittens. They were weaned. In fact, Mrs. Hubble said with a shrug, "It'll be into the river with 'em any day, Mrs. Rossiter."

They were a collection of delightful, roly-poly creatures, and Judith felt an almost overpowering urge to take them all before this dreadful fate occurred. She was certainly happy to let the children pick one. As Rosie had fallen in love with a playful white kitten with a scattering of black patches, that one came home with them.

Magpie, as it was christened, certainly took their minds off the rogue by the riverside.

Not so Judith, but she had to serve supper and get through the evening ritual—some reading, and tonight the construction of a bed for Magpie—before she was alone and could take her rage out on the raisins.

Now the rage was mostly gone, leaving only bitterness and sadness. For a moment there by the riverbank she had liked the man, and that was why his cruelty had hurt so much. He was a good-looking young man with a distinctive air, and despite her reputation she was not immune to such things. He had seemed troubled in some way, and she had truly wanted to help him if it were in her power. Then he had played that vile trick.

At first she had thought he was another of the silly poets, and that was bad enough. Though her husband had never made money from his work he had gathered a small following of admirers who wrote, and occasionally visited.

Over the past twelve months a steady trickle of them had come to Mayfield to visit his grave and stare at his Judith, his Angel Bride. Four of them had proposed marriage, three of them in verse.

In truth if any of them had appeared to be in funds she might have been tempted for the children's sake, though to be the subject of endless derivative odes to her eyes would have been torture. But they were all short of money and so she had sent them on their way.

If that had been it, if today's encounter had been poetic nonsense, she would have been disappointed, but nothing more.

But it had been worse. It had been some kind of cruel joke. Had it been a wager? The Marquess of Arden appeared to be a typical London buck, and there had certainly been some wild goings-on at Hartwell before his marriage, but would even he sink so low as to make such a cruel wager with a guest?

Could they seriously have expected her to believe such an offer? Or to accept, no matter how poor she was? Her rage was returning. She threw the last of the raisins into a bowl and paced the tiny room, thinking up a great many unpleasant things she'd like to do to a certain gentleman with a charming smile, mesmerizing eyes, and no conscience at all.

Then she stopped her pacing and laughed. She had to confess she was enjoying this brief spurt of honest fury. Sebastian had not liked to have strong emotions about him, especially anger, but there were times when it was cathartic.

She went over to the dresser and opened the last bottle of the previous year's rich elderberry wine. She had been saving this one for Christmas, but the indulgence of an early glass wouldn't hurt. She raised the glass high. "Thank you, Mister Whoever-you-were for an excellent reason to let fly."

The next day Judith was in the kitchen with Rosie, grinding the suet for the mincemeat, when there was a knock at the front door. "Bastian! See who that is, please." She helped Rosie stir the fat into the fruit, smiling with her at the rich aroma.

Rosie sighed with satisfaction. "We have a cake,

and a pudding, and now mincemeat. It's going to be a lovely Christmas, Mama.''

"Yes, it is, dear . . .''

Bastian dashed in and hissed, "It's Lady Arden, Mama! I've put her in the front room.''

Judith let the spoon fall. What now? She encountered the new marchioness now and then, mostly after Sunday service, and liked her well enough. There was no question, however, of intimacy with one in such different circumstances. She had thought sadly that if Lady Arden had come among them while Sebastian was alive it might have been possible to be friends.

"Mama!'' prompted Bastian. "You can't just leave her there.''

"I suppose not.'' Judith rose and took off her work apron. She washed her sticky hands in the bowl in the sink. "Boil the kettle for tea, please, children, but don't pour it on the leaves unless I say.'' They couldn't afford to waste tea. "Lady Arden probably won't stay above a minute.''

The cottage only had two rooms downstairs and so they called the front room exactly that, though some might call it a parlor. It boasted two upholstered chairs, and three hard ones at a table. That was about all it could hold.

As Judith entered, her visitor rose and smiled. "I'm very sorry to drop by unannounced, Mrs. Rossiter, but I felt we had need to talk.''

Judith knew then that it was something to do with yesterday's adventure. Had the marchioness come to apologize on her husband's behalf, or to complain? Her tormentor had said he was a guest at Hartwell. Perhaps he was deranged.

"We had better have tea, then,'' Judith said, and called to the children to complete their work. She waved Lady Arden to one chair and took the other.

"Mrs. Rossiter,'' said the marchioness. "Yesterday

I understand you had an encounter with a guest of ours."

Judith kept her face blank, still unsure what was to come of all this. "He did say he was staying at Hartwell, my lady."

"Indeed he is. We are talking, of course, of the Earl of Charrington. He is an old school friend of my husband's. He fought at Waterloo, and has not been back in England very long."

Judith let go of some of her tension. So that was it. The poor man was suffering from battle-madness, or the like. She knew she had sensed some terrible need. "I'm very sorry," she said.

Lady Arden wrinkled her brow at this. "I don't think he particularly minded being abroad."

"I meant about his . . . sickness, my lady."

"Sickness?" Beth stared at her then laughed. "Do you think him mad? Poor Lee, though I fear he deserves it, rushing his fences like that."

The conversation halted as Bastian came in, carefully bearing the tea tray, followed by Rosie with a plate of biscuits. Judith was glad of an opportunity to review the situation. It was clear she still had no idea what it was about.

Lady Arden smiled at the children and asked to be introduced. After chatting she said, "I quite forgot. I brought a cake. It is in the carriage. Perhaps you could bring it in for me, my dears. I shouldn't think your Mama and I particularly want cake at this time of day, but you may have a small slice if you are allowed."

Judith gave a nod, and the children were off in search of their treat. As soon as they were gone, however, all good humor fled for she could not see a pleasant interpretation to put on the affair. She poured the tea with a steady hand. "I can't imagine what part you have in all this, my lady."

Beth took the cup. "An honorable one, I assure you, Mrs. Rossiter." Her tone compelled Judith to meet her eyes. "I can assure you that I would never be part of anything designed to injure another woman."

Judith was tempted to believe her. "What is going on, then? The man was clearly wicked or mad."

Beth shook her head. "You have every reason to doubt Lord Charrington's sanity, but he is not mad, or wicked. I cannot speak for him, but he has reasons for wishing to marry. He wishes to marry a woman who will accept the arrangement in a practical rather than a romantical way. When he heard about you, he thought you would suit his requirements. As for *your* requirements, I can only tell you that he is wealthy and willing to support you and your children in generous style. I think you have seen for yourself that he is not an unpleasing man."

Judith stared, her tea untouched. "But half the women in England would be willing to marry him if that's what he wants! Why me?"

Beth looked at her cup for inspiration and found none. "To be honest, I don't really know." She looked up. "I can assure you, Mrs. Rossiter, you will do yourself no harm by at least discussing this matter with Lord Charrington. He is in earnest and his plan offers you many advantages. Let us be frank. You are poor, and poverty is unpleasant. It will make life very difficult for your children. Marriage to the earl would change that dramatically."

"Too dramatically. I'm no fool, Lady Arden, and there must be a price to pay."

Beth shrugged. "I would feel exactly as you do, but I think you should at least let him speak. Perhaps he can make the price clear. Perhaps it will not be too high to pay."

* * *

Thus Judith Rossiter found herself within the hour anxiously awaiting the Earl of Charrington in the library of Hartwell.

It was a small room—for Hartwell was a small house, though many times larger than her cottage—and had a pleasant, lived-in feel to it. The carpet was even worn in places, and the leather chairs had the shine of long use. Many of the shelves were slightly disarranged and missing a volume. Three books lay on a mahogany table looking as if they had recently been opened and enjoyed.

A fire burned in the hearth. Judith went over and held her hands out to the heat, more for comfort than for warmth. She didn't know what to do.

She had allowed Lady Arden to persuade her to this appointment. The marchioness had brought her back in the carriage, insisting that the children come, too. Bastian and Rosie were now being entertained by the marquess and marchioness in the stables, and Judith wasn't at all sure this wasn't a subtle form of pressure.

Bastian's eyes had shone at the mere thought of being around horses again, for his pony had been sold on Sebastian's death. Judith couldn't ignore the fact that as Bastian's stepfather the earl would surely provide him with another one. For that, almost any sacrifice seemed worthwhile.

But she wouldn't allow herself to forget that there was always a price to pay, and it might not just be herself who paid it. If she married Lord Charrington she would be putting herself and her children in his power, and he was undoubtedly powerful. If things went wrong they could end up in an even worse situation than at present, and perhaps with more children to be hurt . . . .

The door clicked open and she whirled around.

He halted, hand still on the knob, expression very

serious. "My dear lady, I cannot have frightened you so badly, can I?"

Judith pulled herself together. "Of course not, my lord. You just startled me."

He closed the door and came over to join her. "That was only too obvious."

She knew he referred to the day before, not the present, and felt color in her cheeks. Her reaction had been entirely reasonable, but she feared she had ranted like a fishwife. She had no intention of apologizing. She glanced at him, trying to study him without being ill-mannered.

"Please," he said, extending his hands gracefully. "Look your fill. It is only natural."

That hardly helped her compose herself, but she raised her chin and did exactly that.

He was only a little taller than she. His build was slim, but his shoulders were wide, his legs strong, and she had noticed that he moved with lithe ease. His face had a fine-boned elegance, but no remarkable feature except his eyes, which were of a bronzish color and caught the light. Set a little deep under elegantly curving brows they had the power to capture the attention.

In looks he was not extraordinary, and yet he had *presence*. He seemed like a creature from another world, more so even than the marquess. Lord Arden was very handsome and had the air of the *haut ton*, but he was somehow comfortably *English*. Without ever having met a foreigner, Judith sensed that Lord Charrington was *foreign*.

He also appeared to be completely in control of the situation. The impetuous young man of the day before had gone, and in his stead was this polished aristocrat.

"I am twenty-five years old," he said calmly, "wealthy, of equable temperament, and with no particular vices. I was born in Istanbul, raised in many places with English attendants, and educated at Harrow. I did not go up to university here but spent brief spells at Utrecht, Lucerne, and Rome. I served with Lord Silchester, mainly in Russia, before joining the Guards. I fought in the Peninsular, and then at Waterloo. I was wounded three times but only slightly. I have scars but no lingering disability.''

Judith looked at him during this astonishing recital thinking that this surely must be a fevered dream.

Matching his tone, she said, "My dear sir, I am twenty-nine. I will be thirty in two months. I have two children and have never been more than fifty miles from this spot. I have no remarkable features or accomplishments other than housewifery. What can you possibly want with me?''

He was undisturbed and even smiled. He gestured to a chair. "Please, Mrs. Rossiter, will you be seated.'' When they were settled he said, "I told you yesterday. I wish to marry you. I cannot explain my reasons in full but I assure you there is nothing in them that will be to your disadvantage. To be blunt, I wish to marry and settle down, and I do not want a bride who will expect more from me than I am able to give.''

Judith's instincts told her he was telling the truth insofar as it went, but she could hardly believe it. She was almost afraid to believe it. She had not admitted to herself how much her situation frightened her until now when a door was just possibly being opened, being opened to a blindingly bright future. "And what is it that you are able to give, my lord?''

He considered it carefully. "Respect, care, and kindness.''

What more could anyone want? "And what will I be expected to give in return?''

"I hope for the same, but the bare minimum of good manners will suffice.''

She took in a deep breath. "You ask so little. I must question this."

He raised his brows. "Very well then. You will curtsy to me when meeting, prepare my food with your own hands, and dance naked before the fire for me every night."

She thought she saw teasing humor in his eyes, but she wasn't entirely sure. It was nervousness that made her laugh at his words. "Can you not make it make better sense of it for me, my lord?"

He raised a hand in an expressive gesture of helplessness. Really, he spoke with his hands in a way she had never seen before. "It makes me sound a coxcomb," he said. "But . . . I have always had the talent of putting people at their ease, Mrs. Rossiter. It was partly inherited, for my father possessed it, but growing up in diplomatic circles honed it. That upbringing also gave me, I am told, a Continental air which Englishmen distrust, and Englishwomen admire. I did not realize until recently, however, that my talent and my air appear to have a somewhat devastating effect on susceptible young Englishwomen."

"They swoon at the sight of you?" she asked skeptically. He was an attractive man, but hardly stunning.

"That, thank heavens, happened only once. But they lose their hearts with alarming frequency."

She stared. "Someone actually swooned at your feet?"

He smiled in self-derision. "Devilish embarrassing. I was escaping an amorous heiress and thought I'd be safe with a very dull-looking wallflower. I asked her to dance. She stood, took two steps, and passed out."

"Well at least you are trained to handle the vapors," she remarked, and his lips twitched in acknowledgment of her sally.

He shook his head. "In this case, I flunked. Her

chaperone rushed to attend her and I slipped away. In fact, I slipped away to Hartwell.''

Judith felt sorry for them both. ''You do realize she had probably been watching you from afar, weaving private romantic dreams, safe in the knowledge that you would never even notice her existence. The reality was just too much.''

''I suppose that's how it was,'' he said with a grimace, ''but you can see why I fled. Apart from anything else I have no taste for hurting people. In fact I have an aversion to it. In the circles in which I grew up, hurt feelings and arguments could lead to massacres.''

Judith was rapidly becoming fascinated. ''Strange then that you became a soldier.''

''Oh, fighting's not the same,'' he said, with a dismissive gesture. ''In fact, I welcomed the honesty of it. It's hurting people's feelings I can't abide. That's why I want to marry a woman who won't expect too much.''

How does one hurt bodies without hurting feelings? Judith wondered. ''And you think I am such a woman?''

''Are you not?''

Judith considered him thoughtfully. It all rang true, and though she couldn't quite understand this devastating effect he appeared to have on the beauties of Almack's, she did not find it incredible. He was having something of an effect on her with his moments of mischievous humor, his aura of sophistication, and those sleepy, catlike eyes.

It was still ridiculous. She had never even dreamt such a man existed and she was supposed to marry him?

But if this was an honest offer it was an answer to a prayer she would never even have dared to send on high.

She sickeningly realized that he was only offering

this golden opportunity because of a misapprehension, and she had always been an honest woman. What was she to do?

"So you wouldn't want me to fall in love with you," she said.

"Absolutely not."

"And you don't believe you will develop such feelings for me?"

He hesitated but then said, "Correct. That is no reflection on you, Mrs. Rossiter. I simply seem to lack the faculty of romantic love."

Could she believe anything so unlikely? Why should he lie?

She had once been a mad romantic, which was how she had ended up married to Sebastian, who had shown her that romantic love left a great deal to be desired. It would not bother her at all to be free of such foolishness, especially when promised respect, care, and kindness. And freedom from want.

She still felt there must be a fly in this sweet-smelling ointment.

"You will care for my children?" she queried.

"It will give me pleasure to do so. They seem excellent specimens."

Judith was very aware that in considering this match she was, in a sense, considering it, too, on her children's behalf. Her marriage would give Leander a father's power over them. Even sweet-natured Sebastian had turned petulant occasionally, said hurtful things to them, and even hit them. He had once spanked little Rosie with what Judith thought most uncalled for severity.

"They are not above being naughty, my lord. What are your ideas on discipline?"

He considered her question carefully. "Being a parent would be completely new to me, and I assure you I would listen to your advice, Mrs. Rossiter. You are much more familiar with the business than I. As

I see it, however, there would be two ways of dealing with such things. I could leave the management of Bastian and Rosie entirely up to you, but would not expect to do so with my own children. You do realize that I would hope to have children with you?"

"Of course." She had never expected otherwise and yet could feel her cheeks heat at the subject. It was very difficult to imagine the intimacies of marriage with this elegant stranger. This young, elegant stranger.

"However," he continued, "it doesn't seem to me desirable that Bastian and Rosie be made to feel different. I think I should counsel and discipline your children as I will those we have together."

"That seems wise," she said from a dry throat, burningly aware of that word discipline. "Er . . . what form would any discipline take?"

Leander was aware that this question had some importance, and guessed it came from a mother's tender heart. Doubtless the poet had been soft-hearted, too, but Leander would expect to raise children, particularly boys, as he had been raised.

"You are wise to raise this before any decision is made, ma'am. If you are asking if I believe in corporal punishment I would have to say yes, particularly for boys."

Judith felt a sinking feeling. She should have known this was too good to be true. Despite some angry slaps and spanks, Sebastian had never really hurt the children. Was she now to hand them over to a man who would flog them?

"It would be cruel," she said.

"My dear lady, I think it cruel to do otherwise. With luck and perfect behavior Bastian might get through school unscathed, though I know no one who has managed it, not even the Rogues. The simple fact is that if Bastian is mischievous he will be beaten at school, and had best learn to take it like a man. I can assure you, it is not in my nature to be cruel."

Judith was distracted. "Why on earth should rogues escape?"

He laughed. "The Company of Rogues—a schoolboy group. We protected each other from unfairness, but our leader, Nicholas, was very firm that we were not allowed to gang together to escape just punishment."

The magic word *school* was beginning to penetrate Judith's mind, and her certainty that she must reject this offer wavered. "You would send Bastian to school?"

"Of course. To Harrow, I would think." Then he looked at her with a frown. "My dear Mrs. Rossiter, I know it will be a wrench for you to part from him, but it would be for the best."

Did he think her that much of a fool, that she would cling to her son rather than see him given such a magnificent start in life? It had been her worry and her dream ever since Sebastian's death.

But school, she now realized, was where he would be up against masters, and even senior boys, armed with birch and cane. Her brothers had gone to school, though a much less grand one than Harrow, and brought home horrendous tales.

"Oh dear," she said and stared at him, seeking some kind of reassurance.

He seemed to read her mind. "All I can say, Mrs. Rossiter, is that I will treat your children as I will my own, as I was treated. My father permitted physical punishment only for serious wrongdoing. Unless a child is steeped in wickedness, I'm sure most crimes can be handled by admonition and a suitable penalty. However, if I think a caning is called for, I will administer it, or order it when Bastian has a tutor. In fact," he said with a rueful smile, "I remember as a boy I was generally quite glad of it, for it made me feel I'd paid and it was quickly over. I found it far more hurtful to feel under a shadow of shame for hours, or even days."

Again she wavered. "And Rosie?"

"I will leave to you. Perhaps girls have purer souls. They seem to get up to mischief much less often."

Judith raised her brows. "I think you said you had no sisters, sir. That is obvious."

"Then flog her if you wish, but I won't do it for you."

Judith looked at her work-worn hands. This impossible, ridiculous plan was taking on an almost irresistible reality.

But it was still ridiculous.

Leander rose and came to her, took her hands, and raised her to her feet. "It comes down to trust," he said. "You are going to have to trust me as I am willing to trust you. Bastian cannot inherit my title or estates, but in every other way he will be my son. I will cherish him, give him every advantage, and ease his way into whatever life he seeks. Rosetta will be my daughter. If, that is, you will be my wife."

Judith bit her lip, still afraid to take the step. "I'm older than you."

"That matters not. Grasp fate, my dear. It is here before you, and I have been scrupulously honest in presenting it."

And I have not been honest with you, she thought. How could a marriage prosper based on lies? Judith sought the conventional escape. "I need time, my lord."

He looked a little disappointed, but nodded. "Of course. Shall I call on you tomorrow?"

She would like to ask for weeks, but she sensed he would refuse that. "Why is there such hurry?" she asked.

A hand expressed unease, but he answered. "It is past time I took up my responsibilities as earl, and settled in my home at Temple Knollis. I have spent too long abroad, however, and I need both a chatelaine and a helpmeet by my side there. But my land cannot abide delay. It has been neglected too long."

Helpmeet. It was a lovely word and implied a real need that she could fulfill. "Tomorrow then," she said, looking into his mysterious eyes.

"I will come to your cottage at eleven o'clock." He raised her hand and kissed it. "I hope you are going to say yes." He seemed to mean it. He tucked her hand in his arm. "Let's walk down to the paddock to find the children, and then I will arrange for a carriage to take you home."

Chapter Four

Judith was aware before she was back at her cottage that she really had no choice. When she'd seen Bastian's face as he fed apples to the marquess's magnificent horses, and the wistful longing on Rosie's, she'd known she couldn't reject this miraculous opportunity.

Again she was glad of the kitten. Magpie obligingly played with some tangled yarn, and distracted the children from their delirious reflections on horses, cake, and lemonade.

That evening, when she'd settled them in bed and begun the ironing, she admitted that she couldn't even claim that their present simple life was tenable. Because there had been no alternative she had persuaded herself that she could manage, but the fact was that they always needed a little more money than they had, and she was eating into her small savings at the end of every quarter. Heaven help them if anyone fell sick.

Could she risk the poorhouse just because of foolish qualms about total honesty? All the same, she would feel a great deal easier in her mind if she could tell him the truth.

That, however, would be to ruin everything.

Lord Charrington had sought her out as the Weeping Widow, the inconsolable one. He would withdraw his offer immediately if she confessed the truth: that she had fallen out of love with her husband many years ago; that she had been only slightly sad for his death, as at the death of a mere acquaintance whose life had been cut short.

When she was sixteen—the daughter of an impoverished curate and living a very simple, country life—Sebastian Rossiter had entered that life like a vision from heaven. With his flowing hair, his gentle brown eyes, and his elegant, romantic clothing, he had seemed straight out of a novel.

She had met him when he stopped to view the tomb of Sir Gerault of Hunstead, their crusader and only claim to fame. She was in the church laying out the prayer books, and directed him to the marble effigy, relating what was known of Sir Gerault.

Sebastian visited the parsonage that evening to present her with a poem he had composed about her. *"Sweet angel by the tomb, about you glows/ The everlasting beauty of the rose./ A virgin standing in a holy place/ With sapphire orbs in alabaster face."*

These days she didn't think it one of his better efforts, but at the time it had practically made her swoon with delight. Nothing so utterly romantic had ever happened in her life before, and at that tender age she had been primed for romance. From the wisdom of almost-thirty Judith shook her head at the foolish girl she had been.

Her parents had been confused, and a little awestruck. They did not quite like the reference to a virgin—her mother because she thought it indelicate, her father because it smacked of popery—but they were not about to object to such a wonderful suitor to their daughter's hand. Any lingering doubts were soon soothed by his impeccable behavior, and his assurance of his firm adherence to the Protestant faith.

Judith and Sebastian were married six months after their first meeting. She was wafted off in dreamy delight to Mayfield House, a solid modern structure of red brick with five bedchambers and a conservatory.

She knew now it was not a particularly grand house, but coming from the crowded, ramshackle parsonage it was heaven. She was mistress of this comfortable home with money to purchase all that was required. She was married to a man who took endless pleasure in looking at her, and composing poetry about her.

It began to pall.

At first, in her youth, she thought she was at fault. How could anyone object to being adored, even if it meant sitting for hours under a particular sunbeam as he contemplated her? Perhaps it wasn't reasonable to want to entertain, to visit neighboring houses, to dance, to laugh, to have friends.

All Sebastian wanted was peace and quiet and her company.

Even if she played the piano, which was not a favorite occupation of hers, she must only play slow, dreamy pieces. Lively music, laughter, and running were all forbidden for they would disrupt the flow of words in his head.

It took her some months to find the courage to question the physical side of her marriage. Though she was hazy as to details, she was country-bred and knew there had to be more than kisses if there were to be children. Children had become increasingly attractive as something to occupy her time.

The subject had embarrassed him, but he had come to her bed that night, and at regular intervals thereafter, and eventually Judith had conceived a child.

At first Sebastian was delighted by the thought of

children. He wrote a number of anticipatory verses about sleeping cherubs and tender mothers. Not long after Bastian's birth he had written "My Angel Bride." But children are not by nature peaceful. They are noisy, and as they grow, they are naturally energetic. Bastian was no exception. Nor was Rosie when she arrived.

The children were a great joy to Judith, but they did not improve her marriage. Life became a constant struggle to allow them the necessary freedom, while maintaining tranquility in the house. It was an impossible situation which led to fretful complaints from her husband, and increasingly sharp bursts of his peevish temper.

It wore away the romance until there was none left. Judith had realized one day that she didn't love Sebastian anymore, and perhaps never had. She didn't even like him, and perhaps never had. She thought his precious poetry sentimental nonsense, and his affected looks ridiculous. When she saw him in his curling papers she was hard-pressed not to laugh.

There was, however, nothing to do about it. She had made her bed and must lie in it. She could at least be grateful that he rarely joined her there, for the fascinating activity that had been the subject of endless girlish, giggling debates had turned out to be a tedious, rather messy business with no pleasure attached. The only wisdom she had seen in Sebastian was his disinclination to indulge in the first place.

The failure of the marriage wasn't even Sebastian's fault, for he was generally kind and generous, and his poetry evidenced his love. It was hers for being such a romantic twit at sixteen. So she continued to do her best to create a home for all her family, regarding Sebastian as another child rather than a mate.

In public she carefully maintained their reputation as a devoted romantic couple, for there would be no advantage to anyone in disturbing it. Sebastian didn't seem to be aware that there was anything false in it, and continued to produce the verses that made her the envy of many women.

At least after Rosie's birth the marital duties ceased entirely, and Sebastian once more restricted himself to kissing her cheek, or occasionally cuddling her on his lap. Things being different Judith would have liked more children, for they were now the light of her life, but not at the price of yet more disharmony in the home.

Her life had been stable and not particularly unpleasant until Sebastian developed pneumonia and died. Her first reaction, she had to confess, had been a sense of liberation of which she had been ashamed ever since. Like a canary in a cage, however, freedom had been a frightening shock, and in the first days she had numbly obeyed the pressure of everyone's expectations, and acted the part of the inconsolable widow. Her distress had become real when she had discovered he had left her almost destitute.

Her poor father had had the task of arranging her affairs, and it had taken its toll on him, too.

Judith had allowed herself and the children to be taken back to the parsonage, where she had languished in despair for weeks. When she began to pull herself together, and wrote to Timothy Rossiter for help, she discovered she had the name of the Weeping Widow. She had not cried for well over a year, but the name had stuck. She knew a part of it was the fact that she continued to wear unrelieved black, but what else was she supposed to do?

Virtually penniless, she hadn't dared buy anything for mourning and had simply thrown all her clothes into a vat of black dye. It had served well enough. Now there was certainly no money to buy new clothes until these were worn out, little money to buy new clothes even then.

Then there was the monument. She had almost had the vapors when a stonemason had arrived with it, saying that Sebastian had ordered it years before, had designed it himself, leaving only the date of death to be filled in. What kind of person did such a thing?

At least he had paid for it in advance. Judith had ordered it set in place, relieved that Sebastian had been provident in one respect, even if a macabre one. She winced, however, whenever she visited the churchyard and saw how out of place it looked there.

She sometimes dwelt on the fact that ten years ago Sebastian had received a legacy from an uncle, and had spent it all on installing a rose garden at Mayfield House. He had even commissioned a rose from a breeder, a rose called Judith Rossiter. It was a pale cream bloom of delicate form that had nothing in common with her. She sometimes wondered whether Sebastian ever saw *her* at all.

When she'd left behind that rose garden at Mayfield House, and thought of the money it had cost, she had felt a spurt of pure hate. But she had fought it, and buried it. Hate served no purpose at all.

Lord Charrington was proposing marriage to an inconsolable widow, and she wasn't that. But she was certainly turned off romantic nonsense for life.

She assured herself that to accept would be honest, after a fashion.

Judith stacked the last of the ironing, and rubbed a hand over her tired eyes. She should go to bed. Apart from anything else she couldn't afford to be burning candles like this.

But if she married Lord Charrington, there'd be candles to spare forever. And servants, and new clothes, and schools, and entertainments, and horses. And no fear of the workhouse. . . .

How could she possibly say no?

She went up to bed prepared to accept Lord Char-rington's proposal, then spent a fretful, sleepless night changing her mind a dozen, a score, of times.

The next day, Judith was hard-pressed not to snap at the children for no reason at all. In fact, with impeccable instinct, they faded into the background and neither so much as raised the subject of Lord Charrington, or Hartwell, or riding.

This strengthened her determination to accept the earl's offer. Both her children clearly wanted it so. Weren't children supposed to have an instinct about people?

In fact, she was a little doubtful about that. Children were creatures of the moment, and these children had been bribed with lemonade, cakes, and horses.

In the end she lost patience with their quiet expectation and sent them off to glean any remaining rose hips in the hedgerows. If they didn't become part of the aristocracy they would need the healthy tonic in the winter. That told her she still had doubts, and she couldn't afford doubts. For once in her life she had to be hard and firm and, as he had said, grasp opportunity.

It wouldn't be melodramatic to say it was a matter of life and death.

She settled to wait, working on a pair of slippers for Rosie's Christmas gift.

When the knock came at the door, it felt like a welcome end to a period of torture. She should have given him his answer yesterday. Any notion of choice had been illusory.

It was a chilly day, and he was dressed in a beautifully tailored greatcoat, a glossy beaver, and supple leather gloves. He looked more handsome, more substantial, more polished even than before. Though he was not a big man, his presence seemed to fill her small front room, and the notion of the marriage became once more absurd.

She looked rather helplessly at her two shabby chairs. "Please be seated, my lord. Would you like some tea?"

He smiled quizzically. "Delaying still? Mrs. Rossiter, please give me your answer, or perhaps *I* will have a fit of the vapors."

She turned away. "You sound as if this is important to you, whereas I know you could find a woman to marry you under any hedgerow."

His tone was amused. "I assure you, I would never consider marrying a woman I found under a hedgerow."

He let the silence run and in the end she had to turn back to face him.

"Mrs. Rossiter," he said, "the whole point of this marriage is to avoid sentimental flummery, but I can say with complete honesty that I want you to be my wife. In fact, you are the only woman I have ever encountered whom I have wished to make my wife."

He seemed so sincere.

"And do you promise never to write odes to my eyes?" Now why on earth had she asked anything so ridiculous?

Indeed a spark of laughter lit his eyes, and he placed his hand on his heart. "On my honor as an English gentleman."

She was smiling at him, enjoying the twinkle in his eyes. The words escaped without her conscious volition. "Very well then."

He smiled. It was a shining smile, and it startled her that she could cause it even in a simple matter of practicality. He put his hat and gloves on the table, and shrugged out of his coat to lay it on a chair. He came over and placed a finger under her chin. She realized he was going to kiss her. She swung away.

"Oh don't . . ." Then she looked back, knowing that had been singularly foolish.

He was frowning slightly. "If this is to go any further, ma'am, you must come here and be kissed."

"We are still virtual strangers, my lord."

"Even so."

Judith had taken the impression that he was young and overcivilized, unlikely to assert his will. She was learning her error. She remembered he was a veteran of the wars. Her doubts resurfaced but she brutally shoved them down. A betrothal kiss was a silly matter upon which to balk. She slowly returned to stand in front of him.

He took her hands in a firm, warm grasp, capturing her with those intense eyes. "I understand that you loved your husband dearly, ma'am, and I don't expect to supplant him in your heart. In fact his hold on your affections is one of your greatest recommendations. But I expect you to be able to accept my kisses and my attentions in bed without shrinking. If you cannot do that, then tell me now."

There was always a price to pay, but marital duties would not be an unbearable burden. She just didn't much like to be kissed on the lips. It was such a sloppy business.

"I will be happy to do my duty," she said.

He nodded, though a brow quirked slightly at her tone. "There is another condition of which I should have told you yesterday. If we are to be married, I insist that you leave off mourning entirely.

Judith thought how strange, and pleasant, it would be to be out of black, then remembered she must not let that pleasure show. He was offering for the inconsolable widow. "Very well," she said with just a trace of reluctance, then added frankly, "but you will have to pay for my new wardrobe."

He stared at her. "Do you mean you are in black because you cannot afford new clothes?"

"No," she lied quickly. "I could not have borne to wear colors. But I understand now that you will wish it. I merely point out that I have nothing else, and if you wish me to be in colors you must provide them."

His expression lightened. "It will be my pleasure to do so." He stepped back slightly and studied her. "Blue, deep rose, warm browns, peach . . ."

His frankly roaming eyes were flustering her. "Are you going to dictate my wardrobe, my lord?"

"Great ladies have begged for my advice, Mrs. Rossiter."

He was dangerous in a funning mood. She raised her chin and said dampeningly, "I think you should apply your mind to more important matters, my lord."

"Slavery and the national debt, no doubt." He released a plaintive, and insincere, sigh. "Very well. I leave fashion to you. But no black, beige, gray, or violet. I forbid it."

She thought it was ridiculous to have this young man forbidding her anything, even in jest, but she sensed that he could enforce his will. What on earth was she letting herself in for? She waited tensely for his kiss, but he hesitated thoughtfully then drew her toward a chair. He sat and pulled her onto his lap.

"My lord! What are you doing?"

"Forgive me for being forceful," he said while holding her with quite remarkable strength, "but I need to be sure we are physically compatible."

With a gasp Judith braced her hands on his chest. "If you think for one moment that I . . . that we . . ."

He relaxed his hold and laid a hand over her lips, laughter in his eyes. "Of course not. In broad daylight, in your parlor? You could have avoided all this, you know, by accepting a decorous betrothal kiss." He captured her hands so she could not push away, and turned serious. "You see, ma'am, despite your best intentions, you may not be able to overcome a natural reluctance to be intimate with a man other than your first husband. That would be fair neither to you, nor to me."

Judith wondered just what he did intend, and what she should do about it. She didn't like to be sitting on his knee like this. In his fondest moods, Sebastian had taken her on his knee in this very chair, calling her his angel. In the first years she had loved it, but then later it had become ridiculous, and ridiculous was what she remembered.

"It would help," he said dryly, "if you would relax a little, and not sit like an apprehensive child on a surly great-uncle's knee."

She thought perhaps she saw a way out of this situation. She composed herself piously. "My husband used to hold me like this in this very chair," she told him, and glanced soulfully at the portrait hanging over the mantel.

He followed her eyes and studied the picture. Judith wished she hadn't drawn his attention to it after all. It showed Sebastian at his most absurd. He was dressed "poetically" in a loose lilac dressing robe, with a soft cravat knotted at his neck, and his hair in its best curls. He held a Judith Rossiter rose in his left hand and a quill in his right as he stared into the distance seeking inspiration.

She looked at manly, vital Lord Charrington, wondering if he would withdraw his offer on the spot.

He met her eyes with a flicker of naughty humor that startled her. "You are uncomfortable to be watched by him? Then it will make this an even better test, won't it?" He abruptly moved his supporting arm so she swayed back, and had to go limp or strain her spine. Sebastian had certainly never done that! She felt positively carnal to be sprawled across a man's lap in this manner.

The fingers of his left hand curled around her neck

to play gently there, but she was perfectly aware that they could also hold her down. His right hand came to stroke the side of her face. "Judith," he said softly, using her name for the first time. "Judith, my wife to be, within weeks we will be naked in a bed. Can you welcome me?"

Naked! She felt herself go stiff. She and Sebastian had never disrobed. *Never.* But she forced herself to relax. She had come too far to retreat. She reminded herself of all the advantages there would be for the children. "Willingly," she lied.

He looked understandably dubious. "Then call me Leander."

Judith swallowed. "Leander," she muttered, studying the pearl pin in his crisp cravat.

He turned her head up to his. "*I* am more interesting than my clothing, as you will find."

Judith knew she had colored at this blatant reference to bodies, but hoped it did not look as if she were afraid. Nor was she precisely afraid. She would prefer that their marital duties were performed in the manner to which she was accustomed, but if he wanted her clothes off that was no reason to balk.

She remembered his remark about her dancing naked before the fire, and wondered if there had been any teasing in it at all. Well, even that would not be too high a price to pay.

Somewhat hesitantly, she raised a hand and touched his cheek.

He relaxed and turned to kiss that hand. Then he frowned at its roughened, reddened state. "We will have to give this poor member some loving care." Holding her eyes, he pressed a kiss into her palm.

Nothing like that had ever happened to Judith before, and she found she was well and truly relaxed in his arms, as limp as a rag. She gasped as his moist, warm tongue tickled her, tracing up from palm to fingertip. Goodness gracious! It must be his Euro-

pean upbringing. Everyone knew they were a strange
lot abroad.

He placed her hand against his heart, and raised
her slightly to put his lips to hers. They were not
puffy and moist, but dry and firm. The taste of him
was not unpleasant. Unlike Sebastian, his teeth must
still be good. She just lay there in a daze, allowing
him to do as he willed.

Then she realized his other hand had released hers
in order to touch her breast. She tried to gasp a
protest, and his tongue invaded quickly then
retreated. Returned, then tickled her lips. It was all
strange but Judith recognized wickedness. Vague
whispered scandals of the goings-on in London came
to mind, and even the ancient stories of the Hell-
Fire Club.

As she had been warned as a child, however, wickedness was not without its attractions. Judith felt the
power of something . . .

Judith knew she should close her mouth and clench
her teeth tight, but with a clever mouth on hers and
a hand teasing her breast, she was trapped in a surge
of hot, inexplicable sensations. She closed her eyes
and let the feelings take her. When he drew back she
kept her eyes closed, afraid of what they might reveal
to him.

That she was shocked? That was certainly true.

That she had wanton impulses? That was true, too,
but he had no one to blame but himself for discovering it.

That she was afraid of this difference, this newness?
That he must never know for he might withdraw his
offer.

She was set on her feet and only then did she open
her eyes to find the room unsteady around her. "My
goodness."

"My sentiments entirely."

She looked up, startled, to see he was both flushed

and amused. "I promise not to challenge you again until we are married, Judith, but I am satisfied that we are compatible. Are you?"

Judith wasn't sure at all, but she was determined on this marriage. She cleared her throat. "Er . . . entirely."

"I thought so."

She flashed him another wary glance. "You still wish to marry me, my lord?"

"Most definitely." He shrugged on his coat. "Will we have banns read, or would you prefer a license?"

"Banns," said Judith quickly. With a license they could be married in days and she needed time.

"In three weeks then," he said.

"Three weeks," she repeated numbly. "That . . . er . . . does not give much time to notify people. Will you not want to invite anyone?"

"I had not intended it, no. Do you have family whom you wish to be present?"

Judith seized on this point, like a person dragged by a runaway horse digging their heels into the dirt. "Yes, I do, actually. You have not asked me about my family."

"They don't have any bearing on my decision. You are more than welcome to have them at your wedding."

"I have three brothers and two sisters," she said with a rush. "My father's the curate at Hunstead, and I wish him to perform the service."

"Very well. Perhaps we should drive over there soon, and tell them the good news."

Judith bit her lip. Would he change his mind when he met her impoverished family? But he knew her to be poor. Would her family reveal what a silly romantic she had been at sixteen? But he would think all that sentiment expended on Sebastian.

"That would be pleasant," she said, gathering her well-practiced composure around her like a cloak.

He put his stylish hat on his head, achieving a precise, elegant angle without apparent effort. "I'm sure the Ardens will allow a gathering at Hartwell after the ceremony. Will three weeks from today be convenient?"

Judith nodded.

"You can leave everything in my hands," he said, then added with a smile, "except, of course, your wardrobe. I suggest you let Beth Arden take you into Guildford. There must be someone there able to furnish some tolerable gowns. I'll pay the accounts, of course. Don't stint yourself. There is money to spare. And buy clothes for the children, too, if they need them, and any other treats they would like."

"You'll spoil them," she protested.

"A little indulgence won't spoil them. It will merely bring them closer to their future station in life. After Christmas, I will arrange for Bastian to have a tutor to prepare him for Harrow."

The runaway horse was off again, despite her dug-in heels. "Thank you."

"And a governess for Rosie."

"Of course." This all seemed like the wildest dream. Judith sought a point of solidity. "My lord, where are we to live?"

He was engaged in pulling on his soft leather gloves. "Why at Temple Knollis, of course. Where else? We should be there in time for Christmas."

"You're going to marry Lord Charrington, Mama?"

"Will you be 'my lady'?"

"Will he live here with us?"

Judith faced her excited children in their kitchen. "Yes, yes, and no."

"Where will we live, then?" asked Bastian with the

anxiety of any child facing change. "Back at Mayfield House?"

"No, dear. In Somerset, at Lord Charrington's house. It's called Temple Knollis and it's supposed to be a splendid place."

"Somerset's a long way, isn't it?"

"Yes."

"So I won't see Georgie again."

She ruffled his curls gently. "I'm afraid not. But you will make new friends."

Rosie said, "Will we dine off golden plates?"

Judith laughed. "Not if I have any say in the matter."

"Will I have silk gowns?"

Judith took in her patent longing and kissed her brow. "Not for every day, darling, but you may have one for the wedding, and for special occasions."

"Pink?" asked Rosie.

"If you wish."

"With lace and roses?"

Judith grimaced inwardly at the thought. "We'll see."

She looked at Bastian, who was somber, but then he suddenly said, "There'll be lots of horses, won't there?"

"I expect so."

And that seemed to settle that.

Chapter Five

The runaway horse was fully in action. The next day Leander escorted Judith and the children to church to hear the banns read for the first time. She was pricklingly aware of the stares of the villagers, and the wandering whispers.

After the service, some came forward to offer good wishes, and be introduced to her intended, but his aristocratic presence, and the attendance of the marquess and marchioness deterred most from anything but staring.

Judith knew they must be wondering about such a strange twist of fate, but she raised her chin and smiled as if it were the most commonplace of matters.

On Monday, Judith found herself in a coach with Beth Arden heading into Guildford on a shopping expedition.

"You probably think this a silly extravagance," said Lady Arden as they roiled along the Guildford road.

Judith considered the state of her wardrobe. "No, I don't think that."

Beth looked at her with surprise. "I was poor when I married Lucien, and the de Vaux virtually had to torture me to make me accept anything."

Judith didn't know what to say to such an extraordinary statement. If she admitted what a joy it would be to buy new things, she feared to be thought mercenary. In the end, she said, "Perhaps you were not in quite such desperate straits, my lady. One day these clothes are going to shred off my back."

Beth's attention was arrested. "You are correct. I was never truly poor. There was always food, and decent clothing, with two new dresses every year."

Judith smiled sadly. "And time."

"Well, I was employed as a teacher, but yes, there was time." She smiled warmly. "I'm pleased to see that you are not being coerced to this. Now we can have fun. I must confess, I am still opposed to wanton excess; but a modest selection of becoming garments cannot be a sin, particularly as we will be patronizing local workers. In these hard times that is a duty."

Judith fretted she might have sounded too enthusiastic about giving up her blacks. "I would prefer to wear sober colors, of course, but I fear Lord Charrington would not like it." Dear heaven, but she hated duplicity.

"No, he wouldn't," Lady Arden agreed. "It is not my place to advise you, Mrs. Rossiter, and probably impertinent as I am some years your junior, but I would suggest you try to think of yourself as a bride, rather than as a widow."

Judith felt defensive. "And could you do that scarce twelve months after Lord Arden's death?"

Lady Arden paled.

"Oh, I'm sorry," said Judith. "You are newly-weds. It isn't a fair comparison."

"Not at all. I hope time doesn't make an alteration. . . You are right to take me to task, but still, if you are to do this at all, you must make the attempt to put the past behind you."

"I am willing to do that."

"And are you willing to call me Beth? I would like

it very much, and that would give me permission to call you Judith, and be comfortable.''

With this arranged Judith almost felt like a girl again. She had left behind a number of good friends upon her marriage but made none thereafter, for Sebastian and the children had demanded all her time. Since his death there had been even less leisure, and there had been the problem of her confused social station. By marriage and birth she was a lady, but in reality she was one of the village poor.

It would be pleasant to have a friend, even if only for a few weeks.

The carriage took them to the premises of Mrs. Lettie Grimsham, Guildford's foremost dressmaker. ''I haven't patronized the lady,'' said Beth as they alighted, ''but I am told she is the best in the locality. I would suggest in any case that you order only the essentials. When you are settled in your new life you will have more idea of what you require.''

Lettie Grimsham was short and very fat, with half a dozen jolly chins, and fingers like sausages. She clearly knew her business, which wasn't surprising as her thick accent revealed her to be French. She explained that she had come to England during the Terror and married Josiah Grimsham, a local corn factor.

When the lady waddled away to pick up her tape and pad, Beth leant sideways and whispered, ''I've encountered a number of modistes with Gallic names who have clearly never been closer to France than Brighton. And here we have a Lettie Grimsham, no less, who is the genuine article.''

The dressmaker took measurements which were noted by an assistant. Madame Grimsham was perceptive and shrewd. She made no comment about Judith's well-worn clothes, but produced swatches of cloth in the sober colors of half mourning.

Beth said, ''I think we want something brighter.

Mrs. Rossiter is to be a bride in a few weeks. In fact, why don't we start with a wedding gown?"

Madame Grimsham's black eyes brightened with delight. She studied Judith for a moment then called, "Sukie! Ze Lyons silk. Ze peach."

In a moment the assistant was back with a bale of wonderful silk, a golden peach figured with embroidered cream sprigs. Judith gasped at the beauty of it but said, "I don't think that is my color."

But she was herded into a private room and ordered to strip down to her shift. Then the dressmaker flung a length of the silk over her shoulder and wound it around. "Zere!" she demanded of Beth. "Am I not right?"

Judith looked at Beth as Beth's eyes widened "Madame Grimsham, you are a genius," Beth said.

"C'est vrai," said the woman complacently. "I could 'ave gone to London, me, but Josiah would not like it zere, and I would not like it zere wizout 'im." She turned Judith to a mirror, and Judith's mouth fell open.

"I always thought blue my color."

"Because of ze eyes, yes? But your eyes need no extra glory, madame, and see how zis color lights up ze skin."

Indeed it did. Judith's complexion was good, though a little browned from outdoor work and walks, but she had thought it ordinary. Warmed by the peach silk, it had radiance, and the deep blue of her eyes stood out even more in the frame of it.

It gave an illusion of beauty.

The wedding gown was soon agreed on, in a simple, high-necked style. They chose a velvet spencer to go with it, and in view of the season, a brown Russian wrapping cloak, hooded, trimmed with fox, with muff to match.

Consulting pattern books and dolls, and riffling through swatches of materials, they had soon chosen:

a deep green cloth pelisse with braid; two muslins with frills and lace; a warm round gown of soft pink cloth; another spencer of maroon gros de Naples; and an excessively fine evening dress of ivory lace over a peach satin slip. The latter had a vandyked bodice and a rouleau of brown and peach ribbon around the hem. In the illustration the bodice was cut to reveal a great deal of the bosom and Judith tried to amend this, but the other two ladies firmly overruled her.

"Judith," said Beth, "we have only chosen such a gown in case you should wish to attend an evening affair. In such a case a low neckline is *de rigueur*."

"At this season?" Judith protested. "I'll freeze!"

"Such occasions are generally overheated, but we must purchase you some shawls in case." She looked at Mrs. Grimsham.

"Zere are places in Guildford where one can buy such items, milady, but perhaps not of ze quality . . .?" An expressive hand gesture dismissed such places, and reminded Judith of Lord Charrington's foreign manner. "As I will have to send to London for some of my materials for zis order," the dressmaker continued, "perhaps I could have suitable items sent . . . ?"

Judith supposed the woman would make a handsome profit on this arrangement, but took some comfort from the fact that her good fortune was being spread. As Beth had pointed out, in these hard postwar days it was the duty of the fortunate to help others.

A perusal of Ackermann's led to a choice of an ivory silk scarf and a cashmere shawl, both English made. Mrs. Grimsham was sure she could procure something very similar.

The dressmaker promised that all items would be delivered by the wedding day, and sooner if possible, and offered to complete the pink dress quickly if required. Judith dismissed this. She had no desire to suddenly be peacocking about Mayfield in this finery, and in fact would find it ridiculous when there was so much work to be done. She would change her style when she changed her name.

Judith also gave Mrs. Grimsham Rosie's measurements and requested a warm wool dress suitable for traveling, and one of pink silk, *lightly* trimmed, for the wedding.

The dressmaker directed them to a tailor, a milliner she allowed to be tolerable, a shoemaker who knew his trade, and a good haberdashery establishment. Within a few hours, Judith had ordered or bought:

From the tailor—a smart suit, a warm coat, gloves, and cap for Bastian.

From the milliner—two bonnets for herself and two for Rosie.

From the cobbler—a pair of half boots for herself and Rosie, three pairs of slippers each, and a pair of shoes and boots for Bastian.

From the haberdasher—all the intimate items any of them could possibly require. By this time she was beginning to feel a little numb at the sheer quantity of her purchases, and tried to be moderate.

She had no problem with replacing her patched shifts and drawers with new ones of fine lawn, prettily worked with embroidery or threaded with ribbon. Nor with the purchase of three pairs of silk stockings to go with the dozen of lisle. She balked, however, at the purchase of silk nightgowns.

"How impractical," she said, adding in a mutter, "especially as he says he wants me to be naked."

Beth heard, and her eyes twinkled. "But perhaps," she said softly, "he will want to disrobe you himself."

Judith didn't know what to make of this, and knew she was pink at the thought. Sebastian had always announced before bedtime his intention of visiting her, and then come to her in the dark. Even if Lord Charrington—Leander—wished to take off her nightgown, would it make much difference in the dark if it were silk or cotton?

Being distracted, she found she now owned two silk nightgowns, and two of cotton flannel. "For occasions," said Beth, "when warmth is of more importance than looks."

Beth's footman shuttled backward and forward to the carriage with packages.

Judith felt that perhaps she shouldn't, but she stopped at the small shop that sold toys and books. She bought each child a new book for their studies, and some paper and pencils. How pleasant it would be not to have to ration such things anymore. Then, feeling they should share in the general frivolity, she bought Bastian a hoop, and Rosie a top.

When they left the shop she said, "Heavens above, let's go home before I buy the town! I daren't think how much I have spent."

They were both content to settle in the carriage, but Beth said, "Whatever the sum, I assure you Lord Charrington will scarcely notice it. Besides, you have bought only the bare necessities. It would be pointless and foolish to be going about looking shabby, and it would upset him. I suspect that, apart from the army, his life has been rather rarefied."

Judith looked at her in surprise. "I thought you were well acquainted."

"Oh no. He is an old friend of my husband's, but I met him for the first time a week ago. Lord Charrington has been out of England since he was eighteen."

Stranger and stranger, thought Judith with sudden concern. "Do you think he will want to go abroad again?"

Beth looked at her. "You would not like it?"

"No, I don't think I would."

"You had best ask him, though I understand that he intends to live in England now."

Judith felt sick. "But I've just spent all that money!"

Beth put a hand over hers. "Don't let it count with you for a moment, Judith. I'm sure he would not be so petty as to make an issue of it, but if he does, I will pay your bills."

"I couldn't let you do that," said Judith, though she had no idea what else she would do.

"Of course you could. I don't forget that I persuaded you into this."

However, when the subject was raised, Leander said without hesitation that he intended to live in England. He suggested they might want to visit the Continent at a later date, but only for a brief visit.

He was delighted with the account of her purchases, and dutifully admired the children's new toys. Then both she and he were coaxed out to admire Bastian's expertise with the hoop, and Rosie's with the whip and top. Rosie found it hard to keep the top spinning, and so Judith went to help her.

When she heard Bastian asking Leander for help, she suspected that it was more a plea for equal attention. She heard Leander confessing that he knew nothing of hoops, and looked over at him, sad for the childhood he seemed not to have had. What had his parents been about? Even if they had little time for him, could they not have hired better attendants?

Rosie demanded her attention again, and so she concentrated on the girl until the top was spinning well under the lash of the whip.

When she looked up, it was to see elegant Lord Charrington running down the lane, bowling the hoop under her son's tutelage. She bit her lip to hold back a laugh, and hurried into the house to put on the kettle.

When they all came in at last, bringing frosty air and laughter, she poured tea and served cake. She only realized when she sat that she'd cut a piece of cake and placed it before Leander without asking him, just as if he were another child. Heavens, she'd be cutting his food up next!

He didn't seem to notice, nor did he seem put out by the indignities in which he had participated.

He raised his brows, however, when introduced to Magpie. "Perhaps not the wisest acquisition when we are about to go on a journey. . ." But then he grinned at them all. "But we'll manage. Remind me to tell you sometime of a bunch of piglets we transported across the Pyrenees. . ."

She remembered again that he'd been a soldier, and presumably there he'd not been able to preserve his perfect gloss. And he'd been a schoolboy, and had surely been in some rough and tumbles.

She had the feeling, however, that she didn't know him at all, and it frightened her. She had been raised in the country where strangers were a five-day marvel. She'd married Sebastian after a six-month engagement, and even then she hadn't known him aright.

What, in time, would she discover about this mysterious man who was to be her husband? And would she only discover it too late?

On Tuesday Leander borrowed the Arden's carriage for the ten-mile drive to Hunstead. He insisted on taking the children. This made Judith nervous for it would be his longest continuous exposure to them, but Bastian and Rosie were on their best behavior to an almost painful extent. It seemed they, too, couldn't quite believe this good fortune, and feared it would slip away.

When they approached the parsonage Judith watched him anxiously. Hunstead Glebe House was a plain building, and never in good repair. The diocese was supposed to maintain it, but didn't. Judith suspected that the Vicar of Bassetford, whose curate her father was, misspent the money.

She saw no expression on Leander's face at all, though she suspected those strange amber eyes were not missing any detail. The children were hanging out of the window, unable to suppress their excitement, for visits to their grandparents were rare. Leander grabbed the back of Rosie's gown to make sure she didn't tumble out.

As soon as the carriage stopped, the children were out and running over to their gray-haired grandparents. Plump Reverend Millsom and his tiny wife were both delighted to see them, but plainly bewildered by the visitation, especially in a grand carriage.

The two of Judith's siblings who lived at home came out to see what was going on.

She made the introductions and explanations. Her sister, Martha—an uncomplicated soul—practically fainted with excitement. Her brother, John, however, was suspicious. That was hardly surprising. He was very like her.

Her parents said all that was proper, but they looked a little dubious without having the nerve to question such a wonderful surprise. For the first time she wondered what they'd really thought of her marriage to Sebastian.

When they went into the house, Leander proved his diplomatic abilities. He accepted without a blink a seat on a threadbare sofa, deaf to the objections of the two cats who'd been moved to make room for him. He discussed with equal ease the terrible lack of employment, the question of absentee churchmen, the prospects for lasting peace, and the difficulty in obtaining good currants.

When Martha made a sweeping gesture and mashed a cake against the sleeve of his Melton-cloth jacket, doubtless finer than anything that had visited this room before, he passed it all off smoothly, somehow giving the impression that a smear of cream and jam was just what the brown fabric had always needed to be complete.

He had said he had a gift for putting people at ease and he proved it. Soon, all of them were gathered around him like doting sheep, even John.

Judith was not entirely sure why she resented this until she realized that her family were not being visited, they were being skillfully handled. They were one of the prices *he* had to pay in this arrangement.

All her doubts resurfaced. Perhaps he was handling *her,* and in such a subtle way that she hadn't noticed. Perhaps she would be handled all her life—which brought to mind the events following her betrothal, where he had indeed handled her. And brought to mind Beth Arden's comments about him undressing her, and nakedness. . .

She could feel her color rising. She was horrified to be sitting here in her parents' parlor with the man who had . . . who would . . . She had never felt this way about Sebastian.

She took a deep drink of tea and choked. John slapped her back so heartily she almost fell off her chair. She stared at Leander who was perfectly straight-faced. She could see the laughter bubbling behind his eyes.

She resented the fact that he was holding in the laughter, laughter at her family.

Before she said something better left unsaid, Judith concentrated on gossip with Martha. Unfortunately it was interspersed with whispers like, "He's like the hero from a novel, Ju." "Will you have to wear a coronet?" "How many servants will you have?" "If you set up in London, will you have me to visit?"

She didn't know the answers to these questions, and they frightened her. Perhaps Leander should marry Martha instead. But then she realized that Martha, for all she was twenty-five, was just the sort of young widgeon to fall in love with him, and perhaps was already on that road.

Judith made a solemn vow never to embarrass him and herself in such a way.

Concentrating on Martha, Judith only slowly realized that Leander was encouraging her family to speak of their financial situation. The Millsoms were not grasping, but when there is never enough money it soon becomes the focus of existence. Judith knew that all too well.

It was suddenly just too much. She put down her cup and rose. "My lord, a word with you please."

The room fell silent. Somewhat surprised, Leander followed her out into the dim narrow passageway. "Is there some problem?"

Judith faced him and whispered tightly, "You have my family all wrapped around your fingers already, my lord. There is no need to *buy* them, too."

His chin rose under the attack. "Why do you object? Do you think I'll take the cost out on you?"

She winced at that, which came too close to the mark. "I don't want you to feel any obligation. My family was no part of our agreement."

In the familiar, dim, cluttered passageway he looked as out of place as a diamond in the ashes. He acted it, too, brushing a crumb from his sleeve, and drawling, "You see me as a very feeble fellow, don't you? But I assure you, Judith, I am never put upon. Am I to leave your family in straitened circumstances when funds I would consider loose change could make all the difference? The fifty guineas for your sister and brother-in-law's lease, the hundred for John's articles. . . These are nothing to me." He gave one of those expressive Continental shrugs, and it seemed to dismiss her family entirely. "I don't expect, or want, gratitude."

She wanted to hit him. "How absolutely *splendid* for you!"

She would have swept by him back into the room, but he grasped her shoulders. "We are to be wed, Judith. With all my worldly goods I will thee endow. Do you *not* want me to ease your family's lot?"

Anger quivered in the chill air. Alarmed, she stepped back, but in the narrow passage there was nowhere to go. She ended up pressed against a wall between the hook holding his greatcoat, and that holding her mother's old musty cloak. Symbols of their different lives.

He let her go, but put his hands at either side of her head, caging her. "Well?" Bred-in-the-bone authority rang through the word.

Her knees were knocking. She didn't know how to handle this, only wanted to escape. "Yes, I want you to help them," she said thinly. "We should go back."

For a moment he leant closer, as if he would demand more. But then he drew in a deep breath and straightened. "What is this all about?"

The anger, the danger, faded, but her heart still pounded madly. "I don't know."

He studied her. "I have frightened you," he said stiffly. "I apologize. I don't know what came over me. Perhaps this is the notorious bridal nerves. Thank heavens there are less than three weeks to go."

Three weeks, thought Judith, until she and her children were in his power forever.

That evening, Leander found himself alone with Lucien drinking port. At Hartwell, it wasn't the practice for Beth to leave the men for this ritual, but this night she had pleaded a headache, and gone early to bed.

Leander was deeply troubled by that moment of anger at the vicarage. It was not part of his nature at all.

"Luce, excuse my probing into personal matters,

but it would appear that you and Beth sometimes fight."

Lucien grinned. "It has been known."

"Do you not find it makes your marriage difficult?"

Lucien topped up their glasses. "It makes it lively. It don't bother us, and we enjoy the reconciliations. I suppose the battle lines are well drawn and familiar, and in no danger of getting out of control. You must have experienced the same in war."

"Yes. A large part of it is maneuvering and posturing."

"Well, I wouldn't say Beth and I are precisely doing that. She's protecting her territory, and I'm protecting mine. By good fortune we discovered we have a large amount of middle ground that we are happy to share. Why the interest? I wouldn't have thought Judith Rossiter particularly militant."

Leander leaned back. "I suspect she could be, particularly in defense of her children. . . But I found myself angry with her today."

"You can hardly expect to never be angry with her."

"I am not used to losing control."

"What did you do?"

"Nothing terrible. But I laid hands on her. I wanted to shake her. I frightened her."

"Well, I'm no adviser on matters like this, but I'd think while a marriage without love would be tedious, one without some anger would be dead. You are right to be concerned that she fear you, though. We are stronger, so they must be able to trust us."

Leander glanced up, caught by something in Lucien's tone, but his diplomatic instincts told him to let it pass. "It is not in my nature to be brutal, you know that. That is why I am concerned. Do you think it means Judith and I are unsuited?"

Lucien grinned. "In a similar situation, Nicholas suggested that my desire to throttle Beth was a sublimation of more earthy needs, and he could well have been right.''

Leander reacted swiftly to that. "I am not mad with desire for Judith Rossiter. This is a marriage of practicality. I have no cause to lose my temper over trifles.''

Lucien laughed out loud. "To me, it sounds as if for once you are being human, Lee. You are finding marriage involves two individuals, and a hell of a lot of compromise." He raised his glass. "Enjoy the fireworks.''

Three weeks, Judith was discovering, was both not long enough and far too long. She could hardly sleep for second and third thoughts. She needed a lot more time to be sure she was making a wise decision, and couldn't have it. Leander wanted this marriage quickly, and that in itself was suspicious. How could she tell what her future would be like when she met him so briefly and generally in company?

On the other hand she wanted it done, for every day brought the danger that she would somehow reveal to him that she was not a grieving widow. That would put an end to the plan. She could not bear that.

Already there were too many changes. The children had their new books and toys, and were beginning to become accustomed to having things as opposed to doing without. Leander visited the cottage nearly every day, and always had a gift—an orange, a book, a ball.

Often he would carry the children back to Hartwell so that, as he put it, they could become used to their future state. If that was so then their future was to be on horseback, for she saw little evidence they ever progressed up to the house.

Despite Leander's urging, she did not spend her

days at Hartwell, for there was far too much to do preparing for the wedding and the move. And perhaps, she admitted to herself, she was avoiding him for fear of making a mistake.

At least the children were getting to know and like him. Lord Charrington says, Lord Charrington does, echoed in her head every evening.

She worried about them. They were fizzing with excitement and at times becoming unruly. Judith would have liked to keep them to a more orderly routine, but that made her the one to say no, and besides, she lacked time to supervise their studies. Leander had insisted on hiring the Hubbles to work for her, but she still had hardly a moment free, and could get more done in a day with the children elsewhere.

One day Bastian begged her to come up to Hartwell and see how well he was doing in his riding. Judith knew nothing of horses, was afraid of them, and secretly thought riding a foolish, dangerous practice when feet and wheels would take you anywhere. She agreed, however, and knew it was a good idea when she saw how pleased Leander was to see her there. Avoiding him might in itself make him suspicious.

He kissed her hand and cheek, then led her over to a place at the paddock rails.

"Is Bastian progressing as well as he thinks?" she asked.

"Yes. Rosie will do well, too, when I can find her a better mount. This one is a lazy dumpling but she seems content."

Rosie rode out from the stables, bouncing happily on a fat little piebald, and waving at her mother. Judith waved back, her anxiety diminished. There was no danger there.

Then Bastian came out, perched on the top of an absolutely enormous chestnut. It scared Judith half to death. Her voice was thin as she said, "He looks so small up there."

Leander leaned against the paddock fence watching the boy put the horse through his paces. He didn't look in the least apprehensive.

"He's a natural rider," he said absently, "and Boscable's a safe mount, trust me. But all the horses here except my stallion and Beth's mare are Lucien's, and you can hardly expect Lucien to ride a pint-size horse. I'll buy Bastian something smaller when we're settled, but there's nothing suitable in this area at the moment." He glanced at her, seeming to notice her feelings for the first time. "Believe me, a vicious pony would be much worse than a well-mannered hunter."

But there would be less far to fall. "Is that what that is? A hunter?" Judith knew about hunting. It killed people.

He nodded. "An old one. Lucien's retired him down here." He turned to her. "You don't know much about horses, do you?"

"Is that a crime?"

"Please don't snap at me," he said in that *handling* voice. "I hear your husband kept a stable."

Judith moderated her tone but was unable to take her eyes off her son, who looked so small and helpless on the huge horse. "A carriage pair and a hack. But he didn't really care to ride unless the roads were too bad for wheels." She too wished she could control this urge to snap over every little thing. It was nerves. It would surely be easier when they were wed. For better or worse it would be done.

"I'd like you to take riding lessons, too."

"Now?" asked Judith in alarm, then could have bit her tongue, since he had clearly intended no such thing.

"Why not?"

"I don't have a habit."

"You have a habit of being difficult. You don't need a special garment to just sit on a horse. Scared?"

Judith looked him in the eye and said, "No."

Satisfaction shone briefly in his eyes. "Good. Stay here."

She knew she'd been handled again.

He was back in an alarmingly short time with a daintier chestnut with white markings. "Beth's mount," he explained. "Come on. Let's get you up."

The horse was relatively small, but still looked enormous.

"Why isn't Bastian riding this one?"

"It's a lady's mount, trained to the sidesaddle. Put your foot in my hands."

Judith stood beside the horse and looked up at the sidesaddle. A stable boy was holding the bridle and the horse was quiet, but she had no desire at all to be up there.

"No," she said. "I don't want to ride."

He looked at her a moment, then nodded to the boy to take the horse back to the stables. At the look in his eye, Judith beat a strategic retreat back to the paddock rails.

He came up beside her. "Why lie?"

"Lie?" she queried ingenuously.

"You're terrified of horses."

"Nonsense. I just don't care to be on one."

"Look at me!"

A shiver ran down her spine, but she obeyed, meeting his still, watchful eyes. They appeared almost yellow at this moment.

"If you are frightened of riding, Judith, I won't press you to ride, but I object, most strongly, to you lying to me about it."

It was said quietly but firmly. Judith felt like a naughty child, and knew she deserved to. "I'm sorry. I just didn't want to admit it."

He looked at her soberly. "I feel as if you are trying

to be something other than yourself, Judith Rossiter. You never relax your guard.''

Judith felt the clutch of fear. Would he poke and probe, and dig out her secret? ''It's just nerves. It was you who insisted that our marriage be so speedy.''

''Do you want to delay it, then?''

''No,'' she said sharply.

He looked as if he would pursue the point, but Bastian called for their attention and set his horse at the tiny obstacle, a plank on two small barrels.

The horse hopped over it with a bored air. Bastian, however, was paying more attention to his audience than to his riding, and didn't stop when the horse did. He slid forward and off Boscable's neck.

Judith gave a scream and dashed out to him. Leander shook his head, and ran over to take charge of the surprised horse before it decided to create a fuss over all these alarums, and absentmindedly trampled the unharmed boy.

He then insisted that Bastian remount, over Judith's desperate opposition. It might have been the make or break battle of their relationship if Bastian hadn't been even more determined than Leander that he get back on the horse and do the jump properly.

Judith stood there, white as a sheet, as her son took the jump three times.

Leander was seriously wondering whether this marriage was going to work at all when she turned to him and summoned a gallant smile. ''I must apologize. That was a great piece of foolishness, wasn't it?'' Her color was now high with embarrassment, and she was staring fixedly at a point somewhere around his ear. ''It is just that I am unaccustomed to horses.''

She tentatively, and then with more confidence, met his eyes. ''As I seem to have given birth to two little equestrians, perhaps I had better take up the practice myself. But not, I think, until after we are more settled. One can only ask so much of one's nerves at once."

She offered a tentative smile, and he knew with relief that it would be all right after all. There are few things more difficult than admitting one has made a mistake.

However, later that day when Leander found himself alone with Lucien over a game of billiards, he raised a question. "Do you think Judith's hiding something from me?"

Lucien looked up from his shot. "Everyone's hiding something. You can't expect her to be an open book on such short acquaintance." He leant down again and potted a red.

"What would you feel like," Leander asked, "if Beth died and you were forced by circumstances to marry another?"

Lucien straightened. "I don't care to even contemplate it. But it's hardly the same. I suspect if the widow has qualms, it's not just because of remarriage, but because of the power you will have over her."

"Power?"

"It's a matter Beth and I have discussed at length," said Lucien dryly, "both before and after our marriage. She has somewhat strong opinions about it, being a follower of Mary Wollstonecraft. She can wax fiery about male domination."

"I have no intention of dominating anyone."

"I don't think I had either, but when it came down to it I expected my word to be law. And, of course, we have the law on our side. The legal ruling is, I believe, 'In law, husband and wife are one person, and the husband is that person.' We control the property and the money. Even if our wife should earn money we can take it for our own purposes. We have the right to her body, and even the right to beat her, though we might get into trouble if we did her serious harm. We can dictate where she may and may not live, and if she should choose to flee from us, we can keep her from her children forever. I'm not sure," said Lucien, "whether in your case the courts would give you control over your stepchildren, but I fear it is very likely. If Judith Rossiter has qualms, it merely proves that she is a rational woman."

"Put like that, it's astonishing women marry at all."

"They mostly have very little choice." Lucien leant on his cue. "This has nicely raised a touchy subject. Judith appears to be unadvised. Beth wishes me to have marriage contracts drawn up to safeguard her. They would chiefly be financial, and as she brings nothing to the marriage that would mean that you would be paying for your own shackles."

"Of course I intend to provide for her—pin money, a jointure . . ."

"Beth, being of a suspicious nature, would like it in writing."

"I have no objection as long as the terms are reasonable." But Leander could hear the stiffness in his own voice.

Lucien grinned sympathetically. "You'll get used to it. And at least you're not marrying someone who was raised on this stuff instead of mother's milk. On the whole, I think you're wise to have a speedy wedding. Less time for Beth to infect Judith with her philosophy."

"How on earth did you two come to be married?"

Lucien raised a brow. "That, I'm afraid, is as undisclosable as your real reason for this marriage." He moved around the table to line up a shot and continued smoothly, "By the way, if I'm representing the lady's interests, don't you think you should buy Judith a ring?"

"Good heavens! How could I have forgotten?"

"Probably because she's still wearing Rossiter's."

Chapter Six

Leander decided it was definitely time to buy Judith a ring, and bury her first husband's jewels in the bottom of her jewel box. He was disconcerted by just how strongly he felt on the subject. He was disconcerted by a great deal these days. He was achieving a practical marriage based on honesty and respect, so why was he constantly on edge?

The matter of the rings, however, was a simple one to correct. He borrowed Lucien's curricle, and drove down to the cottage. He was accustomed by now to just walking in, using the back door as everyone seemed to, and so he entered the kitchen unannounced—to find his future countess, damn her, stretching precariously on a stool to clean a high shelf.

He grasped her by the waist, and swung her to the floor.

She gave a squeal of alarm, and then collapsed against his chest. "Leander! You frightened me to death!"

"So I should. I thought I hired a couple to help you."

Judith moved back, but he held on to her. "You did," she said, "but they can't do everything."

"Of course they can. If there's too much work, hire more."

"It doesn't bother me at all to work in the house. I'm accustomed to it."

"Then become unaccustomed. You will hardly be dusting out cupboards at the Temple."

Judith raised her chin. "If I wish to, I will."

He gritted his teeth. "No, you will not." It's happening again, he thought.

Then Judith chuckled. "Am I really fighting you for the right to scrub and clean? I'm sorry, Leander, but there's so much to do if this place is to be left neat for the next occupants, and it simply won't be done if I don't help."

He didn't know what to say to this sort of foolishness.

"Besides," she added, "I don't like to see those old folk up on stools."

"And I don't like to see *you* up on a stool." But he could feel his anger fading and other feelings growing. She looked surprisingly fetching, rosy with embarrassment and humor. "Or at least," he said softly, "not for cleaning." He picked her up, and sat her on the stool, then brushed back a tendril of her silky hair. "Was I bullying you?" he asked.

She nodded. "Yes, I think you were."

"I'll try not to." He wanted to kiss her, but he wanted it so much he distrusted the impulse. He moved away and leant against the oak table facing her. "The Ardens think you are worried about the power I will have over you as a husband."

Judith nodded again. "A little, but mostly for the children's sake. The children are a weighty responsibility, one I cannot just shrug off."

"I've never thought of these matters. All I can say is that I have no intention of being a despot."

"I sense that, which is why I'm willing to trust you."

"Then I hope you will let me buy you a new ring to symbolize a new start." He watched for her reaction.

"Of course." She did not seem upset.

"It will mean," he pointed out, "that you will have to remove those you wear now."

Judith looked at her rings, so familiar as to be a part of her, and wondered why this had not occurred to her. She was blushing with embarrassment that she hadn't removed the rings sooner. What a fool he must think her. The thin-shanked sapphire came off quite easily, but the broader gold band, which had never been removed since her wedding day, didn't. With a worried look at him, she rubbed some soap on her finger and worked it off.

There was a mark where it had been, and she felt naked without it.

He took her hand and rubbed at the mark. "We will have to find one a little looser."

"Twelve years and two children bring changes, my lord."

"Leander," he reminded her gently. "I doubt I could wear anything bought for me when I was sixteen. I have the curricle, and would like to drive into Guildford now to buy you the rings."

Judith didn't feel able to protest or delay. The Hubbles were here for the children.

Perhaps she should take time to change her gown but there was little point, for they were all as shabby, and this one was not particularly dirty. She put on her bonnet, and took her red cloak off the hook. He placed it around her shoulders as if it were a priceless ermine wrap. Perhaps being treated as a countess would one day make her feel like one. She doubted it.

The matter of the rings was bringing a finality to all this that she should have welcomed. Instead it made her nervous, and scruples assailed her again.

She tied her bonnet strings, fighting the scruples down, but in the end they won and she turned to him. "This marriage is a cockeyed idiocy and everyone knows it. As you've seen today, I'm not fit to be the Countess of Charrington, the mistress of Temple Knollis. I know convention says you may not, but I have no objection to you withdrawing your offer. I'll say it was my decision."

His face had gone blank, which doubtless meant he was trying to hide his relief. She felt a pang of loss, but held to her course. She knew him a little by now, and added, "After all, my lord, if you were to give us a small annuity, we would go along famously, and you would not need to worry about us at all."

"But, my dear Judith, that would be money for nothing. Don't you think that a little grasping?"

Judith gaped at him. He smiled blandly and held out his arm. "Let us go purchase rings."

As they rolled through the crisp autumn countryside, Judith told her troublesome conscience that she had done her best to steer him from this course. What's more, though she had allowed him to retain a misconception, her intent was completely honest. She would do her best to make him a good wife and countess, and she was certainly past the age of falling in love.

Judith was surprised to find she was given her choice of betrothal ring, and it presented something of a problem. Though the jeweler did not have a large stock, there was considerable variety. She knew Leander would not consider a trumpery piece, and suspected that it would have to be clearly of more value than the sapphire to satisfy him.

The ring that most appealed to her was an antique ruby heart held in two hands, but that would be a disastrous exhibition of romanticism. The other choices were a marquise sapphire, a triad of emeralds, and a large square-cut diamond.

She chose the diamond as likely to be the most expensive. The jeweler's beaming satisfaction argued that she was correct. She felt a momentary qualm, but assured herself that in this marriage, money was the one thing she need not concern herself about.

When it came to wedding rings, she ignored value and picked out a narrow one. Sebastian's ring had shown that wide ones were impractical for an active woman. Leander might think she was going to laze her days away in idleness, but she could not imagine it.

He had been investigating on his own as she chose, and now he added a pearl pendant and a filigree parure set with blue tourmalines. A protest hovered on Judith's lips.

She knew it was ridiculous, but she was feeling *bought*—perhaps because she was not doing anything for all this largess, and was not at all sure what she was expected to do in the future. It was as if a ledger were being constantly drawn up with endless debit on her side.

But she said nothing. It would be pointless.

As he dealt with the financial matters, she stood looking down at her hands, her strange hands. At Leander's urging she had been using an expensive cream on them every day, and trying to remember to use protective gloves when working. They did look a little paler and smoother, which she supposed was how a countess's hands were supposed to look.

Now the square diamond caught the sun and flashed rainbows. It mesmerized her like a child's kaleidoscope.

He came over and gave her one of his radiant smiles. They had the power to convince her that she really was making him happy, strange as that may seem. He raised her left hand to his lips and, holding her eyes, kissed her finger by the ring. Judith's heart gave a warning tremble. She sternly ordered it to behave.

She was ready to return to Mayfield and work, but Leander insisted she show him the town. It was market day and they had to weave their way through crowds, stalls, and animals. The noise, dirt, and smell were overwhelming. She thought this would soon dissuade him from the venture, but he was fascinated.

He didn't seem to know what many of the items were. He didn't even recognize a turnip, and wasn't entirely sure he'd ever eaten any. "Have you heard of Brummell's response when asked if he liked vegetables?" he said. "He replied that he didn't know, as he had never eaten any."

"Are you claiming you have never eaten vegetables?"

"Oh, I am sure a few have passed my lips, well disguised by heavy sauces. . . ."

Judith wasn't sure if he were teasing or not. She paid the tuppence for a turnip, and had the stallholder slice it. She gave Leander a slice.

"Raw?" he asked plaintively. "Surely it's eaten cooked."

"It's palatable raw. Try it."

He bit off a lump, and chewed with a doubtful look. "I prefer melon."

"So do I. What has that to say to anything? Have you had it before?"

"Definitely not raw, and probably not cooked. And," he added pointedly, "I am not in a passion to do so."

"You'll find buttered carrots and turnips an excellent dish," she assured him.

He did not look convinced, and steered her away from the vegetable stalls.

"I don't understand," she said, "how anyone can not know a turnip when they see one."

He slid her a glance. "Perhaps I find it hard to

understand how anyone can mistake beluga for lump-fish, or a Côte de Nuits for a Côte du Rhone."

Judith stopped and faced him. "And what are they?"

"Fish eggs and wine."

She shrugged. "Well, I don't like cod's roe, and elderberry is good enough for me."

"Cod's roe and elderberry wine!" He looked pained, but she could tell that now he was teasing.

"Yes, your highness. You can see how unsuited we are."

"Nonsense." He took her elbow to steer her out of the way of a barrow. "We are superbly well matched. If I had married Princess Irina Bagration, neither of us would have known a turnip, and Lord knows what disastrous consequences could have ensued."

"Were you supposed to?"

"What?"

"Marry a princess."

He was momentarily distracted by a man demonstrating the sturdiness of his earthenware by bashing it against his head. "She thought it a good idea," he said absently, then turned back. "Don't look so impressed. Princesses are two a penny in Russia, and I think she only wanted a ticket to London so she could become another Lieven."

He was fascinated by an ironmonger's wares, and picked up a metal cup with a silent question.

"Egg poacher," Judith said.

Another item.

"Potato masher."

Another.

"Sausage stuffer. My lord, have you never been in a kitchen?"

"I've been in yours."

"Apart from mine."

He smiled. "No. You see, you are bringing endless useful knowledge as your dowry. It never previously occurred to me to wonder how the meat found its way into a sausage.''

Judith began to feel she had a schoolboy in tow rather than a frightening future Lord and Master.

Like a schoolboy, he unerringly detected a cake shop, and they took a table and set to enjoying tea and cream cakes—eclairs, savoys, horns, and sandwiches. Judith was amazed at the number of cakes this slim young man could put away. She must have looked wistful, for he said, "Don't worry. We'll take some home for the children."

She frowned at him. "Do you know everything I think?"

He was suddenly serious. "I wish I did."

"And I most certainly do not."

"Why? Are you hiding something?"

There was a serious tone behind the question. Judith wanted to look away but forced herself to meet his eyes. "Not particularly, but everyone needs privacy in their thoughts."

He nodded. "I don't read minds. I'm sensitive to feelings, that's all. It's a gift I inherited from my father. It's very useful in diplomacy."

And in handling people, thought Judith, but didn't say it. "You've never told me about your family."

She thought he might avoid the broad hint but he didn't, though she noted he looked down as he spoke. "I was the only child. My mother was a great heiress, and it was her money that enabled my father to launch his diplomatic career. It's an expensive business, you know, for the government is rarely generous." He fiddled restlessly with a spoon. "My father loved to wander, never wanted to put down roots. My mother would go anywhere to be with my father."

Judith smiled. "It sounds like a wonderful love match."

His hand stilled. "On her part it was."

Was that, thought Judith, why he'd developed his

aversion to one-sided love in marriage? "And were you always with them?"

"Oh yes. My father was often busy, and my mother became accustomed to my company. She wouldn't leave me anywhere, even if they were going into a dangerous situation. My father virtually had to use force to send me to England for my schooling."

Judith felt her skin crawl at this vignette of his family life, but she tried to be charitable. "Poor woman. She knew she was losing you for years. Surely it is possible to gain a good education abroad."

"Most definitely. But not what one learns at a good English school."

"Which is?"

He looked up. "Why, to be an English gentleman."

Judith studied him, head on one side. "I'm afraid, my lord, the teaching didn't take."

His eyes widened. She thought for once she might have shocked him. "Are you saying I am not a gentleman?"

"All I know is," she teased, "an English gentleman would know a turnip when he saw one."

He laughed in a delightfully open way. "How true. So you are completing my education most admirably. Let us go and continue it."

But when they were out on the street, complete with an absurdly large box of cakes, she said, "I really must get back to Mayfield, Leander. The Hubbles will be wanting to go home soon."

He looked around wistfully. "This has been fun. There will be other days, other markets. . . ." He looked down at her. "But I've learned that these special moments do not come again."

She knew exactly what he meant. For a while today she had been happy as she had not since her girlhood. "There will be others," she promised.

He nodded. "There will be others."

Judith returned home in a very perilous state. She

knew now that it would be possible, and all too easy, to fall in love with Leander Knollis.

The children were delighted with the cakes, but ecstatic to see the ring, solid proof that all was to go ahead. Judith had not even realized they had doubts.

Bastian took a formal stance in front of Leander, hands clasped behind his back. "Lord Charrington?"

"Yes, Bastian."

"If you are to marry our mama, what are we to call you?"

Leander looked across at Judith, but she gave a small shrug. She had not considered the matter.

He looked back down at the boy, and at Rosie who had come to stand by him, very much interested. "What would you like to call me?"

Bastian glanced at his sister. "We're not sure we should call you Papa."

"I see. Well, you can call me my lord, or sir."

Another meaningful glance. "We'd *like* to call you Papa, but . . ."

"But I'm not your Papa. I understand. Let's see, there's pater, which as you know is Latin, and pere, which is French. Padre is Spanish. Vater is German . . . Or simply father might do."

The children were clearly discontented by the offerings and fretted by the problem. "I . . . We wondered whether we could call you Papa Leander. . . ."

Judith almost laughed at the expression that flitted over Leander's face but of course, with his training, he hid it well. "If that is how you wish to address me, I am amenable. . . ." At their continued anxiety he said, "Yes, you may."

They broke into smiles and disappeared into the front room with a cake each. A bundle of black and white fur trotted after in the hope of crumbs.

"Good Lord," said Leander, "it makes me sound like a buffoon in the *commedia dell'arte!*"

Judith let the laughter out. "Hopefully with time

they'll shorten it. Perhaps when there are other children who just call you Papa."

They stilled, and looked at each other. He came over and cradled her face in his hands. "I knew there would be dimples. . . ."

Her lips were still parted with laughter, and he kissed her briefly, but openmouthed. It spoke of intimacy far more strongly than a probing tongue for it contained no striving, no anxiety. It was one kiss among many, part of a lifetime of kisses.

Judith was left shaken, and trying to hide it.

He turned for the door, then stopped and pulled some papers out of his greatcoat pocket. "I forgot, Lucien drafted these, and he wants you to look at them before he has his solicitor put them into final form." He added dryly, "Beth scrutinized them, so they should be in order."

"There's no need . . ."

"Don't shake my faith in you as a practical woman. It's best to have these things clear."

When he'd gone Judith ignored the papers. She wasn't sure she could cope with more largesse. She went mechanically through the business of preparing vegetables to go with yesterday's cold mutton, but her mind was elsewhere.

She had discovered an overwhelming desire to break through Leander's sleek veneer and see him laugh, and play, and that pointed to her danger. She could no longer be sure she wouldn't fall in love with him, hadn't already fallen in love with him. It was ridiculous not to be in control of such a thing, but it was like shivering in a draught, or perspiring in the heat. A simple reaction.

And, of course, the very affliction made it less possible for her to cut free of it all, for then she would lose him forever. More than that, she could leave him vulnerable to a woman far less well disposed than she. She at least meant to deal honestly with him.

He did need her. She could sense, ridiculous as it seemed, that in her he found something to fill some of the gaps in his life.

Gaps left by his parents? His mother had clung to him, but she clearly hadn't given him what a child needs. It sounded as if she had used him to try to fill the gap left by a neglectful husband. In the process she had stolen his childhood. She could imagine him at Bastian's age, already the perfect gentleman, squiring his mother to functions in Rome, or Vienna. . . .

"Mama, what's the matter?"

Judith realized she was just standing with half the potatoes in the water, and the others turning brown on the chopping board. She quickly threw them in the pot, and turned to the children. "I'm just tired after such a long day, dears. Set the table, Rosie. Bastian, fill the kettle. Supper will not be long."

Like a dam bursting, the questions started. "Will we have rooms of our own?" "How many horses do you think Papa Leander owns?" "Will we have servants?" "Will we have cream cakes every day?" "Is Temple Knollis bigger than Hartwell?" "Bigger than Lord Faversham's house?" "Will we meet the king?"

Judith could answer a definite no to the last one, for the poor king was mad. For the rest she said, "I think we should treat this as a mysterious adventure, dears. We'll discover each new thing as it happens, together. I'm sure, however, that all the discoveries will be wonderful."

When they sat to the meal, Rosie said, "Well, I hope when we go to Temple Knollis, we'll *never* have to eat cold mutton again."

Judith frowned, but thought how silly it was of her to be continuing with her frugal housekeeping while preparing for opulence. But it seemed important for some reason to go on as they usually did. Perhaps it was a talisman against the bubble bursting.

When the children were in bed she reluctantly unfolded the papers. After reading them she let them fall. And she'd been feeding her poor dears cold mutton!

Her pin money, just for personal expenditures, was to be in the thousands of pounds, and hers to spend as she wished. There was a meticulous note in parentheses that the arrangement was that she be responsible for ensuring that this money did cover her requirements. Beth Arden apparently believed that rights were best guarded by responsibilities.

There was a generous allowance for the children in addition to the provision of their household of servants, which would be Leander's responsibility. The allowance was to be under Judith's direction. There was even a small personal allowance for each child's independent use, with provision for it to increase at each birthday. That was added in a separate hand, and she suspected it to be Leander's work.

She would be hard put to prevent him spoiling her children beyond belief.

Every eventuality was allowed for, including future children, and widowhood. Her widow's jointure would ensure a life of ease.

There was even, to her surprise, a provision for them living apart. If either or both should decide to live apart from the other, Judith was to have custody of Bastian and Rosie and receive two thousand pounds per annum, regardless of the cause of the separation, or any legal actions of any party.

Even though this implied that he would take custody of any children born of their union, it was extraordinary. She could turn around the day after the wedding and never speak to Leander again, and he would be obliged to pay her this money. That he was willing to sign this document was a great act of trust in itself.

For a moment she wondered if he perhaps was too

sweet-natured, almost to the point of foolishness. But then she remembered that moment in her parents' house and the way he had said, ''I am never put upon.'' She had not doubted him then.

He trusted her. He trusted her to deal honestly with him in financial matters. He trusted her to deal honestly with him in all ways, and she was betraying that trust.

She closed her eyes and rested her head on her hands. It was a tortuous situation, but all she could do was trust that she could give what he wanted, without, by mischance, giving more.

Chapter Seven

One afternoon, Patrick Moore, the local carrier, drew up before the cottage and unloaded a stack of boxes into her front room. Judith knew they contained the clothes. Called by children's natural instinct for treats, Bastian and Rosie came running to help her open them.

Rosie was ecstatic over her pink dress, Bastian a little self-conscious about his suit, which was made in imitation of a grown-up one, but pleased all the same. They couldn't be expected to be thrilled about new underwear, and yet she sensed their satisfaction at yet more tangible signs of the change in their lives.

Rosie absolutely *had* to try on her lovely dress, and so Judith helped her into it. She combed her daughter's hair out into a gleaming fall of pale gold silk and ran her hand over it. It was lovely hair but she feared that Rosie, like her father, would have to resort to curling papers to be fashionable.

Rosie stood on the kitchen table in an attempt to see herself in the small mirror, then jumped down to set her skirts swirling in a dance. Judith had to capture her before she dirtied her finery.

"Now you, Mama. Show us your dress."

Judith gently took out the peach silk gown, marveling again at the beauty of the fabric. It slithered through her fingers like sin. The gown had only simple ruffles and piping to decorate it.

"Put it on, Mama!"

"Not now . . ."

"Please!"

In the end she gave in and went up to her small room under the eaves to slip into the gown. In the same box there was an underslip of creamy silk, butter-soft cream kid gloves, sheer silk stockings clocked with peach butterflies, and white lace garters, threaded with peach satin.

Judith looked around at her iron bedstead, the warped planks of the floor, and the damp-stains on the whitewashed walls, and thought the clothes should crumble like fairy gold to be in such surroundings.

In the end, though, she put on every item, wincing slightly as the silk caught on her still-roughened hands. She put the gloves on to save the fabric from damage.

She couldn't fasten the buttons at the back, but looked in the cheval mirror all the same. She could see herself from the waist up, and the gown was utterly beautiful. Even in the dim room it made her skin glow, though the effect would be improved if she didn't have a smudge on her forehead from black-leading the grate.

She made her way carefully downstairs, gathering the skirts up to her knees to be sure they would not be soiled or snagged on the wooden steps.

The children gasped. "You look lovely, Mama," Bastian said with a seriousness that caught her heart.

"Fasten the buttons for me then, dear."

She bent slightly so he could reach the tiny buttons that went all the way up to the high neck. When he'd finished, she glanced in the mirror and saw the frilled collar made her neck look long and slim, and framed her face becomingly.

"You look like a bon-bon in a frilled cup." Rosie giggled with delight.

Judith broke into laughter, too. "I hope someone doesn't decide to eat me up!"

Filled suddenly with excitement as joyous as the children's, she dug through the boxes and pulled out the Russian mantle and flung it around her shoulders. It was lined with soft fleece and wonderfully warm. Apparently one did not have to be plain to be practical. She pulled up the hood with its fox trimming then glanced in the mirror again.

The heart-shaped face peeping out of the rich russet fur did not look like Judith Rossiter at all. It almost looked like a countess. . . .

"Mama," said Bastian excitedly, running to the door. "I hear a horse. It must be—"

"Leander!" shrieked Judith. "He mustn't see me in my wedding gown." She flung off the mantle, picked up the skirts of her dress, and fled up the stairs.

She heard his voice as she reached her room.

"Mama's run upstairs," said Rosie. "She's in her wedding gown."

Judith leant down the stairs to listen.

"And so are you, I think. That is a very pretty gown, Miss Rosetta Rossiter, but it scarcely does justice to the pretty wearer."

"Oh, Papa Leander, you do say lovely things."

"Only to lovely people. And Bastian is going to put me into the shade, I fear."

"What will you be wearing, sir?"

"Do you know, I haven't thought to purchase something special."

"I'm sure you have lots of fine clothes."

"Yes, I'm afraid I do. I'm something of a peacock

at heart. I could send to London for a special suit if I knew what your mother would be wearing. . . .''

"Don't you dare!" Judith called. "Don't tell him. It's to be a surprise."

He came to the bottom of the stairs, and so she ducked into her room. "Are you coming down today? I thought we could go for a walk."

"In a minute," said Judith, and tried to unfasten her buttons. It didn't take long for her to realize that it was impossible. She stuck her head around the door again. Leander was still at the bottom of the stairs, leaning against the wall, arms smugly crossed. "You can't undo your fastenings, can you?"

"How did you guess?"

He just smiled, somewhat wickedly.

"Send Bastian up to me, please."

"I'm closer."

"You cannot see my wedding dress before the day."

"Will it disappear in a puff of smoke? Delightful thought."

Judith thought of the children. "Leander!"

"Even in this dim light, I can see you're blushing. Do you realize it's only three days until our wedding? It really wouldn't matter if I came up and helped you out of your gown . . ."

Judith remembered Beth's comment about him wanting to undress her, and thought her face must be like a scarlet beacon. She saw him put one foot on a stair. "Don't you *dare!*"

He laughed and said, "Pity," then went to get Bastian.

Judith retreated into her room, shaken.

She'd just been well and truly teased, but the promises for the future were real. Her own vague imaginings alarmed her, but she could not deny a tickle of excitement. It was like when she and her sisters had slipped down to the river to swim in their shifts, terrified that some male would chance by to see them, but enjoying that very terror as part of the treat.

She felt like a girl again. . . .

Bastian came in and undid the buttons. "I think this is a silly way to fasten a dress," he said. "What if you were alone? You'd be stuck in it."

"Then I would never have dressed in it in the first place, would I? Anyway, this is a lady's gown, and ladies have maids."

"You don't."

"I will. Go and take off your finery, dear, and be sure to put it away neatly so it doesn't crease."

Judith hung up her dress carefully, draping a sheet over it to protect it from dust, then put on her black again and went downstairs. Rosie was just about to go up, her everyday clothes in her hands. Judith gave her the same instructions then joined Leander in the kitchen, feeling somewhat fluttery

"Do you think I'll need a maid?" she asked.

He kissed her hand and her cheek in that foreign manner to which she was still unaccustomed. "Of course. But there hardly seems any point in hiring one here, when a local girl will be happier at the Temple. Unless, that is, you would prefer a highly skilled dresser from London."

"But I will need one on the journey, as you see."

His smile was wickedly lazy. "Not at all. You'll have me. I don't intend to take my valet."

Judith didn't know what to say. She turned away. "I still am not sure it is wise to take the children. It will be a long journey for them."

"But they will be our family, and they will have to make the journey one day. We are in no hurry, and won't set too hard a pace."

Judith's concern was that he would lose patience with them, confined in a carriage for days. Even her children, good though they were, were bound to com-

plain, and squabble, and whine. She turned back.
"But it won't be much of a wedding journey for you."

"It will be your wedding journey, too."

"You forget, I've been married before."

"I never forget that." Something dark flashed in
his eyes, but then she decided she must have imagined it, for he smiled as he took her hands. "Though
I confess, sometimes I wonder . . ." He lowered his
lips and touched them to hers, something to which
she had become accustomed, and which she found
quite pleasant. He released her hands and grasped
her waist, slowly sliding his hands up until his thumbs
brushed her breasts.

A shudder rippled through her. She gasped and
stared at him.

The children clattered down the stairs. He sighed
and let her go.

As they all left the house he said, "Surely you must
have something in one of those boxes that you could
wear for this expedition."

"Nothing suitable for tramping the countryside,
no."

"Then you haven't ordered enough clothes."

It was one of his dictatorial statements. Judith
raised her chin and marched ahead. "I'm sorry if
you feel ashamed to be seen with me, my lord."

He grasped the back of her gown. "Don't be hoity-
toity or I'll kiss you here and now, and the vicar's
coming down the street."

Judith smiled tightly at Reverend Killigrew, and he
beamed back.

As soon as the vicar was past she glared at Leander.

He tucked her hand in his arm, but his eyes were
cool. "We have an agreement. You are to stop wearing
mourning."

"And so I will," she said, *"when* we are married."

He sighed. "I'm sure your first husband would not
begrudge you a pink dress."

He still thought she was attached to her mourning. It seemed to her ridiculous that Leander could think Sebastian's memory challenged the reality he represented. But then immediately she felt guilt. Sebastian had adored and cherished her in his own way, and given her two wonderful children. How wrong for her to brush his memory aside for this rather facile young man.

"I'm sorry," he said rather bleakly. "I won't pester you about it again."

She looked at him, wishing there was something to be said that would comfort him without being disloyal to Sebastian. If there was such a phrase, she couldn't find it.

They walked across fields in the brisk air, talking of everyday impersonal things. The children gathered colored leaves, and nuts. Bastian ran over with a handful of horse chestnuts.

Leander pulled out a knife and cut off the outer shell. Unlike a hoop, this was apparently a matter he knew about. The two males assessed the glossy conkers like connoisseurs, debating which would prove to be strongest in battle. Bastian would carefully thread string through them, and then swing them against those of his friends, to see which would break first. The winner would have a knot in the string, one knot for each victory.

"Georgie has a grand one," said Bastian. "A tenner. I think this one might beat it, though."

"I think so, too," said Leander. "Do you know, I'd never heard of conkers before I went to school."

"Really? Why not?"

"It's not played in other countries. I had a lot to learn besides Greek. Actually," he added thoughtfully, "my modern Greek was rather good."

Bastian looked up at him with a frown. "Will I like school, Papa Leander?"

"I hope so. It can't all be perfect, though, and

enduring the hard times is part of the education. But be assured, Bastian, that if you really find it miserable, you may change your school, or even come home and be taught by a tutor."

Bastian gave him a sideways look. "A tutor who'd teach me to endure the hard times, and I'd be stuck with him all the time? I'm not sure I'd care for that."

Leander grinned. "I see we understand each other."

Judith wasn't sure *she* understood. It pleased her to see Bastian growing to trust Leander, and yet she felt as if a little male enclave was growing up which might exclude her.

Bastian looked down at the conkers, but said, "Will I be beaten at school?"

"I never knew anyone who avoided it, but you're welcome to try."

Bastian looked up again. "I've never been beaten. Does it hurt?"

"What do you think?"

Bastian was quiet, and Judith seriously thought of announcing then and there that her child would go to school over her dead body. She began to have more sympathy for Leander's mother, who had not perhaps been trying to cling to her son, but trying to save him from this cruel life. But then life *was* cruel as she well knew, and she had been fortunate. She had never witnessed it, but people were whipped through the streets for crimes, and flogged in the army and navy. As a curate's daughter she was well aware of the hardship to be found among the poor.

What path would Bastian take in life? The law, the military, the church? Even as a landowner he would be a magistrate. There were few careers that did not expose a man in some way to harshness.

Bastian looked up resolutely. "It's not that I'm a coward, Papa Leander. I'm just afraid I'll cry."

Leander ruffled his hair. "Grit your teeth and stare at something, then run away afterward and find a place to bawl."

"Is that what you did?"

Judith saw that Leander's cheeks had colored. "Probing rather deep, aren't you? Yes, that's what I did."

Bastian ran off, apparently happy.

"Was that the truth?" Judith asked.

"That I bawled? Are you too fascinated by my wickedness? Yes, but not at school. I'd been sufficiently hardened before then, and trained out of most foolishness."

Judith felt chilled, both by what this said about Leander's childhood, and by its implications for the future. "I thought you said your father was not cruel."

"Nor was he. I was not a particularly easy child."

She swallowed against a lump. "I find that hard to believe. You'll be telling me next you want to whip Bastian daily to toughen him up!"

His glance was hooded by his heavy lids. "Of course not. Instead, when we're in Somerset, I'll take him to visit Nicholas Delaney. Perhaps he can advise Bastian on how to set up a new Company of Rogues. Our punishments were few and far between, and never excessive."

"It is perfectly natural," snapped Judith, "for a mother to be tenderhearted about her children."

"Of course it is," he agreed, and spoiled it by adding, "that's why children have fathers."

Judith glared at him and marched ahead. But despite that, she knew Leander would not be cruel, and she felt he would be able to guide Bastian's steps toward a successful, productive, manly life better than Sebastian ever could.

It made her sad and proud at the same time.

* * *

It was only three days to the wedding, and Judith had almost finished readying the cottage for departure. In consequence it had a rather bleak look. A few larger items had been crated and already sent to Temple Knollis by carrier. This included Sebastian's portrait, his books, and various boxes of notes and unpublished verses. It had seemed strange to send them to her new husband's home, but she could hardly throw them away, and one day the children might value them.

Their new clothes were neatly packed to travel with them. The children had each packed a small box of books and toys as well. Judith had seen some rubbish slipped into those boxes, but had made no objection. It was strange what people treasured.

She herself had fought battles over such things as her first wedding dress, worn out now and too tight around the chest, but kept folded in lavender all the same. She had thrown it away. She had kept, though, the handwritten poem Sebastian had brought to the vicarage that first day, fourteen years ago.

She was now faced with the last decisions—her Christmas baking, and her elderberry wine. There was absolutely no reason to keep them, and they would be appreciated by some of the village people who were even more impoverished than she had been. On the other hand . . .

Rosie came in, Magpie in her arms. "Why are you scowling at the pudding, Mama?"

"I'm just wondering to whom we should give it, dear."

"Give away our pudding?" protested Rosie. Magpie hissed when he was squeezed too tightly.

"There is no point in taking it to Temple Knollis, Rosie. I'm sure the cook there has baked dozens, all much better than this."

"But this is *ours!*" Rosie cried. "We stirred it. I made my wish! It's got a silver sixpence in it!" She burst into tears. Magpie slithered out of danger and ran away. Bastian came running.

"Mama wants to give away our Christmas pudding!" Rosie wailed.

Bastian didn't cry, but his eyes showed his hurt.

Judith knew when she was defeated. "No, no," she said. "We will take it with us. And the cake. And the mincemeat."

The children cheered, and Judith found herself grinning. She, too, had longed to keep these things. They might be nothing at Temple Knollis, but they had been made with love, and paid for with sacrifices. If necessary they would have a secret Christmas feast in some corner of the great house.

"You have to take the wine, too," said Bastian. "You always have wine with Christmas dinner, and you said this year I could have a little."

Judith looked dubiously at the ten bottles of this year's vintage, and the one, opened, bottle of last. "Lord Charrington will have many wines, Bastian."

"But they won't be the same."

She gave in again, hoping the coach would hold all this.

"And what about the Christmas ribbons, Mama?" Bastian asked. "And the Chinese lantern."

All their little Christmas treasures. Judith swallowed. "They are gone, dearests. They really were falling apart, and we will find new ones. . . ." Before they could protest, she hurried on, "We are starting a new life, and must accept that many things will be different. Perhaps Lord Charrington will have Christmas treasures of his own." She rather doubted it, which made her sad. He would have, in the future.

"When we arrive at Temple Knollis," she said firmly, "we will have to spend time making new decorations. As it is such a large house, I'm sure there will be lots to be done.''

They weren't happy, but they accepted it. Judith sent them off to the Dog and Partridge to ask Mr. Hopgood how best to pack eleven bottles of wine.

Later, they were engaged to take tea at Hartwell, and Beth drove over in the carriage to collect them. Judith was very tempted to put on one of her new gowns, but she stuck to her resolution. She would change her dress when she changed her name.

She found she liked Beth Arden very much and desperately wished she could talk to her, but she couldn't see how to raise the subjects that concerned her. She herself was not sure which fretted at her most—the raising of boys, or different approaches to the marriage act.

As they alighted and the children ran ahead, Beth touched her hand. ''You look very worried, Judith.''

Judith pulled herself together. ''Just nerves. Any marriage is nerve-racking, I suppose. This more than most.''

''I think it will work out very well. You are both quite levelheaded people, not given to extremes.''

Judith swallowed. ''I suppose so.'' But she wondered if it wasn't just their backgrounds—his diplomatic training, and her years under Sebastian's control—which were keeping a lid on things. She sometimes felt the potential for extremes boiling up.

They were in the house and taking off their cloaks and bonnets. Beth said, ''It would be a kindness to him, you know, if you would put off your mourning.''

''I suppose so, but it seems symbolic to keep to my blacks until my wedding day.'' Beth didn't seem overly impressed by this explanation and so Judith added, ''And of course the new gowns are so beautiful, and impractical, that I can't bear to wear them for work around the house. And though Leander wants me to be a lady of leisure, he doesn't realize how much there is to do in vacating a home, packing possessions, and preparing for a journey.''

Beth laughed. ''That is true, and not so long ago I would have felt much the same. It took me an age to grow accustomed to being casual with expensive things. My hands would tremble just to be handling some of the china. And we couldn't explain it to them,'' she said with a smile. ''They've been surrounded by riches all their lives.''

''Was your life really that simple before your marriage?''

''Oh, yes. Did you not know? I was a very ordinary teacher in a girls' school in Cheltenham.''

''You make a wonderful marchioness.''

''Do I? In the thick of London Society, I still feel like an impostor.''

Feeling more at ease than ever before, they linked arms and went to join the gentlemen. Judith hugged to herself the fact that Beth Arden had transformed herself. She could do it, too.

They all ate together, but toward the end of the meal the children became restless, and so Judith gave them permission to play in the garden. ''Bastian,'' she said, ''you are to keep an eye on Rosie. And don't go near the horses without an adult.''

When the children had left, Leander queried, ''Not even *near* them, my dear? Do you think they'll be eaten?''

Judith felt foolish, and annoyed to be taken to task before others. ''Horses have been known to bite.''

''Not these. Lucien's are impeccably well-bred, just like him.'' He turned to his friend. ''Aren't they?''

But the marquess said, ''Don't bring me into it.''

Beth diplomatically rose. ''We are going to have tea in the garden room. Come when you've settled the issue.''

As she and Judith left, Lucien laughed. ''Trust Beth to make it look as if it's we men who are quarreling.''

"Instead of me and my sweet bride." Leander gazed at the door through which the ladies had exited. "She's dangerously overprotective."

"She's had to care for the children alone," said Lucien. "She seems to be a very sensible woman. I'm sure she'll come around, especially when there are tutors and governesses to share the burden. For heaven's sake, I rarely saw my parents except at set hours, and I'm sure you were the same."

"That was certainly true of my father. I suspect that pattern won't please Judith, though. To tell the truth, I'm not sure it would please me either. I've grown to like having the creatures underfoot. What about you when you have children?"

As they rose from the table and headed for the garden room, Lucien considered. "I think I'll try to have more to do with them than my father. It could be, though, that I'm taking Nicholas as my example. Have you met his daughter, Arabel?"

"No. I've not seen Nicholas. He seems fixed in Somerset. I was going to visit when I finally get down to the West Country. But surely the child is not yet one. How does one 'meet' a baby?"

Lucien grinned. "In this case, one just does. She's a living advertisement for the infantry, and definitely one to be enjoyed to the full. Beth warns that not all children are such delights, but I'm determined that anything Nicholas can do, we can do, too."

"Somewhat rash," murmured Leander as they joined the ladies.

Judith found being with the Ardens intriguing. The conversation was always lively and amusing. Often the discussion became intellectual and political, but Judith was never entirely left out, for someone would explain or redirect.

Lucien and Beth had minds like twin blades—meeting, but often in sharp opposition. She was surprised to see that such disagreements didn't cause offense. They were surprisingly well-read—Beth for a woman, and Lucien for a social creature—and often cited erudite support for their arguments. At one point Lucien leapt up to go and look for a book, bringing it back to triumphantly make his point. In Greek.

Leander briefly entered that discussion to question the translation, but he preferred anecdote to debate, and Judith was glad of it. She had no desire to live in a never-ending debating society. His anecdotes were invariably amusing, but often a little risqué.

At one point he broke into verse. *"The Grand Duke's been known/ When his passion's full blown,/To seek solace in any spare corner . . ."* He looked at Judith and broke off. "Ah, I promised no poetry, didn't I? Let me continue in prose."

His story about the state in which a certain grand duke and duchess had been found during a ball in St. Petersburg made her blush, as much at the hints it might give to their future as at the naughtiness of the tale. He must have noticed for he laughed and suggested a stroll in the gardens.

By the time Judith and Beth had put on their cloaks and bonnets the gentlemen, more hardy—or better clothed in their wool jackets—were already outside and strolling down toward the river. Judith wanted to ask Beth whether she ever had, or had even considered, doing such things behind an arras at a public affair, but didn't dare.

She decided she had best make it clear to Leander at the earliest opportunity, that she would never agree to such a thing.

They walked along a laburnum path toward the river. Suddenly they heard raised voices. A tearstained Rosie hurtled toward them, and flung herself, wailing, at Judith.

She knelt to hold her. "What is it, love?"

"Bastian!" cried the girl, and a hundred horrible

prospects flashed through Judith's mind. "He went to look at the horses, and Papa Leander's ever so cross, and Bastian's run away, and Papa Leander's shouting at him . . . I'm *scared!*" She broke into heart-breaking sobs.

Judith felt her heart break, too. The bubble had finally burst. She stood up, and pushed Rosie into Beth's arms. "Look after her."

"Judith . . ." said Beth. But Judith was already off at a run down the path toward the river.

She saw no sign of Lucien, but she could hear Leander shouting in the distance. He sounded furious. She picked up her skirts, and raced over the meadow toward the orchard.

She came upon Leander in the orchard, hands on hips. "Bastian," he was saying crisply to the air. "I do not expect to have to search you out. Come and face the music."

Everything was still. Poor Bastian must be terrified. Perhaps Leander had already hit him. And just because he wanted to look at the horses.

Judith marched forward, fighting tears, and pulled off the diamond. She arrived in front of Leander and held out the ring. "Take this, if you please. Our engagement is at an end."

He eyes flashed a dangerous yellow. "What the devil's the matter with you now?"

"How *dare* you swear at me!"

"You're enough to drive a saint to imprecation, believe me. Are you seriously objecting to me taking Bastian to task?"

"I'm objecting to you terrifying him!"

"I've done nothing to terrify him, though perhaps I ought to. Do you know what he did?"

"Yes! It was hardly a cardinal sin!"

"Oh, wasn't it? And I thought you were the protective mother. If I had the right, I probably would whip him, but that would bruise your tender sensibilities, wouldn't it?"

Judith pushed the ring into his clenched fist and turned away, throat aching. "Bastian, come here, my dear," she called out. "It's safe now. I won't let anyone hurt you."

"I don't believe this," muttered Leander.

Not a leaf stirred.

Judith pressed her hands to her face. "Oh God, where could he be?"

"Doubtless he's sneaked off home."

Judith turned on him with an annihilating look. "You, sir, have a heart of stone!" She ran off to collect her daughter.

Leander leant against a tree and contemplated the ring in his palm. He really should feel that he'd had a lucky escape from Bedlam.

But he didn't.

Chapter Eight

Judith retrieved Rosie and grimly accepted the offer of the Arden carriage to take her home. It was as much the Ardens' fault as hers that she had become entangled in this disaster. She found tears streaming down her face and angrily scrubbed them away. She hugged Rosie. It was not a loss. It was a lucky escape.

Look at her daughter. She was still shaking.

Through the carriage window, she searched the landscape for the figure of a lonely, scared boy, apologizing silently to him for exposing him to this terror. There was no sign of him.

Perhaps he was still at Hartwell. Perhaps she should turn back. But the Ardens had promised to look for him, and take care of him. She trusted them that far, or rather she trusted Beth. She didn't know about men anymore.

As soon as they arrived home, she searched the cottage but Bastian wasn't there, not even in his favorite hiding places. Of course he wasn't. He couldn't walk home as quickly as the carriage had brought her. Judith was tempted to start back for Hartwell again, hoping to meet him on the way.

Rosie began to sob again, and so Judith took her

onto her lap and forced herself to be calm. Leander wouldn't harm the boy now that he no longer had the right. The *right!* What right did anyone have to bully an innocent child.

Well, not entirely innocent.

Judith looked at her sniffing daughter and stroked her hair. "It'll be all right, darling. Everything will be all right." She didn't know how. Perhaps she should have kept the diamond.

Rosie ducked her head. "It's all Bastian's fault for going to look at the horses."

"No, dear. It wasn't such a terrible thing to do."

Rosie wailed. "Then . . . then it's *mine!*"

She would have buried her face again in Judith's bodice but Judith held her off to look at her as she handled this. "No, dear. How could it be yours?"

But Rosie was sobbing beyond coherence. Eventually Judith caught one word. Boat. The Ardens' punt.

She felt a chill shoot through her. "Did you get in the boat, Rosie?"

Gasping sobs, and a frightened look.

"You know that's not allowed."

A nod.

"If you'd fallen in the river, you could have drowned. You can't swim."

"Papa Leander stopped me falling in."

Judith swallowed against an ache in her throat. "Did you nearly fall in?"

Rosie looked down. "I was just looking for fishes."

Oh, sweet heavens. The whole picture was filling in. No wonder he'd been furious. She tried to tell herself this was all Leander's fault. Bastian would never have dreamed of sneaking off to the stables and leaving Rosie before he'd been indulged in daily rides.

"What did Lord Charrington do to Bastian, Rosie?"

"He called him back. Then he told him off something terrible. He told him he was irr-e-spon-si-ble."

"And then what?"

"Bastian started blubbering," said Rosie not without a touch of satisfaction, for Bastian was always accusing her of being too quick to cry.

"Bastian *cried?*"

Rosie nodded. "And ran away."

"Lord Charrington must have done something else, or threatened to. Bastian doesn't cry, and he doesn't run away. What did he do?"

Rosie shook her head. "He just said things. But he was so cross."

Judith stood Rosie up and went to the door, not knowing what to make of any of this. "Oh, where are you, Bastian?"

Instead of her son, she saw Hubble walking toward her with a large packet. For a second she thought it was some bizarre parting gift from Leander, but then she saw it had come on the mail.

Hubble smiled cheerily. "This come yesterday and got forgot-like, Mrs. Rossiter. Asked if I'd bring it over on my way back from the Dog. I'll set it in the house, will I? It's a mite heavy."

"Yes," said Judith absently. "Have you seen Bastian, Mister Hubble?"

"Aye, the lad's down in the graveyard, ma'am."

Judith was swamped with relief, and said some heartfelt prayers of thanks. She went to collect Rosie and found her studying the package with interest, her spirits reviving rapidly. She clearly didn't understand the consequences of this day's work.

Judith glanced at the package without much interest. There was no sign of what it could be and she didn't care. She had more important matters on her mind.

She had to admit there had been some justification for Leander's anger, but not for whatever he'd done to terrify her child. She should be glad she had seen the truth before she had committed herself to him. In fact, she felt a sickening sense of loss.

She took Rosie's hand and went out to find her son.

He was sitting on the lump of granite, staring morosely at the water, tearstains on somewhat grubby cheeks. Judith sat beside him and gathered him to her side. "It's all right, Bastian," she said gently. "It will be all right."

"No it won't," he muttered.

"Yes it will. Lord Charrington and I are not going to be married."

He put his head on his knees and started to sob. For a moment she thought it was relief, but then she began to have doubts. She grasped his shoulders. "Bastian, what is it? What's the matter?"

"It's all my fault!" he choked out. "I knew he'd not want me as his son!"

She pulled him up against her breast. "It's *not* your fault, dearest. You don't have to put up with his cruelty. We'll manage . . ."

He drew away and fought to control himself. "He wasn't cruel, Mama, but I could tell he didn't like me anymore. And he was right. I *was* irresponsible. I *shouldn't* have left Rosie. I *do* deserve a whipping."

"No, you don't," she said fiercely.

He looked miserably down. "I think I might rather that than no riding. But I don't suppose there'll be any riding anymore. . . ."

"Bastian," said Judith, "you can't let him bribe you with horses!" Then she paused, taking it in. "Is that what he threatened you with, no more riding?"

He glanced at her. "Not threatened. That's what he said. No riding until we got to his home, Temple Knollis."

"And that's why you ran away?" She had to admit

that it was a fair punishment, and one that would hit home.

"No," said Bastian scrubbing at his eyes. "I ran away because I could see he didn't like me anymore. Then he was angry 'cos I'd run. And I knew I'd torn it for sure."

"Oh darling," Judith said and gathered him in again. "Of course he likes you." It was an inane thing to say and yet she knew it was true. Leander had doubtless been disappointed in Bastian's behavior, just as she was, but his feelings in the orchard had been more worry than anger.

She had misjudged him again, and this time emphatically put an end to the whole affair. As Bastian would have said, she'd torn it for sure.

She gave him one last hug then rose wearily to her feet and began the walk home, an arm around each child. It was as well she hadn't worn any of her finery. Perhaps Lettie Grimsham would take the clothes back for part of the cost. . . .

Back at the cottage she wondered dully whether there was any point in apologizing, but despaired. He was surely pleased of a lucky escape.

The children asked if they could open the tantalizing parcel, and she absently said yes. She mechanically set about preparing their supper, thinking about the complications and embarrassment of canceling the wedding, wondering if she could hold on to the cottage. There were new tenants ready to move in.

She would receive her quarterly allowance from Timothy Rossiter in the New Year. Thank heavens she had not yet written to tell him it was no longer necessary. She added figures in her head, and wondered whether she should start to wear Sebastian's rings again now, or whether she could sell them to keep them all from the workhouse.

She realized there had been no comment from the children on the package's contents, and turned. Any distraction would be welcome at the moment. "What is it, then?"

They were using the string to play with Magpie. "Just more of Papa's books."

Judith wiped her hands and went over, puzzled. As soon as she saw the contents she recognized the handsome editions in blue leather and gilt. Sebastian had paid for his poems to be produced in this opulent style, and then given them away as gifts. He had always sent one to the Regent, and received a brief acknowledgment from a flunkie.

No wonder he'd never made any money. She wondered what on earth she was supposed to do with this belated batch, and picked up the letter which accompanied them.

Dear Mrs. Rossiter,

I hope these elegant volumes of your husband's exquisite poems are a cause for sweet remembrance, not renewed grief. It has been a cause of some distress to me that these special editions of his last opus were delayed by problems in acquiring precisely the leather he requested.

I knew, however, that as in life his standards had been immutable, so in death he would wish to be the same.

I know you take comfort from the warm regard in which your husband's work is held by all who read it, and who share in your loss.

There is a small sum outstanding for these specially bound editions.

Algernon D. Browne

Judith appreciated the careful phrasing. So Sebastian's work was held in warm regard by all who read it. Perhaps true. What a pity it was such a small number. Probably readers were put off by having to purchase the poems in cordovan leather with heavy gilding.

There was another sheet of paper. With horror she saw it was a bill. For twenty specially prepared issues of *Sweet Light of Angels*, A.D. Browne, printers, was owed one hundred and four guineas.

Judith looked at the books as if they were a nest of vipers. A hundred and four guineas! That was nearly two quarters' allowance. Could she return them? No, even if it were legally possible, how could the Weeping Widow do that? Oh, did that matter anymore?

Could she sell them? She laughed aloud at that thought. Would Prinny be disappointed not to receive his copy? She couldn't even afford the cost of sending it.

Could she preserve her dignity, and pay for them? Only by destroying any chance of solvency. She wanted to weep, but fought it for the children's sake. They mustn't know how frightened she was.

There would always be a place for her with her parents, she reminded herself, but there would be little money for training or dowry. Her throat was aching. This cruel twist of fate on top of a cruel day, was almost too much for her.

There was a knock at the door. Judith simply couldn't take any more. "Bastian, please . . ."

He went to answer it, and she saw he wasn't fooled. Both her children were very sensitive to atmosphere. Dear heavens, but only a few weeks ago they had possessed a kind of contentment, a satisfaction with so little, and a joy in simple things. Then Leander Knollis had turned their lives upside down.

But that wasn't fair, it really wasn't.

Bastian returned and gave her a note. "From Hartwell," he said.

She turned the crisp white paper in her hand. It was simply addressed to Judith Rossiter. It could be from one of the Ardens, or from Leander. It could be from the butler if it came to that. She knew none of their hands.

Her own hands were shaking as she broke the seal. She didn't know what to expect, what she hoped for.

My dear Judith,
    We've bounced into absurdity again, haven't we? I could offer you an apology, but I am not sure what I would be apologizing for. There are clearly matters that need to be discussed, but I am convinced our separation is due to a misunderstanding rather than intent.
    If you are of the same opinion, I will be in the churchyard until the light goes.

                        Leander

Judith found that she was standing staring at the books and knew it was not by accident. Absurdity, tragedy, she wasn't at all sure a marriage between her and Leander Knollis was practical at all, but now she had no choice. She had to marry him.

She looked up and saw Rosie and Bastian watching her with solemn, fearful hope. They at least had no doubt as to the desirable outcome.

She glanced out of the window. The light was already beginning to go. She picked up a woolen shawl and flung it around her head. "Bastian. Look after Rosie. And this time, *do* it."

He was leaning sacrilegiously against Sebastian's tomb, looking tall and formidable in a long riding cape, and solemn enough for a graveyard.

"One can't expect much," he remarked, "from a courtship that mostly takes place around graves."

Judith came to a halt, facing him across the grave, not knowing what to say.

He straightened. "I gather Bastian is safe?"

"Yes."

"Was he terrified of me?"

She swallowed. "No." She was aware of an atmosphere of misty gloom and ghosts.

"I should perhaps have left the matter in your hands," he said, "but I was first on the scene, and scared by what-might-have-been. I have begun to think of myself as his father. In addition, I felt somewhat responsible as I had reintroduced him to horses."

Judith seized on it. "He wouldn't have been so thoughtless a few weeks ago."

He raised a brow. "Are you laying that at my door?"

Quite apart from the fact that she *had* to reconcile with him, that wasn't fair. "It's the excitement," she admitted, "and you are only the indirect cause."

"Strange, I thought I was the heart of it."

She could tell he was in a dangerous mood, and yet with his skills, she couldn't read him. She didn't know what to say or do. She was reminded that he had recently been, not a diplomat, but a soldier; that he was a veteran of that bloodiest of battles, Waterloo. She shivered, and gathered her inadequate shawl tighter around her shoulders.

He frowned. "We shouldn't be here like this. It was the only neutral territory that came to mind."

"It is the only peaceful spot hereabouts."

He looked around at the ranks of gravestones. " *'The grave's a fine and private place,'* " he quoted, " *'But none, I think, do there embrace.'* " He took out the ring and turned it in his fingers. "You're going to have to trust me a little, or this won't work at all."

"I do trust you."

"Do you?"

His silence demanded some explanation for the afternoon's debacle. "I'm used to handling the children alone," she said. "I'm not used to letting anyone else decide if they are in the wrong or right, and what should be done about it.''

"You must have shared such duties with your first husband.''

She looked down. "No. He was too busy."

Night was falling fast. She heard bats squeaking out from the church belfry. She looked up at him, half seen in the gloom.

"If you say your vows to me," he said, "you will be giving me the right to help you with the children, a right I intend to claim. You will have to trust me. I won't always be right, but then neither, with respect, will you. It may be the cause of some fights between us, but I will always try to act for their good. If you cannot believe that, then we cannot marry. Which I think would be a shame.''

Judith felt her heart melt at his tone. Oh my dear, I think a braver, better woman would let you go. But she lacked that strength, and she had a bundle of costly useless books to pay for, and new dreams that only he could make true.

"I, too, think it would be a shame.''

He stepped across the grave to join her, and slipped the ring back on her finger. He clasped her hand. "You're chilled." He took off his riding cape, and draped it around her shoulders. It was warm, and had a slight aroma of horse, and another she recognized, with a stir inside, as his. It was also heavy.

"Lord," she said, "my knees are like to buckle!''

He put an arm around her waist to support her. "I'll help you bear the weight." He turned her into his arms. "I'm glad we've only tomorrow to get through. You won't jilt me at the altar, will you?''

She shook her head.

His head swooped down on her and he kissed her fiercely, using his whole body to overwhelm her senses and demand a response. She felt seared. "Now my knees *are* buckling," she said shakily.

"Good. Sometimes I think you mistake me, Judith, and the time for mistakes is almost over. This may be a marriage without love, but that does not mean I do not care, or that I do not desire you. I desire you very, very much. I am looking forward to our wedding night, to when I have the right to explore your body, and learn your ways, and see you lost in the senses. . . ."

Her body was still humming from that kiss, and his words made her head swim. His hand was absently tantalizing her nape to devastating effect. She felt she had to warn him. "I think it's going to be a bit different with you. . . ."

"Good God, I hope so." He cast a grimacing look at the grave, and led her away toward the lytchgate. "You see how you've destroyed my composure? A few weeks ago, I would never have been so maladroit as to make love to a lady in a chilly graveyard."

Not to mention over her husband's grave, thought Judith, though more with humor than with guilt. The past was the past.

He'd ridden down, and the big gray horse stood like a patient ghost. When they reached it, Leander said, "Will you ride with me?"

She supposed it was a kind of trust, and nodded. He took off the cape. She shivered slightly, as much from the loss of the essence of him, as from the loss of its warmth. He put his hands at her waist and lifted her onto the saddle.

She clutched at the pommel, nervous to be alone on the horse, and surprised again at his strength. She found herself wondering what kind of body was under the covering of excellent tailoring, then suppressed such wickedness.

On the other hand, if he expected her to be naked, perhaps he would be, too. . . . He swung up behind her, then shifted them around until she was in his lap, and they were both enclosed in the cape. She was snuggled against him like a child, and imagined she could feel the slow beat of his heart. Perhaps she could. She could certainly feel the solid strength of him.

He set the horse to amble slowly back down the misty village street toward the lane where her cottage was. Fuzzy rectangles of light marked the houses, but the street was deserted. It was as if they were alone in the world.

"I'm going to make you a good wife," she said suddenly.

"That sounds dauntingly worthy."

She glanced up at him, unable to read his tone. "I mean, the sort of wife you want."

She saw the white of his teeth as he smiled. "That's more like it. Is that a promise?"

She hesitated, then said, "Yes." And meant it.

"Good. And I'll try to be the sort of husband you want." He looked down and blew gently at her forehead. "Would you care to give me some hints?"

He was perfect as he was, but she couldn't say that. As they turned into the lane she teased, "Serious, sober, and sensible. And faithful, of course."

He swung off the horse and helped her down. "One out of four will have to do."

She fought a smile. "Which one?"

He let his smile free. "You choose."

She tilted her head on one side. "Serious," she said.

He laughed out loud. "You chose wrong." He tilted her chin and kissed her. "I'm going to hide from you tomorrow, wife-to-be. I daren't risk any other problems until we're wed. But I think I should speak to Bastian. Will you send him out?"

She felt that pang of alarm, and yes, of possessiveness. She didn't want to share the children in this way. But she suppressed both feelings. This was where she proved her trust. "Of course. Good night."

"Good night." He somehow invested the words with sultry promise that sent shivers down her back, and curled her toes.

The children had laid the table, and put out the bowls for the soup that was simmering on the hob. They both looked at her with wide-eyed anxiety. They saw the ring, and their faces lit up.

"It's going to be all right!" Rosie squealed.

Judith hushed her. "Yes, it's going to be all right." She turned to her son. "Bastian, you are not to think this quarrel between Leander and me was your fault, for it wasn't. On the other hand, you hurt him by not believing that he will care for you even if you disappoint him by your behavior. He wishes to speak to you. I wish you to apologize."

"Is he still angry?"

She hugged him. "Not at all."

He came back in a few minutes. *"He* says I'm to apologize to *you* for causing you distress!" Despite his exasperation at the ways of adults, his apology sounded heartfelt. He improved on it by apologizing to Rosie for leaving her, assuring Judith that it was his own idea entirely.

Not to be outdone, Rosie apologized for getting in the boat and almost drowning.

Judith hugged them both. It would be all right.

Chapter Nine

Rosie woke Judith on her wedding morning, bubbling over with excitement at the day, her part in it, and the future. Rosie had followed the pattern of all young ladies and fallen head over heels in love with Leander Knollis. But for Rosie he was Papa.

Or rather, Papa Leander.

And here the day was upon them all. The banns had been read. The church was decked with garlands and flowers, mostly courtesy of Hartwell. Her family were doubtless on the road.

Judith thought back to her first wedding day, when she'd woken in her old room at home, sharing the bed with her sister, Anne, vibrating with nerves and excitement, unable to think of the future for thinking of the night ahead when she would experience the mysterious wickedness that was the marriage bed.

And then Sebastian had done nothing for weeks until she'd prodded him to it.

It had hurt the first time, but she'd expected that. What she had not expected was that it be so dull, and that it never become pleasant. Nor had Sebastian appeared to enjoy it. He had seemed to be every bit as embarrassed about what he was doing as she was, even in the dark.

In time, Judith had overcome her self-consciousness about the act, though she was not sure Sebastian ever had, but she had never understood why people could be so excited about it.

Tonight could hold few surprises, and there was no reason for nervousness. Despite twelve years of marriage, however, she felt as if she was once more embarking upon unknown waters, and was unable to think of the future for wondering about the night.

She acceded to Rosie's excited pleading and got up. It was early and there was little to do other than dress, for all the packing had been taken care of. She had no intention of putting her lovely dress on so early and getting it creased or soiled, so she dressed in black. Soon Bastian was up, too, equally full of nervous energy.

They all made a last check of the cottage, to be sure nothing was left behind, though they'd done it before. There were surprisingly few boxes, and she wished she hadn't been quite so ruthless. What harm would there have been in taking those old Christmas baubles, even if they just ended up decorating the schoolroom at Temple Knollis?

It had been much that way at Mayfield House. Judith's attempts to introduce her family's boisterous Christmas traditions there had met with frosty disapproval from Sebastian, and had been reserved for the nursery.

Christmases with Sebastian had followed a bleak pattern. There had never been any guests. When the village carolers came to the door, Mrs. Polk, the housekeeper, took them into the kitchen for a slice of cake and, Judith suspected, some rum punch. Sebastian didn't keep any spirits, but Mrs. Polk established that she could not make a Christmas cake without rum. When Judith did the accounts she saw that it took a quite remarkable amount of rum to make the cake, but she made no issue of it.

Judith had often longed to spend more time down in the servants' quarters where there *was* laughter, and singing, and rum punch. She made her elderberry wine, as her mother always had, and that was the only wine in the house. At Christmas, she insisted in drinking a toast with it, and Sebastian relented so far as to take one small glass.

On Christmas morn, she and Sebastian exchanged gifts, and they then gave each member of the small staff a present. It was always something practical such as stockings, or a length of cloth, but that was common enough. Sebastian would also give them a copy of his latest book of poems, though the kitchen maid at least was not a good enough reader to enjoy them. The staff had been pleased to get them, though. Upon his death, the servants' grief had been rather more substantial than her own, for they had felt there was a real cachet to serving a poet.

Judith wrinkled her brow when she thought of those slim volumes in plain cloth bindings. It had never occurred to her before, but he must have had them specially bound that way rather than give the staff ones in cordovan. At over five guineas a copy, the good ones were expensive, but it seemed to her positively nip-farthing to have had servants' editions produced.

She pushed the thoughts away. She did not want harsh thoughts of Sebastian on this, her wedding day.

"Is it time to dress yet, Mama?"

Judith sighed. It must be the tenth time Rosie had asked that. She was twitchy with excitement, and it would only get worse. She decided they should all go for a walk, to pass the time and get rid of some of the energy.

They ended up by the river near the graveyard for, as she had said last night to Leander, it was the only peaceful spot in Mayfield. The street was busy, and the nearby fields were plowed. One had to go some distance to find another open space suitable for children to run around.

The clock struck ten and she knew it was time to return home for the last time, and prepare for the wedding. As they retraced their steps they passed by Sebastian's grave and stopped. Judith didn't suppose she would visit it again, and there'd be no one to put flowers there anymore.

Unless devoted admirers came by to do homage.

The children stood still with their solemn, mourning faces on, but she knew they didn't particularly mourn their father, and neither did she.

Again she felt a pang of guilt. Sebastian had, she supposed, done his best.

Leander had been sent by Beth to the church with another basket of hothouse flowers. Now he sat on his horse and frowned at the sight of Judith in her black standing by that damned grave.

"Well, even if she still weeps for you, Sebastian Rossiter," he said softly, "you shan't greet her at the gate soon if I have any say in it. And perhaps when that day comes you'll get a surprise. It's clear you didn't reach the depths of her senses. Tonight I'll wipe all memory of you from her mind."

The small church was tolerably full when Judith walked into it on her brother's arm, Rosie and Bastian preceding her. Bastian was carrying the ring on a satin cushion. Rosie was strewing petals down the aisle.

Most of the village was present, of course, and Leander had made arrangements for them all to make jolly afterward at the Dog and Pheasant. Judith's family occupied the front pews, for with spouses and children it now counted over twenty souls.

There was no one for Leander other than the Ardens. At least after today he would have a family.

It felt so strange to be in colors. In the peach dress, with a high-crowned bonnet lined to match and boasting three plumes, Judith felt a different person. She saw the congregation stare at her and come to the same conclusion.

At the end of the short aisle waited her husband-to-be. He was handsome in biscuit and buff, with a cheerful bronze cravat. It all toned pleasantly with her outfit; she supposed Beth had told him.

If she was a bundle of nerves, he looked calm. But that in itself, she decided, was a sign of nerves. When himself he was boyish or formidable according to his mood. This blandness was his diplomatic face, and if a wild man of the jungle were to walk down the aisle, he would handle it calmly, and with impeccably good breeding.

At the thought, she felt a giggle bubble up. The struggle to keep her lips straight was positively painful. She reminded herself that she was not a sixteen-year-old virgin, but a mature woman of nearly thirty making a practical marriage. She had no intention of giggling and simpering. She raised her chin and marched forward.

Leander fought a smile when he noted what he had come to think of as her ship-of-the-line walk, all guns rolled out for action. He supposed she was still uneasy about this course, which annoyed him, but if she'd come this far he had her.

Which made him inordinately pleased.

Her gown was a delight. The warm peach color picked up the tone of her skin and deepened the blue of her lovely eyes. In the frame of frill and bonnet she looked like a pansy, but he doubted she'd like to be told that.

The stylish gown also showed off her figure properly for the first time. Though it was high-necked, there was no denying that there was a magnificent bosom beneath it. He'd known that day in her cottage, when she'd accepted his proposal and he'd tested her, that making love to Judith would not be hard. Now he knew it again.

And tonight he would do it.

This anticipation was an altogether unexpected bonus of his plan.

Bastian did his part and went to stand by Leander's side with the ring, but Rosie stopped and looked up at him with quivery excitement, wanting to say something, but shy. He bent down and kissed her brow, then pushed her gently to where her grandmother was sitting.

Then he could take Judith's hand and lead her to the altar.

Judith did not shame herself. She said her vows with clear, mature precision. Leander did the same, then slid the ring onto her finger to make her his.

Judith had found it strange not to have a wedding ring there for a few weeks, but it was even stranger to have this different ring in place. Because of the daily care, her hand was paler and smoother; the rings were completely different. This wasn't the old her at all.

She realized she was staring at the rings, and looked quickly up at him. He leant forward and lightly kissed her lips. In some way he made the brief movements of his lips over hers a promise of other things to come, and she felt hot blood rush into her cheeks. As if she were a nervous sixteen-year-old again.

Back at Hartwell there was a meal spread and ample drink. Judith chatted with her family but she felt strange and nervy. Three-quarters of her attention was on the children, who were overexcited and eating too much.

She was glad when the time came to leave to begin the first day of their journey to the Temple. Then she couldn't find Bastian.

"He's in the garden with Georgie," declared Rosie.

Judith hurried out and called him. After a moment he came running. "I was just saying good-bye, Mama."

"I know, dear, but we must be off now."

A giddy round of farewells, a shower of rice that the children thought hilarious, and they were off to a new life.

Judith's head was still whirling. The children were positively fizzing, and chattering about everything. Rosie had Magpie in a special basket, but the kitten mewled to be allowed out, then scrambled across everyone's laps. It seemed to particularly want to be in Bastian's lap, which upset Rosie.

Judith took the kitten onto her own lap to stop the argument.

Now Bastian and Rosie craned to see what was left behind, then craned to see what was coming ahead. They waved to villagers as they passed. Judith lifted the kitten to rescue her silk from Magpie's claws. Leander took Magpie in a firm grip and lectured him on manners.

Judith looked at her husband apprehensively. He appeared relaxed and amused, but she prayed everything would simmer down.

Soon they were out of Mayfield, heading for the turnpike, and the children settled to watching this new world unfold around them. At last, Magpie curled up on Rosie's lap and peace arrived. Judith still couldn't help but be concerned as to how things would go when the novelty wore off. She wondered if Leander had seriously thought what three or four days in a coach with two children and a cat would be like.

"I suggest you ladies remove your bonnets," he

said, and they were only too happy to comply. "I think it all went very well," he said to Judith. "I hope you were pleased."

"It was lovely.

"What was your first wedding like?" he asked abruptly.

Judith was surprised he would raise the subject. "Not very different. . . . I was a lot more nervous, of course. . . . We left early then, too."

He looked at her. "Did you not want to leave? I thought it better for us to be on our way."

"I didn't mind."

It was clear that scintillating conversation was beyond them, and so by tacit agreement they fell silent except for answers to the children's occasional questions.

But he took her hand once and smiled at her in a way that told her he was still happy with the state of affairs.

They planned to go only as far as Winchester this first day, and so they stopped at Farnham to eat. Not long after leaving Farnham, Rosie complained of a tummy ache.

Judith's heart sank. That was all they needed, a sick child.

At her suggestion, Leander moved over to the other seat so Rosie could lie with her head in Judith's lap. The girl was soon feeling more comfortable, but they didn't bother changing places.

When they arrived at Winchester there was daylight still, and Leander suggested they walk around the splendid old city, and visit the famous cathedral. Judith welcomed the opportunity to stretch and enjoy the fresh air, but she wondered how much longer the children would last. It wasn't late, but they'd had an extremely exciting day.

All seemed well, however. Leander had a ready store of stories about the ancient times when this had been the capital of Wessex, and therefore of England. Judith was as fascinated as the children, and her anxiety was eased by the tolerant way he answered the children's questions.

Eventually, as she had feared, they started one of their rare fights, but he soothed that, too, with firmness and a touch of humor. She should have known a diplomat and soldier could cope.

He looked over at Judith. "A long day for them."

She nodded. "And an overexciting one. They will be better in bed."

He did and said nothing, but as they retraced their steps to the inn, Judith was aware of the word *bed* reverberating like the cathedral bells chiming five.

Judith and Leander had a large bedchamber and a private parlor which was every bit as grand as her drawing room at Mayfield House, and almost as grand as Hartwell. There were damask curtains at the window, and upholstered chairs set before a blazing fire. A table was laid ready for their supper.

The children were in an adjoining room with two smaller beds. It, too, was grand, and Bastian and Rosie were very impressed.

Leander ordered a simple supper, but even so the children ate little and drooped in their chairs. Judith shooed them off to wash and change, first Rosie, then Bastian.

Rosie came back in her new nightgown to kiss Leander. "Good night, Papa."

He hugged her. "Good night, moppet. More adventures tomorrow."

Judith tucked Rosie in her bed, and Bastian emerged from behind the screen somewhat quickly. Her mother's instinct warned he was up to mischief, but she couldn't imagine what. Though he'd been quick about it, he looked as if he'd washed properly. He, too, went to wish Leander good night. He came back speedily to scramble into bed.

Judith looked closely at him and checked Magpie's basket. The children had been told they could not have the kitten in bed with them. The little bundle of fur was there, fast asleep.

She decided it was her nerves that were making her suspicious, and tucked them in. Then she read to them for quite a while. She was making sure that they were ready for sleep and unafraid in a strange place, but she was aware that she was also delaying her return to her bridal chamber and the moment of truth.

Rosie was asleep and Bastian almost there when she finally closed the book and rose. As she extinguished the candles something ran across her feet.

She let out a yelp. A mouse! She grabbed the poker and pursued it.

"Mama don't! It's Blucher!"

Now Rosie was awake again, too.

Judith stared at Bastian. "I said no rat!"

"He's Georgie's goodbye present!"

Leander came in. "What's the matter?"

"Bastian has a rat!"

"I don't! Mama's chased him away, and he'll get lost and eaten by a cat. He's only a baby!"

"It went behind the washstand," said Judith tightly.

Leander went over, knelt down, then eased the washstand away. Lightning fast he snared the little creature before it could squirm away.

"Don't kill him, please," begged Bastian tearfully.

Leander held the baby rat up, quite gently she noticed, and said, *"Morituri te saluti.* Thumbs up or down?"

A moment ago Judith would have walloped it with the poker without hesitation, but now it looked so defenseless and Bastian was so desperate. Magpie had turned out to be largely Rosie's pet. . . .

"We can't have a cat and a rat," she protested. "One of them will eat the other!"

"I don't think either of them is a predator yet,"

said Leander, and she noticed he now had the rat in a hold that allowed stroking.

"You're as bad as Bastian!"

He twinkled at her like a mischievous schoolboy. "Bread and water for both of us?"

Judith gave in. "But it is not running free."

Leander pushed back the screen that concealed the washstand, and put a dry cloth in the bottom of the empty bowl. He placed the rat there and covered the bowl with a towel. "That should keep him for the night. Tomorrow we'll find another basket of some kind."

Bastian scrubbed at his eyes. "Thank you, Papa."

"Don't thank me. If your mother had wished, I'd have broken his neck. Now, go to sleep. Your mother and I want some time to ourselves."

He left, but his words stayed behind, drying Judith's mouth. Despite the fact she'd known this night would come, despite the wedding and the vows, she still found it difficult to imagine the intimacies of marriage with this man who was still in many ways a stranger.

She stayed for a little while until she was sure the children were settled. She checked on the rat, which was not asleep but didn't appear to be able to climb the smooth china walls of its prison.

She wondered if Bastian had managed to sneak it some food during the day, and supposed he must have. Probably the creature needed water, too. She found a small china pin bowl on the dressing table, filled it with water and placed it on the cloth. The silly beast nuzzled at her fingers.

"I don't like rats," she hissed, and covered it again.

Then there was no further excuse for delay, so she joined her husband in their bedchamber.

She found Leander in his shirtsleeves, drinking wine as he stared out of a dark window. He looked over at her, giving no evidence of impatience. "Settled?"

"Yes. Fast asleep. Except the rat. I'm sorry about that."

"It's not your crime to apologize for. The children are ours now, Judith, not just yours. Do you want me to dispose of it?"

"How could we?"

"Quite easily."

"I mean, how could we be so heartless?" She looked at him. "I thought you seemed quite taken. I'll never understand men. Rats are vermin!"

He laughed. "In the plural, yes. One rat won't ruin the world. We'll just have to hope it really is male."

Judith closed her eyes. "I don't even want to think about it."

A silence built up and so she said, "They are not used to being out of their accustomed beds. They may wake in the night. . . ."

"Then one of us will go to them and reassure them," he said calmly. "Would they be frightened to find me looming over them in the night?"

"I don't know." She stood there, clasping her hands in front of her, unsure of what to do.

He dropped the curtain and went to a table to pour her some wine. He held it out. "Come. Drink to our happiness."

She took it, and they clinked glasses and drank. Judith blinked. "My, but that's good!"

He laughed. "You have excellent taste. It's a Clos Vugeot from Burgundy. I thought you no oenophile."

"An expert on wines? Nor am I. In fact," she said, taking another sip, "I don't believe I've ever before tasted a wine made from grapes."

"Never . . ." He looked lost for words.

She shrugged. "My family could never afford it, and Sebastian disapproved of strong liquids. He said they overheated the blood."

"Did he, indeed?" he asked lazily. "And why was that such a bad thing?"

It was as if the air in the warm room were growing heavier. Judith turned away from him. "I hardly feel it is right to discuss my husband at such a time, especially in such a tone of voice."

He turned her to face him. "Your *first* husband," he corrected. "I am your husband."

Judith could have bitten her tongue. "I'm sorry. I didn't mean . . ."

He sighed, and laid a hand over her lips. "I know," he said. "I'm sorry, too. This day doesn't leave my nerves untouched, you know."

"No, I didn't."

He took her hand. "This has been a long day for all of us. Let's to bed."

He said "let's to bed" but his eyes said something different, and he was drawing her toward him. Judith panicked.

"Yes," she said, and pulled out of his grip. She disappeared behind the dressing screen, snatching her nightgown as she went. Probably his intention had been to disrobe her, but she simply wasn't up to that tonight. She'd get into her nightgown by herself, and into bed. Hopefully then it would all be like it had been with Sebastian.

She soon realized her mistake. After trying and failing to find an alternative, she peeped around the edge of the screen. He was standing, waiting, his face bland, but laughter in his eyes. "Do you perhaps need some help, my dear?"

Only in certain respects, she wanted to say. She swallowed. "The buttons . . ."

He came over. She turned. His nimble fingers undid the long line of tiny buttons; each brushing touch against her spine set nerves quivering. Judith knew her wifely duty was to let him strip her if that was his pleasure, but she couldn't. Two lamps were burning, and there was a fire in the hearth. The room was as bright as day!

He finished. She would have moved away, but his hands grasped her shoulders. She froze. His lips brushed the top of her spine and she caught her breath at the sweetness of it.

He released her. "Don't be long," he said softly.

Judith took off her lovely clothes. She quickly used half the water in the jug to wash with, and put on her nightgown, one of the new silk ones. She'd never worn silk next to her skin before, and the chill slither of it made her shiver. But it stirred her senses in unexpected ways. Every movement she made seemed to set the cream silk whispering and stroking.

With trembling hands she poured her dirty water into the slop bowl, and checked she had left all ready for him. It was time to leave the cover of the screen.

She did so, and with only the briefest glance at him went directly to the bed to scramble under the covers. She felt like a fox gaining its earth. From the protection of the bedcovers she could look at him and give what she hoped was a calm, mature, and mildly encouraging smile.

He looked nothing so much as tender. He smiled back and went behind the screen.

Judith realized she was in bed without having done her hair. She eyed the screen, but he was clearly washing, and should be a little while. She slid from under the covers and tiptoed to the dressing table. She pulled out the pins and brushed out her hair. She normally would plait the mass of dark curls, or put it under a cap, but she didn't have a cap and feared she didn't have time to plait it.

She heard him pouring out his water, and dashed back under the covers.

Leander came out from behind the screen and felt his heart speed. His wife was flushed and rosy, and her hair was a shining dark cloud about her pillow.

Her lips were slightly parted, and she looked shy and apprehensive. She might be shy—he was a little shy, too—but he was safe in the knowledge that she couldn't really be apprehensive.

How could he ever have contemplated marrying a young virgin? This was much more fun.

He was in a nightshirt, since it was clear that she would prefer it at first, but he badly wanted to be naked, with her naked beside him. Soon, he told himself. Soon. It will just take a little while to overcome her reserve.

He tended the fire then extinguished the lamps. He would have preferred to leave them burning but he sensed that she would be more comfortable with the dark at first. Not that it was really dark with the fire still blazing. By the time he reached the bed his eyes had accustomed themselves and he could make out her pale face and her big eyes.

Desire swelled up in him and pounded in his veins. He wanted to lean straight over her and take her lips and her breasts, and roll swiftly into passion, but that wasn't the way for a first time.

He just wasn't sure what was. Following his father's precepts, his lovers had been older and experienced. By the very nature of things they had been bold. Judith might be older, but she had experienced only one man, and she clearly wasn't bold at all.

He had to do this right.

Tonight he wanted to make her completely his.

He joined her in bed and lay on his side looking at her. Then he kissed her.

Her lips were surprisingly tentative against his, but they were soft and delicious. He could be happy for some time just with lips. At least, he thought he could. He found his hand was playing with her breast, but her lips had became more active and he didn't think the two facts were unrelated.

He pulled back and smiled. "You're even more

beautiful than I knew. Your hair's like a cloud of midnight. . . .''

Judith lay looking at him, at sea in more ways than one. She *still* didn't know what to do, and she felt as if she were being swept out on a sea that was growing increasingly stormy.

His hand on her breast was truly extraordinary. Silk seemed to be a magical fabric capable of transforming a simple touch into . . . into . . . She didn't have words for what was going on inside her. His kiss had been tender, and she'd felt cherished as never before.

Still, despite differences, she knew the act would be the same. At any moment he would enter her and then it would be done with.

Not quite yet it would seem.

He was putting his mouth to her breast like a baby! She gave a choked cry of astonishment at the sensation that shot through her.

He looked up, smiling brilliantly. ''Ah, you like that?''

''Do I?''

He turned serious. ''You must tell me.''

Like didn't seem quite the right word but she wanted to please him. ''Yes, I liked it.''

So he did it again as his hands stroked the silk and used the silk to stroke her. She melted. She wasn't on the sea, she was the sea, a soft, swirling sea. She gripped his shoulders as the only firm spot in a liquid world—

"Mama!"

The sudden shriek had her bolt up in bed. Rosie cried again, and then there were the unmistakable sounds of someone vomiting. With one, bereft, horrified look at Leander, Judith raced for the children's room.

Leander lay back and started to laugh.

Chapter Ten

Judith found that Rosie had at least made it to the washstand, and Bastian had grabbed Blucher in the nick of time.

She wiped the girl's face and felt her head. There was no fever. This was just an upset stomach, doubtless the result of too much rich food and excitement.

Judith sent Bastian back to bed, but he sat there anxiously as she settled Rosie. "She'll be all right, Bastian. You go back to sleep." She decided to ignore the rat on his pillow. One crisis was enough at a time.

"She'll throw up again," Bastian predicted gloomily.

Judith feared he was correct. She found one of the chamber pots was unused and kept that close by, then sat on Rosie's bed and stroked her head as the girl began to drift back to sleep. She found herself thinking of Leander and what they had been doing. It had been extraordinary and rather pleasant, but it had left her feeling unwell. She ached. She felt a little sick herself. Perhaps there had been something wrong with the dinner.

Then there was the fact that they hadn't arrived at the significant part, and she feared he would be annoyed. She wasn't sure, for nothing like this had ever happened to her before. She told herself defensively that it was he who had insisted on bringing the children on their wedding trip.

She heard the door and looked up anxiously. He didn't *look* annoyed.

"How is she?" he asked.

"Not too bad. It's just the excitement, I think."

"Should we send for a doctor?"

"No, I don't think so."

"I'll call someone to clean away the mess."

"It's late."

"Not particularly."

He came back in a moment with her wrap and draped it about her shoulders. Soon a manservant came in and quietly cleared away all the slops, leaving clean bowls and water.

Leander returned with a glass. "Try this for her."

"What is it?"

"Just warm water with a little sugar and brandy. It should settle her stomach."

Rosie sipped it dubiously, but then began to drift off. When Judith tried to move, however, the girl's eyes flew open and she whined, "Don't leave me, Mama!"

Judith looked up helplessly at Leander.

His smile was rueful, but he bent down to kiss her and said, "You stay here. I'll take Bastian to sleep in our bed."

The boy had fallen asleep and Leander picked him up and carried him through, shutting the door between them. Judith sighed and got into Bastian's bed.

She hoped this wedding night wasn't a sign of things to come.

Judith was wakened the next morning by something tickling her chin. Thinking of rats, her eyes flew open. Leander was sitting on her bed fully dressed, tickling her with a hothouse rose.

"You're pretty in the morning," he said lazily.

"No one's pretty in the morning."

"Children are," he said with a grin at Rosie, who was just waking up, too, "and so are you."

She couldn't help but smile, but said, "I'm sorry about last night. . . ."

He shook his head. "I wanted a family and must take the rough with the smooth. We'll have many more nights."

Judith suddenly realized from the light that it was late. She sat up. "We'll be ready in a moment."

"No hurry. I never intended us to travel on today, and it is Sunday, you know. I thought we could go to service at the cathedral if Rosie is up to it."

Rosie bounced up. "Oh yes, Mama. I'm as right as rain."

She certainly looked it. Judith checked her temperature again then said, "Very well, but you must eat a little something first. Perhaps some toast."

"It all awaits next door," said Leander. "I stole the flower from the table."

He tucked the rose in her hair, and left.

Judith looked in the mirror and saw a stranger, a Gypsy creature with rosy cheeks and wild tangled hair adorned with a crimson rose. Who was this? Not Judith Rossiter, but hardly the Countess of Charrington either.

A knock at the door brought a maid, sent by milord to assist milady. Judith was duly assisted into one of her elegant new muslins, a white figured with spring flowers, and her hair was brushed and worked into a becoming arrangement of knots and curls.

"Why thank you," she said, surprised. "That is lovely."

The woman looked pleased at the compliment but said, "Your hair's a treat to handle, milady. I'm sure it would do anything with just a brush and a few pins.''

Judith had always found it an unmanageable mop.

She asked the maid to do Rosie's hair, too, and so she brushed it into a topknot of silky curls, decorated with a white ribbon. Rosie was delighted and ran off to show Papa.

Judith followed more decorously, but she, too, was pleased to show Leander how fine she looked. ''Very elegant,'' he said softly with a kiss on her cheek, ''but I prefer you tussled and rosy in bed.''

Judith was certainly rosy as she sat down to breakfast.

She had never been to a service in a cathedral before, and the echoing vaults were overpowering. The voices of the choir floated and soared, and Judith mouthed the hymns. Though generally she enjoyed singing hymns, she knew she had no voice and did not dare disturb this excellence with her efforts.

Leander, she noted, had a rich baritone. Bastian had a clear sweet voice that blended in with the choirboys. Rosie piped up merrily, but Judith winced. Her daughter had inherited her lack of ear.

After the service, they strolled about the town and took luncheon, then headed back to the inn. On the way they found a small lidded basket for Blucher, and some rags to line it, for rats could not be expected to be trained in these matters.

The Crown had gardens, and the children and animals were allowed to play there for a while. Blucher seemed content to run about on Bastian's shoulders, but Magpie chased leaves and straw, and Rosie chased Magpie.

Bastian was more interested in the comings and goings of the busy inn yard. It was a staging post, and there was a constant stream of carriages of all kinds halting to change teams.

At one point one of the ostlers called out, "You can come and help us, young lad, if you like."

Bastian looked at Judith and Leander eagerly. They shared a glance and Leander said, "No horses, remember?"

Bastian's face fell but he said a polite, "No thank you," to the ostler.

Judith and Leander shared another look and a smile. She really thought it would work out, and hopefully this night would see no more sickness.

It was warm in the last of the sun and so they sat. The only convenient place was on either side of a stone chess table.

"Tell me about your home," she said.

"My home? Oh, you mean the Temple. It's said to be the most beautiful house in England." His tone was extraordinary for its very blandness.

Any mention of Temple Knollis seemed to cause unexpected reactions but Judith pursued it. "Is it really?"

He shrugged. "Beauty is in the eye of the beholder, but probably. My grandfather was much taken by Azay-le-Rideau in France. As a result Temple Knollis has perfect proportions reflected in a glassy moat. It's built of a particular pinkish stone that changes in the light. Every cloud, every change of the hours and it changes, too. The lake, or moat, is part of a tamed river so the house is in effect on a peninsular. It is built around a central garden set with rare and fragrant plants."

Beth Arden had shown her a picture of Temple Knollis in a book, so Judith knew most of this. What she wanted to know was why Leander's tone became so strange when he spoke of it. "You must love it very much," she said.

He turned to her. "I? I hardly know the place. We can explore it together."

"You hardly know it?" she echoed.

He smiled at her in that charming, blank way he had when he was handling a situation. She'd hoped such days were past. "Didn't I tell you?" he said. "I've only visited it once. Earlier this year, when I returned to England."

"But a visit is long enough to love such a lovely place."

"Not a visit of two hours," said Leander coolly. "Do you play chess? The innkeeper doubtless has the men."

Judith admitted to knowing the moves, wishing she knew the moves of this marriage. As she waited for him to return she accepted that he had virtually slammed a door on that topic, and yet it was a topic that could hardly be avoided.

For the first time she wondered if there was something wrong at Temple Knollis. Could it be cursed or haunted? That seemed so melodramatic, and yet there was clearly some problem.

To what kind of place was she taking her innocent children?

He came back with chess men and news, apparently restored to good humor. "There is to be an assembly at the George tonight. Mine host was of the opinion that such exalted guests as we would not care to be bothered with a mere provincial affair, but I am decidedly interested." He smiled down at her. "I want to dance with you, Judith."

He invested the simple words with subtle power, but she answered. "I fear it won't go so well. Except for some old country dances, I don't know how."

He sat opposite. "You must have attended dances with your first husband, if not balls."

"Very rarely. And Sebastian didn't care for dancing, and liked me to stay with him." She shrugged. "I'm sorry."

"Do you think to escape so easily? There'll be many country dances, and you'll manage them without trouble. Just in case it is danced here, I think we should practice the waltz."

He raised her to her feet. She looked at the small lawn and said, "Here?"

"Why not?" He took her hand. "Place your other hand on my shoulder, so. Step to the side, and back . . ."

Judith obeyed his instructions, but she was soon attuned more to the gentle guidance of his body. She turned and swayed like a tree in his breeze, and if she made a misstep he somehow corrected so their movement hardly faltered. He began to hum a lilting tune and it all seemed as natural as breathing.

The tune came to an end, and he stopped. "There, see. It's easy."

She was still in his arms, and rather closer than when they'd been dancing. "Only with you, I fear."

His lids drooped in a lazy, suggestive manner. "Only with me, I hope . . ."

Giggles distracted them, and they found Bastian and Rosie on the grass in a tangle, having tried to copy them. Rosie scrambled up. "Bastian trod on my toe!"

"You didn't move, you noddy! You can't dance for toffee."

"I can so"

In one accord, Judith and Leander moved in and separated the two to steer them back to the inn. "Time for tea," said Judith, "and then some quiet activity."

The children were happy enough with books and puzzles until supper time. After the meal they all played a guessing game until bedtime. Leander asked to tell them a story, rather than read to them.

Judith was supposed to be preparing for the assembly, but the door was open and so she didn't ring for the maid but listened tenderly to his story. It was all about a clever German child who outwitted the giant who wanted to eat her family.

Judith had to admit that the young lady was not always ladylike in her actions, but the children were soon giggling and joining in with suggestions of other ways for Olga to trick the giant.

When it was over, she heard him say, "Now, that didn't send you to sleep, so I'll sing you a little song. This is German, too, and is appropriately about a rose. *'Sah ein knab ein Roslein stehn, Roslein auf der heiden . . .'*"

Judith listened, smiling. Peace and quiet fell.

He came into the parlor, and shut the door. He looked at her and raised his brows. *"Nach was du willst . . ."* He broke off with a laugh. "Sorry. You must do as you please, Judith, but that dress is not quite in the right style."

Judith tried to imagine what it must be like to forget what language one was speaking, and couldn't. "I know it," she said. "I was enjoying your tale and song too much. I have the wedding gown or a fine ivory silk. What do you think?"

"The neckline of the wedding gown is too high," he said with certainty. "At such events as these, low necklines are *de rigueur.*"

"That's what Beth said." She rose and went toward the bedroom to change. With a twitch of her lips she asked, "Is your neckline, too, to be low?"

"No. It's to be high, starched, and soon wilted. Perhaps I should dispense with it and show my décolletage, too."

Not totally sure he was funning, Judith beat a retreat.

She had not put on the gown of ivory lace over peach satin before, and was a little startled by how low the neckline was, though at least it meant she could get into it without assistance.

The frill of the neckline skimmed the edges of

her shoulders above puffed sleeves, then plunged between her breasts to a rosette that gathered the fabric there. A few twists and shrugs reassured her that it would not actually slip off and reveal all, and when she looked in the mirror it was not too bad, but when she looked down she thought she looked naked.

Before summoning the maid to do her hair, she went nervously into the parlor. "Leander, is this dress . . . acceptable?"

He looked up and his eyes both brightened and darkened at the same time. He came over to her. "My dear, it's exquisite! Such wonderful . . . material."

"That's not what catches the eye and you know it!"

His eyes shone with laughter and appreciation, and he let them wander caressingly over her breasts. "Don't worry. Most of the other ladies will be as exposed, I assure you. They just won't have anything quite so magnificent to show off."

Judith put her hands over the exposed flesh. "I knew it. My bosom is too large for this style."

He captured her hands and pulled them down. "Nonsense. You'll be the envy of all the women, and I'll be the envy of all the men." Holding her hands at her sides, he bent forward and placed a kiss in the exposed crevice between her breasts. He straightened. "Enough of this, or I'll ravish you here and now. Hurry, or we'll miss the first dances."

Judith went back to have her hair dressed, stunned by the word *ravish*. After last night she had some notion of what it might mean.

When they entered the rooms where the assembly was being held, Judith saw that he and Beth had spoken the truth. Nearly all the ladies wore low necklines, and many had little to support their bodices.

She also noted that there were few men to match Leander in looks, and none to match his style. He was completely unostentatious, and yet there was an air about him which set him apart.

The company was as mixed as one would expect at a country affair, with all kinds from well-to-do farmers to aristocracy. The master of ceremonies greeted them and steered them over to a corner of the ballroom where the local lions, Lord and Lady Pratchett, and Sir James and Lady Withington, held court. This was clearly supposed to be their natural milieu.

The Withingtons were a comfortable middle-aged couple with a son and two daughters present. The son, about twenty, looked bored, though he brightened at the sight of Judith, and ogled her bosom. He suddenly stopped, and she guessed Leander had done something about it.

The girls were about sixteen and eighteen. The older one had an air of ennui, but the younger was bright-eyed and fidgety. Judith guessed it was her first grown-up event, and gave her a warm smile.

The Pratchetts were clearly used to lording it at these events and were not entirely pleased, their title being a mere viscountcy, to have an earl in their midst. On the other hand, the connection could not but do them credit. They were still quite a young couple, but acted old and cold. Judith rapidly tired of Lady Pratchett's disparaging comments about everything, accompanied as they were by, ". . . as you and I both know, my dear Lady Charrington."

"In fact I don't," said Judith at last. "Until a few days ago, I lived in a cottage, and my main concern was where the next meal was coming from."

The lady gaped, but was rescued from having to respond by the first music. Leander bowed, and asked Lady Pratchett for the dance.

As Judith allowed Lord Pratchett to lead her out to the country dance, she was sickeningly aware she'd disgraced herself. Lady Pratchett was doubtless even now complaining to Leander about her behavior. She'd known this would never work.

Well, she told herself bracingly, both this marriage and this assembly had been his idea, so he could take the consequences. She set to enjoying herself.

As she'd told Leander, she'd rarely danced since her marriage, but she remembered now the jolly village hops of her youth. For a brief moment she wondered if a countess was supposed to romp, but then consigned such thoughts to the devil. How else was one supposed to do a country dance? A glance around showed her lots of bouncing and laughing.

After a cooling promenade, in which she conversed only with Lord Pratchett, as others seemed nervous of intruding, she danced the next set with Sir James, who despite his portly build was well able to swing and pass.

As she stood and chatted to him, another couple joined them—the Dean and his wife. When the Countess of Charrington proved to be approachable, there were more introductions. News that she had children thawed the ladies in no time, for children are the same no matter what their station.

She saw Leander at ease among another group. She was sure he was *hundling* everyone perfectly. He looked up and smiled across the room in a way that was as good as a kiss.

The next dance was a waltz, and not everyone was able or willing to take part. Judith was trying to tactfully refuse an invitation from the Withingtons' son and heir when Leander was at her side. "So sorry, my dear fellow, but Lady Charrington only dances the waltz with me."

In seconds they were on the floor and the music began. For a few minutes Judith was nervous, for she could see any number of eyes on them, but then she relaxed into his guidance and floated. They didn't speak, and yet she felt this was as public a declaration of their joining as their wedding vows.

When the music stopped, they just stood smiling at each other for a long moment.

Then he led her to the next room where refreshments were laid out, and found her a glass of negus. Before he could speak, they were interrupted by a nervous young man. "Lord Charrington, I understand."

He was of sturdy build, with neat brown hair, and tolerable clothes, but very young to be accosting an earl. About twenty.

Leander admitted his identity, but with a reserve that would have chilled away most intruders.

"I'm James Knollis," the young man said. "Your cousin, don't you know. . . ."

Judith thought then that she saw a faint resemblance. Why had she heard no mention of cousins?

There was a strange pause, but then Leander warmed and held out his hand. "What a pleasant surprise. Delighted to meet you, James. And this is my countess, Judith."

The young man blushed and bowed. "A pleasure to meet you, my lady." He turned back to Leander. "We received your message that you were married, cousin."

"We're on our way to Temple Knollis," Leander said smoothly. Judith recognized his diplomatic manner, and wondered just what problem he perceived here. Was it the reason he had let her believe he had no family? "Are you heading to Somerset, too?"

James tugged at his high cravat. "No," he said sharply. "Leaving. Fact of the matter is, there's sickness there. Diphtheria."

Judith caught her breath. Diphtheria! That was a killing disease.

"How terrible," said Leander in a strange tone. "Who is afflicted?"

"The two youngest. Matthew and Elizabeth. And it was feared Thomas might be taking it. I'm off to stay with a friend."

"Very wise," said Leander. "I hear music starting up and I have promised Judith this dance. But I would like to talk more later. Will you meet me in the tap room for a drink after the assembly?"

The young man agreed, but without gushing enthusiasm. As they went toward the ballroom, Judith whispered, "Diphtheria! We can't possibly take the children there!"

"Of course not. If it's true."

Judith turned to look at him. "Why should he lie about such a thing?"

This strange encounter with his cousin was building that impervious manner she resented. "I don't know."

"I am not willing to take the risk. The whole area could be infected."

He led her to join a line of dancers without answering.

Judith was perfectly prepared to fight over this, but not in public. She was angry at his manner, though, and that he had kept his family secret. What was there about them that she wasn't supposed to know?

She danced stiffly and in silence. He hardly seemed to notice. When the dance was over he said, without consulting her, "Our wisest course will be to go to London and make inquiries from there. The children will enjoy it, and you will be able to add to your wardrobe."

Judith had no real objection to this plan, but resented the manner of its announcement. She couldn't wait to get him alone.

The assembly was just about over, and he escorted Judith up to their rooms, but then turned to go to his appointment with James Knollis. Judith couldn't stand this.

"Why didn't you tell me you have cousins?"

His brows raised. "Doesn't everyone?"

"Everyone doesn't keep them a secret."

"You've never mentioned yours."

That was indubitably true. "They have no bearing on our life," she protested.

"I rather hoped mine would have no bearing on it either."

Judith felt as if she were beating against polished marble. Everything he said was reasonable, and she hated it. "Do I gather that these cousins of yours live near Temple Knollis?"

"My dear," he drawled, robbing the endearment of warmth, "they live *at* Temple Knollis."

Her heart was pounding. "And you didn't think to warn me?"

"I told them to leave."

Judith took a deep breath, afraid of hovering disaster, determined to be reasonable "So why are you so anxious to talk to your Cousin James?"

"To see what he's up to."

"Do you suspect that there's mischief afoot?"

He met her eyes coolly. "I'm not sure what I suspect."

"But you do suspect something," she insisted.

His lips tightened with annoyance at her persistence. "All I know is that my uncle has done his damndest to keep me away from the Temple since I returned to England."

Judith wanted to drop the subject, but this could be crucial to her children's safety. "What has he done?"

He raised his brows. "What are you imagining? Poison? Hired assassins? He has merely written a number of strange letters designed to make the place unappealing."

"And you think diphtheria is another such ploy. Why would he do this?"

"It need not concern you. I have set a number of inquiries in train which may be bearing fruit. A return to London will serve its purpose."

He was speaking, but telling her nothing. "Don't you think you should tell me all about this?"

He looked at her, blankly. "No. It is nothing to do with you."

"I am your *wife,*" she protested. "I am your partner in life."

"You put it too strongly," he said coldly. "Do not concern yourself about my personal affairs." With that, he left her.

Judith felt chilled to her soul. She was seeing his other face with a vengeance, but had no one but herself to blame. He had always made it clear that this marriage was one of practicality—how could it be anything else? It was her foolishness to succumb to his practiced charm and grow fond. When she had promised not to, as well.

One thing was sure, she could not bear intimacy with him tonight. She didn't bother to try and move Bastian, but slipped into bed with Rosie.

For a while she lay nervously, expecting Leander to charge in and drag her to his bed. But time passed, the fire died, and the town clock chimed midnight. Judith began to drift off to sleep.

What was she to make of this business at Temple Knollis? If he wanted his family out he had but to ask them to leave. And what were his family up to that they were trying to scare the rightful owner off?

Leander returned to their rooms and found an empty bed. He checked the parlor in case she was sitting up waiting for him, but he already knew she'd be with the children. That was one thing to be said about marrying a woman with children. She was unlikely to flee into the night.

Which was about what he deserved.

He couldn't imagine how he could have been so discourteous. He was discovering that if Judith was possessive and touchy about her children, he was the same about his family problems.

Can the Ethiopian change his skin, or the leopard change his spots? He had wanted a home, a family. He had wanted to belong to his place in the world. But can a man who has learned to walk alone learn to lose his self in others? The thought of sharing his personal problems with anyone made him flinch. But Judith was not just anyone. . . .

He'd hoped his family would obey his instructions and leave the Temple. He and Judith could have moved into the place without contretemps, and begun to build their new life.

"Hell," he muttered, and it was an assessment of the whole situation.

He rubbed his hand over his face, knowing he was drink-sodden. Young James had a surprisingly strong head and it had taken a while to loosen him up. Unfortunately, after all Leander's efforts, there had been only a brief interval between the drink taking hold and unconsciousness. But one piece of information had been obtained. Whether or not there was diphtheria he didn't know, but Uncle Charles had apparently been recently struck down by a seizure and it wasn't sure he would live.

How that fit into the pattern, he didn't know.

He stripped off his clothes, and since he had no modest wife to consider, climbed into bed naked. All in all, this wouldn't have been a good night to consummate the marriage, but he regretted having hurt Judith, and wished he could tell her that.

He would make it up to her tomorrow, and then take her to bed. Lord, if he didn't get round to bedding her soon, she'd begin to doubt his ability.

* * *

His intentions were good, but by the time he awoke the next day, Judith and the children had been up for hours, and had already been for a walk. He had a headache.

He settled to a late breakfast, aware of his wife's chilly formality, and the pain behind it, trying to ignore the throbbing behind his temples.

Temples. Lord save him from temples of all kinds.

He needed to put everything right with Judith, but they couldn't possibly discuss their problems in front of the children. There were clearly reasons why God designed children to come after the honeymoon.

"Did your mother tell you we have a change of plan?" he asked Bastian and Rosie. "We are to go to London for a little while, instead of to the Temple."

She clearly hadn't told them.

Rosie pouted. "But I wanted to see the Temple ever so much."

"Don't be silly, Rosie," said Bastian. "We'll be living at the Temple sooner or later. In London there's all sorts of things. Parades, theaters, Astley's."

Rosie brightened. "Will we see the king and queen?"

Judith answered calmly. "Not the king, dear. He's not well. But you might see the queen, and the princes and princesses." She glanced at Leander. "When will we leave, my lord?"

He noted her use of his title and his head throbbed even more. He abandoned breakfast. "As soon as you are ready. It's a full moon. By pushing hard, we can reach London today. I'll make the arrangements."

Chapter Eleven

It was late and long dark by the time they arrived at Montague Square in London, and Judith was travel-weary. Both Rosie and Bastian were asleep. She and Leander had scarcely exchanged a word all day, which was probably as well, as his mood had not been of the best. She knew he probably had a drinker's head, but she wasn't inclined to be sympathetic.

Their stops had been brief and neither of them had made any attempt to be alone together. They could hardly hiss their grievances over the children's heads, even when the children were asleep. Anyway, she didn't know what she wanted to say. She was sick with despair at the situation in which she found herself, and not at all sure what to do for the best. She was very tempted to take the two thousand pounds per annum and leave him to his family and his *personal affairs*.

The groom opened the carriage door, and Leander picked up Bastian, but the boy awoke and said he wanted to walk. So Leander picked up Rosie, who slept peacefully on.

The groom rapped at the door, for the knocker

was off, and after a pause they were confronted by a startled footman in shirt and breeches.

"My lord! we didn't expect . . ."

Leander strode into the house. "I didn't expect to be here myself, George. Have the bags brought in."

He led the way through an elegant narrow hall to a chilly reception room, where he gently deposited Rosie on a sofa. Moonlight was the only illumination, but the room, and the house, looked expensively furnished.

Leander walked into the hall and shouted, "Ho, the house! The master's home, so stir yourselves!"

A somewhat unorthodox way of announcing oneself but it worked. Within minutes a portly butler and two maids appeared, all very flustered.

"My lord. . ." stammered the butler.

"Yes, I know. You didn't expect me. It's all right. But I have my wife with me and two children, and we're all bone tired. We need candles, tea, and food of some kind. Soup, if it's available. Air the necessary beds, the children's first. Put them on the main floor near the master suite in case they wake in the night. I don't suppose anywhere has a fire except the kitchen?"

"No, my lord."

"Never mind. We'll be in bed soon, but find a couple of blankets for the children while they wait."

Soon all was bustling.

Bastian had slumped back to sleep at an awkward angle, but Judith didn't move him for fear of waking him. The footman brought a branch of candles and lit them. A maid hurried in with two blankets and tucked them gently around the children, then left with a curtsy and a curious look.

Leander disappeared, to reappear with two glasses and a decanter. "Brandy," he said and offered some to Judith.

Judith shook her head. She wasn't precisely cold

in her sumptuous Russian mantle and muff, but she felt chilled. It was mostly exhaustion, for she hadn't slept well last night, and it had been a terribly long day. But it was also the rift between them.

Here they were in his house, where the fact that they were married had rocklike reality, and yet their relationship was more brittle than it had ever been.

To avoid sitting facing him she walked about the room. It was expensively furnished, yes, but in the style of a generation ago, and had all the warmth of a neglected furniture showroom. She wondered if the house was hired, but even such a simple question was beyond her.

Over the mantel was a splendid portrait of a young woman with anxious amber eyes. The clothes, the style, the pose all spoke of arrogant wealth, but the eyes pleaded.

"My mother," Leander said quietly from behind her. "Henrietta Delahaye, only inheritor of two large fortunes. This house was part of her dowry."

Henrietta could only have been about sixteen when this portrait had been done. Judith wondered what kind of woman she had become, other than a clinging mother. She thought she saw a physical resemblance to Leander in the finely curved lips, amber eyes, and soft brown hair, but his character must have come from his father.

As if reading her thoughts, Leander said, "She learned to shield her vulnerability better, but she never lost it. She was too easily hurt."

By then the food was being laid on the table. Judith turned, realizing that she had not contributed to that "conversation" at all, and yet it had thawed the ice a little—as he doubtless intended.

But she wouldn't be *handled* out of her distrust.

As the butler, Addison, finished laying out the food, a maid came in to say the children's beds were made.

Leander told the footman to carry up Bastian and took Rosie himself. Judith brought up the rear.

The rooms were chilly, but what else could be expected, and new fires at this point would do no good. The maids were passing two warming pans through Rosie's bed, and when Judith ran a hand between the sheets she found no damp. With the help of the maid she just took off the girl's outer clothes, her boots and dress, and tucked her up.

When she went into the next room she found Leander had already done the same for Bastian.

"We can leave the doors open between their rooms," he said softly, "and into yours as well, so if they awake in the night they won't be too frightened."

She was to have a room of her own? Judith went through the next door and found the maids making up the big bed there. The hangings were of blue Chinese silk, the wood heavy and dark. Again there was the excellent, old-fashioned quality, but the deadness of an unused place.

Leander opened another door. "Your dressing room. My bedchamber is beyond. Come downstairs and we'll have some supper. It will help you rest."

As they went downstairs Judith said, "I don't think I will need help to rest." Her voice sounded strange, and she realized it was the first time she'd spoken since she entered the house.

It was only the lightest of touches on her elbow to steer her back into the room, and yet her very awareness of it illustrated the gulf between them.

"Still," he said, "I think you should eat."

There was a hearty vegetable soup, doubtless the servants' fare, some wedges of cold ham pie, and toasted cheese. And tea. Judith drank three cups but only picked at the food. She knew this would be a disastrous time to talk of their problems, and yet it seemed wrong to sit here in silence ignoring them.

But they weren't ignoring them. The silence spoke eloquently of that.

She stood. "I must go to bed or you'll end up carrying me up, too."

His look responded to her words, but he only said, "Good night, then. Sleep well."

A maid was waiting to help her out of her gown and brush out her hair. Within moments, as it seemed, Judith was in bed, too tired to even worry about the future. Despite a remarkably lumpy, sagging mattress, she fell fast asleep.

Judith was woken the next day by a maid making up the fire. She had accepted this small luxury at the inn without thinking, but now she realized it was part of her new life. If this was to be her new life.

Rested, however, her more despondent musings of the day before seemed unreasonable. These last few days had been strained and hectic; it was hardly surprising if everything had not gone smoothly. Surely the Leander she had come to know in Mayfield could not be the monster of her worst imaginings.

When the maid had finished her work, she curtsied and made to leave.

Judith said, "Is it possible to have some tea?"

The woman looked startled, but said, "Yes, milady."

With daylight and leisure, Judith studied her bedroom. It was just as she had thought the night before, and not particularly appealing. The furniture was heavy and dark, the hangings faded by time. As neither Leander nor his father had been in England much, she supposed no one had brought this room up to date since the last occupant. Had that been his mother? His grandmother, even? The mattress certainly felt as if it could date back fifty years or so.

She was surprised to experience a touch of nostalgia for her cramped but cozy cottage. Then she took herself to task. She was a countess now, and this was a fashionable house. Doubtless cottage homeliness would be very out of place.

As if to prove it, the maid from the night before came in, a different creature entirely from the flustered girl faced with unexpected duties. Back ramrod stiff, the starch in her apron rustling, she set a silver tray by the bed and curtsied. "Good morning, milady. I am Emery, and I'll be honored to act as your maid for as long as you wish. I have brought your tea. Is there anything else you require?"

This was said with a challenging edge. Clearly, Judith had disturbed some aspect of servant etiquette by asking the undermaid for tea. On the other hand, the undermaid had been just the sort of servant she had been accustomed to at Mayfield House. This high-in-the-instep young woman was very daunting.

"I will require my clothes, of course," said Judith as firmly as she could. "I have no idea where my trunks were put . . ."

"All your clothing has been unpacked and cared for, milady," said Emery crisply.

Judith flashed a look at the window, but the dimness of the light confirmed her belief that it was still early in the day. This was a tightly run household, alarmingly so. Still, she was determined not to be browbeaten in her own home.

"How efficient," she congratulated with a mild smile. "Then I will take a bath in half an hour, and will wear my rose wool gown. Has someone been given the task of seeing to the children?"

The maid already seemed to be thawing, so Judith assumed her manner had met with approval. "Yes, milady. Betty is to look after Miss Rosetta, and George is to look after Master Bastian. The children are not yet awake, however."

Judith nodded and wondered what else she should

say. Ah, yes. "And Lord Charrington? Has he risen yet?"

"Not as far as I know, milady."

Further decisions were clearly called for. "I will breakfast downstairs when I am ready, Emery. The children may join me when they rise. After breakfast I wish to have a tour of the house, and discuss management with the senior staff." She nodded. "That will be all, thank you."

When the maid had left Judith sighed and poured tea from a silver pot into a transparently thin china cup. She would be much happier to be friends with the servants here, rather than a distant mistress, but she knew that would be disastrous. The style of management suitable for Mayfield House would not do for here, and particularly not for Temple Knollis.

She shivered at the thought of the staff of the Temple. They probably thought themselves lords of creation. What would happen if all these proud servants learned of her poverty before her marriage? As Leander had been in Mayfield without his own servants, there was always the chance that word would not spread, but she doubted it. When the Ardens returned to town, their staff would carry the word.

Judith cradled her warm cup for comfort. In all her doubts about the marriage she had never considered this, the daily effort to establish her right to her place.

She pulled herself together. It was merely a challenge, and a lesser one than others she had faced in her life. She had promised Leander that she would be a good wife, and a good countess. Even if all else was falling apart, she could at least fulfill that part of their contract.

What should a good wife and countess do?

Manage his households for prosperity and comfort.

This house, no matter how well run, would not be ready for children, nor could Bastian and Rosie be allowed the freedom they had enjoyed in Mayfield.

If they were only to be in London for a few days it might not be worth hiring a governess or tutor, and yet someone would have to look after them.

If this had been a bachelor household, there might be any number of ways in which she could improve it. . . .

On the other hand, Leander could well be happy with it as it was and resent interference. . . .

Judith rubbed anxiously at her temples. Just a few days ago she would have discussed these matters with him, but not now. She heard again the way he had said, Do not concern yourself with my personal affairs. Were his houses his personal affair?

She remembered the Leander who had teased her, the fellow explorer of the marketplace. How had they come to this disastrous state?

Judith sat up in bed and shook her head. Really, this was a great deal of nonsense. She balanced all their days—during which he had appeared honest and kind—against that one hurtful moment, and pushed down the hurt. She was old and wise enough to know that sometimes people said things in a way they did not mean, particularly when they were laboring under strong feelings

So, under what strong feelings did her husband labor?

It was something to do with his home at Temple Knollis, and his representative there, his Uncle Charles. He thought his family were trying to keep him away, even by fabricating stories of disease. He had described them as grasping.

But why would he not discuss it all with her?

That, she decided, was what lay between them, what really hurt. That he appeared not to trust her.

Emery came in to say Judith's bath was ready. Judith went into her dressing room to find it warmed by a fire. The tub was steaming and thick towels hung on a rack to warm. Sheer heaven.

As she washed she considered her situation. Sebastian had never discussed his personal affairs, including his family, with her and she had not objected. Why was she upset now? Because Leander had seemed different.

Because Leander was important to her in a way that Sebastian had never been. Her hand stilled and her heart missed a beat.

She mustn't feel that way. It was the cardinal principle of this marriage, that it be untarnished by love. She knew how much he would hate to be put in the unfair position of having to be the object of her devotion, but unable to return it. He had lived with his mother's pain. He did not want to relive it in his own marriage.

She had promised. She had promised.

And it was more than a matter of keeping a promise. She knew Leander needed her. In many ways, he was alone in the world, and a stranger in his own country. He distrusted his natural family. No one should be so alone.

She would not let him be so alone. She would make a home and family for him, and be his link to his heritage.

The water was cooling. As Judith hurried to use the washcloth to remove days of traveling, her lofty resolves echoed hollow in her mind. *Do not concern yourself with my personal affairs.*

Perhaps all he wanted was a housekeeper and a body in his bed.

At the thought of bed, Judith cast an anxious glance at the door to his bedchamber and hastily stepped out of the tub and into the huge towel held by the maid. She didn't know when he would decide to complete their marital duties, but she hoped it would not be now, not before they had regained their balance.

She was soon securely dressed. Emery, too, had no

trouble in arranging her hair into a becoming style and when Judith assessed herself in the mirror, she decided her husband would at least have no complaint as to her appearance.

However, Judith felt very much the interloper when she ventured down the stairs of her new home. The staircase was wide and uncarpeted, with heavy, bulbous dark oak balusters. It was overhung by darkened landscapes against parchment walls. There was no speck of dust anywhere, but no speck of warmth either. Judith wanted to order in the painters, and carpet the stairs a rich red. She wanted lighter pictures and some bright ornaments.

The stately butler was in the chilly tiled hall to welcome her again to the house, and direct her to the breakfast parlor. Judith looked around and wondered again if it was just because she was unused to grandeur that she found this house so cold and unwelcoming.

Perhaps it was just her nerves.

In the breakfast room she found Leander reading the paper.

He put it aside and stood with a careful smile. "Good morning, my dear." It was a *handling* smile, and there was none of the friendly ease they had once enjoyed.

"Good morning," Judith replied as she sat.

She allowed Addison to serve her breakfast. Leander did not return to the protection of his paper.

"Did you sleep well?" he asked.

It hardly seemed the moment to complain of the mattress. "Tolerably," she replied. She sought something else to keep back silence. "This is an interesting house," she said at last. It sounded inane.

"It's quite old by Mayfair standards. This block was built by my great-grandfather in the early seventeen hundreds. It's not in the latest style, I'm afraid."

Judith glanced at him, wondering if that comment implied dissatisfaction, or was just a statement of fact.

"It must be interesting to have a house with such a long family history."

Then she winced. What a *stupid* thing to say to a member of the aristocracy, particularly in front of a servant.

He poured himself more coffee. "My mother's family is not particularly interesting. A few generations ago they were small craftsmen, then they made money in ironmongery, coal, and, I'm afraid, slaves."

Judith didn't know what to say to this.

"I've always thought this house reflected more money than taste, though if you like it, I'm pleased." His cup stopped partway to his lips, and it was his turn to wince. "That sounded amazingly rude."

A bubble of laughter burst from Judith. "And you the perfect diplomat."

He smiled back at her, and the temperature raised a good many degrees. His tone was almost a caress as he said, "You destroy all artifice, my dear."

Judith looked hastily down at her eggs, not at all sure what to make of that.

"The house has some advantages," he remarked. "It is large, and has adequate stabling, and a spacious garden. It also," he added, "has the best stair rail I've ever encountered for sliding down."

Judith looked up. "Don't tell Bastian!"

He laughed. "If he doesn't perceive it immediately, he's not the boy I take him for."

Judith then caught the sounds he had heard—a smothered giggle and a hushing sound. Then a muted, *wheeee*. She rested her head on her hand.

In a moment, Bastian and Rosie presented themselves, looking like perfect angels. "Good morning, Mama. Good morning, Papa Leander."

Judith accepted kisses from both of them, and directed them to their chairs. Addison came forward to serve them.

To Judith's amazement, this august personage

thawed in the presence of children and seemed inclined to offer them the entire contents of the pantry. Judith intervened. "Just eggs, toast, and tea, I think, Addison."

The butler accepted that, but then asked the children if they had any preferences for future meals. Judith shared a glance with Leander, and saw he, too, was amused by this unexpected side to the butler. She saw no harm in allowing Bastian and Rosie to list all their treats, however, for their recent diet had been such plain fare that their treats were mostly inexceptionable—oranges, Scotch eggs, shrimps, steak pie, and, of course, ices.

When all these matters were settled, Leander dismissed Addison, then said, "I hope you are all recovered from the journey."

"I feel a great deal better for a good rest and a bath," Judith said.

She was rewarded by a smile. "I confess, you were right all along. A long journey straight after our wedding, with two excited children along, was not the wisest enterprise."

Rosie's face puckered and she said, "I'm sorry for being sick."

They had to take time to reassure her.

Bastian said, "But will we not be going to Temple Knollis soon, sir?"

He, too, needed to be reassured. "We certainly will, Bastian, but I have to check first that there is no sickness. It would be no fun to get there only to be sick."

He amiably answered a stream of questions about the Temple, and about London, but then rose from the table. He turned to Judith. "I am going to arrange for someone to check on the state of affairs at the Temple. We should know what's toward within the week."

She wanted an opportunity to talk to him, but this

clearly was not a good time or place. He was on his way to the door. There was one subject that must be raised, however.

"Leander," she said, "we have to consider what arrangements to make for the children, what sort of attendants to provide for them. Also," she added tentatively, "it may be necessary to make changes in the house for our comfort." There, that should be subtle enough.

He shrugged in a manner expressive only of mild surprise. "You must do as you wish. This is your home."

Men. That was little help at all. "Will we entertain?" she asked.

"I hadn't considered the matter. Do you wish to?"

He seemed genuinely unconcerned and so Judith gratefully said no. She had enough novelties and tangles to handle without trying to take her place in society as the Countess of Charrington.

"In that case," he said, "we'll leave the knocker off the door, and neglect to give any notice of our arrival. I suspect we will be here only for a couple weeks at the most." He came back to the table and placed a conventional kiss on her cheek. "Do just as you like, dear. The place has been neglected for years. Even the staff was hired only months ago. There was only a caretaker before that."

With that he was gone and Judith was left exasperated. He said, do just as you like, but if she did so he would doubtless object to some change she had made. Moreover, it was not clear whether by change he meant moving a sofa, or having a wall knocked out. Not that she was contemplating anything that drastic, but still . . .

"May we go to the Tower, Mama?"

Judith turned her attention to Bastian's question. She knew her frustration was less about household matters than about her problems with her husband, but he seemed to have put his coldness aside, and there would surely be time at a later date to talk to him.

When the children had finished their breakfast, she let them come along on the tour of the house. Mrs. Addison was the housekeeper, and just as portly as her husband but less awe-inspiring. She bustled them cheerfully over four floors and the basement.

It was all the same—solid, clean, decorated in expensive, old-fashioned style, but lacking any personality at all. Many rooms looked as if they had hardly been used.

In Judith's opinion, it was also distinctly ugly.

There was a nursery area, but it had clearly not been used for a generation. Judith decided it would be pointless to try to refurbish it for Bastian and Rosie, especially for what promised to be a short stay. There were some boxes of books and toys there, however, and a rocking horse. After making sure that the latter was sound, she left the children to play.

The basement was in many ways the most comfortable part of the house, being the most thoroughly lived in. Judith admired the new closed stove.

"Just about the first thing the earl bought," said Mrs. Addison approvingly. "You wouldn't believe this kitchen, my lady, so old fashioned as it was. He hired Addison and me, and told us to do the rest, but I told him straight out, there'd be no chance at all of getting a cook worth her salt with such a kitchen. He asked what was needed and ordered it, just like that."

"And what of the rest of the house?" Judith asked. "It would appear that no changes have been made there."

"The earl hasn't asked for any, my lady. Being a single man, he's not been entertaining more than a friend now and then." She glanced at Judith and seemed to make a decision. She progressed to gossip. "There was only one old man living here until about

five years ago, or so they say. A Mister Delahaye—
the earl's grandfather on his mother's side. He was
a bit of a recluse, as I understand, though the earl
visited here as a boy. When he died, the present earl
and his father were abroad and so the place was just
shut up. It was cared for well enough, but I tell you, my
lady, it was a mite of work to bring it up to scratch.''

''I'm sure it was, Mrs. Addison, but you appear to
have done a wonderful job. The house is spotless.''

''Just doing my job, my lady.'' But the woman
preened.

Judith couldn't help wondering if her manner
would be so cordial if she knew that a few weeks
ago Judith had been scrubbing her own floors. She
silently thanked Leander for insisting she care for
her telltale hands.

Judith returned to the ground floor thoughtfully.
She needed a place to make plans.

If they were to spend much time in this house, she
rather thought she would have a boudoir near her
bedroom, but for the moment the nearby rooms were
being used by the children. After considering the
limited possibilities, she appropriated a small ante-
room to the library, and requested that a fire be laid
in the hearth.

She considered her new quarters. The hand-
painted wallpaper was faded with age, but did not
offend; the curtains were a gloomy maroon brocade,
but would do for the winter months; the carpet was
a tolerable Aubusson, hardly worn at all. It was the
furniture she did not like—a squat, heavy table, four
hard wooden chairs, and a couple of low, uncomfortable upholstered Queen Anne chairs.

A mental review told her that there was nothing
more comfortable in the house, except in the library.
She rather thought that room, however, had been
the old man's haven, and was now Leander's. It would
be wiser not to raid it.

If she wanted a pleasant nest she would have to buy at least a comfortable chair.

That reminded her of her overgenerous pin money. When would it appear?

It also reminded her of the money owed to the publisher, and her allowance from Timothy Rossiter.

Now she was in London, she could easily send a note to Timothy's address to tell him to stop paying the allowance. On the other hand, she could use the money to pay some of the bill for the books. It seemed more appropriate to use money from Sebastian's family for that purpose than money from Leander.

She wondered how penny-pinched her brother-in-law was. His address, she remembered, was Clarges Street. She would ask Leander what that implied.

No, the only immediate solution was to pay the bill out of her pin money. She still begrudged such a waste of funds and yet it must be paid. Which meant she would have to remind Leander about the money. She hated that thought, even if she was entitled to it. Especially as she hadn't earned it.

She shivered. That was a horrid way to put it, but until she really was his wife she wasn't entitled to anything.

She pushed away those thoughts and raided the library as far as a pen and paper went. She was very tempted to curl up in the big chair before the fire there, but couldn't be entirely sure Leander would not object.

She lost track of time as she noted down what was needed: two comfortable chairs, in case of company; a lady's writing desk; calling cards; stationery; more books and games for the children; a guidebook to London; a means of transportation . . .

She sat chewing the pen. How exactly was she to get to Mister Browne's to pay that bill? The fact of the matter was that she had not the slightest idea how to get along in London. She had always lived in villages.

Leander would know how to get along. He doubtless would discharge the debt for her if she asked. Judith was guiltily aware that she did not want Leander to know anything about it. He could never guess what part it had played in sending her to reconcile with him, but she felt as if it would be obvious on the instant.

As if summoned by her guilty thoughts, Leander came in.

"Busy, Judith? You deserve a rest, you know."

He was so much the pleasant man she had married that she relaxed. "Making lists is hardly work," she said.

"Lists? Sounds ominous. But why here? Is this room really to your taste? I've always thought it extremely ugly." Then he put his hand over his eyes. "I've done it again, haven't I?"

Judith struggled to keep a straight face. "I think this chamber charming."

Incredulous dismay flashed over his face, before being skillfully masked. "I must be pleased, then," he said smoothly, all diplomat.

"Yes," said Judith, looking around. "The colors are so evocative of past eras, aren't they? And the furniture is so very . . . substantial."

He came over, a strange light in his eyes. He raised her chin, and Judith's heart skipped a beat.

"My Lady Charrington," he said softly. "Are you being so bold as to tease me?"

"I protest, my lord. Not a word I said was false."

He pulled her to her feet and into his arms. "You're growing saucy. Here in my grandfather's house, I remember women should know their place."

His lips were hot and skillful, but quickly gone. It was a branding.

"And what is my place, sir?" Judith asked shakily.

"Why, beneath me, of course."

She caught her breath. Had he intended that double entendre?

He raised her chin again so she had to look at him. "Beneath me in bed," he said. "In case you've forgotten, we have unfinished business."

Judith swallowed, but was determined not to be difficult. "Now?"

He was startled. "Here, perhaps? You must have led an exciting life, my dear. No, tempted though I am, I'm not risking disturbances again."

Deeply embarrassed, Judith tried to stammer a disclaimer, but he overrode her. "I need to talk to you. Let's go into the library. Much though you love this room, my sensibilities aren't up to it."

Leander walked behind Judith into the library, wondering if he should take up her invitation to bed her now. She must be thinking him the worst kind of fool to be four days into the marriage and it still unconsummated. Doubtless Sebastian had been much quicker off the mark

Chapter Twelve

There was only the one armchair in the library, and Judith went to a wooden library chair, but Leander insisted she sit in the big chair, then sat on the footstool at her feet. Judith felt a strange urge to stroke his wavy hair, as if he were Bastian. What an unpredictable man her husband was. Dangerous man one moment, boy the next. But it was going to be all right. The warmth was back.

He took her hand and kissed it. "It's been a strange few days, hasn't it?"

"A strange few weeks."

He was serious as he said, "Do you regret it?"

She met his eyes. "No. Do you?"

"Not at all." He looked down at her fingers and played with them a moment. "I must apologize for my behavior the other night. I was unforgivably rude."

This time Judith raised *his* chin. "No you weren't, for I've forgiven you."

"You are generous."

"I am supposed to hold a grudge over a few ill-chosen words?"

There was a particular query to it and he registered it. "You would be within your rights, but you are

right. It was a case of ill-chosen words. I do not want
to exclude you from my life."

"Good, for I wouldn't like it."

He looked away into the fire. "The truth is that
it's a strange story, and must reflect badly on some
part of my family. . . ." He toyed with her fingers
again. "I'm probably not doing this well. I'm not
accustomed to baring my soul."

"I don't want to intrude. . . ."

"It's no intrusion. . . ."

He leapt to his feet, and in one movement, as it
seemed, he was in the chair and she was in his lap.
"I much prefer this position," he said smugly.

"Do you?" But Judith felt very comfortable, snuggled against his chest. Then she remembered another
time and looked at him warily. He began to sway her
back, but she could see the teasing light in his eyes.
"Don't you dare!"

It was the wrong thing to say. He laughed and
tipped her back to ravish her lips most thoroughly.
A wandering hand added to the work so Judith was
humming with desire when he straightened her, and
rearranged her clothes.

She realized she was gaping when he closed her
mouth. Then he kissed her again, a delicate, tantalizing play of lips that left her breathless. "I'm enjoying
this," he said softly,

"You are?" she asked weakly.

"Having someone to play with."

Judith choked at that description. *"Play* with!"

"Oh, don't worry. I won't torment you forever."

"But . . ."

"Tonight," he said.

"Tonight?"

"Definitely." He kissed her again.

Judith began to wonder if they would wait until
tonight. When he released her lips, she said, "Leander, are you avoiding our main concern?"

"Dear heart, are you saying this is not your main concern?"

"Leander!"

Laughter in his eyes, he sighed and capitulated. "Very well." He became serious once more. "I probably was trying to avoid this. Believe me, Judith, I never knew how hard it would be for me to admit someone deep into my life. I am resolved to be open with you, but I may falter. Have patience. . . ."

Judith couldn't answer this with words, so she answered with a kiss. They were almost distracted again, but she said, "Leander."

"Very well, tyrant. Let me see if I can explain my predicament, without making my entire family, myself included, sound like lunatics."

Judith gathered together her scattered wits and tried to pay attention.

"It started, I suppose, with my grandfather—my paternal grandfather, the first earl. He conceived the desire to have the most beautiful home in England. He'd seen Azay-le-Rideau in France, and as his family home, Knollis Hall, happened to be built on a kind of promontory into the River Farnham, he decided to build something similar for himself.

"This was back in the seventeen-sixties, and he wasn't a young man. All the same, he managed to marry an heiress, and with that money to tear down his Elizabethan hall, and begin the building of Temple Knollis. Rather incidentally, I've always thought, he begot himself two sons—though I suppose an heir to carry on the work was part of his plans.

"My father was his oldest son, and was raised to his position, which was not so much Earl of Charrington as Guardian of the Temple. My view on this may be rather jaundiced, as it comes from my father, who hated the place. You see, my grandfather was obsessed with his Temple. My father, however, God knows why, grew up obsessed with travel. As long as

I knew him, he hated the countryside in any form, and to stay in one city for more than a year or two was tedium. The thought of all the cities he hadn't seen was constant torment to him.

"Grandfather, however, kept him chained to Somerset and the Temple except for his school days, and even there he was sent to Winchester, instead of Eton or Harrow, both much closer to the temptations of London. There was, of course, no question of a Grand Tour, though my father made private arrangements to learn as many languages as possible. He had a gift for it, one that I appear to have inherited. My impression of my father's youth is that it was a constant war, and he regarded himself as a prisoner with a sacred duty to escape.

"Eventually my grandmother's money began to run out, and the Temple was yet unfinished. A new heiress must be found for my father to marry, so he could carry on the great work. Research threw up Henrietta Delahaye, heiress to two large fortunes, and in the guardianship of her reclusive father. A plum ripe for the picking. The courtship was strictly by negotiating, and my father was commanded to marry her. He dragged his feet, seeing it as yet further confinement, until he realized that Henrietta's fortune would be his. He married her with alacrity, and they immediately went abroad where he found himself a diplomatic position, and almost incidentally, his area of genius."

Judith had followed this carefully, but saw nothing particularly strange in it. "I would say it served your grandfather right."

"Oh, probably, but he never saw it that way. I read some of his letters to Father, and they were violently vituperative, bordering on the insane. On one line he would beg piteously for him to come home and bring the money with him. On the next he would threaten to shoot him on sight." He glanced at her ruefully. "I really should have told you this before you married me."

"For fear of inherited madness? I see only a thwarted tyrant. There is no sign that you have inherited a tendency to megalomania."

He smiled slightly. "You haven't tested me yet, wife."

Judith felt a shiver down her spine that was, strangely, largely excitement. "Your grandfather could do nothing to your father, though, could he?"

"Nothing at all, especially as Father rarely stepped onto English soil thereafter. I, however, was eventually sent to England to school."

"What happened?"

"My father gave me dire warnings before I left, the gist of which were that if I ever went near the Temple I'd never be free again. Now I wonder if he wasn't warning me I'd be caught up in the wonder of the Temple, but at the tender age of twelve I thought my grandfather would kill me, or at least throw me into a dungeon. I wouldn't have gone near the place for a thousand guineas.

"Grandfather tried to draw me down there by every means, which terrified me even more. I was sent tempting invitations, offering sport and horses. When I was older, I was even offered women. Twice I received urgent messages that he was on his deathbed. I felt terrible then, but I kept my word."

He dislodged her onto the chair and moved restlessly in front of the fire. "He even came to see me once," he said, "and put on a most touching scene. It finally convinced me that my father hadn't been mistaken; Grandfather was mad. It was clear the old man could imagine nothing more worthwhile in life than to cherish the Temple."

Leander shook his head. "It was bizarre, and frightening for a fifteen-year-old. His white hair and yellow nails were long, his clothes were almost threadbare.

He spoke in a rambling way, and he spoke of the building as if it were his lover ... You can see," he said reluctantly, "that when my father suggested my Uncle Charles might kill me to get the place, I couldn't quite disregard it."

"*Kill* you?"

"That was on Father's deathbed. I was in the army at the time. To be honest, since I was dealing with death and danger every day, a crazy man in England didn't concern me greatly. It was after Waterloo, when I found myself still alive and the earl, that I had to consider the situation." He stopped his roaming and sat down on the stool again. "Let me tell you about Uncle Charles."

"He was the second son."

"Yes, and apparently inherited his father's love of the Temple. He willingly stayed on to help with the work. He, however, did not marry an heiress—I suppose it's not so easy for a second son who is merely his father's steward. He married a local girl, Lucy Frome. Good peasant stock. Produced babes like rabbits."

"Leander!"

He colored slightly. "I'm sorry, I'm echoing my father who was somewhat bitter that my mother produced only one."

"Why," mused Judith, "is it always the woman's fault?"

"Pax!" he cried. "You're right. But in this case, to be charitable, an infusion of yeoman blood was clearly good for the line. I have ten cousins, and eight are boys."

"Good heavens, that is quite a family. Is the problem that they are hard to provide for?"

He frowned and looked into the distance. "The problem is that I don't know what the problem is." He laughed and looked back at her. "I'll have you concluding that if anyone's mad, it's me, won't I?"

He picked up his story. "My grandfather died in eighteen-ten, and at that point the nonsense stopped as far as I was concerned. Shortly after that, I joined the army and had other things to worry about. It was only at my father's death that the matter raised its head again. Father was convinced that Uncle Charles would do anything to have the place for his own, and that the letters he had received begging him to return to the Temple were part of a dastardly plot. He was also bitter that his requests for extra funds from the estate were always ignored, and believed his brother was stealing from him. As I said, I didn't give the matter much thought at the time, but when I found, to my surprise, that I had survived the war, I had to do something. I am the earl, and it is all my responsibility.

"I decided the most sensible thing to do was to go and see the Temple for myself, and if possible assess my uncle and his family. Years of warnings had left a residue, however, and I went incognito.

"As it worked out, I saw only the housekeeper who showed me around, and a couple of young children whom I assumed to be two of my cousins. They looked perfectly normal children but for being rather subdued. I would have thought that echoing, pillared hall ideal for running games, but they tiptoed through it like a pair of nervous mice in a cathedral."

"They'd doubtless been told to behave when guests were around."

"I suppose so," said Leander with a frown, "but the thing that struck me about the Temple was its silence. It was like a museum, or a cathedral even— an unused one—though the housekeeper assured me the family was in residence. It felt like this house, but here we have a place that stood empty for years. . . ."

"So you didn't like it."

"To be honest," said Leander, "I don't know. It's undoubtedly very beautiful."

He rose and took a portfolio out of a rack, to open it on a table. "Come and look at these. I commissioned them after my visit. It is a truly awe-inspiring place."

Judith looked at the watercolors, so much larger and clearer than the small print Beth had shown her. They were of a fairy palace on a promontory, with only a causeway allowing access to an arched gateway. That gateway cut through a wall into a garden courtyard. The walls encircled that courtyard like a modern castle, with a substantial house at one end decorated with fairy-tale turrets.

It was difficult to pinpoint what made Temple Knollis so striking, but even in the pictures she could feel it. It was, she thought, a matter of perfect proportions.

Leander spoke softly. "These pictures can't capture the stone. It's a pinkish granite, and it changes with every shift of light. The river there is generally smooth and reflects the house like a mirror. The courtyard garden is full of aromatic plants alive with butterflies. It's a beautiful part of the country anyway. The air is soft and sweet, and always seems to be full of birdsong. The pastures are lush, the hedgerows have grown high and deep over centuries. It is the very picture of England."

"So why aren't you living there?" Judith asked.

He made a business of putting away the pictures. "It was tempting at first, but I decided to think about it. My father's warnings had taken root, and I felt I should resist such a powerful siren call. Also, there was the problem of Uncle Charles."

He slid the portfolio into the stand. "When I arrived in England, I contacted my uncle by letter, and received a reply. It was disconcertingly reminiscent of my grandfather's letters—begging me to go down there, threatening dire consequences if I didn't, though these seemed to more along the lines of the house crumbling like the walls of Jericho. Now I had seen the place, I had to wonder if he *might* be willing to kill for it. I'd learned in war to be cautious. It would have been absurdly easy to stage an accident, and who would question it?''

She shivered at the thought. "So, what did you do?"

He shrugged. "Nothing. I was thrown off balance by it all and there seemed no hurry. I had come home to settle, but I was new to England, and new to my responsibilities as earl. I set myself to learning about my properties, and that was quite a task. I visited them all—Cumberland, Sussex, and Rutland. I started learning about estate management. What a quagmire that turned out to be.

"All the money of the earldom still passes through the Temple, you see, and my grandfather and Uncle Charles had developed a very strange form of accounting. The Knollis man-of-business here in London seemed to have no trouble with it, but I couldn't make head nor tail of it, and couldn't be sure I could trust him either. He could well be in league with Uncle Charles. I seriously thought of going down to the Temple to demand a clear accounting, but then I received a letter from my uncle showing he was aware of my interest in the business of the estate, and asking me to do just that."

He laughed, self-consciously. "I must confess that I began to wonder if it wasn't a Machiavellian plot to get me down there by one means or another. So instead, I hired a new man here to straighten it out, and explain it to me, in particular why there wasn't as much money as there should be."

Judith put on an expression of mock alarm. "Are you trying to tell me you're under the hatches, sir?"

He grinned. "Don't worry. That's not likely, but even I could tell there were shortages, as my father had claimed. The Earldom of Charrington is very wealthy, but my income is merely handsome. As long as I was with the army, it was more than enough for my needs. When I came to London, however, it was obvious that the income wasn't as much as it should be. . . ."

"So you, too, think your Uncle Charles is stealing from you," Judith said.

He grimaced at such bluntness. "I don't like to think that of my family, but it looks more and more likely."

Judith heard in his tone how much family meant to him. He had perhaps hoped to become close to his uncle and cousins, and was hurt by their actions. Perhaps his generosity toward her family hadn't been a buying of favors, but a desire to become part. And she had objected . . .

"Does your uncle have an income?" she asked.

"Yes. He's always received a generous income as steward, plus the fact that he's lived free at the Temple. But on my grandfather's death, he received an unentailed estate called Stainings. Its income is over five thousand a year. I'd have thought it adequate. There were inheritances for his children, too."

Figures like that were enough to make Judith dizzy. What, she wondered, was the income of the earldom of Charrington if it could dispose of such an estate without concern? "What do you intend to do now?"

He picked up a book, then put it down. "I don't know. I haven't proof of illegality and I'm not sure I could prosecute my family."

Judith faced him. "And what part does our marriage play in all this?"

He met her eyes but ruefully. "All ways, and no ways. You see, one of the things I noticed at Temple Knollis was that the land there is neglected. Weeds grow in the fields, drainage is poor, cottages ramshackle. I intend to correct that, but I don't know much about such things. I needed someone to help me who belonged to the land.''

"A good steward would be more use than I.''

He sought refuge in the fire again. "I didn't just want an employee,'' he said softly. She could hear the struggle in his voice. "I was tired of being alone, Judith.''

She took his hand, too moved to speak. His fingers tightened on hers. Then he looked up, smiling derisively. "Don't melt for me yet. I had other reasons to marry. Since they appeared to be untrustworthy, I wanted my family gone. But I couldn't quite see myself descending on the Temple, whip in hand, like Christ. I thought it would be cleverly subtle to acquire a wife, and ask them to leave. I also thought that the sooner I married and set up a nursery, the less likely it was that they would inherit. When I met you, I realized a wife and family would be even better.''

"Why?'' asked Judith, still holding his lax hand.

He gave a Gallic shrug. "I'll confess it all. I thought that any marriage, even a recent one, would give them pause if they did have evil plans. You could already be with child.''

Her look must have remarked on that. His hand turned to hold hers. He smiled lazily and raised her hand to his lips. "We really will have to work on it.''

Judith was in no mood for dalliance. "Good heavens, Leander. If they're of a mind for one murder, why would they balk at two?''

His lips stilled and all humor left his face. "Believe me, Judith, I never considered that. I suppose two deaths would be bound to raise questions, but still . . . I never intended to put you in any danger, I swear. Anyway,'' he said with a reassuring smile, "I'm convinced that part of it is nonsense. I've not seen any evidence of anyone wishing me harm since the last French bullet flew, and killing someone is not a tricky business if one is set on it.''

"I hope you're right," Judith said. "There's the children, too. . . ."

"There's certainly no cause to touch a hair of their heads." He took both her hands firmly. "Don't look so anxious. I never meant to frighten you. You see why I was reluctant to tell you all this? When I put it into words, it all sounds a farrago of nonsense. When, as I expect, we hear that there's no sickness at the Temple, we'll post down there and sort it out once and for all, even if it means I have to snarl, and scowl, and be thoroughly undiplomatic."

They heard children's voices asking for their mama.

"Don't worry," he said. "I'll take care of you, and them." He dropped a kiss on her lips as the children burst in.

"Mama . . ."

"No." Leander's voice was quiet but firm. "You will both go out to the hall, count to thirty, then knock. You will enter when you are given permission."

Both children's faces fell. Bastian scowled angrily, and Rosie looked close to tears. They went, however, and closed the door.

"Leander . . ." said Judith hesitantly.

He was formidable. "We are married. We can't have them feeling free to burst in on us whenever they please, unless you wish them to see more than children should."

She colored. "They would hardly burst into our bedrooms."

"I think they are probably accustomed to making free with yours." A flash of wicked humor lit his eyes. "And what makes you think I intend to reserve our intimate moments for a bed?"

Before Judith could respond to that there was a soft knock on the door.

"Enter," said Leander.

The children crept in. Rosie was subdued. Bastian was angry. Judith wanted to hug them both, but knew that wouldn't be wise.

"Well?" said Leander with a smoothly diplomatic smile. "How do you like your new home—or one of them?"

Rosie looked silently down at her slippers.

Bastian said, "It's ugly." It was a sweeping condemnation of more than the house.

Leander flashed Judith a cry for help but she shrugged slightly. He'd caused this, and would have to handle it. Had he expected it all to be easy?

Leander sat down. "Bastian and Rosie, come here, please."

They dragged themselves over as if they had chains on their ankles.

"Bastian, Rosie, I know you feel hurt that I had to reprimand you, but you must realize we are all making changes. You have had your mother to yourself since your father died, but now I want to share her with you. I want to kiss her sometimes as married people do, and we would be happier to be alone at those times. That is why you must not burst into rooms without knocking. You must also remember that your mother and I may have adult guests, and not want to be disturbed."

Bastian looked up, still scowling. "I liked it better at the cottage. I wish we'd stayed there."

Leander carried on gamely. "Then we'll have to work at making things better for you here. What do you lack?"

It was clear the children couldn't actually think of anything. Rosie looked up shyly. "I don't mind it here, Papa Leander."

"Bastian?" Leander prompted.

The boy was clearly reluctant to let go of his grievance. "I don't think it's *fair,*" he said.

"What?"

"You said I couldn't ride until we got to Temple Knollis, but we won't be there for months!"

"Ah," said Leander, relaxing. "In fact, I am determined to be there for Christmas, but you have a point. Bastian, whenever you have a legitimate grievance, you must feel free to discuss it frankly, rather than sulking. What do you think would be fair?"

Bastian looked at Leander directly for the first time, surprised by the question. His sullenness fell away to reveal hope. "How long would it have taken for us to reach Temple Knollis, Papa?"

"Four days, perhaps."

Bastian counted in his head. "This is the fourth day!"

"Then if your mother agrees, we could consider resuming your riding tomorrow."

Two pairs of young eyes swung to Judith. "That appears fair to me," she said soberly.

The children whooped.

"Now," said Leander. "What do you really think of this house? Your mother and I are perfectly agreed that it is ugly and old fashioned, so you need not hold back your feelings."

"I like the banister," said Rosie with a giggle.

"There's a super rocking horse," said Bastian.

Leander grinned. "I remember. It has scarlet reins and stirrups."

"Not anymore. There aren't any."

"Mama," said Rosie, clearly recalling the reason they had sought her out in the first place. "Bastian wouldn't let me ride after I fell off!"

"Well, I'd get blamed if you hurt yourself, gaby!"

Judith rushed to stop them with a hug. "Hush, hush. If we can find some reins and stirrups you won't fall off, Rosie. And Bastian, if we find a companion for both of you, you won't feel so weighed down by responsibilities."

"You'll be with us," he said, scowling again.

Judith glanced at Leander but decided it was her turn to handle trouble. "As Lord Charrington says, darlings, things will be a little different now. There'll still be lots of times for us to spend together, and of course now you have Papa Leander to take care of you, too. But I have many new responsibilities. I wondered if Betty or George would suit you for a while. To look after you, and show you around."

The children looked distinctly dubious about it all, but Rosie said, "Betty's fun."

"George is all right, too," admitted Bastian. "He knows boxing, and he likes Blucher."

Leander spoke up. "Then one or the other or both can look after you when your mother and I are busy. I'll go odds they both know London a great deal better than we do. Now, it's time for nuncheon, and you are both rather dusty. Why don't you go and wash. Do you know how to ring for the servants?"

They nodded.

"Off you go, then."

When they had gone, he turned to Judith with a rueful look. "I confess, I never thought they would resent me so."

"A blow to your ego?" she asked, but then said, "I'm sorry. That's hardly fair. They are bound to have problems with some of the changes, and I'm afraid they'll blame most of them on you."

"I suppose I can cope. It should toughen me up for the Battle of the Temple. I don't like it when they look at me with that reserve, though, as if they expect me to turn into a two-headed monster at any moment. But I can't always indulge them. It wouldn't be wise."

She went and linked her arm with his. "Of course it wouldn't. They're in the middle of a great many changes, and still working out for themselves what it will all mean. So are we. I'm finding it hard to be a countess, and I'm sure it must be very hard to become a father overnight. I think you're doing splendidly."

He grinned like a schoolboy. "Thank you. I think you're doing well at the countess trade, too."

"Though I've hardly started." Judith meant that she'd not attempted to take her place in Society but she saw him read another meaning. He gave her a sleepy, sultry look that had her heading straight for the dining room. She hadn't forgotten that comment about not restricting intimate moments to bed.

After the meal, Leander went over Judith's list, and made arrangements for the hire of a carriage and horses from a nearby livery, and riding horses for the children. He also gave her a roll of bills as part of her pin money, and authority to bid the merchants send their accounts to his man-of-business for settlement.

Judith looked at the bank notes, more than her quarterly income before this marriage. "You are very generous."

He dismissed it with a gesture. *"De nada."*

When he discovered she intended to visit a furniture warehouse, he put aside his plans and came with her. While Bastian and Rosie were sent off with both escorts to explore the nearby streets and parks, Judith and Leander rolled off in the carriage to the establishment of Waring and Gillow.

Judith discovered she had the schoolboy back on her hands. Leander, it turned out, had not done a great deal of domestic shopping in his life. As long as he had lived with his parents, they had taken care of household matters, and the family had always lived in temporary, hired accommodations. As a single diplomat or officer, he had had little need of domesticity.

He was charmed by the variety of designs and fabrics, and the selection available. He tried any number of chairs.

"What a marvelous idea," he said when he'd found one he liked. "I always thought the furniture one ended up with was at the whim of the gods." He winked at her. "Perhaps we should try out the beds. I definitely need a new one. Mine must have come off the ark."

Judith cast an alarmed glance at the clerk, and frowned at her mischievous husband. "Waring and Gillow do not provide mattresses, only frames, and the frames in your house are in perfect condition."

"A bit somber, though, aren't they?" He leapt up and headed toward the beds. Judith gave up discretion and grabbed his jacket. He stopped and looked down. "No?"

"Not today. Leander, we're only likely to be in London for a few weeks. When we return, our tastes may be quite different. I just want a couple of chairs and a desk, though I don't suppose I'll even have them to use during this stay."

She saw the twinkle in his eyes and wondered just how much of the boyishness was acting, how much was real.

He turned to the clerk. "We want three chairs. That one and those two." He indicated the one he'd liked and the style Judith had chosen.

"Yes, my lord. Perhaps you would care to select a fabric. . . ."

"No. We want *those* chairs."

The clerk blanched. "But they are our display models, my lord."

"So?"

The man looked even more harassed. "But any number of people have sat in them."

Leander burst out laughing. "I should think the whole world's sat in the ones we're using now. They certainly feel like it. If you can't authorize it, find someone who can."

"No . . . no. If you're certain, my lord. Of course . . ."

"Good. Then on to desks. And don't show us anything you're not willing to deliver today."

Judith was half inclined to hide under a table at this

display of aristocratic arrogance, and half inclined to cheer. It was clear Leander thought absolutely nothing of it, and so she tried to look as if she scarcely noticed the incident either.

Unfortunately the desks were situated close to the library furnishings, where ingenuity seemed to run wild. While she was choosing between a number of delightful escritoires, he was exploring. When her choice was made, he insisted on demonstrating chairs that turned into steps, and steps that turned into desks.

"I can't understand why this principle hasn't been extended," he said merrily. "We would only need one piece of furniture. We would merely have to operate a lever and the bed could become the breakfast table, then the desk, then the sofa. . . ."

"There'd be crumbs everywhere," said Judith dampeningly. "And what would be the point? We have room enough for furniture."

"But then everyone could live in one room. Doubtless the population of England could all live in London."

Judith shook her head. "And that would be an improvement? Anyway, my lord, a great many people do live in one room, whole families in one room, but I doubt they can afford your fancy furniture."

He chose to look subdued. "Yes, ma'am."

Judith steered him out of the establishment and to the carriage. He gave the coachman an address.

"Where are we going?" Judith wasn't much concerned. She could not remember ever feeling so free, and having such fun. The children were well cared for, she had no money worries, she was with a madcap who would doubtless make her laugh all afternoon.

"Mattresses," he said. "The clerk supplied an address."

"Are we to have mattresses, too, that the world has used before?"

"No," he said, "at that I draw the line. But we'll order them so that when we return here the beds will be free of lumps."

"There was really no need to bully that poor man. I could have survived without new chairs for a few days."

"But why should you, when there are perfectly good chairs there? If you don't like the coverings, we'll order others, then they can have their samples back." He grinned at her. "Are you feeling sympathy with the *sansculottes?* Do you want to hang me from the nearest lamppost?"

"Of course not. I suppose I'm a little envious really."

"Then at the mattress maker, you play the tyrant."

"I wouldn't know how, and we don't expect to get mattresses today."

"See what you can do."

It was a challenge. Judith found she responded to challenges. At the mattress makers they were shown miniature samples stuffed with hair, felt, feather, and down. She had always wanted a down mattress. The expense was terrible, but she was a countess now. . . . "Oh, the down, I think," she said with a casual air. She turned to Leander. "Unless you prefer a firm mattress, my lord?"

He was smiling at her in a way that made her think of the coming night. "We should probably have one of each, and then sleep how the fancy takes us. . . ."

She hastily looked away. "Well, I intend to have the down."

"Then I will have the best hair. I certainly don't mind a firm bed."

Judith turned to the clerk and made the orders. "We would like them immediately," she said, trying for a haughty manner.

"Immediately!" the man said, almost dropping his pencil.

Judith found haughty did not come naturally, and she turned to appeal. "Is that impossible?" she asked sweetly. "You see, my husband and I have just moved into this house with the most terrible beds. I have not had a wink of sleep. . . ."

The young man blushed and fidgeted. "Well, milady, I'm not sure . . . Just hold on a minute."

He disappeared into the workroom. Leander bent over to whisper in her ear, "I must remember to be on my guard if you ever decide to wheedle me, my dear."

Before Judith could reply, the clerk came back, bashfully pleased with himself. "We . . . er . . . have a couple of mattresses just completed, my lady, and the customers not expecting them yet. They'll be delivered today."

Judith was hard-pressed not to laugh, but she managed to give the young man a beaming smile along with her gushing thanks.

When they were in the carriage, Leander touched her nose, "Beginning to appreciate your charms?"

Judith did not know what to think. "I suspect it is the title rather than any attribute of mine."

"Do you think so?" He took her hand and kissed her fingertips. "So, my Lady Charrington, which do you prefer tonight? Hard or soft?"

She could not think of anything to say, but he appeared to be very content to have rendered her speechless. He progressed from thoroughly kissing her fingers to kissing her lips. Judith found any tendency to object to this outrageous behavior was swamped by the sweet pleasure of his lips.

He gently disengaged. "If we are to wait until tonight, as a proper married couple should, I must now recollect that I have a number of matters to attend to hereabouts. Would you mind returning home alone?"

Judith felt decidedly reluctant to see him go, but

she knew he was right. "A coachman and footman is hardly alone. Of course not."

He pulled the cord, and the coach stopped to let him off.

Judith watched him go, still tingling from his kisses, and more nervy than ever about the night. She knew, from their interrupted wedding night something of what to expect, but whenever she thought of marital duties her experiences with Sebastian always came to mind. She could neither separate the two entirely, nor mesh them to make sense. . . .

It was only after a few minutes that she realized that this was an opportunity to get the matter of the wretched bill over and done with. She had the roll of bills he had given her, and there was over two hundred pounds. He'd told her to indulge herself. To be rid of this burden would be the greatest indulgence possible. She pulled the cord.

When the coachman opened the trap, she directed him to the establishment of Mr. Algernon Browne, Printer.

Chapter Thirteen

She half expected somewhere shady, but when the coach drew up, it was outside a handsome stone building, with a shiny brass plaque announcing the proprietor. The footman let down the steps and handed her out, then accompanied her into the building.

It was doubtless the coach and footman who conjured up such gratifyingly warm attention. Soon she was closeted with Mr. Browne, the footman awaiting her outside the office.

"Some wine, my lady," the man gushed. "I had not heard of your happy nuptials. Please accept my warmest felicitations."

Judith took a glass of wine. Mr. Browne was in no way shady either. He was a handsome, rotund gentleman in his forties, giving every evidence of prosperity. And why shouldn't he, she thought waspishly, with idiots willing to pay a hundred and three guineas to have twenty volumes of their poetry bound in cordovan leather, heavily gilded?

She smiled sweetly, however, as he praised her late husband's art and sensitivity, and reiterated how much Mr. Rossiter was missed by his devoted readers.

"I have wondered, dear lady," the man said at

last, not quite able to hide the hungry gleam in his eyes, "whether Mister Rossiter left any unpublished works . . . ? I did ask Mister Timothy Rossiter, but he denied the possibility. Even if the poems were in an unpolished state, we would be willing to publish them. . . ."

"No," Judith lied firmly. "I'm afraid not." For all his apparent respectability, the man had the instincts of a shark. He scented money now she had married well, and hoped to gain a commission for another extravagant edition. "I have merely come to pay what was owed for the last edition." She pulled out the money, which she had already counted in the coach.

He took it, flicked through it with apparent casualness, and wrote a receipt. "How sad," he said, with a good assumption of sincerity. "I was sure that he had been working on something, and even his brother—"

"I cannot imagine how his brother should be expected to know," said Judith. "My husband had little contact with his family."

"But Mrs. Rossiter . . . I mean, Lady Charrington . . . Mister Timothy Rossiter was executor of your husband's will, and he acted as your husband's agent in the matter of his poetry. It was always he who delivered the manuscripts, and handled any moneys."

"Oh." Judith thought it strange that she had not known this, but Sebastian had told her little of his affairs. As he always received the post, and only gave her any items addressed to her after opening them, he could have maintained extensive contact with his family and her none the wiser.

"Well, I can assure you, Mister Browne, that there are no further poems available," Judith said. "If Sebastian was dissatisfied, he burned his work." This was untrue but she had no intention of using Leander's money to have Sebastian's remaining works published.

Mr. Browne sighed lugubriously. "Tragic. Tragic."

Hypocrite, thought Judith. She put down her glass and rose. "No," she said, "I'm afraid our professional association is at an end, Mister Browne." She couldn't quite keep the satisfaction out of her voice. "Good day."

When she emerged, she took a deep breath. Something about that interview had been disquieting, and she feared Mr. Browne must be a rogue after all, but at least she was done with it. Though she felt badly that she had not told Leander all about the shipment of books, it was tidied up now, and she could put it out of her mind.

Now the only deception in her marriage was the little matter of her overly warm feelings for her husband, but presumably she could keep them under control.

The children ate with them at dinner, but Leander warned them that there would be many occasions when this would not be the case. Judith thought she saw some discontent on Bastian's face at this, but he said nothing. She suspected he was afraid tomorrow's riding would be called off if he misbehaved.

She sighed a little. There would be constant small irritations, caused as much by the remarkable change in rank as by the marriage, and there was nothing to be done but struggle through them all.

She had to confess that she couldn't concentrate on the children's feelings when a good part of her mind was upon the coming night. How would it be managed? She hoped she would be able to retire as usual, and have Emery prepare her for bed, then be waiting properly in the dark when Leander came to her.

How soon should she retire? Earlier than usual? Or would that appear shamelessly eager? If she delayed, would she appear reluctant?

Leander seemed to be in no hurry to be rid of the children. After the meal, he shepherded them into the library. Once there, however, he didn't seem quite sure what to do with his family, and yet he clearly wished them to spend some time together.

Judith felt lovingly tender. "Perhaps we should play a game of cards," she suggested.

"Whist?" he asked with surprise.

"I'm afraid not. . . ."

"Matrimony!" yelled Rosie excitedly.

Leander's brows shot up, and Judith knew she was blushing. "It is a perfectly unexceptionable game," she assured him. "Bastian, do we have some cards?"

Before he could reply, Leander went to the desk. "We have some here somewhere." He returned with a pack.

"And I will need some sheets of paper," said Judith, already doubting the wisdom of this suggestion. The simple gambling game was a favorite with the children but always generated excitement and noise, and this was such a dignified house. "And something to serve as counters. We generally use beans."

"I can do better than that," he said and produced a black enameled box. He unlocked it to spill beautiful painted ivory counters onto the table. Judith almost felt she should object, but there was no damage the children could do to them, and they were already enthralled.

"Is this Chinese writing?" Bastian asked.

"Yes."

"Can you tell me what it says?"

"No, though I understand they are mostly numbers."

"Then would these two lines be two?"

"I think so."

Judith smiled and left them to their exploration as she made up the five sheets: Matrimony, Intrigue, Confederacy, Pair, and Best. When the children had been persuaded to divide the counters evenly, she laid the papers on the table and told Leander, "We all put some of our counters on each."

"Ah, I've played games of this type, but generally for high stakes."

"Really?" she said. "How foolish to risk money on something entirely dependent on chance."

"That's the basis of most gambling, my dear. And do you mean you are not backing these counters with gold?"

"Assuredly not."

He turned to the children. "What about you, young 'uns. Do you have any money to lose, or am I wasting my time?"

They saw he was teasing, but still looked worried. "I have three ha'pence," offered Bastian.

Leander shook his head. "I see that as your father I'll have to frank you. I'll back you to a penny a counter."

Rosie stared at her pile of discs. "I've over two shillings!" she declared.

"Aye," said Leander with a menacing smile. "But only until I win it from you, my little pigeon."

Rosie's face assumed the determination worthy of a hardened gamester.

"So," said Leander. "Explain the rules to me."

Both children complied, in an excited babble, so it was a wonder he understood anything. But in the end he said, "Marriage is any king and queen. Correct? Intrigue is any queen and jack." He glanced at Judith with a wicked glint in his eyes. "I thought you said it was perfectly unexceptionable? Smacks of wickedness to me."

Judith wondered how she could not have realized this before. And it was played in the vicarage!

"Confederacy is any king and jack," he continued, then paused meaningfully. "I really must decline to comment on that."

Judith wanted to sink through the floor.

"Any pair wins pair, and the ace of diamonds wins Best. Have I that right?"

When the children noisily assented, he began to deal with a slick action which invested the nursery game with hellish overtones. Perhaps that was why they all became enthralled in the winning and losing. Or perhaps it was his promise to back the counters with money. Pennies were still riches to the children, even though they would soon be receiving their generous allowance.

That did not explain why Judith herself found she was watching the piles of counters on the different sheets with all the avidity of a gamester. She called herself to order.

Once she regained her wits, she saw that Leander was cheating.

When he shuffled the deck, he turned the pack so he could see the cards. When he dealt them, he sometimes slid one from the bottom. The net result was that the children neither won nor lost excessively.

She really should object, but in fact her heart swelled at this kindness.

The children were laughing and shouting with excitement, and she wondered whether to admonish them, but Leander didn't seem to mind.

In fact, he seemed as excited by each small win, as disappointed by each loss, as the children. A good part of it was acting, but he *was* having fun. He still had the capacity to enjoy simple things even though they had rarely been part of his life.

Judith resolved to bring these simple things into his life, and lay them before him as gifts of love.

Love . . . She really mustn't . . . But she admitted it was already far too late.

She went through the motions of the game distractedly, oversensitized to his every movement. The children were delighted with her confusion, and proud to show off their expertise by prompting her when she had a winning combination.

When Leander pushed some winnings to her and brushed against her hand, it was like fire. She pulled her hand away.

This was a disastrous situation, especially when he had shown an eerie ability to read her feelings. She struggled desperately not to betray herself by any gesture. How was she to behave in bed so as to be a warm and willing wife, but not allow a trace of this deep and frightening longing to show?

If she could have thought of an excuse to avoid the planned consummation, she would have used it, but nothing came to mind that would not be obviously specious. And it wasn't just one night she had to face, but the rest of her life.

At last Leander announced the game over, and counted the winnings. He gave the children a penny for each counter. Bastian received one and fourpence, Rosie a whole two shillings.

"You have to give Mama her winnings, too," said an ecstatic Rosie.

"So I do," said Leander, "but your mama's mind was clearly not on the game. She is left with only sixpence." He placed the pennies in her hand, closing her fingers gently over them. Judith besottedly thought she would treasure the coins forever.

She shook off her silly thoughts long enough to send the children to their rooms, promising to look in and read to them. She looked nervously at her husband, wondering if he would object. "I think it important to try to keep to their usual ways."

"I'm sure it is," he said, apparently unconcerned. He was putting away the cards and counters. "Now, are you content with your chairs and desk, not to mention the mattresses?"

"They all seem excellent."

"And are you sure there is nothing else you need for your comfort?"

"I can think of nothing at the moment."

It seemed ridiculous to be having this prosaic conversation when her nerves were all on edge. "Do you know how long we will be fixed here?" she asked.

"No, but not for long, I hope. I spoke to Cosgrove, my solicitor today, and told him to put more clerks onto going over the Knollis books. There should be some sense out of it soon. I certainly don't recommend that you unpack anything but essentials." He leaned over to tend the fire, then rose. "By the way, among our belongings, there is apparently a case of wine of some kind."

"Oh yes, my elderberry."

"Elderberry," he said blankly. "What are we supposed to do with that?"

"Drink it, I expect." She wasn't sure how to explain the impulse that had caused her to bring it.

He shrugged. "We can give it to the staff."

Judith stared at him. "Are you saying it's not good enough for your noble lips?"

His face went blank. "Of course not. We'll have it with dinner tomorrow."

"It's not ready for drinking yet," she pointed out, "besides doubtless being shaken by the journey."

"Then we'll drink it when it is ready."

He was desperately *handling* an embarrassment. Judith had been hurt for a moment, but now she loved him even more. "Yes, we will," she said sweetly, trying not to laugh. "You'll like it. Truly you will."

She almost saw the wince. "I'm sure I will."

At that moment, Judith resolved to blend a mixture of fig juice and vinegar for his first taste, just to test his diplomatic abilities. "One bottle will be ready by Christmas," she said.

"Then we'll toast the season with it at the Temple," he said bravely.

"Or perhaps we should save it for some special guest," she mused. "After all, elderberry wine is so much less *common* than grape. Perhaps if the Regent comes to visit."

He actually gaped, and shut his mouth with a snap. "Er . . ."

Judith burst out laughing.

His eyes lit in response. "You—"

But before he could retaliate, Betty came in to curtsy and say the children were in their beds. Judith was glad of an excuse to escape. "I will go up, then." She looked to him for some hint, but then bit the bullet. "I . . . er . . . I think I will retire when the children are settled, if that is all right."

"Will it disturb them if I, too, stop by to wish them good night?"

"I am sure they'll like it."

He smiled. "And will it disturb you if I stop by to wish you a good night . . . ?"

Judith swallowed. "No. No, not at all."

When she had heard the children say their prayers, she read them more of the story of Little Peter, who was stolen by Gypsies, but was well on his way to making his fortune in the navy. Then she checked that both animals were safely in their boxes, and went through to her own room, carefully closing the adjoining door.

It felt like crossing the Rubicon.

She smiled, though, at the sight of her thick down mattress. That had been a success. It showed, surely, that she could cope with this new life. Once she had this next step over with, and was truly his wife, everything would be perfect, and the new bed seemed an auspicious sign.

She rang for Emery, and prepared for bed. She

put on one of her silk nightgowns, shivering slightly at the thought that he might want to take it off again.

Then she had a strange thought.

Would Sebastian have *liked* her to wear silk nightgowns? Was it possible that his lack of enthusiasm for his marital duties had been because she had not been doing things right? Her mother had said nothing of such matters. . . .

But then she had no indication, other than a large family, that her father had enjoyed his duties. She knew from her own experience that very few connubial visits were needed to start a child.

Was it possible she, and her sisters, and her mother, and possibly her mother's mothers through the generations had all been doing it *wrong*? Fluttery panic started in the pit of her stomach. Had Leander's calmness about Rosie's sickness on their wedding night been a reflection of *relief* that he did not have to go on with it?

Had not been able to go on with it?

Judith remembered now those embarrassing occasions when Sebastian had come to her bed and nothing had happened. Sometimes he had hurt her then, squeezing at her and pushing, but he hadn't entered her, and she had known it was because he hadn't stiffened properly. The stiffening was the sign that a man wanted his wife, and Sebastian clearly hadn't wanted her. . . .

The panic spread, and she started to feel sick.

She remembered her wedding night. Had all that playing around been because Leander had been trying desperately to stiffen himself, and it hadn't been working?

The maid had finished dressing her hair in two plaits. Now she bustled off to pass the warming pan around the bed one last time, then left, taking the pan with her. Judith just sat there, looking at herself in the mirror.

He'd danced with princesses, probably bedded them, too. What could he want with Judith Rossiter, even in silk?

No, not Judith Rossiter. Judith Knollis.

No, not that either. He'd explained that a countess used her title as her surname. She was Judith Charrington.

She swallowed and raised her chin. If she was, it was completely at his insistence. If he found he did not like it, he had no one to blame but himself. She would do her duty, and give what she had promised as best she was able, and if he couldn't perform his duties, well . . .

Judith pressed her hands over her mouth. It would be so *embarrassing.*

She extinguished the candles, and slid into the warm, cloud-soft bed. She was immediately snuggled in a silky hollow like a mouse in a nest, but even that sensual delight could not soothe her. She felt chilled as she waited for him.

She heard the clock ticking away the minutes, and distant noises, but she could not tell if they were Leander preparing for bed, or the servants about their tasks. Her eyes became accustomed to the dark, so the fire-lit room did not seem dark at all. She wished it were pitch black.

Leander put on his nightshirt and velvet dressing gown, surprised at how nervous he felt. Their wedding night debacle had not been his fault, but all the same, he felt if he didn't carry off tonight with panache Judith would have reason to wonder at him.

This decorous bedding in the dark wasn't his normal style though, and he wasn't comfortable about it. He was resolved, however, to do it this way the first time for Judith's sake. Then he would gently try

out some more interesting approaches if she were
willing.

If she wasn't, he wouldn't insist, though he would
be disappointed. . . .

He realized he was delaying, and shook his head.
He extinguished the candles in his room and headed
for his wife's room.

Judith heard the door open and turned to look.
He was far from the fire, and just a dark shape. He
came over to the bed.

"Good heavens," he said. "Are you in there?"

It summoned a chuckle even in her anxious state.
"Very much *in*. I'm not sure how I climb out, but
it's wonderfully comfortable."

He shed his robe and slipped between the covers.
Now the warm hollow held the two of them, snuggled
together. He pulled her into his arms. "I think I like
this. Like frolicking in the clouds."

Despite all her fears, Judith reacted to the comfortable cheerfulness of his voice, and the pleasure of
his embrace, and relaxed.

He dropped a kiss on her cheek. "Betty is sleeping
with Rosie. If anything occurs short of imminent
death, she is to handle it."

That further reassured Judith. "You were disappointed, then?" she asked shyly.

"Did you think I wasn't? And I thought you'd have
appreciated my noble forbearance. Were you not disappointed?"

"Yes," she admitted softly. In this private hollow,
deep in down and under blankets, the firelight hardly
glowed. It was a private place.

He kissed her lips, gently, but openmouthed. His
tongue teased at her lips so she could not help but
part them. He moved back. "I won't disappoint you
again," he promised.

"It wasn't your fault. . . ."

He silenced her with another kiss, harder, more

demanding. Judith knew what she must do, and
opened her mouth. His tongue explored her. She
allowed it, not knowing if there was anything more
she should do. This was all unlike Sebastian, even
their position. With this soft, silkily shifting mattress,
there seemed no possibility of lying neatly on her
back; they just seemed to roll together.

He kissed her neck. He kissed her ear. His hands
wandered gently over her body. His lips explored her
neck. A warm tide flowed through her, loosening all
bonds and she had to struggle to keep her wits about
her, to try to do things right. Then his palms passed
lightly over her nipples, and she gasped with surprise
at how sweet that fleeting touch had been.

He drew back for a moment. Then his hands came
up to hold her head as he kissed her. His tongue
became hard, and he slid it in then out, again, and
again. At this blatant simulation, Judith made a chok-
ing protest. His lips freed hers. "Good," he said. "I
was beginning to think the children were a product
of virgin births."

Judith struggled away. "I'm sorry . . ."

He groaned. "God, I am, too. I didn't mean it like
that. I suddenly had an attack of funk. I've never
done this before, you know, and you have."

"*What?*" But a moment's thought assured her he
couldn't be saying he was a virgin.

She heard the humor in his voice. "Made love to
a spouse, in the dark, in nightclothes. . . ."

She *was* doing it all wrong. "I'm sorry," she said
again, trying to struggle up, to get out of her night-
dress, to go light the candles. . . .

"Oh hell," he said and kissed her again, pressing
her back into the bed. It was a hot and powerful kiss,
and denied any attempt at struggle. A hand took
possession of a breast and made magic there as it
had on their wedding night. Then it traveled down,
over silk, exciting every scrap of skin it tantalized,

found the hem, traveled up again under silk, agitating nerve endings, to end in the curls between her thighs.

Sebastian had touched her there when he'd wanted to enter her. Judith tried to roll onto her back and spread her legs, but Leander's body and the mattress wouldn't let her. She made a little sound of distress against his lips.

Leander didn't know what the hell he was doing wrong, but if they stopped to talk about it, they'd never get this done, and that would be even worse. He broke the kiss. "Am I hurting you?"

"No, but . . ."

"Hush then," he said, and moved his lips to her breast.

Judith caught her breath at the sweet sensation, but remembered he didn't want noises. It was hard. His hand and mouth made her want to make noises.

She couldn't stop the gasps.

She was feeling hot and dizzy, and her heart had begun to pound in the most alarming way. She was feeling sick as she had the last time. She almost asked him to stop until she had herself in hand again, but that would be disastrous.

He did not so much move on top of her, as pull her under him as they rolled in the billowing bed. They ended up in the familiar position at least, and she felt him hard against her. At least he'd stiffened.

She was breathing in deep gasps, and strangely aching there, where he touched. She wanted him in her, as she had never wanted such a thing before, but she couldn't say so. It would be indelicate, and he'd told her not to speak . . .

"My wife," he said softly, and slid into her.

Judith rose to help him seat himself, and gave a long sigh. Nothing had ever felt quite so right in her life. It must be because she loved him . . .

But that he must never know!

She worked at staying calm as he did his duty, biting

her lip to hold back noises, controlling a need to thrust up at him, draw him deeper and deeper. . . .

He gave his seed with a gasping shudder, and swooped down to kiss her deeply and hotly so that, despite all her efforts, a shudder passed through her, with something else hovering in its train. She felt raw, and aching, and still rather sick, which had never happened to her before. Would it always be this way?

But at long last it was done.

He moved them so they were back in one another's arms, side by side. His hand cherished her face. "I'm sorry," he said. "That wasn't quite what I intended."

Judith didn't know what that meant, and had never even contemplated discussing the act. It probably meant she'd done it wrong.

"I just wanted to do it in the way you'd be comfortable with," he said, "but I don't think I did it right. . ."

Was it possible he was a virgin? Had been? "It was fine," she assured him. What else could she say?

"It can be better," he said dryly.

No, not a virgin.

Just disappointed.

She had done it all wrong. She swallowed tears. She'd thought she was all grown up, but she felt like a young, scared girl again. "I'm sorry," she gulped.

"Stop saying that!" His voice was sharp. He took a deep breath. "Judith, it's no one's fault. We just have to learn how to get along. It was doubtless the same with your first husband. No," he suddenly said. "It was my fault. I became obsessed with getting it done, making you my wife. I should have taken more time." He kissed her gently. "But now you most certainly are my wife, aren't you?"

Judith had to smile, for he did sound truly pleased about that at least. "Yes, I most certainly am your wife."

He rolled slightly, so she was lying half over him.

''That's good. But I can't take this sort of strain. Next time we're doing it my way.'' His hand gently rubbed her bottom. ''You'll like it, I promise you.''

On the whole, Judith thought it would be good to see how it was really supposed to be done. She wondered sleepily if when she found out, she should tell her mother and sisters. . . .

Chapter Fourteen

Judith awoke to find herself alone in the bed. Deep in her downy nest, she ruefully contemplated the consummation of her marriage. It had been a muddle, but at least it was done, and it would appear he had experienced no particular difficulty in stiffening himself. That soothed her pride.

And it would appear Leander knew how it was supposed to be, and was going to show her. The only problem she had with that was the alarming tendency she had developed to lose control in his arms. She was going to have to think of ways to prevent it.

The undermaid crept in to light the fire. A little later, Emery appeared with her morning chocolate. Judith struggled into a sitting position with the bed billowing about her. Emery draped a soft shawl around her shoulders.

"The children are awake and would like to visit you, milady."

Judith gave permission, and soon the children bounced in. They climbed on the end of the bed and gave a whoop of delight as the mattress shifted about them. "This is like playing in clouds, Mama!" Rosie declared.

Judith blushed. "Yes, isn't it?"

Bastian giggled. "It looks as if the bed is eating you, Mama."

"Oh no!" Judith screamed. "My toes! It has my toes!"

She was claiming the bed had her as far as her knees when Leander burst in, in shirtsleeves. He stopped when he saw them all in giggles.

Rosie called out, "The bed's eating Mama, Papa Leander! Save her!"

He came over and grabbed Judith under the arms, hauling her up. Judith caught some sheet between her legs to stop him. "Aah! It's no use! Save yourselves, my innocents!"

Leander was laughing so much, he had little strength. "Bounce on the bed, children," he commanded. "Make it let go."

They gleefully obeyed, and with a great tug, Judith emerged into Leander's arms to be swung around. "All still there?" he asked with a grin.

Judith solemnly inspected her toes. "Saved in the nick of time."

"Good," he said, and winked at her. "Perhaps you should sleep with me until we have that carnivorous bed tamed."

"What does carnivorous mean?" Rosie asked. Both children were still bouncing on the bed.

"Meat eating," said Leander.

"Oh," said Rosie, unconcerned.

Bastian leapt off. "Silly! People are meat, too, you know."

Rosie scrambled off too. "I am *not* meat."

"Yes you are. Just like a silly sheep."

"No I'm *not!*"

"Yes, you are!"

"I'm not. I'm not!"

"Stop!" Judith commanded, horrified at the monsters her children were becoming.

They both stopped, but glared at one another.

"Bastian," Judith pronounced, "after breakfast you will write thirty times in your best plate, I must not be rude to my sister. Rosie, you will prepare to explain to me in what way people are not meat."

"Yes, Mama," they said in sullen unison.

"Good. Then go and dress."

When the children had gone, Leander drew Judith into his arms for a kiss. "How stern you are. In what way are people not meat?"

"In no way at all," said Judith, flustered to be behaving in such a way in daylight. "Though Rosie may bring in the matter of our immortal souls. I merely hope she will think on the subject."

He grinned. "May I hope to hear her dissertation?"

"Of course, though you mustn't expect too much from a six-year-old."

The children continued to be subdued throughout breakfast, though Leander's reminder that there would be riding later did raise the clouds a little. When they were finished, Bastian went off to do his punishment, and Rosie was told to say her piece.

She stood, hands clasped in front of her. "I have considered, Mama, and it would appear that people *are* meat, except that God made us special and gave us immortal souls. God also gave us dominion over the animals," she added firmly, "so they *don't* eat us."

Judith decided to leave that error uncorrected for the moment, and was about to congratulate her daughter on her thoughts, when Rosie said, "But this has made me wonder about Daniel, Mama."

"Daniel?" queried Judith with a sinking feeling.

"In the lions' den. The lions were going to eat him, weren't they?"

Before Judith could answer that, Rosie carried on, "And the Christians in Rome were thrown to the lions.'' Her lips started to quiver. ''Mama, I don't want to be eaten!''

Judith opened her arms, and Rosie ran into them. ''Truly, Rosie, people are very rarely eaten, and never in England.'' She looked to Leander, hoping that was true.

''Absolutely,'' he said. ''There are no large carnivores in England except in menageries.''

Rosie peeped at him. ''Truly?''

''Word of a gentleman.''

''And the bed wasn't truly eating Mama, was it?''

''Absolutely not. We were playing.''

''Grown-ups don't play,'' the little girl said with authority.

He smiled at Judith in a way that made her hot. ''Oh yes they do.''

''Papa didn't play,'' said Rosie.

''Well, this papa does.''

Reassured, Rosie went off to prepare for her ride. Judith shook her head. ''How strange it must be to be six, and not sure what is real in the world, and what is not.''

''Are you sure what is real and what is not?''

''Of course,'' said Judith, then wondered. She wasn't sure of much in some areas.

''Look at my situation with the Temple. What is real, and what is not?''

''We will find out as soon as we get there,'' said Judith firmly.

''Yes, of course.'' But he didn't sound convinced. ''What are your plans for the day?''

''I have none in particular. I did think I might buy some Christmas items. We are used to making some decorations for the house . . .'' She trailed off at the thought of the Temple. ''The children will like to put up wreaths in their rooms, at least,'' she said.

''I hope you will put up wreaths everywhere. I want

a rollicking English Christmas. Spiced ale and sugar-plums, holly and mistletoe."

Judith saw he was serious. "Very well, then," she said, but she couldn't quite imagine it. "I would like to send something special to my family if you do not object," she continued. "Some food and gifts. And I suppose I will find more interesting toys for the children here than in Somerset."

"Toys," he said, bright eyed. "I, too, must look into it."

"There is no need for us both to buy them a gift. They will be spoiled."

"No they won't. And I, too, want an excuse to rummage around in a toy shop."

Judith shook her head at him. "Then buy gifts for your cousins, sir."

"But they want to kill me," he protested, in a way that showed he did not take the matter seriously at all.

Judith, however, felt a frisson of alarm at his words. "Don't joke about it."

"Why not? I've told you it's nonsense. They doubt-less hope to keep me away so they can continue to live at the Temple, and shave off large amounts of the earldom's income, but they would not go so far as murder. It hardly seems appropriate to take them gifts, however, when I intend to throw them out."

"I would have thought it very desirable. Even if you have to be firm with them, you'll want to turn them up sweet afterward."

"How well you know me already," he murmured, advancing for another kiss. "How easy is it to turn you up sweet, true wife of mine . . . ?" But then they heard the children returning and moved apart. Bas-tian presented his lines for approval, and then Lean-der took them away to the equestrian center.

Judith ordered the carriage and went shopping.

She was modest in her purchases, for after settli

her bill with Mr. Browne, she did not have a vast amount of money, though it was more than she would have dreamed of weeks ago. On consideration, she was resolved to inform Timothy Rossiter immediately that she had no further need of his money. It was hardly his fault his brother had been an improvident fool, and she could not in conscience take any more of his money. Her overgenerous pin money, even what was left of it, would surely be adequate for all her needs.

It was a joy to visit the shops with money in hand. She bought both children one of the new jigsaws.

She also bought Rosie an ark, complete with little wooden animals, and Bastian a castle with wooden soldiers.

She purchased ribbon and wire to make wreaths and kissing boughs, smiling like a fool at the thought of Leander stealing a kiss under the mistletoe. Oh, she, too, wanted an old-fashioned, rollicking Christmas. She hoped there were carolers at Temple Knollis, and perhaps a mystery play nearby.

Walking by more emporiums, with her footman in tow, she couldn't resist a white fur muff and hat for Rosie, which meant she had to buy an equivalent gift for Bastian. In the end she bought him a pair of York tan gloves, an exact replica of the style Leander favored.

At the last moment, she bought Leander another pair. She was sure he had plenty, and probably had them custom made, but she had to give him something, and could think of nothing else. Perhaps she could make him something, but couldn't imagine what he would find acceptable.

Embroidered slippers? She hardly thought so. Look at his reaction to her elderberry wine. Her high spirits flagged a little. Would his idea of a merry Christmas and hers really mesh?

* * *

The children were home when she returned, bubbling with excitement at their first ride in a school. Rosie proclaimed that she *had* to have a proper habit if she was to hold up her head. Judith's first thought was that it was a ridiculous extravagance when she would grow out of one every year, but then she threw caution to the winds and agreed. She supposed she would need one, too, if she were to learn to ride.

Leander had gone out again, leaving a message to say he would not be in for luncheon, and so the three ate together just like the old days. Except that the meal was cooked and presented by servants, and served on fine china plates.

Judith looked around her with satisfaction. She was growing used to this life of comfort, and her marriage was proving to be a delight. How had she come to be so fortunate?

After the meal, the children wanted to take her on a tour of the local area and show off their explorations. Judith agreed happily and only delayed long enough to put her resolution into action, and write the note to Timothy Rossiter. Addison assured her it would be delivered to Clarges Street, which apparently was not very far away.

Judith felt liberated, as if the last entanglement of her first marriage had been cut. She set off merrily with the children and George to explore Mayfair.

It was as they watched the Guards parading in Hyde Park that a vague sense of malaise, and an ache in her back, resolved itself for Judith. She thought back in her mind. Yes, it was time for her monthly flow.

Her first reaction was disappointment that it would be some days before Leander could show her the right way to perform the marriage act.

Following that came embarrassment. She would have to tell him, and it was not a matter women discussed with men. It had been simple with Sebastian. He had always asked permission to visit her. She would merely say, "I am sorry it is not convenient tonight."

Oh well, if Leander came to her room, she would say the same. Surely he would understand.

But when Leander came to her before dinner, where she sat in her study writing a letter to her mother, he kissed her and touched her in a way that seemed to be laying down promises for the night, and she blurted out, "I'm afraid it is not convenient . . . I mean, it's my time of month!" Then wished the earth would swallow her.

"Is it?" he said, just slightly red himself. "I hope it doesn't take you badly."

Judith had never imagined discussing such a matter with a man. "No," she said, looking fixedly at her pen. "I have little trouble."

He turned her face up to him. "Good. It doesn't preclude kissing, though, does it?" And he proceeded to kiss her very thoroughly. "Now," he said, "I thought you might like to visit the theater tonight, but if you are unwell . . ."

Judith felt a thrill of excitement. "I would *love* it. I have never been to a real theater."

He shook his head, but smiled. "It is a joy to me to show you the world, Judith."

"May the children come, too?" Judith asked. "They have never been to a theater either, and who knows when they will next have the opportunity?"

He was a little taken aback. "I'm not sure. The main play is *Hamlet,* which may be a trifle somber for Rosie."

"That's the one with ghosts, isn't it? But I would like to try. We could take George and Betty, and they could bring the children home if they don't care for it." His quizzical look penetrated her excitement, and she flushed. "Oh, I'm sorry. It doubtless isn't done at all, is it?"

"I can't imagine why not," he said with a sudden smile. "Introducing the children to Shakespeare. Educating the servants, too. We'll set a fashion."

Judith bit her lip. "I'm sorry. Disregard it, please."

"Not at all. I think it an excellent idea. You must never be governed by what is common practice. Most people have no imagination. But, if we're to venture among Society, I must insist that you play the countess. Wear your wedding dress and these." He casually produced a parure of topaz and amber.

"Oh, how lovely." She carelessly added, "They remind me of your eyes."

He looked at the jewelry in mock alarm. "Good lord, woman. Next *you'll* be writing odes to *my* gleaming orbs."

Judith and the children were entranced by Covent Garden Theater, as much by the handsome chandeliers, the ornamented ceiling, and the glittering audience as by the stage. Bastian and Rosie had to be restrained from leaning out to study the merry activity of the pit.

The pit was a maelstrom of fashionable bucks, and lively ladies; the circles and boxes were chattering ranks of silk and jewels. Betty and George sat quietly at the back of the box, but they were wide-eyed and their excitement could be felt. Judith was delighted that her plan had brought them here.

Their box was near the stage, and seemed in an excellent position.

"How does one obtain a box at the theater?" Judith asked Leander.

"Many people hire one for the Season, but it costs a great deal. Others rent them for the night. After all, no one attends the theater every night, so people who have a box rent it out when they don't require it. The theater insists on it, or they'd have half-empty houses most of the time.''

"Did you rent this one then?''

"No, I used my influence.'' He grinned at her. "It's the Belcraven box. The duke is Lucien's father. As neither the duke nor Lucien are in town, I was easily able to arrange to have it.''

"Without paying?'' she teased. "How cheap.''

He placed a hand dramatically to his brow. "My conscience is suddenly assailed! The House of de Vaux is doubtless even now crumbling for lack of the guinea.''

They both burst out laughing, and the children demanded to be told the joke.

Judith became aware that their laughter had drawn attention. Any number of eyes were focused on their box as people whispered to one another. She put her chin up and tried to look like a countess, but she was relieved when the lights were dimmed, and the curtain drawn up.

The first item was a farce, and the children thought it very funny. Judith was pleased they didn't understand all the jokes. In truth, there were some she didn't understand herself, but she had no intention of asking for an explanation.

At the intermission a number of people stopped by, and Leander introduced her, but he always said, "We are not officially here, mind. We have merely stopped off for a day or two before going down to the Temple.

"Otherwise,'' he whispered to Judith, "you'll have them all leaving cards.''

Two young men, however, refused to be fobbed off that way. Blond, fine-boned Sir Stephen Ball said, "None of that. I'll be by tomorrow.''

And Irish-eyed Miles Cavanagh winked at Judith. "With me at his side, dear lady.'' He kissed her hand with devastating flare. "A truly charming addition to the Rogues."

The music signaled the resumption of the program and the visitors departed. Judith looked at Leander. "Are they saying I have been recruited to your Company of Rogues? I'm not sure I approve."

He took her hand. "Apparently Nicholas has decreed that wives are given the privileges of membership. Without the penalties, you'll be pleased to know."

"Penalties?" Judith asked quietly as the curtain went up.

"Schoolboy nonsense. We scarred ourselves on our right palm." He extended his hand, and even in the dim light Judith could see the white mark.

"That's terrible," she whispered. "I won't have Bastian subjected to such a thing. It could have become infected."

He grinned and raised his hand to her mouth. "Kiss it better then."

Judith did so, thankful that everyone's attention was on the stage. It might be her time of month, but her foolish body didn't seem to realize that. It was seduced by the rough warmth beneath her lips, and the taste of his skin on her tongue.

The children did not flee *Hamlet*. True, Rosie crept over to Judith and cuddled by her side, and hid her face during the slaughter at the end, but she appeared to enjoy most of the play.

When the lights went up, Judith turned to Leander. "Thank you. This has been wonderful"

He smiled back. "You are easily pleased. Will you not give me something harder to do? A dragon to slay? A ghost to face?"

She chuckled. "I come from too simple a background to have ghosts. It is the high aristocracy who are plagued by them, my lord earl."

Bastian asked a question, and Leander turned to

answer it. Judith checked that they had all the wraps and gloves they had come with. She looked over the emptying pit, and gasped.

The sight of Sebastian staring at her brought a darkness around her vision. She clutched the rail at the front of the box, afraid she would fall.

When her vision cleared, and she blinked, there was nothing there. She took deep breaths to calm her racing heart. And she'd thought it would be Rosie whose imagination would be overstimulated by the play!

She checked again, searching the parting crowd, then shook her head. Imagination, or some fleeting resemblance. Now she thought of it the pale-faced man—if he had existed at all—had had darker hair. There had been no true resemblance to Sebastian. The shivery feeling lingered, however, not just from the illusory apparition, but from the expression. Bitter. Vengeful, even . . .

On the way home, there was a lively discussion of ghosts. Judith and Leander strove mightily to convince Rosie that the ghost had not been real, had merely been an actor dressed in flowing cloth, but she was not entirely convinced.

Bastian scoffed, "Next you'll be saying they all died at the end."

"Of course not," said Rosie. "For they stood up afterward to bow."

"The ghost bowed, too, so there. And I don't think," added Bastian rather fiercely, "it was at all fair that Hamlet die. He was only trying to help his father."

Judith and Leander shared a look. From his tone, the boy felt strongly about it, but the rights of deceased fathers was a ticklish debate to get into at this time of night. Judith said, "We can discuss it later. I think Hamlet did some things that were not quite nice."

"His uncle did worse," said Bastian.

Leander ruffled his hair. "Then perhaps he, at least, deserved to die."

By then they were back at Montague Square and the sleepy children were taken off to bed.

Judith and Leander sat down to a light supper. "I'm surprised at how seriously they take it," said Judith. "But then I confess, as long as the players were on the stage, I was convinced it was all real. I felt all Hamlet's anxiety, and poor Ophelia's despair. I'm glad we took the children. Thank you."

He touched her hand. "It was my pleasure. I'm somewhat jaded, you know. It's delightful to see these things again through fresh eyes."

"Yes, children are like that, aren't they? They gift us with the world afresh."

"I wasn't just speaking of the children."

Judith glanced at him uncertainly. "I'm sorry I'm so unsophisticated."

"Don't be. The children will grow up, and you will grow worldly. Let us enjoy this little innocence while we can." His eyes twinkled. "One day before we leave, I am going to take you all to the circus. I can hardly wait."

The next day the two Rogues did call, accompanied by a third—a handsome, one-armed man called Hal Beaumont. Judith began to wonder if the Rogues hadn't been chosen for their looks. The Marquess of Arden, after all, must be one of the most handsome men in England, and Hal Beaumont could run him a close second in dark-haired fashion, even with his infirmity.

There was no question, it would appear, of proper calls of twenty minutes' duration. The three guests made themselves thoroughly at home. She gathered this was another way of the Rogues, and she had no particular objection, though she sensed she was being assessed almost as if she were joining a family.

That's what it was, she thought. A kind of family, with the same loose yet powerful bonds. She could see why Leander, with his lack of home, placed such store on the group.

When the children came back from their walk, they sent Addison to ask if they might enter the drawing room. Judith found this painfully awkward, but when permission had been given, and they came in, Leander complimented them on correct behavior.

Rosie, incurably honest, said, "We asked Addison and he said that would be the correct thing to do."

"Even better," said Leander with a grin. "To seek good advice and follow it is a sure path to success. Now, let me introduce you again to my friends, for I am not sure you could drag your thoughts away from the stage last night long enough to pay attention. This gentleman is Sir Stephen Ball, and he is renowned for his brilliant speeches in the House of Commons. This is Mister Miles Cavanagh, who likes to pretend to be an Irish rascal, but in fact is the owner of vast acres there. If you make up to him he may one day be willing to sell you one of his magnificent horses. And this is Mister Hal Beaumont. He should call himself Major, for that was his rank in the army, and he positively covered himself in glory until he lost his arm, and had to let some other fellows have a chance."

Judith gasped at this blunt reference to the infirmity, and she saw Rosie's eyes grow wide. It was clear, however, that Mr. Beaumont preferred to have the matter dealt with honestly. His only comment was, "Not lost, dear fellow. Makes me sound dashed careless."

"And these, as you know," said Leander proudly, a hand on each child's shoulder, "are my new children, Bastian and Rosie Rossiter."

Bastian gave a bow and Rosie a curtsy, though they were tongue-tied.

"Two new Rogues!" declared Mr. Cavanagh. "Well, that's almost outdoing Nicholas, my boy."

Leander laughed. "I suppose that could be true. Bastian will be going to Harrow soon, so he can keep the Rogues's traditions alive. I've already arranged his admission, so I suppose those masters who remember us are already shaking in their shoes."

They spun off into schoolboy tales, to which Bastian listened with rapt attention. The tales mainly involved merry japes and sporting feats, so his enthusiasm for his school days grew visibly, despite occasional mention of retribution.

Rosie sat quietly, sneaking looks at Hal Beaumont's empty sleeve.

When the groupings shifted, Judith found herself talking to Stephen Ball, a quieter man than the other two, but with eyes that missed little. "Are you perhaps related to Mister Sebastian Rossiter, Lady Charrington?"

"Please," she said, "I can see how it is with you, and you must call me Judith. I am not accustomed to a title anyway. As for Sebastian, he was my first husband."

"Really," he said. "Then if you wish to live quietly while here in town, we must keep that to ourselves."

She must have looked her bewilderment, for he added, "He had devoted admirers, don't you know, who would be inclined to view his widow and children as living shrines."

Judith thought of the trickle of devotees who had made their way to Mayfield, and supposed he might be correct. She certainly didn't want any more silly poets dogging her footsteps. She was surprised, however, that such a man as Sir Stephen had even heard of Sebastian. She wondered if he were a secret poet himself.

She was distracted when Rosie was drawn to Hal Beaumont by a welcoming grin. She tensed, wondering what her daughter would say.

"You may ask about it, you know," said Hal kindly. "I don't mind talking about it. In fact, I like to milk it for every scrap of sympathy I can get, particularly from pretty ladies."

Rosie leant against his leg. "I'm afraid it must have hurt."

"Yes, off and on." Then he burst out laughing "Gad's, what an awful pun!"

"What happened?" Bastian asked eagerly. "Was it a cannon, sir?"

"Yes. Took it right off. Luckily, my sergeant had the presence of mind to tourniquet me, and I made it through."

"When was this?"

Mr. Beaumont went on to describe a minor skirmish in Canada. Judith could not feel comfortable with this frank discussion of such a thing, but she could see no one else minded. For the most part, she watched Rosie, all her maternal instincts clamoring the alarm. But since Mr. Beaumont seemed so at ease talking of his injury, she couldn't think what the girl might say to embarrass.

Then Rosie piped up. "Sir. What _happened_ to your arm?"

He looked blank for a moment, and then said, "Oh, you mean, where did it go? Do you know, I don't know. It was left on the field."

Rosie looked up at him with big eyes. "Then do you suppose it was eaten?"

"Rosie!" exclaimed Judith, and saw Leander struggling to keep a straight face.

"Eaten?" echoed Hal blankly. "What a thought . . . But if so," he said briskly, "I'd be glad of it. Always hated waste."

Talk swung onto other matters. Judith snared Rosie

before she could say something worse. "I'm sorry if I shouldn't have said that, Mama," Rosie said warily, "but I wanted to know." After a moment she added, "I suppose there are more carnivores in Canada than there are in England."

"Yes, I believe that is so," Judith said faintly, pleased to at least have the specter restricted to a distant land. "Wolves and bears."

There was a lengthy silence and Judith began to relax. Then Rosie said, "Do you think it is wasteful to be buried, Mama?"

Judith groaned.

Bastian had come over. "Silly. When we're buried, we're not wasted. We're eaten by worms. It's in Job. 'And though, after my skin, worms destroy this body . . .' "

"Mama!" wailed Rosie.

Judith quickly shepherded her two children away. That night she had to sleep with Rosie and try to put into perspective her new realization of mortality. It was as well there had been no question of sleeping with Leander this night.

Chapter Fifteen

The next day, despite her words to Leander, Judith wasn't feeling quite the thing. She chose to spend most of it in front of the library fire with a book— Sir Walter Scott's *Waverley*. Novel reading had not been a large part of her life, and she enjoyed herself tremendously, especially as there was nothing to do but drink the tea, and eat the meals prepared for her.

She was consequently a little put out when told her brother-in-law had come to call. On the other hand, she welcomed the opportunity to thank him for the money he had sent. Without it, she did not know what she would have done.

The gentleman who was ushered in was a stranger, though she supposed she must have met him at her wedding all those years ago. Timothy Rossiter was as slight as his brother, but had a paunch, and rather puffy eyes. His hair was short and mousy, but his features were very similar to his brother's.

"My dear Lady Charrington," he gushed. "Or may I still call you sister?"

Judith could hardly hold back a gasp. His voice was exactly like Sebastian's except for a slight drawl. "Of

course . . ." she said uncertainly, for he had never
called her sister to her recollection. She would have
sworn that at the wedding he had not addressed two
words to her. "Please be seated. Would you care for
tea?"

He accepted, his eyes darting around. She thought
he looked disappointed by the simple, old-fashioned
room. Wryly, she suspected that he had come in
hopes of bolstering his fortune. Perhaps she should
offer to repay the money he had given her, for he
did not look prosperous. His suit of clothes was plain
and rather worn; the kind of thing one would expect
of a servant. She realized she had no idea what he
did for a living.

She was shamed to find she didn't care for him,
when he had been so kind, and she strove to inject
warmth into her voice. "I am so pleased to have this
opportunity to thank you in person, Mister Rossiter.
The money you sent made all the difference to me
and the children."

He smiled warmly. "I did not grudge a penny, dear
sister. I only wish it could have been more, but . . ."
He sighed. "Where are Sebastian's little angels?"

Was that how Sebastian had described them to his
brother? "Bastian and Rosie are out at the moment,
riding. You must come back another day and meet
them."

The tea tray was brought in and Judith poured. As
she passed the cup, she said, "You must forgive my
ignorance, Mister Rossiter, for Sebastian spoke little
of his family. Do my children have other relatives?"

He sipped. "Alas, no, sister. Or only very distant
ones. There was only Sebastian and me, and our
parents died before your marriage. That is why I feel
we should keep in touch. Your children are the only
chicks in the Rossiter nest."

Judith couldn't deny that his words made her
uncomfortable, and she found she was pleased that

they would soon be removing into Somerset. Timothy Rossiter was part of her family, and she was truly grateful for his help, but she did not want to become close.

"As I said," she murmured, "I will arrange a time for you to visit and meet the children. Now, forgive me for mentioning it, but is there any way I can repay you for your help over the past year? I am sure my husband would be delighted—"

"No, no, dear sister," he cried, rather sharply. "I would not dream of it. I am just happy to see that your cares are over, and I know Sebastian would be so, too." He put down his cup and rose. "It has been the greatest pleasure to meet you again."

With that he took his farewells and Judith could not help but be grateful for it. It was strange, she had never before had to contend with a relative she did not care for. She had no idea how to handle the situation, and could only hope that it would sort itself out.

She contentedly returned to her book.

The children returned, but Leander had dropped them off and gone about his business. After luncheon they went off happily with both Betty and George to yet more explorations. Judith approved the evening's menu, and authorized a purchase of spices. Then, feeling lazy, but unrepentant, she returned to her book.

When Leander arrived home he shook his head. "I've married an idle wretch."

"I fear you have," she said, accepting a cozy kiss. "I could become accustomed to this."

"I doubt it. If I commanded you to live like this for a week, you'd be in revolt in a few days."

Judith had to admit he was probably correct.

"Where are the children this afternoon?" he asked.

"Out again. Their attendants are proving to be marvelous. Today they are to see St. Paul's. I confess, if I were feeling more sprightly, I would have gone with them."

"Betty and George are probably viewing this as a jolly holiday themselves. Now, I have been invited to dine with some friends this evening, fellow officers in the Guards. Will you feel terribly abandoned if I accept?"

She was happily able to assure him that she had no objection, and felt that their married life was settling into a comfortable pattern if he felt free to take himself off now and then. "But is there any news from the Temple yet?"

"No, but we should hear tomorrow. With luck, and barring diphtheria, we should be able to leave soon after, but you must say if you don't feel up to it."

She dismissed this. "I am not usually so frail, I assure you, and any tiredness lasts only the one day."

"Good, then are you up to looking over these papers with me?" he asked, producing a folder and untying the string. "These are some of the estate records, and they make no sense to me."

"Leander, I know nothing of such things."

"But you have a good head on your shoulders, and you've lived in the country all your life. My solicitor and accountants aren't making much headway either, so don't feel badly."

He laid out the sheets of neatly scribed details. "Look, there are four principal estates, and they all have income and expenses. The income has been going to the Temple, and then any amounts for repairs, new purchases and such has gone back, though all on paper through various banks around the country."

"But how ridiculous," said Judith. "Surely the estate managers should be able to take reasonable amounts for management."

"You'd have thought so. My grandfather set up things this way. He became obsessed with control of the money—miserly even—probably because he didn't care what happened anywhere except at the Temple. I fear the lesser estates have suffered.''

''But still,'' said Judith, leafing through the bewildering sheets of paper, ''I would have thought it possible to see if money was missing.''

''In theory, but with it all going round and round in circles like a whirligig, and through so many hands, it's a conundrum. The simple fact, however, is that at the end there doesn't seem to be all the money there should be. Look, the steward of the Cumberland property is complaining that he has not received money he requested for repairs. This account shows the money was authorized and withdrawn. Yet it never arrived in Cumberland. . . .''

Judith shook her head. ''I'm sorry. This kind of thing makes no sense to me.'' In fact, she was staggered by the amounts being moved on the papers. Hundreds of thousands of pounds.

He gathered the papers up with a sigh. ''I confess, I wish I'd been raised to this rather than to waltzing my way through diplomatic mazes. Ah well, doubtless when we get to the Temple, and I get my hands on the central accounts there, it will begin to resolve itself.''

''If there's anything left to resolve. One interpretation of all those papers could be that money is being skimmed off like cream.''

''Yes, I have thought of that,'' he said with a frown. ''I really would like to get there before Uncle Charles sails away, leaving only thin milk behind.''

That evening Judith played a game with the children, and read to them, and it was almost like the old days, but much better. They told her excitedly about St. Paul's. ''It's ever so big, Mama,'' said Bastian. ''I'd really like to go to service there some day.''

"Then we will. Perhaps this Sunday, if we are not already on our way to the Temple."

"Are we leaving so soon?" Rosie protested. "I wanted to see Westminster Abbey!"

"Then I would suggest that you go tomorrow."

"But we were going to go to the Tower tomorrow," said Bastian. "Do you know they have effigies of all the kings of England, in armor!"

Judith sighed and said firmly, "Today is Friday, and we surely will not begin our journey on Sunday, but if Lord Charrington wishes us to start our journey on Monday, children, then we will. You will have to choose what you want to do tomorrow, and if you cannot decide, you will have to stay at home." She saw their unhappy faces and said, "We will come to London again, you know, dears."

As she went to her own room, she hoped this was true. What would she do if Leander was entranced by Temple Knollis as his grandfather and uncle had been? She would live with it, she supposed, though the place was beginning to loom ominous in her mind.

The children settled their difference by lot, and Rosie's Westminster Abbey won. Bastian's disappointment was soothed when Leander announced that he would take them to the circus that evening. He told them they would definitely be leaving on Monday.

Later, he explained to Judith that he had finally received the report from Temple Knollis. There was no trace of sickness in the area, though his uncle was apparently ailing from a seizure, as James Knollis had said.

"It seems pretty conclusive," said Leander to Judith with a frown. "Why the devil would they try such a trick? It could only buy them a few days."

They were cozily on either side of the library fire.

Judith had needlework in hand. Leander was sipping brandy. She liked this togetherness very much indeed. "I suppose a few days could be crucial," she said. "Perhaps they're even now packing up the artwork, and preparing to flee the country."

"I'd almost say they're welcome—the place is too much like a museum of objets d'arts at the moment—except for the amount of money it all represents. With so much to be done to bring the estate back into good heart, and help the people through these hard times, I may need all those treasures."

"Did your man see any sign that the family were preparing to flee?"

"No, but they've become reclusive. They've dismissed most of the staff, and are hardly seen. It's all dashed odd."

"Well," said Judith with a supportive smile, "within the week we'll be there, and we can set it all to rights."

He smiled back, fire flames dancing golden in his mysterious eyes. "I like that *we*."

Yes, thought Judith, I like this very much.

The circus was a roaring success. The children loved the acrobats, the equestrian feats, and the animals, and so did Judith, though she kept trying to remember to behave as a countess should. Sometimes she didn't feel as young as Leander, she felt as young as Rosie.

There was a real lion, however, and the handler put his arm into the beast's mouth. Rosie hid her face. "It's going to eat him!"

Afterward, despite the trainer's safety, she had to be reassured that there were no lions roaming free in England.

When they arrived back at the house, the children were both excited and exhausted. They drooped over their soup, and made no objection to seeking their beds. Judith and Leander had just settled to enjoying a cup of tea when both children raced downstairs again. "Mama! Betty is sick. Very sick!"

Leander and Judith hurried to Rosie's room, where the maid slept. Betty was sprawled on her truckle bed fully dressed, breathing in a harsh, shallow way. Her skin was pallid and felt chill, and she had vomited.

Judith looked at Leander. "Drunk?" she murmured.

He shook his head. "I don't think so." He put his fingers to the woman's neck. "Her pulse is strange. It could be her heart. I'll send for a doctor. Rosie had better sleep with you."

Judith calmed the children as best she could and sent them to prepare for bed. She sat by the maid anxiously, expecting the faltering breathing to stop at any minute. Betty was little older than herself, and it was frightening that she suffer heart failure.

It seemed an age before the doctor arrived. Dr. Northrop was a stocky man, with strong, capable hands. He examined the maid carefully. During the examination, Betty came round, though she didn't seem able to speak.

"Indeed, it does look like the heart, my lady," the doctor said, "but I think she'll do with care. She must rest and eat sustaining broths when she is able. When she feels more the thing, I will see if there is a lingering weakness. It is generally the case, however. You will doubtless find she had a childhood illness that would account for this. You will likely have to discharge her."

Judith almost rejected this out loud, but held her tongue. Still, she hoped Leander would not look at it that way. She knew what it was to be poor, and she couldn't throw the woman onto the street.

When the doctor had gone, Leander assured Judith that he would not dismiss the woman. The maid was moved to the attic quarters, and the undermaid was given the job of caring for her.

Judith reassured both children that Betty was not too ill, and then went downstairs to the library. Leander joined her there.

"I have asked Addison," he said, "and he reports that she seemed completely well up to an hour ago. Though he admitted that it was unusual for her to go up to Rosie's room before she was summoned, so perhaps she was feeling sickly." He poured brandy for her. "Here, this should steady your nerves after all that excitement."

Judith sipped gratefully, though she gasped at the fire of the spirits. "I do hope she recovers fully. If we are to leave for the Temple shortly, Betty should have plenty of opportunity to rest and get well. I don't know what we should do if she proves to be unable to work, though."

"We'll cross that bridge when we come to it. We'll see what the doctor says."

The next day, as promised, they all went to service at St. Paul's. Winchester last week, thought Judith, St. Paul's this. How her life had changed.

After church the children were permitted to visit Betty, for the woman did seem remarkably recovered, though frightened by the whole thing. "Oh, my lady. I really must speak to you. I'm ever so sorry . . ."

Judith hastened to reassure her. "Betty, you must not fret yourself. We will see what Doctor Northrop has to say, but no matter what your condition, provision will be made for you."

The woman began to weep.

"There, there," said Judith. "I'm sure you still feel most unwell. I will return to speak to you when the doctor has seen you."

She sent the children off with George. They could

not visit the Tower on a Sunday, unfortunately, but they were to take the carriage there and view it from London Bridge.

When they were gone, Judith settled to arranging the last of their packing, but as Emery folded her spare silk nightgown, she found herself distracted. Her courses were almost over, and she wondered if she should tell Leander this. That embarrassed her even more than the original need to tell him they had started, for it could appear to be an invitation to her bed.

She would leave it. He seemed to be familiar with these womanly secrets, and would doubtless realize in a week that it must be done with.

She went to the storage room to check the boxes which had never even been unpacked. She would definitely take her wine. She hesitated over her box of Christmas baking, however, for having become used to Leander's style of living she could not imagine such things being needed at Temple Knollis. But in the end she directed that they be sent in the spare carriage. They still had meaning.

Leander wished to take his valet on this trip, and a number of possessions from the London house, and so Rougemont, the valet, would travel with this extra baggage. Emery, after fretting over it, had sadly announced that she did not want to leave London, so Judith would hire a maid in Somerset.

With a spare carriage, there would be ample room. What else would be needed?

She had no idea whether the Temple boasted a good library, and so she decided to take some volumes from the library here. She set about the selection, often distracted by an interesting volume. Such a quantity and variety of books had not been part of her life before.

She was disturbed by a commotion, and Rosie's voice calling frantically for Mama. She ran out into the hall to see George shepherding along a very wet Bastian, wrapped in a horse blanket. Rosie ran to her. "Someone pushed Bastian into the river!"

"What? George bring him in here. . . ." Then the smell hit her. She hugged her son anyway. "Bastian, darling, are you all right?"

"Yes," he said boldly, but he looked rather white and shaken. "A boatman fished me out pretty fast, and I can swim."

"Thank heavens for it. We must get you warm and dry." The foul smell of the river was all over him. "In the kitchen, I think." She sent Bastian off with other servants, keeping George and Rosie back. "Now," she said, "tell me what occurred."

"Someone pushed him off the bridge!" Rosie yelled.

Judith gathered her into a hug. "Let George tell me, dearest."

"Well, milady," said the young man, who looked pretty shaken himself, "I don't know rightly what to say. After we'd looked at the Tower, the young 'uns wanted to walk across the bridge, and watch the boats. Master Bastian ran ahead. I didn't see no harm to it. I stayed with Miss Rosie, and I were watching some boats go under the bridge when she screamed. I looked around and there was no Master Bastian. When I looked down, sure enough, there he was in the water. But he were picked up in seconds. I'm right sorry, milady."

"I'm sure you cannot be blamed," said Judith, wondering why these strange accidents were being visited upon them.

"A man pushed him," said Rosie firmly. "I *saw* him."

Judith looked at her daughter, who was not in the habit of lying, or even exaggerating. "You saw someone push Bastian into the river?"

Rosie nodded vigorously. "He sort of threw him. Picked him up and tossed him over."

Judith could hardly believe what she was hearing. "What did the man do then?"

"He ran away."

"Could you tell what he looked like?"

Rosie shook her head. Judith looked at the footman. "Did you notice this man, George?"

"No, milady. I were taken up by watching them fish Master Bastian out of the river, and giving thanks when I saw he were all right. By the time I understood what Miss Rosie were saying, any man was gone."

Judith felt chilled. "Were there many people on the bridge? Would anyone else have seen?"

"There were only a few, milady, and none nearby with anything to say about it. One old biddy was going on about rascals who climbed on the parapets, but I'm sure he didn't do that."

Judith wondered if Rosie would lie about this strange attacker to cover up the fact that Bastian had been so foolish, but she knew she certainly wouldn't without much coaching, and this hardly seemed a preplanned adventure. "You must have some idea what this man looked like, Rosie. Was he big or small?"

"Just ordinary, Mama." She wrinkled her brow in powerful thought. "He looked like Papa Leander, I suppose."

Judith felt a chill of shock. "Like Papa Leander!" she echoed.

"Yes," said Rosie. "About that size, and dressed ever so nice."

Judith's heart steadied.

"And like Papa, too," added Rosie helpfully.

Judith decided there was nothing of use to be learned from Rosie except that the man had been a gentleman, and no ancient. It was all most peculiar. She took Rosie with her to see to Bastian, and found him scrubbing himself cheerfully in front of the kitchen fire, rather proud of his adventure now he was safe.

"Excuse me, my lady," said Addison faintly, "but what are we to do with Master Bastian's clothes?"

Judith considered the pungent, soggy pile in the corner. She hated to waste new clothes, but said, "Throw them away, Addison."

The ruler of the house passed on the order with a gesture, and the kitchen boy gathered up the garments and scurried off. Something about his manner made Judith think that it would all be washed and used, but she had no objection.

Like Hal Beaumont, she hated waste.

"Begging your pardon, milady," said Addison quietly, "but it is quite likely that Master Bastian swallowed some river water, and that could make him ill."

First Betty, now Bastian. "Bastian, do you think you swallowed any of the water?" Judith asked.

"No, Mama. George had just been saying how dirty the river is with all the city using it as a cesspool, so when I was falling I thought I'd better take a breath and keep my mouth shut. And I did." The pride drained out of his voice. "It was funny, Mama. It seemed to take forever to fall."

The thinness of it caught at her heart, and she hugged him. "I think you did marvelously, dear. Now, tell me. Did someone push you in?"

"Well of course they did," he said indignantly. "Did you think I'd jumped?"

"No, of course not," she said hurriedly, trying to hide her fear. "Do you know who?"

"No," said Bastian with a frown. "But do you know, Mama, all morning I kept seeing the glove man again."

"The glove man?"

"The one who lost his gloves yesterday. They fell

out of his pocket in Westminster Abbey, and so I ran
after him and gave them back. He was very grateful.
May we have the sweets now?''

Judith wondered if he were wandering in his mind.
''What sweets, dear?''

''The ones he gave us. Betty said we couldn't have
them without your permission. They were marzipan
fruits.''

''Well, she was ill and must have forgotten to ask . . .''
Judith trailed off under her horrified thoughts. She
swallowed, and struggled to remain calm. ''I'll ask
her when I go up. Bastian, you and Rosie are to stay
home for the rest of the day.''

Judith hurried off, wishing Leander was home. Was
it a terrible plot, or just two strange coincidences?
But it was *Leander* whose life was supposed to be in
danger. Oh, lord! What if he were even now under
attack?

''Addison! Do we know where the earl is?''

''I'm afraid not, my lady, but I could send round
to the clubs, and to Mister Cosgrove's office.''

''Do that please. Send a message that I need him
to come home as soon as possible.''

Judith ran up the stairs to Betty's attic room. The
woman was asleep, but Judith ruthlessly woke her.

''Milady. . . ?''

''Betty, did you eat any of the sweets that were given
to Bastian?''

The woman's face crumpled, and she began to cry.
''Oh, milady. I'm right sorry. I only had the one. And
I've been thinking . . . I know it's daft, but could it
have been them 'as made me sick?''

''It could indeed,'' said Judith grimly. ''What happened to the rest?''

''They're in my cloak pocket, milady.''

Judith found them, a gold net bundle of gaily colored marzipan fruits, most attractive to a child. She
was trembling with what might had been. Look at

what had happened to Betty from eating only one, and she was a grown woman. Her darling children could have *died*.

A knock on the door heralded the doctor. Judith quickly explained the course of events.

"Extremely strange," said the doctor, and took the sweets. "I will examine these, but if we are considering a noxious substance . . . Excuse me while I check my patient, Lady Charrington."

The examination was thorough. At the end, he said to Betty, "I believe you will do very well. I detect no weakness of the heart."

"Was it those sweets, then, sir?" the maid asked.

"I fear it could be so, but in that case, your action— improper though it was—may well have saved the children's lives."

Judith led the doctor downstairs and gave him a glass of wine, taking one herself to steady her nerves. "Would one of those sweets have killed a child?" she asked bluntly.

"I fear it might have been so, Lady Charrington."

"Do you have any idea what is in them?"

The man sipped his wine thoughtfully. "There are a number of possibilities, but my guess would be extract of foxglove. It is used medicinally to induce vomiting, and to steady the heart. The symptoms would fit. Lady Charrington, do you have any idea why anyone would try to harm your children?"

"No," Judith lied, and decided not to tell the doctor about the attack on Bastian.

Leander came in hurriedly. "What is it?" He looked alertly at the doctor. "Is Betty worse?"

The doctor explained the situation, and Leander's face became a watchful mask. "I see. It is most peculiar. I will look into this incident, but I fear it must be a case of a madman. The authorities must be informed. As we are leaving London tomorrow, at least our children cannot be at further risk."

As soon as the doctor was gone, he relaxed and let his worry show. "Struth, I never would have believed it. But what gain in harming the children?"

Judith spoke coldly. "Someone pushed Bastian off London Bridge today."

His eyes widened with shock. "Is he . . . ?"

"He's fine. He says they were followed today by the man who gave them the sweets." She was using the words like a bludgeon, but could not help herself.

Leander poured himself some wine and drank it down. "It makes no sense."

"All I know," snapped Judith, "is that my children are at risk because of you and your demented family. Perhaps they think Bastian is your true son and heir."

"They couldn't be so foolish."

"They seem capable of any kind of foolishness. After all, if they realized someone was down asking about diphtheria, they could have realized that trick had failed. What better way to delay us than to kill a child? A mere nothing to a Knollis, I suppose."

"Judith, it makes no sense," he repeated. "You're upset. I understand that—"

"*Upset!* That is to put it at its lowest, sir. I'm in a rage, and a good part of it is directed at you. You were not honest with me. If you'd told me my children could be endangered by your family squabbles, I wouldn't have married you for the Mint!"

"How could I know they would run mad?" he demanded, running his hands through his hair.

"They're your family!" Judith fired, and stormed off to guard her children.

Leander came to see them, and kept the tone light as he went over it with them, encouraging Bastian to see it as an adventure. Then, without further words with Judith, he went out again.

Judith's anger, which had been three parts terror, subsided, but she didn't totally absolve Leander. He had clearly not been honest about the extent of his family's wickedness. When Addison came to say that Mr. Rossiter was below, she denied herself. She was in no mood for guests, especially not Sebastian's brother.

Addison returned in a moment to apologize for the fact that while Mr. Rossiter was waiting, the new footman had gossiped about the accident on the bridge, and upset the boy's uncle. He had apparently been soothed by the news that they were all to leave town shortly for the safety of the West Country.

Safety, thought Judith. It was more like heading into the lion's den.

Chapter Sixteen

As Bastian seemed none the worse for his ducking, they set off the next day as planned.

Leander had talked this over with Judith the night before, offering to leave the children behind, and even suggesting that they all go somewhere else and let others investigate the problems. Judith had no intention of separating from her children, and she didn't feel anywhere would be safe. The only security was in confronting Leander's family and spiking their guns forever.

Leander agreed. "I have informed the magistrates," he said, "in case this should be a case of a wandering madman. I have also given all that we know to the Rogues, and they will pursue inquiries. They will check particularly whether young James Knollis, or any other of my cousins is in town."

Despite the fact that they were talking frankly, his manner, like hers, kept securely within a barrier of formality.

"Do you think we will be safe on the journey?" Judith asked.

"I'm not entirely sure we are unsafe here, but since we will be in the coach, and I do not intend to let any of you out of my sight, I do not see much danger. I'm taking George along, to supplement the hired coachman and postilions, just to be sure. He seems a competent young man, and assures me he is a good enough shot with a pistol."

Judith shivered. "As you said yourself, it takes so little to kill someone." At that moment, she wanted him to hold her, but the walls between them were too high.

"Outright, yes. It's more difficult to make it look like an accident, and that seems to be the intent here. If Bastian had come to grief, and Rosie hadn't been watching, wouldn't we all have assumed he must have climbed up onto the parapet and fallen?"

Judith took a deep breath. "That makes me feel a little better. I will be glad, however, when we expose your uncle and cousins, and put an end to this."

"As will I. Judith," said Leander with a troubled frown, "I am hoping that when we arrive in Somerset, you and the children will stay with a friend of mine while I go on to the Temple alone. Nicholas's place is only about thirty miles away."

Judith wanted to protest, to say that she must go with him, to somehow guard him, but her children must come first. "Of course," she said. "Another Rogue?"

"King Rogue," said Leander with the trace of a smile. "You'll like Nicholas, and I trust him to keep you all safe."

The children, sensitive to atmosphere, were rather subdued at the beginning of their journey, but they soon perked up and then became rambunctious. Judith would be heartily glad to have them in a stable place, and back into a routine before they were totally ruined.

The animals were with them. Since Blucher was

content to live mainly in Bastian's pocket, with occasional tours of his shoulders, Rosie demanded that Magpie be let out. The kitten, however, had killer instincts, and hissed and spat at the rat.

In the end, time out of confinement had to be rationed between the two, which satisfied Rosie, but angered Bastian.

Judith found she had a headache, and she wondered if Leander wished he'd never set eyes on the family. Now that they were not in accord, all the lighthearted fun seemed to have disappeared.

When they stopped for lunch, he would not let the children out of sight, which limited their exercise, so that they were still fidgety when they climbed back into the coach.

They started a fight about which side of the coach to sit on. Judith suggested she move so they could both sit on the same side. Then they fought about who should sit with her. Judith snapped at them to stop it, and they subsided into sullen silence.

Leander was preoccupied with fears for their safety.

He was in a hurry to get to the safety of the Delancys' house, and they pushed on to Andover on the first day, emerging in the gloom, stiff and ill-tempered. Judith and Leander had separate rooms.

By the next day the weather had taken a turn for the worse. It was overcast, and there was a freezing drizzle. Judith felt sorry for those traveling outside the coach.

"If we can make good speed, we could be at Redoaks today," said Leander. Judith wanted to protest such grueling haste, and yet she, too, would be glad to be at a house, and glad to have the task almost done.

When she tasted the tensions in the carriage, however, and saw the detachment Leander had wrapped about himself, when she thought of what Charles

Knollis had tried to do to her children, she was well on her way to giving in to hate.

The sky cleared as the day went on, but that meant it grew colder. Even in the carriage Judith and the children huddled in blankets; she could not imagine what it was like up on the box. At each change, Leander commanded hot bricks to put on the floor against their feet, and hot toddy for all, though the children's was well diluted. Even so, it made them sleepy as the day went on, and their fretfulness decreased.

As they left the post road—the light already fading, and the moon a mere sliver—Judith suddenly asked, "Is your friend expecting us?"

"I sent a rider on ahead," Leander said. "Did you think I wouldn't?"

"I'm not sure what to expect of you Rogues. What if it is not convenient? The Delaneys will not feel able to turn us away."

"Convenience doesn't enter into it," he said flatly. "If there had been no one at home, my messenger would have returned."

She could not like it. "How long is it since you last saw this Nicholas Delaney?"

He thought about it. "Oh, we bumped into one another in Salzburg three or four years ago. We've corresponded."

Judith opened her mouth then shut it again.

Leander noticed. "I turned up on Lucien's doorstep with no warning at all, and I'd not seen him since eighteen-ten. I haven't been in the country much."

Judith sighed. So she and her children were to be foisted on perfect strangers without so much as a please. It was going to be a very difficult visit.

There was just enough moon for them to push on after dark with the aid of lamps, but after ten hours of almost uninterrupted travel, Judith had begun to feel they would roll on forever when they finally turned in open gates. Through immense old trees which must give the house its name, she glimpsed a solid, square house with bright welcoming windows. She prayed it would be all right.

She gently woke the children. Rosie rubbed her eyes miserably, but Bastian leant out to see where they were.

By the time the coach had arrived at the door, it was open, spilling golden light into the cold dark, and people were emerging. Judith had a confused impression of a pleasant man and woman, and cheerful servants, as she and the children were bustled into the warmth. The overwhelming feeling, however, was ungrudging welcome.

They were in a brightly lit room, heated by a large fire, when she had opportunity to take in her companions. The children were sitting on a sofa, being talked to by a handsome, auburn-haired woman. Leander was in conference with a blond man, presumably Nicholas Delaney. Leander looked, she noted, as if a burden had been lifted, and she knew the grueling journey had been as hard for him. Had he really thought they might be attacked?

"Lady Charrington?"

Judith looked up to see that her hostess had taken a seat beside her.

"You must be exhausted," said Eleanor Delaney. "Your children must truly be tired for they are admitting it, and say they only want a little something to eat before their beds. I thought to order bread and milk for them if they like it."

"Yes," said Judith gratefully. "That would be just the thing."

"And there will be food laid out for you in the dining room in a trice, but I'm sure you would like some tea."

Eleanor went off to give orders, and Judith went

to her weary children. "This seems a very pleasant house," she said. "I'm sure we'll like it here."

"Why can't we go to the Temple, Mama?" Bastian asked, almost with a whine in his voice.

"We can, and we will, but this is far enough for one day. Besides, Papa Leander is not sure his relatives will make us welcome, as they have lived there for so long. He wants to handle that before we arrive. It will only take a few days." She decided to give their thoughts a different turn. "When we arrive, it will be time to prepare for Christmas. We will have to make up our decorations, and cut vast quantities of fir, and holly, and ivy, to decorate the house. We'll need to see if we can find mistletoe, too."

"I'm good at finding mistletoe, Mama," said Bastian, brightening.

"Yes, I know, but this will be a new place to explore, so you won't know all the best trees."

She turned as Leander led their host to them. "Judith, may I present Nicholas Delaney. Nicholas, this is my wife, and my new children, Bastian and Rosie."

Bastian and Rosie struggled to their feet to make their bows.

"Trust Lee to do things with such panache," said Nicholas Delaney with a smile for them all. "Not just a marriage, but a ready-made family. You are very welcome," he said, and made the words utterly convincing. "Did I hear some talk of mistletoe? Tomorrow we were planning a foraging expedition ourselves, and we need lots of help."

"I'm good at finding mistletoe," said Bastian proudly. "Apple trees are the best, you know."

"Are they? Well, we have an orchard, and if we had someone to climb the trees . . ."

Judith looked at Leander and smiled. He smiled back. It was going to be all right.

The children ate their bread and milk, and then

were tucked up in warm beds in adjoining rooms. Judith took some soup, but then sought her bed herself. She found she and Leander were to share a room and bed, but the matter was overwhelmed by exhaustion, and she was asleep in minutes.

In the library of Redoaks, Leander and Nicholas shared a bowl of hot punch. "So," said Nicholas, "you think your family is behind these attacks on the boy?"

"What else can I think? Though it convinces me they are mad."

"It would be lunacy," Nicholas agreed. "And almost beyond belief. Are you saying the whole family is ready for the asylum? Even as a means of delaying you it makes no sense, and would be unspeakably callous."

Leander rubbed his hand wearily over his face. "I don't know, Nicholas. It's enough to drive me mad, or do you think it runs in the family anyway?"

"No," said Nicholas plainly, and topped up Leander's cup.

Leander sighed. "Perhaps they meant no real harm to the child. After all, the poison only made the maid ill, and one would expect that the boatmen would fish Bastian out of the river. A sick child would have tied us in London for another week or so."

"It would link in with the story of diphtheria," said Nicholas, "and I have found lowly minds prone to tread the same rut. . . . Still, it doesn't sit right. After all, from what you said, the poison that made the maid ill could have killed a child, and the simple fall from the bridge could have stunned the boy if he'd landed badly. Then he could well have drowned before anyone could reach him. At the very best, your villains have a careless way with human life."

Leander took a deep draft of the potent punch. "A family is a mixed blessing."

"Is it?" asked Nicholas with a trace of amusement. "Yours sounds like an unmitigated curse."

"I mean Bastian and Rosie. I never counted on the weight of the responsibility. If one of them is hurt because of me, I will never forgive myself."

"They'll be safe here. It's you I am concerned about."

"I can take care of myself."

"Haven't you always? But you could be in danger. I'd go with you except that I think I should stay here on guard."

"Assuredly. I'll take my man, George. He's a handy character." Leander looked into his cup, then up. "Nicholas, if something should happen to me, you'll take care of Judith and the children, won't you?"

"I'm offended that you need to ask. I promise more. If you are killed, I'll pursue your demented family to the jaws of hell. Not one of them will benefit from the crime, I give you my word."

It was simply said, but Leander knew it was a binding promise. He took great comfort from that.

Leander woke the next morning beside Judith in the bed. She was still fast asleep, and there were shadows under her eyes that hadn't been there when he married her. He put out a hand to brush a tendril of dark hair off her cheek, then halted the gesture. He mustn't wake her. She needed rest.

He was sorry they were at outs, and would like to untangle all their problems immediately, but this wasn't the time or place. It certainly wasn't the time for lovemaking, though the warm curves of her body close to his were engendering a distinct inclination. Time enough for that when they were settled at last.

At home.

He savored it in his mind. Temple Knollis, not as the bleak museum he had visited, but as a living home. Temple Knollis at Christmas. Children running through the corridors, filling the air with laughter. Judith hanging green garlands on carved and gilded banisters, and a punch bowl ever ready, so the tang of fir and pine blended with lemons and spice. Servants and family gathered to sing carols by candlelight. Perhaps local people coming up to sing for mince pies and wassail.

His home.

But first, he thought with a sigh, he had to win it, and the sooner the better.

He eased out of the bed and went to shave and dress.

Judith woke with his leaving; the bed beside her was still warm. She heard him in the dressing room. Would he leave without a word?

She hastened out of bed and dressed quickly, even though the only garments to hand were her travel-weary ones. When she heard him leave the dressing room to go downstairs she hurried to join him.

He turned at the top of the stairs. "Did I wake you? I'm sorry."

"I always rise early," she said, feeling remarkably ill at ease.

"I hear noise below, so I judge breakfast to be available." He took her hand to lead her down, and the warm comfort of it spread.

"I'm sorry," she said softly.

"What for?"

"For blaming you for Bastian's accidents."

He stopped in the hall to face her. "But it must have been because of me. There's nothing in your life to summon violence."

"Even so," said Judith, "it was not your fault. It was just that I was so scared. The children are all I have. No," she said, distressed, "I didn't mean that!"

He gathered her in for a hug. "I know, Judith.

Don't distress yourself. I'll clear it up, and then we can settle to bucolic happiness.''

She looked up. "And will you really like that?" she asked rather doubtfully.

His eyes sent a warm message as he gently kissed her lips. "I expect to like it very much indeed."

A strange squawk made them spring apart, and they turned to see Nicholas carrying a young child. "Meet Arabel," he said ruefully. "I would have waited discreetly, but she has no manners, and wants her breakfast." He led the way into the breakfast parlor, and put the child down.

She was already walking, though with the wide-legged uncertainly of a beginner. She happily trotted over to Leander and grabbed his leg.

"A terribly forward wench," said her father. "We'll have great trouble with her. She also insists on rising absurdly early, and so we have reorganized our household accordingly. Come along, Bel," he said. "Your egg will be here any moment."

The child looked around and launched herself on a laughing, shaky voyage toward a chair which had been raised on a platform so she would be level with the table. Her father settled her there, and gave her some fingers of buttered toast to work on.

Judith watched this with amazement. She had never imagined a father looking after a child in such a way. When Arabel gaily hurled a piece of toast across the table, Nicholas broke off what he was saying. "No, sweetheart. You must not do that." He took the plate away, and resumed his conversation.

Arabel stared at the plate, then made demanding noises.

Nicholas turned back. "Very well. But you must not throw your food." The plate was returned, and the child settled to eating the toast, albeit in a rather messy manner.

"Does she actually understand what you say?" asked Judith in surprise.

"I have no idea," said Nicholas cheerfully, "but acting on that assumption seems to generally have good results."

A maid came in with a mashed-up egg in a bowl for the child, and hot dishes of bacon, eggs, sausage, and beef for the adults. By that time Eleanor Delaney had arrived. She sat on the other side of Arabel, and helped steer most of the egg into the child's mouth, but it was clear that Nicholas would do as much of the work as she.

Judith felt her whole picture of life was being turned on its head, but she knew this wasn't the normal way to behave. Why, highborn children rarely appeared in adult company until they were old enough to behave. Did the girl not have a nurse?

Eleanor spoke to Judith. "I thought it best to leave your children to have their sleep out, Judith. A maid is sitting up with them, and will bring them down when they are ready."

Nicholas was helping Arabel to drink from a spouted cup, but said to Leander, "You probably should delay your departure until they are up to say farewell."

"They know I'm leaving."

"Even so."

To Judith's astonishment, Leander appeared to take this as a kind of order. She eyed Nicholas Delaney surreptitiously as she ate.

King Rogue. That seemed to be the case in truth.

He was good looking, like all the Rogues, though there was nothing spectacular about his appearance. It was more something in his warm, brown eyes, and something else indefinable that could be called charm. That, however, implied a facile, superficial quality, whereas Nicholas Delaney deserved the word deep.

She found she resented the influence he appeared to have on her husband.

"They won't mind you leaving without seeing them," she said firmly. "I will explain."

At that point, the issue became irrelevant, as Bastian and Rosie, neatly scrubbed, came cautiously into the room. Both of them lit with interest at the sight of Arabel.

Nicholas performed introductions, and Judith would have sworn the toddler smiled directly at each child, a smile of astonishing welcome. This was a very strange household.

Bastian and Rosie were settled with food, and Judith was relieved to see them on their best behavior, though Rosie giggled when Arabel waved a spoon and flung some egg onto her father's face. Eleanor did not appear alarmed. Nicholas merely gave his laughing daughter a look, and wiped it off.

When Bastian understood that Leander was leaving for the Temple, he said, "I do wish I could go with you, Papa Leander."

"Not this time, Bastian."

Bastian glanced at him. "Will the man who pushed me in the river be there?"

"I don't know. I hope so. I'll draw his cork. Any more details of what he looked like? Or the man who gave you the sweets?"

Bastian shook his head. "I didn't see the man who pushed me. The man in Westminster Abbey was all niffy-naffy. High shirt points and a fancy cravat, with a hat tilted down so I couldn't see much of his face. He just looked ordinary really, though I thought perhaps I knew him from somewhere."

That didn't sound like young James Knollis, thought Judith, for he had dressed with country simplicity.

"Did you perhaps think he looked like me?" Leander asked, pursuing the same line, though there was little family resemblance either.

Bastian looked at him and emphatically shook his head.

"Well, it was probably some complete stranger behaving in a peculiar manner, but while I'm gone you are to stay close to the house unless you are with an adult."

"But I was going to hunt for mistletoe."

Nicholas responded to that. "Don't think you are going to leave us behind on that trip, young man."

This sense of encircling peril terrified Judith, but she found she was more terrified for Leander, setting off alone, than for her children, safe in this house. "Leander," she said suddenly. "I want to come with you." Then she shook her head. "Oh, how foolish. I cannot leave the children with the Delancys. . . ." She was feeling a perfect widgeon.

"We don't mind, if Bastian and Rosie don't," said Eleanor.

To Judith's surprise, Bastian said very firmly, "I think Mama should go."

She looked at Leander, who said, "I don't think so. It could be dangerous. . . ."

"Precisely why I should go with you. An accident to a man alone could be believed. To the two of us, much less so."

"On that basis," said Leander sharply, "we should take the children, too."

"No," said Judith sharply, then collected herself. "But I would feel much better if I were with you, and perhaps I can help with your family. I have more experience than you with families."

Leander frowned, but nodded. "Very well. I confess, I would welcome someone by my side."

"A helpmeet," said Judith softly.

" 'It is not good that the man should be alone,' "

quoted Nicholas from the Bible. " 'I will make him a helpmeet for him.' I think it an excellent idea."

As soon as it was agreed on, Judith began to have second thoughts, but she knew she couldn't bear to see Leander heading into danger, and wait behind. She was surprised, however, by the ease with which the children had accepted the plan.

When she was ready to leave, warm in her Russian mantle, Judith asked Bastian why he had been so set on her going.

"You'll make sure he comes back, Mama."

For a moment she thought he meant she would keep him safe, which seemed ridiculously optimistic, but then she realized that the children were still not sure of their future. It had been an unsettled time, and they still seemed to think that it might disappear like fairy gold.

She hugged them both. "Marriages can't be broken, dears. We'll be back in a few days then we'll all go on to the Temple for our first Temple Christmas."

Chapter Seventeen

They made the journey in Nicholas's curricle, with George up behind. It was cold, but swathed in wool and fur Judith did not mind it. Her nerves were chilled, however, for she did not know what to expect, and half feared a pistol shot from every bush.

The journey was uneventful, however, and in early afternoon they crested a gentle hill to see Temple Knollis on its promontory. The day was overcast, so no magic lights played over the dusky-pink stone, and yet the beauty was there all the same. With its perfect proportions and turrets, it was a fairy palace reflected in a glassy lake.

A drive wove through parkland which looked rather bleak and neglected, up to the causeway which led through an arched gateway into the large court-yard.

Though the park had no wall to mark its boundaries and hide the house from the road, there was a gatehouse, built in miniature of the Temple. It was empty and clearly deserted. The blank windows gave Judith a chill down the spine.

They rolled down the potholed, graveled drive. On

either side, the parkland was as neglected as it looked, though sheep were busily keeping the meadow neat.

There was no one to be seen. Judith told herself that wasn't surprising in December when there was little outside work to be done, but she wondered if the family had already fled, and the staff dispersed. In many ways she would be glad of it, but she wondered in what state they would find the house.

There were gates in the gateway, but Judith guessed they were never closed. Instead of going through them, Leander turned the curricle to follow a carriage path that went along the outside of the walls.

"Where are you going?" she asked.

"It looks as if we'll have to fend for ourselves," he said, "so we might as well go straight to the stables."

"But where are the stables? There are no extra buildings here."

He pulled up beside wide double doors in the wall, and George jumped off to open them. "There are chambers all around the wall," Leander explained. "Storerooms, dairies, tack rooms, stables, et cetera. They all have openings into the courtyard, but the main openings are onto this lane. So that the perfect courtyard need not be disturbed by servants, don't ye know." He steered the carriage into the relative warmth of a carriage house, and George closed the door behind.

Judith almost wanted to protest that they might need a quick escape, but brought herself to order. No matter what horrible tricks they had been up to in London, the family were hardly likely to attempt a cold-blooded massacre.

Anyway, with any luck, they were gone. She prayed earnestly that they be gone.

The carriage house could hold ten vehicles, but the only inhabitants were an ancient traveling Berlin, and a dogcart. Leander assisted Judith down and they went to explore.

Next door was a tack room, and beyond that the stables. One horse, a sturdy cob, turned curiously to look at them, alone among twenty or more stalls.

"There were half a dozen or more horses here when I visited," said Leander, going over to the cob. "But this fellow is being cared for, so there must be someone about."

"I don't suppose they'd leave the place entirely empty, would they? I must say, this is a very fine stable." Judith looked around at the Dutch-tile walls, and a ceiling whimsically painted with a scene of Pegasus heaven.

"Nothing too good for the Temple," said Leander dryly. "Come on, let's explore and discover the worst."

They left George to care for the horses, and began to work their way through the wall chambers of Temple Knollis. "All the rooms link," said Leander, as they passed through a fodder room. His voice echoed in the tiled magnificence. And this was simply the workrooms. "Absolutely no need for servants to venture into the courtyard, as you'll see."

Judith peered through a grimy window at the courtyard. "It's so big. A little enclosed park. It must be pretty when all the plants are in bloom."

"Yes, it is."

"And," she pointed out, "I'm sure the servants appreciate not having to go outside in cold or wet weather."

He laughed. "Ever practical. I'm sure you're right. Come on."

They passed though rooms used for storage, and then rooms used to keep fruit. Judith stepped aside to inspect the racks of apples. "No bad fruit," she said. "These haven't been neglected for long."

"The family were here only days ago."

A grape room, with grape bunches being kept fresh in their glass holders, and then a larger door. "The house," Leander said. "Though only, if my memory serves me, the servants' hall, and kitchen. Do you want to go that way, or do you want to nip through the courtyard and enter by the front door?"

For undefinable reasons, Judith felt that Leander should enter his home for the first real time through the front door, and said so.

"Right." He swung open the narrow door onto the courtyard. Judith walked through and looked around admiringly. It was a beautiful space even on a dull day—a private, enclosed heaven. The walls were not square, but an irregular shape, probably following the peninsular, and they were covered by ivy, and the skeleton branches of roses, laburnum, and other plants, so that they seemed a part of nature, not the work of man.

One little tower contained a dovecote, and she could hear the throaty cooings of the birds. She smiled at Leander. "It's lovely."

"Yes," he admitted, "but at what cost?" He led the way up to the carved oak doors and hesitated. "I'll be damned if I'll knock for admittance to my own home." He turned the knob and opened the door. He smiled with a touch of his boyish humor, and swung Judith into his arms to carry her into the house.

She was laughing when he put her down, but her laughter turned to astonishment when she looked around. "My goodness."

"Exactly."

Judith would have been hard-pressed to express what she thought of Temple Knollis. It was undoubtedly beautiful. The entrance hall ran the depth of the house, with large windows at the end letting in light, and an exquisite view of the river. The upper lights of the window were stained-glass flowers in shades of yellow and gold, which cast magical lights about the room.

The floor was a gold-swirled marble, and the same marble formed slender pillars along the length of the room. Embrasures in the painted walls held white marble statues; plinths held exquisite vases in jewel-bright colors. Numerous doors led off this chamber, the wood the rich gold and black of amboyna. To one side, a wide staircase curved gracefully up to yet greater glories.

"My goodness," Judith said again.

"Extraordinary, isn't it?" remarked Leander, strolling into this magnificence. "One has to admire my grandfather's taste, and then wonder why one doesn't like it."

Judith knew she was afraid to touch anything for fear of breaking it. She looked at one of the Etruscan vases on a plinth. "These will have to be moved before the children come here."

He turned to it. "I think you'll find . . ." He tugged it, and it didn't move. "Wired down, you see. But not proof against a flying ball, for example."

"Oh, I would never let them play in here."

"But that's the point," he said, his voice echoing as if in a church. "The whole place is like this. You saw the stables. Neither you, nor I, nor the children, are going to live in a museum." He looked around. "I must admit, however, that nothing seems to be missing."

"These are hardly the most transportable items."

"True. Let me think . . . This way, I believe. . . ." He led the way to a door, and opened it upon a saloon of some kind.

Perhaps, thought Judith, it was the drawing room, but it was hardly the place for comfortable family evenings. Gilded pillars divided tapestry-covered walls. The ceiling was an amazing trompe l'oeil view of the heavens. The furniture was of the finest quality, covered with expensive silk, and looking as if it had just come from Waring and Gillow. She would be afraid to sit on it.

Perhaps the room would be the better for fires in the three fireplaces. The whole house was deeply chilled; she kept her hands tucked well inside her muff.

Leander looked up and said, "The third prophet from the right is apparently my grandfather, forever looking down on the wonders he hath wrought."

Judith looked up at the sharp-faced man with flowing hair, and shuddered.

Leander walked across the room, and opened another door. "Ah, yes."

Judith followed and found she was in a plate room. Glass cases displayed gold and silver bowls and dishes for all occasions. "Nothing missing as far as I can see," said Leander. "Stranger, and stranger."

Judith remembered her words to Rosie, and said, "Will we have to eat off golden plates after all?"

"Of course not." Leander led the way into the next room, where ranks of china—English, French, and Oriental—were displayed.

He put his hands on his hips and surveyed it all. "The place appears to have been abandoned untouched. I can only assume—"

"And what do you think you're doing?" a voice demanded.

Judith and Leander turned sharply to face a young man armed with a pistol. It was young James Knollis. Judith's heart leapt into her throat, and she thought of throwing herself before Leander.

But James let the pistol drop, and paled. "Oh lord," he said.

"Precisely," said Leander, and removed the pistol from the young man's hand. "When did you get back here?"

James went from pale to red. "I came straight back

from Winchester, sir. I'm sorry about that. I couldn't think what else to do."

Leander uncocked the weapon. "Why was there any need to do anything?"

James looked between them and sighed. "You'd best come talk to Mother."

"Your mother is still here?"

"We're all still here," said James with a touch of bitterness. "What choice do we have?"

Leander and Judith shared a puzzled look and followed James as he led through room after room, and into the servants' quarters. It was hard to believe James a murderer. And why was his mother in the kitchen?

The whole family was in the kitchen.

James ushered Leander and Judith in, saying, "Cousin Leander, everyone, and his wife. In other words, Lord and Lady Charrington."

There was a general air of consternation in the crowded room, but no threat that Judith could detect. All the same, she was glad Leander still had the pistol in his casual, but doubtless competent, hold.

"Good day," he said smoothly. "I must assume you are my aunt and cousins. Where is Uncle Charles?"

The woman, Lucy Knollis, rose slowly to her feet. She was a sturdy woman with a strong jaw and very fine eyes. Her face was guarded. "Up, children, and make your bows to your cousin."

The nine youngsters at the table—from a girl of about sixteen, to a little one of about three—struggled up and bowed or curtsied. Most of them were boys and bowed. The family almost rivaled that of King George for fecundity.

Lucy looked directly at Leander, with no hint of apology. "Charles is in bed, of course. He's pretty much bedridden, and it'll only agitate him to know you're here, but Ill take you to him if you insist."

The kitchen was cozy, even hot. Leander assisted

Judith out of her fur mantle, and shrugged out of his greatcoat. "I'll insist on nothing until I've some idea what is going on, Aunt." He pulled two extra chairs up to the long table for himself and Judith, then said, "Would you care to tell me why Cousin James tried to frighten us away with tales of diphtheria, and why you are camped out in the kitchen?"

Once everyone was seated again, the children set to their food—a hearty stew with dumplings.

Lucy didn't answer his question, but said, "Would you care for some stew, my lord? It's all your providing anyway."

"Yes, please," he said, and Judith said the same. She was hungry after their journey. She wondered whether to prompt him about George, but doubted he had forgotten. Perhaps he was keeping the footman a secret, in case of need. She suddenly wondered if the soup would be poisoned, but was reassured when one of the older boys asked for more and had his bowl refilled from the same pot that had filled theirs.

The stew was very good, but it was clearly peasant fare, and contrasted absurdly with the gilded palace they had just walked through, and indeed with the magnificence of the kitchen in which they sat. Judith had heard that the kitchens of the Regent's Pavilion in Brighton were ornate; he obviously had much in common with the first Earl of Charrington.

The kitchen was large and beautifully proportioned, with long windows to let in light, and high ceilings to cope with smoke and steam. Here again the walls were tiled, and the tiles formed handsome pictures of fish, game, and cheeses. Great racks and shelves held dishes of all kinds.

Leander took a few spoonfuls of his stew and then said, "Are you going to answer my questions, Aunt?"

"I would prefer to wait until the children are finished, my lord."

He accepted it calmly. "Very well. Perhaps we would be easier if you were to call me Leander. I am not that much older than your oldest son. Or nephew, if that suits you better."

This did seem to fluster Lucy. "I will try, Lord . . . Leander."

"And you must certainly call me Judith," said Judith, "for I am unused to titles anyway."

"Aye," said Lucy. "Your marriage was not so long ago, was it?"

"A mere two weeks." Judith noted that Lucy seemed to be under no strange apprehension that Bastian was Leander's son.

Lucy wiped the hands and faces of the two youngest, who had finished. "I understood that you had children, Judith."

"Yes, we have left them with friends for a day or two."

Lucy flashed them a shrewd look. "Ah."

Judith was surprised to think she could like Lucy Knollis very much. She was an intelligent, strong woman with a fine family.

"How old are they?" asked Lucy.

"Bastian is eleven. Rosie is six."

"Well, that's nice. My Arthur here is eleven, and little Elizabeth is nearly six. They'll be able to play together."

Judith smiled but said nothing. Were they aiming to stay then? There could be trouble ahead.

"Bastian is to go to Harrow soon," she said. "What schools have your boys attended?"

Lucy's face hardened. "The older ones go to Blundell's in Tiverton. We don't care to send them far from home."

"What a shame," said Leander. "There'd be no question, then, of Arthur going to Harrow with Bastian. It would be good for him to have a friend there. And the younger boys in turn, of course."

Lucy looked dumbfounded. "Well ... I don't know, I'm sure ..."

"We'll have to see if they get along," said Leander smoothly. Judith recognized that he was into the handling mode, and knew the family had no hope. Except his intentions seemed to be benign. Was he going to let them stay on after all? Judith was not happy at the thought of trying to make a home out of the Temple with this tribe underfoot, doubtless objecting to every change she made.

Leander spoke again. "Stainings is not so far away that they will have trouble getting together, I think."

This reference to his uncle's inherited property was slid in so smoothly, it took a moment for it to register with Judith, but then she glanced quickly at Lucy. She caught no trace of pique.

"No, it's but a mile." There was some reservation in it, though, and Judith wished she knew why.

The meal came to an end, and the children departed. They all seemed to have tasks. In some cases it was to look after the little ones, but in others it was a maintenance job around the house. What had happened to the servants?

James stayed behind, seating himself pugnaciously at the table, as if expecting to be sent away. If his father was sick, he doubtless felt it was his place to support his mother.

Lucy poured strong tea for them all, then sat, stiff backed at the head of the table. "I won't apologize, for I don't see that we've done much to apologize for."

"Mother—" said James.

Leander stopped him with a gesture. "Young James here sent us on a wild-goose chase back to London with his talk of diphtheria."

"I can't see as it's done you great harm, Nephew. The truth is, as you'll doubtless have realized, that we wanted time. I had hopes to set things straight,

or at least make head and tail of them. . . ." Her
strength wavered a little. "The truth is that I've no
notion of business. How could I have, who've had
her hands full of babies these twenty years?"

"True. But is my uncle so ill he cannot handle
business?"

Mother and son exchanged glances. "Not in his
opinion. But he's stuck in his bed, and half paralyzed,
so we let him give us orders and then we do as we
think best."

"What's the problem, then?" Leander asked
calmly. "The house seems to be in fine shape."

"Oh yes," Lucy said bitterly, "it's in fine shape, all
right. It's the only thing that is." She fixed Leander
with her handsome dark eyes. "You must have found
out by now that there's money missing."

"There do seem to be discrepancies. . . ."

"Not a penny has been stolen," she said harshly.
"Not a penny. It's all gone into this damn palace!"

Judith saw the woman was close to tears, and knew
she wasn't someone who cried easily.

"What mother's saying," interjected James, "is that
Father has been fiddling the accounts to get money
for the Temple. He's let Stainings, which should be
our home, and even taken a mortgage on it. And all
because you wouldn't come home."

"I would have been here a week ago if you had
not interfered."

"What's a week?" the young man asked bitterly.
"By then, we were desperately trying to tidy up some
of Father's shady dealings."

"Shady?"

"I don't know what else you could expect," said
Lucy, "when you wouldn't take up your responsibilities. We couldn't leave here until you came to take
over. We weren't allowed to stop the work until it
was finished. Once the old earl was dead, though,
there wasn't the money to pay for it, as the income

was first your father's, then yours. So my husband started altering accounts, finding ways to divert money to pay the bills. . . . Then the steward of the Cumberland estate started talking of investigations and accountings, and my Charles realized he'd messed things up so well he'd be hard-pressed to prove his honesty."

She sighed. "That was when he told me what a pickle we were in. The work was finished, so the worst of the outlay was over. We dismissed the servants, and cut back all the expenses, trying to balance the books. Then you announced you were coming, and he had the seizure. Since then, James and I have been toiling over those dratted books, trying to make them make sense, but I don't know . . . If I looked at them afresh, I'd swear we'd squirreled away a fortune. . . ."

Leander looked at the ceiling and shook his head. "Didn't it occur to you to just tell me about this?"

"Why should it? We didn't know you—still don't if it comes to that—and the only thing Charles knew about your father was that he was a top-lofty sort who'd run through his wife's money, and would squeeze every penny he could from the Knollis properties for his silly gallivanting. Charles fair begged his brother to come back and take this place off our hands when the old man died, but not him."

"You should have written to explain all this to me."

"But you had to be here!" exclaimed young James. "Haven't you even read the bloody will?"

Leander looked sharply at him, but his voice was level when he said, "Clearly, not carefully enough. Does it stipulate that I must live here to inherit? No one said anything of that to me."

"Not that exactly," said James more moderately. "But Father isn't allowed to leave until you come here to take over. Grandfather didn't seem to think you would, and he didn't want the place abandoned.

Father was also responsible for ensuring the work in hand was finished. The penalty was that he could not receive Stainings if he did not fulfill the conditions of the will.''

"But why on earth did he not tell me this? I understood that clause of the will only to mean that I must be alive to inherit, not that I had to be here. I would have come down and taken charge.''

"He says he wrote to you. Do you say you never received it?''

Leander looked a little uncomfortable. "I received a letter begging me to come to the Temple. It said nothing of the will.''

"So, why didn't you come?''

"I did,'' he admitted, "but incognito, as a visitor. You must understand, I was raised with some strange notions about this place.''

"As were we all,'' said James bitterly. "It's swallowed up my parents' lives, and it's well on the way to swallowing up us, too.''

"Not anymore,'' said Leander briskly. "It's a house, no more than that. Do I understand you would be happy to move to Stainings?''

Lucy looked up with a glimmer of hope. "More than you can imagine! Do you mean you aren't going to prosecute?''

"For what?'' asked Leander. "The management has been unusual, but I believe nothing has been taken. I'm only sorry this misunderstanding has cost my uncle his health. Tell me, has he loved this place as my grandfather did?''

Lucy frowned. "No, I wouldn't say that. But he's conscientious to a fault, my Charlie. He felt we couldn't leave the old man alone, and so we stayed on and helped make this place what it is. Never cared for it myself, and it always seemed a waste, but *doing it right* became the issue with him. He always thought it'd be finished soon, and then we could live a normal life. He knew he was to get Stainings and thought his father would give it him as soon as the Temple was finished. But the years just dragged on and the place never was finished. . . . Have you any idea how hard it's been to raise ten children here?"

Judith spoke up. "But haven't you been living in the house?"

Lucy shook her head. "Lord no. Old Lord Charrington wouldn't have them around, and anyway, Temple Knollis had to be perfect, see? Every mark, every blemish, had to be repaired or replaced. The job would never have been done if the children had been allowed to run around. We have rooms in the East wall, and the children spent most of their time with the servants. Once the staff were gone, it was easier to move mostly into here."

"Oh, you poor woman. I don't know how we can ever make it up to you."

"Just take this place off our shoulders, dear." Lucy smiled. "You mustn't think it was all so bad. The children had the park to run in. They could boat and fish in the river, and they've plenty of family hereabouts. And Charles and me have had many good times. We had love, see. Well, of course you do, newly wed and all . . . I'm sorry though, to be offloading this place onto you. I hope you can make it a home, but I wouldn't know how to go about it."

She pushed herself up from the table. "Now, I suppose you'd better see Charles. Try not to upset him."

Leander's uncle was a big-boned man, with a pugnacious jaw, but he soon relaxed when he realized Leander meant him no harm. His speech was unclear, and one arm was limp, but the visit seemed to brighten his eyes.

Lucy lovingly straightened his sheet. "We'll be at Stainings in days, love. How fortunate Colonel Manners just left, and we haven't replaced him. A home of our own at last.''

Charles Knollis's good hand curled around his wife's and he smiled.

"Now," said Lucy to Leander, "I suppose you'll be wanting a bed for the night. There's none aired."

Leander agreed, but Judith had a frightening thought. She touched Leander's arm, and when he glanced at her she whispered. "These people clearly had nothing to do with Bastian."

His mind was on other matters. "Some madman, I suppose."

"I don't know . . . Leander, have we time to get back to Redoaks today?"

He looked at her sharply. She thought he might take her to task again for being overprotective, but he said, "Yes. Why don't we? I've no desire to sleep in a chilly bed. From the sounds of it, none but my grandfather's have ever been slept in at all. What a ridiculous place this is."

They arranged with Lucy for servants to be hired, and the house to be made as ready as possible for their return in a few days.

"I'll do that, Nephew, and there's many hereabouts who need the work. But will it be all right for us to move into Stainings? I'd dearly love to have Christmas in our own home.

"Of course. I can understand your feelings, for I share them. I, too, want to have Christmas in my own home. I'm deeply sorry for all the problems my branch of the family has caused yours."

Lucy smiled. "Well, that's family for you, lad. I'm looking forward to having you here, and meeting your wife's children."

As Judith and Leander walked back through the magnificent house, Judith thought it would certainly be a labor of Hercules to make the Temple into a home, and fill it with Christmas cheer, but she would do it for Leander. She rejoiced that he now had family of his own. Her main preoccupation, however, was to be with her children just in case the two attacks had not been random madness.

Chapter Eighteen

They left George to help in the house, and rolled off at a brisk pace.

"I'm sure Bastian is safe," said Leander. "Nicholas will take good care of him, and there is no reason for anyone to wish him harm."

Deep in her muff, Judith's hands were clasped tight. "I know. And yet I cannot see those two attacks as chance. If some lunatic was wandering London giving children poisoned sweets, we would surely have heard of it. And for the same man to pursue Bastian, and push him in the river . . . Oh, Leander, I am most dreadfully afraid. Can we not go faster?"

"Not without risking an accident. Try to be calm."

Judith tried, since railing at Leander was hardly fair, but her mother's instinct was screaming in a way she had never experienced before. Was it just overblown imagination, or was there a reason behind it?

Frost had rutted the roads, and as the light faded, a mist grew so thick that they could scarcely see the road in front of the horses. Leander had to slow down, rather than speed up. It took nearly four hours to return to Redoaks, and Judith was frantic. When she first saw the tall trees and the handsome house with lights glimmering though the mist, she took a deep breath of relief.

She smiled at Leander. "I fear I've been letting my imagination run away with me."

He smiled back. "I can appreciate your concern. But all our problems are over."

By the time they arrived at the door, a groom was there to take the vehicle, and Nicholas was running out to meet them.

"Lee, I'm sorry, but Bastian's disappeared."

"No!" wailed Judith.

Leander helped her into the house. "Where? When?"

"Just minutes ago," said Nicholas. "I'm raising a search, but we can't get sense yet out of Rosie."

"Let me," said Judith, and ran to where she could hear her daughter crying. She found her in the morning room, in Eleanor's arms. Eleanor looked up with concern and relief at the sight of Judith. "Judith, I'm so sorry. They were playing in here, and now he's gone. We never thought there would be danger in the house!"

Judith took Rosie. "Hush, Mama's here. You must stop wailing, Rosie, and tell us what happened to Bastian."

Rosie tried to speak through gulping sobs. All that emerged was Papa and ghost.

"Ghost?" asked Judith, pushing her daughter ruthlessly away. "There are no such things as ghosts, Rosie. This is no time for make-believe. Were you playing a game? Is Bastian hiding?"

Rosie hiccupped, and her blue eyes were immense. "But it *was,* Mama. It was Papa's *ghost.* All in white like in the play. And he took Bastian, and he's dead, too, now! I *tried* to stop him!" She burst into tears again.

Judith hugged the crying child, and looked at the others in bewildered horror.

"Forgive me, Judith," said Nicholas, "but is there any possibility that your husband is not dead?"

"None at all. He died of pneumonia, and I myself helped lay out his body."

"Then who might look like him?"

Judith suddenly remembered Rosie saying the man who'd pushed Bastian off the bridge looked like Papa. Had she meant more than it would appear? She pushed the girl away again. "Rosie, did Papa's ghost look at all like the man on the bridge in London?"

Rosie gulped and thought about it. She nodded. "But he had darker hair. The man on the bridge."

Judith looked at the others. "Sebastian has a brother. He looks a little like him, with darker hair." She looked back at Rosie. "Now, Rosie, tell us calmly exactly where you were, and what happened. I assure you, it wasn't a ghost, just someone playing a trick."

The child knuckled her eyes. "I don't like these kinds of tricks, Mama."

"Neither do I, and we're going to put a stop to it. Tell us all about it."

"We were in here playing with the soldier." Judith saw a brightly painted Grenadier lying on its side on the carpet. "There was a tapping on the French doors. Bastian opened them, and it was Papa! It sounded just like Papa!" She began to cry again, and Judith soothed her.

She looked up at the others. "Timothy Rossiter has a voice very like his brother's. It startled me." She turned back to the girl. "What did Papa do, Rosie?"

"He beckoned. He said he couldn't get to heaven without our help. He sort of wailed it . . ."

"And Bastian went?"

Rosie nodded. "I told him not to, but he said it

was just like *Hamlet!* The ghost reached for me, but I said I wouldn't go. Then they ran away.''

"How long ago was this?"

Rosie sucked a knuckle anxiously. "A little while. I didn't want to get Bastian into trouble. Uncle Nicholas said we weren't to leave the house without an adult . . . But then he didn't come back, and it got darker, and I was scared. . . ."

Judith hugged her. Nicholas and Leander were already inspecting the ground outside the French doors. "Thank heavens for this mist," said Nicholas. "There are tracks in the grass. I'll get a lantern."

Judith could see other bobbing lanterns through the mist, and took courage from the thought that many were searching. "Why?" she asked no one in particular. "If it is Timothy Rossiter, why is he doing this?"

Nicholas came back through the house with a lantern. "I'd guess, money," he said crisply. "The root of all evil."

"Money?" said Judith. "What money?" But the men were already disappearing into the misty dark.

Judith stood. "Come, Rosie. We must go, too. Let's get you wrapped up warmly." In minutes Judith and Rosie were out in the dark mist, trying to follow Leander and Nicholas. Eleanor had disappeared on some other business.

Soon Judith was wishing she had taken time to find a lantern, but she struggled after the dim lights ahead, calling her son.

Nicholas and Leander followed the eerie trail through the misted grass. The lantern cast only finite light, creating a gray wall into which bushes and trees would push and become solid.

Leander worked his way around a mighty oak and

plunged on, then the deepening dark told him Nicholas and the lantern had stopped.

He turned back. "Come on. The footsteps go this way!"

Nicholas was stationary by the big tree, looking up. Leander hurried back. "What's holding you up? The bastard's probably . . ." He stopped as he heard it. A faint cry for help from high in the tree.

"He's up there?" Leander asked. "Why? How?"

"Who knows. But with this freezing mist, he'll fall soon. We'll need a ladder."

"The devil we will," said Leander, and stripped off his greatcoat. "Give me a leg up."

He put his foot into Nicholas's hands and was tossed up so he could grab onto the first spreading branch. "Bastian!" he hollered. "I'm coming. Hold on!" It was like shouting into the void. Somewhere up there in the dark mass of branches that reached over a hundred feet, was a small, terrified boy. How he'd climbed up there was a wonder for later.

Well, actually, Leander decided, the how was not the question. Once onto the first branch the tree was easy to climb if one had a head for heights and strong arms. The rough old trunk and the nobbly boles offered footholds when the gap between branches was too great.

The dark and the mist was a problem, though. He could only see the branches just overhead, and could not plan a path. The ground had already disappeared into a sea of mist. Above him was just another misty sky. This isolation made him shiver. He could imagine how it must be affecting Bastian.

"Bastian? Can you hear me?"

"Yes," came back a thin voice.

"How are you?"

"Cold. I'm sorry but I don't think I can get down, Papa Leander."

"That's all right. Just hold on. I'll be there soon."

But as he resumed the climb, Leander wondered how the devil he was going to get the frozen boy down. It was far too high for a ladder.

The moon winked on and off as clouds scuttered by, and the gusting wind up high blew the mist. Leander thought he saw the boy hugging the trunk nearly at the top of the tree. His heart almost stopped at the sight; Bastian still seemed so far away, and his position looked precarious. But he climbed steadily on.

He wished he'd brought a rope, then he could perhaps have lowered Bastian down. He was aware that his gloved hands were growing dangerously cold. He doubted Bastian had gloves.

He was going to murder Timothy Rossiter when he got his hands on him

"I'm coming, Bastian."

Leander felt he must be getting close, but the moon had gone and there was still enough mist to conceal.

"Bastian?"

"Yes."

"Do you think you can talk to me, so I can find you?"

"Hello," said the wavering voice. "Er, what do you went me to say, Papa?"

Leander began to work around the tree a bit. "Sing then. Can you sing?"

Waveringly, the boy's sweet voice began, " *'At Christmastide so long ago/ An angel came to earth below/ To bring to men the blessings dear./ Jesus, our Lord, is near.'* "

Leander tracked the thin, trembling voice.

" *'The angel's light brought peace on earth,/ A signal of the Savior's birth./ New hope for all and end of fear./ Jesus, our Lord, is near.'* "

And suddenly, there Bastian was, a pale shape, shivering, clinging eyes shut to the branch, and gamely singing.

Leander waited until he was close enough to grip, before saying, "Like the view from up here, do you?"

The boy started, and turned, and Leander just managed to grab the back of his trousers before he fell. Bastian began to cry, and Leander pulled him close.

"Cheer up," he said bracingly. "You can dine out on this for years." But the boy was shaking with the cold.

Bastian sniffed, and Leander managed to extract a handkerchief and give it to the boy. He also gave him his gloves. When their hands touched, Bastian's were icy, and Leander had to fight down terror at what might have been.

When Bastian had finished blowing his nose, Leander said, "Now, if you could steady yourself, I can get out of my jacket, and you can have that, too."

"You'll be awfully cold."

"Grown-ups don't get as cold as children," Leander said briskly. For a moment, pulling one arm out of a sleeve, he almost tipped them both, but then he had the garment off, and could help Bastian to put his arms into the sleeves.

"Th . . . that feels good," said Bastian, shaking more than before, perhaps with reaction. "What do we do now?"

"We get down," said Leander cheerfully, "though I'll tell you truly, I'm not sure how. We'll figure out something. Haloo!" he shouted down into the misty nothingness.

"Ho, the Rogues!" called Nicholas's voice, not seeming very far away. "I'm on my way up with a rope. How are you?"

"In prime twig. In fact, we like it so well we might stay if you're bringing some cake and cider."

Bastian gave a gurgling laugh.

"You'll have to make do with brandy," said Nicholas, clearly very close indeed, though still not visible.

"I feel like a bloody Saint Bernard. Where the devil are you?"

Bastian naughtily piped up with more of the song. " '*A sinner's plight makes angels sigh./ Ungodly words make angels cry . . .*' "

"Stubble it, you impious whelp," said Leander, hugging him close.

Then Nicholas was there—a very fat Nicholas. He took up a perch on the next branch. "I have great hopes for the future," he said. "The boy's clearly a born Rogue." He unwound something from around his body and passed it over. It was Judith's Russian mantle. Leander wrapped it around Bastian, pulling the hood up over the boy's head.

Next Nicholas passed over a flask of brandy, and Leander was glad enough to take a deep swig. He gave Bastian a little.

The boy almost choked them off the branch. "That's horrid!"

"See you keep that thought for at least eight years or so," said Leander. He turned to Nicholas. "We'd better get down." The truth was that the cold was beginning to eat into him and would soon sap his strength.

"Right," said Nicholas. "My plan is that I'll lower the boy, while you climb down to help if he gets caught up."

Leander tied the rope under Bastian's arms and showed him how to hold it. "Not long now," he told the boy.

As Nicholas gently lowered the boy, so the rope could start to take his weight, Bastian said, "Do you think Papa got to heaven?"

Leander and Nicholas shared a look. "I'm sure," said Leander, "that your father is in heaven. But this was a trick. We'll talk about it when you're down."

He then began to lower himself from branch to branch, finding it rather more nerve-racking than climbing up. His fingers were growing distinctly numb and he had to grope downward with his feet, seeking a secure spot. He kept pace with Bastian, though the boy in fact needed no help and managed to kick away to avoid branches that would have stopped him.

Leander knew Judith must be waiting below, and so he called, "We're all safe. We'll be down soon."

Then they arrived at a ladder, with a sturdy servant at the top, but they decided to lower Bastian all the way. Leander was glad enough to use the ladder for the rest of the descent, however.

By the time his feet touched the ground, Bastian was already in his mother's arms, though still trailing the rope like a newborn baby still linked to its mother. Leander gave the rope a couple of sharp tugs to tell Nicholas that all was well and then shrugged into his greatcoat, teeth chattering. "Come on," he said. "Into the house with all of us."

Eleanor had soup waiting, and roaring fires, and they all set to thawing out. Judith, too, was chilled, though someone had found her a blanket while she waited. Nicholas came in, and after a quick conference with Eleanor said, "My delightfully resourceful wife not only thought of soup, but has sent people out around the area to track down our friend. We don't have that many strangers hereabouts, so I'm sure we'll find a trace."

Bastian looked up. "It wasn't Papa? But it looked just like him. It sounded like him. He even had his ring."

"Timothy Rossiter received Sebastian's ring in his will," Judith said. "Why? Why would he be doing these cruel things?"

"For gain," said Nicholas. "Bastian stands between him and something he wants. Does he inherit anything if Bastian dies?"

"No," said Judith. "I mean, he does get the rights

to Sebastian's poetry, I believe, but that has never brought in any money."

"Really?" said Eleanor. "But 'My Angel Bride' was on everyone's lips when it came out. The book was in our circulating library in Gloucestershire, and was positively dogeared with reading."

"In gilded cordovan?" Judith asked in surprise.

"No. In plain cloth-bound," said Eleanor, equally bewildered.

"I think," said Nicholas, "that we have a mystery here that needs investigation, but first the children should be put to bed." He anticipated Judith and said, "For tonight, at least, a servant will keep watch in each room."

Bastian seemed rather more impressed than alarmed at this. "Do you think he'll come back?"

"No," said Nicholas with a grin. "I'm afraid you had so much fun, you'll be off up that tree again."

Bastian grinned shyly back. "And Papa is really in heaven?"

Judith answered that. "Assuredly, Bastian."

"That man," said Bastian with a sliding look. "He said that he'd been thrown out of heaven because you'd married again, Mama, and because Papa Leander had stolen his children. He said if I climbed the tree as high as I could, and renounced Papa Leander three times, he'd be able to go back again. . . ." His look flickered to Leander and away again.

All the adults shared a horrified glance. "Bastian," said Judith, hiding her rage. "That was all cruel nonsense. You mustn't believe such a thing."

"But it was sort of like *Hamlet,*" Bastian muttered.

Leander put his hand on Bastian's shoulder. The boy didn't look up. "I certainly didn't murder your father, lad, and it is not wrong for widows and widowers to remarry, but this would all be better discussed tomorrow when you're rested. Yes?"

Bastian nodded.

"And," added Leander, "I don't hold it against you that you did what you thought necessary to help your father."

Bastian flickered a grateful look at him, but was still subdued. At least he made no objection to both Leander and Judith taking him and Rosie up to their beds.

When the children were settled, Judith and Leander paused on the landing before returning downstairs.

She took his hands. "I'm sorry about that. Bastian will get over it. I could *throttle* Timothy Rossiter. What can he be after?"

"We'll find out."

"It's all so horrible."

"Yes." His hands tightened on hers. "We've sailed close to tragedy three times, haven't we? But it's over now."

"How can you be sure?" Judith wanted him to draw her into his arms, but there was still a barrier between them.

"Because we know who. We'll have him, and make sure he does no more harm. And there I was putting it all at the door of my poor family." Leander wanted to hold her, but wasn't sure how he would be received. That stupid Hamlet business had him feeling as if this marriage had been the cause of all their woes.

"When it was really my family," said Judith. "Or at least, Sebastian's. Do you know, before I went to London, I didn't even know that Sebastian's brother had handled his affairs?" Then Judith found herself confessing about the books, and her visit to Mr. Browne's.

A glimmer of humor lit Leander's somber face.

"My dear, are you saying you married me for one hundred and three guineas?"

Judith looked up anxiously. "I suppose I am."

The glimmer turned to a glow. "I'm delighted. I'm sure it seemed a vast sum to you, but I can't believe you would have married someone you disliked for such a sum."

Judith smiled with relief. "That is true, I suppose. I was glad of an excuse to make up after that silly disagreement. I wanted to marry you for a lot more than money." That came dangerously close to an admission she mustn't make, but she was beginning to feel careless about it. After all they had been through, would honesty be so terrible?

"I," teased Leander, "never pretended I didn't want to marry you." He leant forward and kissed her, a brush against the lips, no more, but a reconnection of significance. "We'd better go down, before Nicholas solves the whole mystery without us."

Nicholas protested that he wouldn't dream of stealing someone else's adventure. "Now," he said when they were settled, "let's recap. Judith believes that her husband made no money from his poetry. I assume that means you never saw his account books."

"No, of course not," said Judith. "He gave me money for the household expenses, and that was all I knew except that he had an adequate income from his family."

"What happened to this income when he died?"

"It stopped. That was why I was in such straits. The only money I had was an allowance from Timothy Rossiter. Why would he give me that money if he wished me ill?"

"How did the allowance come about?" asked Nicholas.

"When I found myself virtually penniless, I wrote to ask if Sebastian's income could be continued. His reply was that it was an annuity that had died with

him, but that he could provide a small income. I had
the feeling the money was not easy for him to find.
I sent a note to him once I was in London, to say it
was no longer necessary. To Clarges Street. Is that a
poor address?''

Nicholas and Leander shared a look. "My dear,"
said Leander, "it's one of the best addresses in
London."

"But when he visited me, he looked quite poor,"
Judith protested. She gave an account of Timothy's
call.

" 'One may smile, and smile, and be a villain,' "
quoted Nicholas. "*Hamlet* again. Could Timothy have
known that the children had seen the play?"

"Yes!" exclaimed Judith. "At the theater, I thought
I saw Sebastian's ghost. It gave me quite a turn."

Nicholas said, "I imagine it would—"

But Eleanor interjected. "You still have not discovered any reason for this, you know. It may all be
moonshine."

"My practical wife," said Nicholas. "Very well.
What happened to the rights to your husband's
poetry, and any income therefrom?"

"There was no income," said Judith. "As to rights,
my father handled all the legal dealings . . . I do know,
however, that all such things were left to Bastian. I
assumed it meant just the copies of his books that
we had—one of each. There seemed nothing else
. . . Except, his papers. They contain his rejected
efforts, and the poems he was working on. Mister
Browne was very interested in them, but I denied they
existed. I had no mind to pay him another hundred
guineas for another issue." She then had to explain
to the Delaneys about the cordovan-covered books.

Eleanor interjected, "But the copies I have seen
are cloth-bound, as must have been the case. I think
we even have one here." She hurried off.

Leander asked, "Who inherits these rights if Bastian dies?"

Judith shook her head. "I have no idea."

"I'll go odds, it's Timothy."

"And I'll go odds," said Nicholas, "those rights are worth a great deal."

"Enough to kill for?" protested Judith. "I would swear that Sebastian never made money from his work."

Eleanor came back with a slim red volume. As she said, it was simply, but elegantly bound in cloth, like the ones Sebastian had given to the servants. On the spine it said, *Heavenly Gifts,* by Sebastian Rossiter.

Judith flicked the pages. "The one containing 'My Angel Bride,' " she said. "I don't understand."

Nicholas slid down in his chair to gaze thoughtfully at the ceiling. "What if," he said, "your husband's work was wildly popular. It's not surprising that you would not know, living quietly in the country. Leander and I have been mostly abroad, and Eleanor lived a restricted life before our marriage. It is quite possible that we would not know about this, though it's interesting that Eleanor had heard of Rossiter."

"So had Sir Stephen," said Judith.

"So had Beth and Lucien," said Leander. "Heavens, Luce could even quote a bit of it, but I put that down to Rossiter being their local lion."

Nicholas straightened in his chair, a bright light in his eyes. "Eleanor, ring for Mrs. Patterson. Our housekeeper," he explained to Leander and Judith, "and a great one for the more sentimental type of literature."

The woman bustled in, thin and bright eyed. "Yes, ma'am?"

"Mrs. Patterson," said Eleanor, "have you heard of a poet called Sebastian Rossiter?"

"Heard of him!" the woman exclaimed. "Why, ma'am, he is my favorite of all. I've bought all his books. 'Twere such a tragedy he died . . . I wasn't myself for weeks. I did wonder . . . Are Master Bastian and Miss Rosie related to him?''

"They are his children."

Mrs. Patterson clasped her hands to her breast. "Oh, goodness." She quoted, " *Two cherubs sent from high to bless our home./ Love's perfect form before us . . .' "*

Judith felt very embarrassed.

"And do you know many others who like his poetry?'' Eleanor asked.

"Oh, everyone," the woman stated. "I was just quoting to them in the kitchen. *'Oh Christmas, time of love and light./ Of diamond stars in sable night. . . .'* Lovely poem, that is."

"Thank you, Mrs. Patterson."

The woman left, muttering, "His children . . . Here . . . Oh, my. . . !''

"Do you mean," asked Judith in a daze, "that Sebastian made a lot of money, and I never realized? But what did he do with it? We lived a very simple life, and he rarely left Mayfield, even to go as far as Guildford."

Before anyone could comment, she added, "And besides, since his death the money should have been coming to Bastian. My father is his trustee, and I assure you he would have told me if there was money available, even if it couldn't be touched. It would surely have paid for Bastian's education, at least."

Leander and Nicholas shared a glance. "I think it more likely," said Leander, "that Sebastian was duped by his brother. You said Timothy was acting as his agent, negotiating with the London printer. I suspect Timothy Rossiter managed to keep all the profits for himself. It was remarkably greedy, or foolish, however, to have Sebastian pay for his special gift editions."

Judith gaped. "You mean he has been taking money, even as I struggled to survive! And he sent me that miserly allowance in such a way that I felt grovelingly grateful? The rogue!''

"Please," said Nicholas, "not rogue. Around here, that is an honorable name. I do look forward to meeting the gentleman, though. I wonder if our people have found any trace of him?"

Leander surged to his feet. "Damnation, what a low specimen. And he adds to it by hunting down an innocent lad. No doubt he fears to have his thievery exposed. Of course!" he said suddenly to Judith. "Your visiting the printer must have scared him to death. Not only were you no longer trapped down in the country where you'd never realize the state of affairs, but you were elevated to a position of power. He must have called on you to see if you had any suspicions. When reassured, he moved smartly on to disposing of Bastian, at which point the rights to the poetry would become his, and he'd have a chance of concealing the past." He looked fiercely at Nicholas. "This one's mine."

Nicholas shrugged. "If you insist. But I claim some rights. He chose to get up to mischief on my territory."

Chapter Nineteen

There was a knock at the door, and a groom entered in stocking feet, still rosy from the outdoors. "We've got him, sir," he said to Nicholas. "Couldn't go far in this mist and dark, and racked up at the Fiddler in Hope Norton. Davy stayed there to be sure he didn't move, but there's little chance, for it's bad out, and he's not what you'd call a hardy man."

When the groom had gone, Nicholas looked around. "Well, what now? Much though I'd like to beat him to a bloody pulp, it may not be wise. What do you want, Judith?"

Judith was shocked by it all. "I'm not fierce, I'm afraid. I just want to be sure he doesn't hurt my children again."

"Do I not get a say?" asked Leander sharply.

"Of course," said Nicholas.

"I want him to suffer. We'd have trouble making anything of his attempts on Bastian's life, but his embezzlement should be easy to prove."

"But Leander," said Judith. "I'm not sure I care to have such a case brought to trial. It would create a stir, and perhaps reflect badly on Sebastian and the children."

She thought Leander would overrule her, but after a taut pause, he said, "Fine. Then we'll take back everything he's stolen. My guess is that will leave him penniless. Then we'll ship him off to some place far from home, to sink or swim as best he can. For such a paltry specimen, that might be suffering enough."

Nicholas looked around. "Seems appropriate. Are we all in agreement? So be it. I see no point in going out in this treacherous weather, though, since we have him trapped. We'll deal with the wretch in the morning, then escort him to London to finish the business."

"But Nicholas," Eleanor protested. "It's only ten days to Christmas!"

"Don't worry. We'll be back, and the villain will be safely disposed of. We'll all celebrate easier for that. As for Christmas," he said, looking at Judith and Leander, "it seems the Temple is not ready for you, so why don't you join us here?"

Judith and Leander shared a look, and Judith answered. "Thank you, but we would like to spend our first Christmas at our home, however makeshift it will be. Leander's Aunt Lucy is arranging for servants, and if the provisions are low, I have my own Christmas baking. There will be cake, and mince pies, and," she added with a smile, "elderberry wine."

Leander rolled his eyes. "Come to that, I could order provisions from London."

"Not to arrive by Christmas, I fear," Judith pointed out.

"Very well," said Leander with an artificial sigh, "I leave Christmas to you."

Shortly after, they went up to their room, peeping in to check on the children first.

Once in bed, Leander drew her into his arms and kissed her tenderly. "It's been a chaotic marriage so far, hasn't it? I'll make it up to you."

"It's not your fault," Judith said, but sleepily. The last few days had left her exhausted.

"I consider it my job to make you happy, Judith. I will."

Judith wanted to make a suitable reply, but sleep stole her voice and sucked her down.

When she woke, Leander was already gone, his side of the bed cold. She hurried downstairs to breakfast and found she was the slugabed. It was nearly ten o'clock and everyone else had breakfasted. Nicholas and Leander had already left, but Leander had spoken to Bastian, who already seemed to be putting his strange adventure behind him.

"Papa Leander's going take care of that man for good," he said with pride and relish.

"I think Papa Leander's ever so brave," said Rosie. "He climbed that big tree."

"I climbed that big tree, too," said Bastian.

"But it's harder for old people."

Judith bit her lip and hoped Leander never heard that. She sent the children off to play.

"You don't think Leander and Nicholas are in any danger?" Judith asked Eleanor anxiously.

"I doubt it. Your Timothy Rossiter does not seem to be a very bold character when it comes to facing grown men, and they can handle themselves well. They have both been in far more hazardous situations."

She entertained Judith with some stories of the Rogues, including a little matter of breaking and entering a few months past. Judith couldn't help thinking it would be a good idea to keep Leander out of contact with his friends, but then she knew it would be as impossible as keeping her divorced from her family.

That reminded her that Leander did now have a

family of his own, and the beginning of a comfortable relationship with them. They would surely all get together over Christmas, as families should, gathered around a table at the Temple.

Christmas at the Temple, she thought, hope rising in her breast. She could do it, and she would.

Leander and Nicholas left early and arrived at the Fiddler Inn in the village of Hope Norton when the place was barely stirring. Davy, the groom, greeted them with the news that their quarry had showed no sign of life as yet.

Nicholas turned to Leander. "Do you want to take charge?"

Leander's jaw flexed, but he said, "Better not. I'd kill him on sight."

"Well, you can if you want," said Nicholas calmly.

Leander looked at Nicholas, startled. "Have you ever killed anyone in cold blood?"

"In cold blood? I recall being angry . . . But yes, I have. There are some people who cannot be let live. I doubt Timothy Rossiter, however, is quite that dangerous."

"No, you're probably right." Leander sighed. "Pity."

Nicholas laughed. "Bloodthirsty, aren't you? A family will do that to you. Speaking of cold, I think we might as well await our friend over coffee." He led the way into the inn.

They took a small parlor, and ordered coffee. Direct questions revealed that the only other guest was a gentleman calling himself Mr. Swithin, who had ordered breakfast in his room at eight o'clock. Nicholas checked his watch. "Ten minutes."

Leander took a sip of coffee, but then leapt to his feet to roam the room. "Why don't we go up now?"

"Disturb the man before he's dressed? Lee, where have your perfect manners gone?"

Leander let out a sharp laugh. "God, Nicholas. I've missed you."

Nicholas smiled. "We had good times, didn't we? And so damned innocent."

"But back then we thought we truly were imps from hell."

"And so we were, but since then some of us have visited hell in very truth. I like your Bastian. A promising Rogue. I like your wife and daughter, too."

"Yes," said Leander, and realized he was smiling. He glanced rather self-consciously at Nicholas.

Nicholas said, "There's no need to be embarrassed about loving them, you know."

"Love?"

"A strange affliction, that makes other human beings essential to one's happiness."

"Ah, that love. . . ." Leander looked down to his coffee. "I am very fond of them of course . . ."

"But you could watch them walk out of your life tomorrow without any great concern."

Leander looked up sharply. "What? Judith's my wife. She's not going anywhere." Then he groaned. "Hell, have I gone and fallen in love with her?"

"I would say so. It presents a problem?"

"You could say that." Leander made a fist and beat once on the table. "She's still in love with the wonderful, romantic Sebastian Rossiter. I only persuaded her to marry me by assuring her that I'd not bother her with sentimental nonsense." He raked his hand through his hair. "How am I to hide it from her?"

Nicholas shook his head. "I doubt it's possible."

"I'll not embarrass her with it."

Nicholas knew a great deal about Leander's family but he only said, "It's a problem that will keep. Let's first deal with Hamlet's ghost."

They walked into Timothy Rossiter's room without knocking. Though they had pistols with them, they did not have weapon in hand, for this villain seemed unlikely to pose such a threat.

Indeed, he rose to his feet, startled but unaggressive. "Gentlemen? This is a private room." He was still in a dressing robe over shirt and breeches. It was a fine, expensive velvet robe. In fact, every one of his possessions appeared to be of top quality, though the man himself was weak of chin and chest.

Nicholas sat opposite him at his breakfast table. Leander closed the door and leant against it. Rossiter's weak eyes flickered between them.

Nicholas said, "My name is Nicholas Delaney, of Redoaks, a house nearby. The other gentlemen is the Earl of Charrington."

Rossiter's puffy face blanched, but he blustered. "So? I do not know you."

Leander smiled icily. "You called at my house not many days past."

"You have the wrong man. My name is Swithin."

"Ah," said Nicholas. "You follow your Bible, sir, wherein it says that a good name is rather to be chosen than riches. Pity you were not so wise before. Sit down."

Rossiter gaped but obeyed.

Nicholas rose and went to Rossiter's valise. Despite a feeble protest, he opened it and extracted a blond wig. He dangled it before his prisoner. "Rejoice. Your nephew Bastian is alive and well and so we do not have to kill you. But Bastian would prosper better with his rightful inheritance, don't you think?"

Rossiter struggled to his feet again, mouth working. "I . . . I will call for help!"

Leander lunged over and assisted him to his feet with a strangling hand in his cravat. He shook him like a rat. "Call, and we'll prosecute for attempted murder, you shit sack."

Nicholas allowed a moment or two before saying, "Lee."

Leander reluctantly relaxed his fingers, and dropped Rossiter to choke in his chair, then brushed his hands distastefully.

"You're mad," Rossiter gasped, clutching his throat.

"Cease," said Nicholas with a sigh. "Timothy Rossiter, have no doubt we could convict you of attempting the life of your nephew, Bastian, on three occasions. It is certain that we can prove that you have been defrauding your brother, his widow, and his heir. A visit to Mister Algernon Browne should inform us as to the amount earned by Sebastian Rossiter's poetry over the years."

Rossiter's expression confessed his guilt. "I never wanted to hurt the boy," he whimpered. "It's just . . . It's all right for you," he spat sullenly. "Born to riches. Idle wastrels. . . ."

Leander snarled at him, and he hunched back in his chair, pallid as a corpse except for the terror in his eyes.

"We're not going to kill you," said Nicholas with disgust. "You're not worth the effort. I'll even stop the earl from beating you to a pulp if you do precisely as we say."

The bulging eyes fixed on him in faint hope.

"We are going to London," Nicholas informed him. "There we will check the accounts, and every penny will be returned. If there is not enough money—and I fear you have been living extravagantly, sir—then all you have must go against your debts."

"But . . . ."

"But how are you to live?" asked Nicholas, almost kindly. "I fear you will have to work. As Horace said, 'Life grants nothing to we mortals without hard work.' Time you learned that, isn't it? And in view of your unfortunate plotting, your labor will have to be well away from your brother's family. You are going to travel, Mister Rossiter. You may choose the destination—Canada, the United States, South America perhaps, or the West Indies. Perhaps you would care for the East Indies? Many opportunities to make a fortune there. Or even Australia. A few people are choosing to go there without the force of law. So much cheap labor."

The man's mouth was working and he looked close to tears.

"You needn't fear. Your generous nephew will provide enough for your passage, and some money to keep you going until you find your feet." He rose to his feet and slapped Rossiter's shoulders with false bonhomie. "Cheer up, man. As the sage said, 'Roam abroad in the world, and take thy fill of its enjoyments before the day shall come when thou must quit it for good.' " He hoisted Rossiter to his feet with an ungentle hand. "And that day shall come with remarkable speed if we see your face on these shores again once you have quit them."

Rossiter was like a puppet in their hands as they dressed him, packed his bag, and thrust him into his coach. They left their horses and joined him there for the journey.

At Redoaks, Judith could not help but be anxious, but Eleanor's lack of fear did much to soothe her. She would not, however, let the children out of her sight and kept them busy making Christmas treasures—wreaths, kissing boughs, and lanterns.

When they tired of that, they all helped Eleanor decorate Redoaks with the greenery and mistletoe collected the day before, and her own Christmas treasures. Little Arabel trotted happily about, entangling herself and Magpie in a length of red ribbon. Rosie abandoned handicrafts to play with the infant.

It was a peaceful, cheerful time, but Judith missed Leander badly, and knew how deep her love had rooted. The thought of trying to conceal that love for the rest of her life was depressing, and she knew she would have to tackle the problem one day soon, but she was frightened. Would he be so distressed he would send her away? It seemed ridiculous, but she knew his feelings on such matters—grown from his difficult childhood—ran deeper than reason.

She didn't know how she would bear losing him, but even worse was the knowledge of what he would lose. He needed her. He needed a companion, a helpmeet, someone able to connect him to his world. Then she doubted herself. Leander Knollis, Earl of Charrington—soldier, diplomat, linguist, earl— surely did not need Judith Rossiter.

On the second day the groom returned from Hope Norton with the news that Nicholas and Leander had captured Timothy Rossiter without difficulty, and taken him off to London. Judith relaxed her vigilance over the children a little and allowed them to play in the grounds near the house.

She stood by the window, however, watching them. "It's terrible," she said to Eleanor. "I don't know when I'll feel at ease with them out of my sight. I used to allow Bastian to wander about the countryside without a care. What if Timothy had taken it into his mind to dispose of him then?"

Eleanor came and wrapped an arm around her like a sister. "He didn't. I think he is a paltry villain, not inclined to action until cornered. You will over-come this fear, and Leander and Nicholas will handle everything."

"I am not used to having someone to take care of things," Judith confessed. Then she realized that it was disloyal to Sebastian. Sebastian, however, had been all too like his brother. Now Leander had all her allegiance, for he had earned it.

"Nor was I," said Eleanor, "until I married. It's rather pleasant, isn't it? But I don't regret my hard years, for they taught me to stand on my own feet, and gave me strength to take care of Nicholas when he needs me."

"Does he?" asked Judith. "Need you?"

"Oh yes. And I'm sure Leander needs you, too, perhaps even more." She drew Judith over to a sofa, and poured tea for them both. "Nicholas has been concerned about him."

Judith looked up in surprise. "I thought they had not met for years."

"True enough, but that has little to do with it. Nicholas tries not to run people's lives these days, but he finds it hard to resist." She laughed. "One reason we live down here in the West Country is to remove temptation. He still keeps a watching brief over all the Rogues, and he took the death of Lord Darius Debenham hard. He died at Waterloo, you know, and Nicholas, being Nicholas, feels that in some way he should have prevented it. . . . Anyway, he has often spoken of Leander, worried about his aloneness. I gather his family was not particularly sound."

Judith decided to be blunt. "I think his parents sound awful."

"Nicholas met Leander's father abroad a few times, and found him to be totally self-centered. He said the man's ability in matters of diplomacy was rooted in an uncanny ability to read people's minds and a habit of viewing them as trained animals, to be made to jump at his command. I'm surprised Leander turned out so well."

Judith nibbled a biscuit. "I suspect he was fortunate in that his father ignored him except for occasional lectures and discipline." She looked suddenly up at Eleanor. "Do you think boys should be beaten?"

Eleanor blinked with surprise. "If they deserve it."

"Oh."

"I was whipped many a time as a girl. I was a sore trial to my parents."

Judith said, "Would you whip Arabel?"

"No," Eleanor said sharply, then bit her lip. "Something to discuss with Nicholas, I think. This concerns you?"

"It is something Leander and I have talked about," said Judith. "He seems to think Bastian will be beaten at school."

"I fear he's correct. I remember a discussion once as to whether this harshness turns men into brutes, or is a consequence of their inborn brutality."

"Leander is not a brute," protested Judith.

Eleanor smiled. "Neither is Nicholas. Nor even Lucien de Vaux, though he has a strong streak of violence in him."

Judith looked into her cup. Having raised one touchy subject, she was wondering if it might be possible to talk about marital duties with Eleanor Delaney. The time was surely coming again, and with all the shocks and troubles in her brief marriage, she felt she must handle it better the next time.

"Was there something you wished to say, Judith?" asked Eleanor gently.

Judith looked up. "I want to talk about the marriage bed."

Eleanor colored a little. "Oh. I do not mind . . ."

Judith licked her lips. "Sebastian . . . Sebastian always came to my room when I was in bed, in the dark. He was quite quick about it. I . . . Leander seems to want it differently. . . . I wondered what was normal. . . ."

"Normal," said Eleanor, and Judith could see she

was a little embarrassed. "I am afraid I cannot say. Nicholas and I . . ."

"Oh, please," said Judith quickly. "I am sorry. I should never have asked. But how is anyone to know," she demanded in frustration, "if nobody speaks of it?"

Eleanor laughed. "How true. Actually, there are books."

"Books!"

"Indeed. But I can tell you that many things are normal for us. Sometimes we make love in the dark, sometimes in the light. Once or twice," she said, rather pink, "out of doors."

Judith struggled not to gape. "I see."

"Judith," said Eleanor, "this is going to be impertinent, but did you enjoy making love to Sebastian?"

"Enjoy . . . ?" Judith had never even thought of it as making love. "No," she said.

"And do you enjoy making love to Leander?"

Judith didn't dare think of *making love* to him. "A little," she admitted.

Eleanor wrinkled her brow. "I think you should encourage him to do anything he wants. You will probably find you enjoy it even more. But I can't be sure. I know some women find it an arduous imposition. As you say, it is not discussed."

Judith realized she was crumbling a biscuit and stilled her hands. "What is the difference between marital duties and making love?" she asked.

Eleanor looked blank. "Nothing, I suppose. I just think making love sounds more pleasant, and more exact. For Nicholas and I it is an expression of love."

"How do you express your love?" Judith asked desperately.

"Judith, I am not sure I know what you are asking."

Judith took a deep breath. In for a lamb, in for a sheep. "When Leander asked me to marry him, it was because I was a grieving widow who wouldn't fall

in love with him. Well, I have," she said defiantly.
"But I am trying not to burden him with that knowledge. I know that his parents' situation—with his
mother doting on his father, and his father not caring
a jot—was very painful for him. I don't want to . . .
to make love, if it will tell him I love him."

"Goodness," said Eleanor blankly. "I'm sure . . .
Oh dear." She leant forward and took Judith's hand.
"I don't know what to say about that, Judith, but I
think what you are talking about is what is called an
orgasm. An explosion of pleasure. At the simplest
level it has nothing to do with love. A man and woman
who hate each other," she said bleakly, eyes looking
into the past, "can give each other an orgasm." She
shook herself. "No matter what you decide to do
about your feelings for your husband, don't deny
yourself, and him that release. Wait a moment."

She left the room and returned with a book. *"Aver-
tino's Postures,"* she said with a naughty twinkle.
"Translated from the Italian. It is what is called erot-
ica. It may help. Now, I must speak to Mrs. Patterson."

When alone, Judith looked at the book warily, then
opened it at random. She gaped. Why on earth would
any two people want to get into that position? And
the text . . . It described the strangest things. With
sudden resolution she closed the book. Perhaps in
time it would be of use, but at the moment she feared
it would terrify her into rejecting Leander entirely.
What if he wanted her to . . .

She leapt to her feet to pace the room, aware of
strange stirrings similar to those she had felt with
Leander in her big down mattress.

She had her answer. Sebastian and she had been
doing it wrong, and she must encourage Leander to
show her how to do it right, and try not to object at
the extraordinary things he would expect. And that
strange feeling she had experienced, and the sense
of aching disappointment, had doubtless all been to

do with this orgasm, which had nothing, at the simplest level, to do with love.

She wondered what Eleanor Delaney had meant by that modifying clause, but put the thought away. At least now she did not have to be afraid of revealing too much during her marital duties.

Traitorously she thought, during making love.

Chapter Twenty

It took Leander, Nicholas, and Rossiter four tedious days to reach London, for they encountered snow on the Downs. On arrival, they went to Nicholas's house on Lauriston Street, where his staff were all well trained to accept the unusual. They locked the cowed Rossiter in a room, then Leander went out to establish the extent of the man's crime. It was Saturday, and if he didn't get to the printer's before they closed, they doubtless would get little information before Monday.

Algernon Browne had no hesitation in providing information to the husband of Sebastian Rossiter's widow, and was aghast to realize what had been going on.

"Believe me, my lord, I know nothing of this. I only met Mister Rossiter—Mister Sebastian Rossiter—once. I gather he did not care for travel, or London. He signed papers to make his brother his agent in all things. See," he said, producing a document. "I have a copy."

Leander looked at it. It was comprehensive. Sebastian Rossiter must have been a damned idiot. "How can he not have realized his work was making money?''

Mr. Browne shrugged. "The only correspondence I ever had with him was concerning the special editions. He paid for them directly. . . ." He blanched. "Good Lord! Do you mean his brother took all his profits and allowed him to pay for those! And his widow . . . The countess . . . My lord, I insist you take the money back!"

Leander found some bank notes thrust upon him. He took them because he saw it would ease the man's conscience, though in truth it seemed he had done nothing wrong.

"And you must believe," said Mr. Browne urgently, "I had no idea that his widow was living in straitened circumstances. None at all."

They sat down with the books and established that over twenty years Timothy Rossiter had diddled his brother out of close to thirty thousand pounds. "Struth," said Leander. "All that from verses?"

"They were, are, extremely popular, my lord. What will you wish to be done about future income?"

Leander looked at him. "Do you mean it's still coming in?"

"Oh yes. He still sells quite steadily." Mr. Browne gave Leander a shrewd look and cleared his throat. "A new volume, a posthumous volume, would sell extremely well, my lord."

"Would it, indeed. But is there anything to put in one?"

"Not that we have." The man cleared his throat again. "I . . . er . . . did ask Lady Charrington about any papers, and she said there were none. A more thorough search . . . ?" he murmured tactfully.

Leander smiled dryly. "With no profit coming in, and over a hundred pounds to pay, I can see why she wasn't enthusiastic. If there are any unpublished works, it will be for my wife to say what is done with them, but I can see no harm in it. It would mean additional funds for the children. I fear that little of the previous profits remains unspent. From Timothy Rossiter's incoherent explanations to date, it was his desperation at the ending of his income that drove him to dire measures.'' He stood and shook the man's hand before taking his leave.

Thirty thousand pounds, he thought, as he made his way back to Lauriston Street, glancing in lamp-lit windows as he passed. He suddenly stopped and laughed. There in a bookseller's was an arrangement of books of poetry by Sebastian Rossiter, and even as he looked one was plucked away to be sold. Another few pennies for Bastian. Someone else to enjoy the poems written about Judith.

He walked into the shop and picked up a volume, opening it at random. *Amid the roses, gold and white/ There's ne're a bloom with beauty quite/Like Judith in my loving sight/ My rose, my wife, my light.*

He tried a different collection. *What joy is Judith, calm, serene./ I know that I am blessed./ Fair jewel of heaven, Eve supreme/ By passion ne'er caressed.*

"Sounds damned dull to me," Leander muttered.

A clerk appeared at his side. "May I help you, sir?"

Leander put the book down. "Sells well, does it?"

"Oh yes, sir. One of our more popular authors. A sure favorite with the ladies."

Leander left the shop. Could he compete with the memory of that devotion? No matter how much of a nincompoop Sebastian Rossiter had been, that sort of sentimental twaddle was clearly the road to a lady's heart, and had Judith's snared forever.

He cursed under his breath, and felt an insane urge to smash his fist through the nearest window. What had happened to all his cool control? How was he to live with Judith without searing her with the passion he felt?

A fine twist of fate. He hadn't wanted to be tied

to a woman who loved him when he couldn't return that love. Now the shoe was on the other foot. He wanted to shower Judith with gifts; he wished he were able to write poetry; he wanted to put his head in her lap and find peace with her. And he, more than most, knew the agony of being the recipient of that kind of unwanted devotion.

He found he was staring in the window of a grocer's. The light was going and soon the shop would close. He laughed at himself. Well, if he couldn't shower her with love, he could shower her with the comforts of life. He went in and bought a vast quantity of supplies.

The sales clerk beamed. "And where shall these be delivered, sir?"

"Temple Knollis, Somerset."

The man's eyes widened. "Yes, sir. I'll have them on the carrier on Monday, sir."

"How long will that take?"

"About a week, sir. Though with Christmas coming . . ."

"Don't bother," said Leander. "I'll send them post."

"Post!" the man gulped.

"That's what I said. Where's the nearest staging inn?"

"Er . . . the Swan . . . But—"

"Then send it there."

Leander made his way briskly to the Swan, and hired a chaise and four, and a man to escort his goods. He warned them there would be more, and went on to buy wine, spirits, fruit, and a collection of livestock—a turkey, two geese, and two ducks. There, that should ensure a degree of comfort for them all at Christmas.

He returned to Lauriston Street and explained the finances to Nicholas. Almost incidentally, he told him about the provisions.

Nicholas's lips twitched. "And you sent it all down by post-chaise."

"How else? Shall we take Rossiter over to his rooms now and see what he's worth?"

"Ah, Lee," said Nicholas with a grin. "I always did admire your panache."

Timothy Rossiter did not appear to be worth much, though his rooms were elegant and his possessions of the best. He even had a valet, who made himself scarce when told to.

A quick search, and a check of the account books, told the truth.

"Spent the lot, didn't you?" asked Nicholas of the man who sat huddled in a chair by the empty grate.

"Not at first," said Rossiter miserably. Leander saw Rossiter had decided Nicholas was someone he could talk to. A common conclusion, and quite correct. Unfortunately for the believers, it did not mean that Nicholas was particularly forgiving.

"At first I only kept part," the man whined. "A kind of fee, don't you know? There wasn't much profit anyway on the earlier books, and Sebastian didn't need the money. He had his income from the pater, while I was supposed to clerk for a living. He lived down in the country where there's nothing to spend it on. . . ."

"You could not say his widow did not need the money," Nicholas pointed out blandly.

"I did give her some," Rossiter protested.

"A couple of hundred a year!" Leander exploded. "You . . ." He bit it off, knowing there was no point on taking it out on the miserable worm. Moreover, he suffered the undermining realization that if Timothy Rossiter had not been a villain, Judith would never have married again.

He would never have found her.

He rested his head on his fist on the mantelpiece. "Let's give up on this, Nicholas. There's nothing here. He might as well take his pathetic belongings with him. I just want to get this over with and get home." He straightened to look at the man. "I'll pay your passage. Just never cross my path again."

They took Rossiter back to Lauriston Street, leaving the valet to pack all his master's possessions, his last task before seeking other employment.

When Rossiter was once more locked away, they settled to their dinner. Nicholas said, "The devil of it is, we'll have to wait until Monday to find him a passage, and hope there's a ship sailing soon. We're going to cut it close for Christmas."

"I'm sorry," said Leander. "Look, why don't you return? I can take care of this."

"No need," said Nicholas. "There'll be a ship going somewhere, and he'll be on it. This will be a first Christmas with our families for both of us. I promise you, nothing on earth will get in the way of it."

On Sunday, Judith attended church with Eleanor, and found that after all simple country churches were more to her taste than cathedrals. They all walked the crisp mile to the village, and joined the congregation. It was a simple, ancient church, floor trodden down by tens of generations, walls crumbling a little under the pressures of time. At the front there was that charming French import, a *crèche*—Mary, Joseph, ox, ass, and angels all waiting for the blessed day when Jesus would come to earth.

There was no trained choir here, but just the congregation composed of all degrees of countryfolk, and of all ages. Encouraged by a number of other discordant voices, Judith joined in lustily as they sang such Advent songs as "O Come, Emmanuel," and "On Jordan's Bank."

Gazing into the *crèche* Judith knew this wasn't the

Season to hold back the gift of love. Perhaps she couldn't speak of it to Leander, but she would show her love in every way possible, and trust that he would not find it too hard a gift to accept.

By Monday, there was some hope that Leander and Nicholas would return, but only if they had completed their business with incredible speed. Judith tried not to watch the road for travelers, but found herself fidgety beyond belief. In their brief acquaintance, she and Leander had never been apart for a day until now, and she found she hated it.

She needed something to do to make the waiting bearable.

She realized she wanted to start the daunting task of taming the Temple.

She felt nervous about going there without Leander, but if she waited until his return, there would be little chance of preparing properly for Christmas. She put it to the children.

"Oh, yes, Mama. Let's!"

When Judith told Eleanor, Eleanor insisted on coming, too. "I'm fidgety, too, waiting for Nicholas to return. We haven't been apart for nearly a year. Anyway, I have always longed to see the famous Temple Knollis. We'll take some of our staff, in case you haven't enough. It will be great fun."

The next day they set off in two carriages: one for Judith, her children, and a maid; the other for Eleanor, Arabel, and Arabel's nurse. For the child did have one, though Judith suspected the post must be close to a sinecure. A cart had gone ahead earlier with more servants and provisions. As well as Judith's baking, Eleanor had contributed some of Redoaks's supplies.

When Temple Knollis came into view, Judith appreciated again its perfection, but it only served to emphasize the magnitude of the task she was setting herself. She might as well try to move the river with a spoon. She'd do it, though.

She was delighted to see a person crossing the courtyard, evidence of human occupation. Perhaps Aunt Lucy had managed to find some servants.

After a hesitation, she directed the coaches into the courtyard, so they could all enter the house by the magnificent hall, and see it in all its glory.

"Oh my," said Eleanor, once they were inside. "It's magnificent. But it is rather terrifying, isn't it? And very cold." Her breath puffed out as she spoke.

"Heavens," said Judith. "I should never have let you come. I very much fear we'll end up camping out in the kitchen like Leander's family."

Bastian and Rosie stood staring, awestruck, but Arabel gave a crow of delight and set off to capture the jewel lights cast by the windows. After a moment, the older children followed.

Footsteps clattered and a plump maid hurried in and stood bobbing a curtsy. "Milady?" she ventured, looking between them for hints.

Judith hesitated, then realized this was her house and her responsibility. "I am Lady Charrington. What is your name?" she asked the woman.

"Jenny Flint, ma'am."

"This is Mrs. Delaney, Jenny. The older children are mine, Master Bastian and Miss Rosie. The little one is Miss Arabel Delaney. Now, how many servants do we have here?"

The woman bobbed again nervously. "There be only ten yet, milady, plus the ones that came over in the cart. Most of us ones 'as worked here afore, so we knows the place. I'm feared there's no upper servants, though, milady. They all moved on to other places, see?"

"Is the Charles Knollis family still in residence?"

"No, milady. They be gone to Stainings, they be. But Mrs. Knollis said to tell you it's close by if you need aught."

"At the moment we need bedrooms prepared. What can be made available, Jenny?"

"All the beds are aired, milady. Mrs. Knollis arranged it. It's but to light fires."

Judith smiled. "Bless Aunt Lucy." She thought of the vast, magnificent drawing room, and how long it would take to warm. "Is there a relatively small room we could use as a parlor, Lucy?"

The woman looked understandably dubious. Small rooms and the Temple did not go together. "There's the casket, milady," she offered in the end.

Judith and Eleanor shared a bewildered glance, but Judith said, "Lead us to it."

They gathered the children and went down a corridor paneled in gleaming golden wood, with borders finely carved. The walls were hung with glowing pictures, and precious objects graced each stand and bureau. Awed again, the children tiptoed cautiously, and even Arabel stayed quiet in Eleanor's arms, studiously sucking her thumb.

The maid opened the door to a room. It was quite dark. She bustled in and flung back shutters to let in some light. It was still rather dark. This was because all the walls and the ceiling were covered with dark paintings in panels.

"Oh my," said Judith. She had a feeling she'd be saying that a lot. But the room was small, only twice the size of her parlor at the cottage—and it contained chairs and a fireplace.

"Please, Lucy, send someone to light a fire in here, and then serve tea."

The maid hurried off. The children gazed around, wide-eyed, then went to sit on the window seat and look out at the river. No one took off their coats.

"Do you know," said Eleanor, inspecting a wall, "I think all these paintings are real. I mean, old. They've virtually been used to paper the walls."

"Extraordinary, isn't it?" Judith responded. "But I quite like it. It's like being in a jewel box." She walked about to keep warm. "You can see how hard it's going to be to make this place into a home, though, especially for me."

"Why especially for you?" Eleanor asked.

"Because I'm not accustomed to this."

"But that could be your advantage. Don't be awed by the place. Do just what you want."

Judith laughed shakily. "I'm not sure I dare. My tastes and Leander's are not always in accord." She told Eleanor the story of the elderberry wine, and they ended up in whoops.

"But that's the point," Eleanor declared. "I'll go odds he loves the stuff when he finally tastes it."

Judith wished she could be so sure.

A lad scuttled in and built a fire, then lit it. In moments it was crackling merrily, and the Temple at least proved its quality, for the chimney drew excellently.

Soon the chill was off the small room, and once they had tea everyone was feeling much more comfortable. "The problem is," said Judith, "I doubt we can all live in here."

She and Eleanor left the children with the two maids, put on their cloaks, and explored. Though Temple Knollis was not a spectacularly large house, it had winding corridors, and they often got lost, but they pressed on, and always found the central hall eventually. As the house was built around it, it provided a focus.

There were ten good bedrooms, two clearly intended for master and mistress. In fact the master bedroom was the only one that showed signs of having been used at all, presumably by the first earl. Judith wasn't entirely sure Leander would want to sleep there, but she allocated it to him anyway, complete with a massive bed festooned with carved cherubs and his coat of arms, and walls frescoed with scenes of Venice.

Her bedroom continued the Venice theme in that it had a bed that resembled nothing so much as a gilded gondola. The pointed headboard swooped up to support pale green silk draperies bunched back against the walls, again frescoed with outdoor scenes. She might never make love outdoors, but she would feel as if she were.

The other rooms were more normal, but decorated with hand-painted wallpaper, or paintings, or tapestries. The carpets and draperies were of the finest quality, and obviously individually made for each chamber. Framed paintings, sculpture, and objets d'art were scattered with deceptive casualness.

Eleanor picked a room at random, and the one next to it for Arabel and her nurse. "Though I fear the girl won't be satisfied with the nursery at Redoaks after sleeping in such splendor."

Judith ordered fires lit in the rooms, then asked Eleanor, "Do you think there is any chance of there being a nursery or schoolroom here?"

They asked, and there was. When Judith saw the children's quarters, her heart was touched. Old Lord Charrington, in the midst of his grandiose plans, had included a perfect nursery. It was even on the plain side for the Temple, though he had not been able to resist some pretty bas-reliefs of cherubs on the walls.

Close by was a schoolroom, large enough for play, but small enough for comfort, and allowed excellent light through large windows. There were also four simple bedrooms suitable for children, two of them having child-size beds, and even smaller rooms for the nursery and schoolroom servants.

The first earl had hoped for children here, and not the children of Charles Knollis, but the children of his heir. What a sad, almost tragic, family this had been.

She swallowed before she said, "I think I will see if the children will be happy to move in up here, with some servants to keep them company. They may as well start as they will go on."

To her surprise, Bastian and Rosie were delighted. They clearly found the main part of the house oppressively grand, and liked the idea of their special domain. It was arranged that two of the local maids would sleep nearby and take care of them.

That settled, they all went on a full tour of the house. It was mostly conducted in silence because their exclamations of astonishment became so very repetitious. It was all perfect, beautiful, and full of carefully chosen, precious items. Judith could understand how it had oppressed Lucy, for to change anything would be to destroy. And yet, as it was now, it was a dead thing.

What on earth was she to do?

The main rooms were still unheated, and so they ate in the little casket, and lingered there until it was time for bed.

That night Judith climbed into her ridiculous bed, wishing desperately that Leander was here to help her with the house. When she sank into a luxurious down mattress she burst into laughter, but there was a distinct element of tears along with it.

She did not sleep well, but she spent the time tussling with the problem of this overwhelming house. In the end she decided a brash direct attack was the only solution, and with that decision made, she fell asleep.

* * *

The next day, Judith summoned her troops, that is, everyone in the house, into the main hall. She had shaped a speech in her head, and now she delivered it, though she was taken aback at the resonant echo the hall produced. The natural inclination was to whisper in this churchlike space, and she thought her firm tone made it sound as if she were giving a sermon.

"Temple Knollis," she said, "is a very beautiful house that has been many years in the building. Now, however, it is finished, and it is time it became a home. To be a home, we must all be comfortable in it."

She tried to gauge the reaction of the servants, but their solid country faces told her nothing. She was concerned that they, too, might regard this place as an inviolate shrine.

"We must all care for the precious things here," she said, "but in a home one must expect wear, and even damage. That will no longer be a disaster." There was a stir among the servants, but she couldn't interpret it. "To ensure our comfort," she continued boldly, "there will doubtless need to be changes. You must come to me with any changes you think should be made."

She left a pause in case someone should wish to make a comment, but no one did. On the whole, she thought, it was good that the upper servants had left. None of these people would dare oppose her, and the servants she hired would be her own.

"The first thing I want is a fire in every hearth. We must drive the chill out of the house. If there are not enough logs, they must be obtained. The word must go out that I will pay for well-trimmed firewood." That did sight a spark in many eyes. These were hard times, and money would be short. "I also want more servants, so if you know any seeking a place, have them come to see me."

That brought cautious smiles.

"Next, I want all these plinths in the hall, and their pots, moved to the corridor leading to the ballroom." At least, she assumed that was what the large mirrored room was.

Still no mutiny.

"Then," she said, "most of us are going out to gather greenery. I want this place to look ready for Christmas. Those behind can prepare mince pies and rum punch for our return."

She saw a distinct brightening among the servants, and knew it was going to be all right.

Since they were so short of servants, Judith and Eleanor unpacked for themselves while the hall was being cleared. Some of Judith's possessions had not been touched since she packed them in the cottage and now they seemed absurdly out of place. What was she to do with a pottery cat Bastian had won at the Michaelmas fair last year? She felt very inclined to *put in pride of place* in the drawing room, but that would be going too far.

In the end, she placed such items in the children's quarters, or in her own room. When she came to Sebastian's portrait, however, she didn't know what to do. Her inclination was to hide it away, or perhaps put it in the schoolroom, and yet that wasn't right. She felt so guilty at the way his memory was being pushed aside.

Then she thought of the library. It would surely be appropriate to have a poet's portrait there, and that rich but formal room was hardly likely to be a favorite haunt. Unlike Beth and Lucien, she and Leander were not particularly bookish. She summoned a footman and had the picture carried down and mounted in place of a French landscape. The landscape by Poussin was undoubtedly a better, and more expensive, painting, but her conscience was eased. Her first husband could forever gaze into the distance, seeking inspiration among these ranks of richly bound, and pristine classics. With any luck, she wouldn't have to look at him more than once or twice a year.

Guilt tickled at her again, but she hurried off to continue her conquest of the Temple.

The whole place was already a great deal warmer, though she was still glad of a wool shawl. The last of the hazardous plinths was being carried out of the hall. The general bustle and the voices of the children were already dispelling the formality.

At the sight of the stripped room, she had a moment's doubt, and wondered if Leander would object. But he clearly hadn't liked the house as it was, and she was doing nothing that could not be reversed. With great satisfaction, she told the children they could now play with a ball here.

Next, she headed to the kitchens for she feared the provisions must be very low. She arrived there and consulted with Mrs. Pardoe, the woman who was serving as cook.

"I tell you true, milady, I'm no fancy cook. I can roast a joint and bake a pie, but I'm not trained to fancy food." She had three large apple pies awaiting their tops.

"Then I think it very kind of you to step into the breach, Mrs. Pardoe, and good English food is just what we want. The question is, what do we need by way of supplies, and where may they be obtained?"

"We have the ordinary stuff, milady. Mrs. Knollis saw to that, and there is fruit and such in the stores. What we don't have is foreign stuff, such as almonds, oranges, and lemons. Nor do we have much in the way of poultry. There's no home farm here, you know, and the local farms haven't been in the way of providing much for the big house."

Judith sighed. "Well, send word I'll buy what there is. We'll make do." She wondered how long the money Leander had given her would last at this rate, and when he would be here to provide more. Presumably the estate itself produced money, but she didn't feel she had the right to dip into that. She supposed the Temple credit was good, but she didn't like to owe money to simple folks.

She filched an apple slice and said wistfully, "I do wish we could have a goose for Christmas, though."

Like an answer to a prayer, George walked in and dumped a hissing, crated goose on the floor. "What do you want done with this, then, Millie?" Then he saw Judith and touched his forelock. "Afternoon, milady."

"Good afternoon, George. Where did that come from?"

The man grinned. "From London, milady, by post no less. I've never seen anything like it. A whole postchaise full of food!"

"A post-chaise!" Judith exclaimed. "Whoever did such a thing?"

The man hid a grin. "The earl, milady."

Judith burst out laughing. "Rarefied indeed. Bring it in, then." She watched with a foolish grin as ducks and chickens, cheeses and potted meats, a ham and a smoked salmon were carried in. Then came huge bags of nuts and fruits.

"Well, Mrs. Pardoe," said Judith. "I don't think we'll starve over Christmas."

The woman grinned. "That we won't, milady. I have mince pies a-baking, and soon you'll have the best lemon tarts this side of London."

Judith went off to relate this story to Eleanor.

"Sending supplies post? How wonderful. Nicholas said Leander lived in his own rarefied world."

Judith's own thought. Leander's natural metier was a rarefied world of treasures and places, and she was deliberately rubbing the gloss off his own private palace.

She looked around anxiously at the drawing room.

A few delicate items had been removed, and chairs had been rearranged for comfort not elegance. A baby blanket draped a gold satin sofa and a rag doll graced the carpet. Magpie was curled up in front of the fire. "Oh dear," she said.

Eleanor touched her gently. "He won't mind. No one could want to live in this place as it was before. It's coming to life."

Chapter Twenty-one

Judith prayed Eleanor was correct, and stuck to her course. She gathered her troops to venture out after greenery. She found a small crowd of local people waiting by the causeway, as if hesitant to cross. They were all looking for work, and some were only children. It was clear many were merely curious, and hoping that a day's casual labor would give them a glimpse of the famous house. Others, however, had the pinched look of the desperate, and worn clothes that were only too familiar.

Recklessly, Judith employed them all. Some were set to bringing in firewood, and a few of the frailest were sent to help in the house, but most came with her to find Christmas boughs. She was pleased to see Bastian and Rosie mixing in with the village children without any self-consciousness. But then why shouldn't they? They had been village children themselves until a short while ago.

As she wandered with her employees, Judith chatted. The people soon lost their awe, and told her of local history and customs. They were proud of the Temple, true enough, but woven through all they said was a message of neglect.

The care of a lord for his land and his people had been missing here for nearly two generations. There was no expectation, for example, that leaking roofs would be soon mended, or Christmas bounty would be given to the poorest by the big house. Such charity was now in the hands of the vicar, and a few of the wealthier tenants, but in these postwar times their resources were stretched thin.

Judith determined that the Temple would do its part as of now; then wondered if she had enough food; then discarded the doubts. If they had to eat bread and cheese at the Temple, she'd make sure the poor had their baskets. She asked Eleanor to supervise the work and set off briskly for the village. She was halfway there when she realized she could have used the gig.

She laughed. She'd grown used to using her feet.

The vicar was in, and was delighted and flustered to meet the countess so unexpectedly. Something else Judith had not taken into account. She caught a glimpse of herself in a mirror, flushed and wind-blown. Oh, she was doing this countessing all wrong.

She brushed it aside. "You must excuse me coming here like this, Reverend Molde, but I must have the names of the most needy people in the locality who have not yet been helped. I wish to give them Christmas charity."

The man provided the list with alacrity. "It will be most welcome, Lady Charrington. We do what we can, but times are hard."

"Yes, and the earl and I are most appreciative. I do assure you, however, that in future we will be taking our responsibilities to the people hereabouts most seriously. We hope you will give us the benefit of your advice."

The man assured her of his willingness.

"Now," she said, "I must return to the house, for we are very busy there. We will, of course, attend

Christmas Day Service. May I hope you will dine with us on Boxing Day?''

She left with Reverend Molde's delighted thanks ringing in her ears. She knew from her own life in a vicarage how hard it could be to fill all the charitable needs of the parish, and still have enough for the family. She knew how flattering an invitation to the big house was.

On the one hand she felt pleasure to be bringing such joy, but on the other she felt most distinctly an impostor. But she *was* the Countess of Charrington. If she shrank from these duties, no one would do them for her.

She enjoyed the brisk walk back, and the brief time to herself. She took a moment to lean against a gate and survey Leander's land.

Leander's home.

Their home.

And he and it were in her loving care.

Back at the Temple she almost staggered with shock. The hall seemed bursting with people, sorting greenery, tying it into bunches, and decorating the place. Though some simply stood gaping. A rumble of gossip filled the air, topped by the high voices of children. She saw one huddle of village children around Bastian, who was showing off his rat.

An enormous silver punch bowl full of spiced ale sat on a walnut table, and all present were helping themselves as they wished. That doubtless explained the high spirits.

There were trays of mince pies and cake, half empty.

Was the whole village here? It was like a market-place.

Perhaps this was going too far.

But the place was positively humming with life.

Judith grinned and went off to the kitchen. She first sent up oranges for the children, then set to making up the charity baskets. She had the ham cut up and shared among them, but could see no way of quickly dividing the living fowl. Despite Mrs. Pardoe's first protests, all the pies went, and a great deal of the fruit and nuts.

"Their need is greater than ours," she told the woman.

Mrs. Pardoe smiled. "You're right, there, milady. It's a blessing you're giving."

"Yet 'tis better to give than to receive. And better still," Judith added, "to make sure there is no want."

She made arrangements for all the baskets to be delivered, then ran upstairs to put her mantle away before joining in the fun in the hall. As she was leaving her room she saw the last of the unpacking, Sebastian's poetry—the single volume of each, and the twenty new ones. She picked them up to carry down to the library on her way. She certainly didn't want her first husband's poetry in her bedroom.

Then she felt guilty at that uncharitable thought. Oh, when would she be free of this rift in her mind?

She found a space on the gleaming mahogany shelves close to Sebastian's portrait, and put the books there. The glossy, expensive volumes looked at home in this elegance. She supposed she could now send one to the Regent, and perhaps he was wondering where his copy was. They said he had a taste for the sentimental.

She took out one of the new ones, and ran a gentle finger down the heavily gilded border. How sad it was that Sebastian had never realized the extent of his renown. Perhaps he would have been less peevish. How sad, how terrible, that she didn't miss him at all, when she had been the center of his life.

She opened the book, feeling the new stiffness of

it, guilty that she had felt no inclination to open it before. It opened at a sonnet, a form he rarely used.

> *The dancing rays of summer sun must fade*
> *And larksong die, shrill loudly as it might,*
> *For Judith steps o'er verdant sward so light,*
> *As raises song as if by angels made.*

She stared at the meaningless words.

Song as if by angels made? But she couldn't sing, and he knew for he had complained of it.

It was a revelation. Not one word of this poetry had anything to do with her at all. Sebastian had written poetry to some ideal woman of his imagining, and complained all the days of their marriage because Judith was not she.

She collapsed down in a library chair—one of those ingenious types that had so delighted Leander.

She burst into tears.

Leander hurried in search of Judith. He was aware of a change in the house—there seemed a devilish number of people underfoot, for one thing, and a hell of a racket— but he was mainly intent on finding his wife. He and Nicholas had ridden to Redoaks, and finding their wives and children gone, pursued them here.

A grinning yokel said he thought the countess was in the library, so Leander headed there. He opened the heavy paneled door and heard weeping. He stopped as if frozen. Damnation. He should have known this house was too much for anyone, even Judith.

She sat hunched over, head in hands, crying as if her heart was breaking. He went over swiftly and knelt by her side. "Judith? What is it? You mustn't cry like this. . . ."

She looked up, her huge eyes awash with tears, her lids red. "Leander? Oh, Leander, I can't sing!"

He was about to laugh at this absurd pronouncement when a book slid from her fingers. Rossiter's poetry. Whatever she said, she was sitting in front of that blasted portrait and weeping for her first husband. The pain in his chest was extraordinary. Did hearts truly break?

He raised her, and took her seat, then drew her down into his lap. "I'll make it right," he said, though it was a damned stupid thing to say. Falling in love seemed to turn everything upside down, and make being an idiot unavoidable. He held her tight as she sniffed and blew her nose on a handkerchief. He stroked damp tendrils of hair away from her eyes. He wanted to kiss her, but she wouldn't want that at this moment.

"I'm sorry," she gulped. "You must think me a perfect fool."

The only thing to do was joke about it. "Why would I think that?" he teased. "You've just realized you are supposed to live in this mausoleum, and are considering the least painful ways to kill yourself."

She rewarded him with a gurgle of laughter. "Not at all. I'm determined to tame it." She looked up cautiously. "I ordered the plinths and vases moved. I thought if the children played in the hall it could start the rot nicely."

"It's worth a try. We appear to have the village fair in there at the moment."

He didn't seem upset, so Judith gathered her courage. "And I did think a billiard table in there would help, too."

He grinned. "Excellent idea. I'm very partial to the game. I also bought the children the equipment for battledore and shuttlecock. That should chase the disapproving spirits away."

Judith smiled and wrapped her arms around his neck. "Oh, Leander, I am happy you're back."

He could feel his own besotted smile stretching his cheeks. "Are you?"

"Very much. What happened in London?"

He quickly related their handling of the situation, all the while wanting to loosen her hair, and kiss her wildly; to explore her, enter her, and lose himself in her. . . .

"Thirty thousand pounds?" said Judith, though she could hardly keep her mind on what he was saying. She wanted to kiss him. She wanted to smooth the hair that fell onto his forehead, and slide her hand inside his jacket so as to be closer to his skin. . . .

"Yes, but it's gone." He rubbed his thumb over her lips.

"Oh dear." She kissed that thumb lightly.

His hand cupped and cherished her cheek. "I thought of lying to you, and saying we'd retrieved some of it, but I don't want lies between us. I do want to put that much money aside for Bastian and Rosie, though. They need never know it wasn't from their father, and it"—he looked again at the book on the floor—"it will keep his memory warm for them."

Judith felt tears welling in her eyes again. "Oh, Leander. Why shouldn't they feel gratitude where it belongs?"

His thumbs wiped away the tears. "I don't mind. I'll have years to plant love in their hearts if I can. Sebastian has lost you and them."

Judith shook her head. "He never had us. Leander, I can't sing."

"What on earth . . . ?"

Judith swooped down to retrieve the book from the floor. She sought for the sonnet, and thrust it before him. "Look. All this stuff about voices made by angels. I *can't* sing, and if I tried, he hated it. Not a word of this poetry is about me!"

Leander didn't know how to handle this tragedy. She must be devastated. "I'm sorry, Judith. Do you think there was someone else?"

She stared at him. "Someone else? Of course not. But I was just an excuse for him to write poetry about this perfect creature. No wonder I could never match the ideal." She laughed for joy. "I really don't need to feel guilty about not loving him, do I?"

"No," said Leander numbly.

Judith froze, then leapt off his lap. "Oh, criminy."

Leander rose carefully. "You've stopped loving him?"

Judith stood straight. "You said no lies, didn't you? I never loved him, Leander. Oh, that's not true. I loved him, I suppose, at the first, but it was a poor sort of love, for it did not last. I hadn't loved him for years when I let you marry me, thinking I was a grieving widow. I'm sorry, I'm sorry. If you want me to leave—"

He grabbed her and swung her high. "Leave! Not on your life! I'll tie you to a marble pillar first. Do you mean there's a chance for me?"

"Put me down! Chance for you?"

He slid her down and said softly, "Chance for me to capture your heart. I've discovered the faculty of love, Judith, and it is all bound up in you."

"You can't . . ."

"I can. I do." He held her tight against his chest. "It's terrifying. I feel as if I would die without you." He pushed her back a little and she saw him struggle for the gloss that had protected him all his life. "Do you mind?" he said. "I'll try not to embarrass you."

Judith cradled his face. "My dearest love, how could you possibly embarrass me?"

His eyes lit, and shone a little with tears. "You can love me?"

"I *do* love you. Oh, Leander, I'm going to cry again!"

"Don't! I can't bear it. Why were you crying when I came in?"

"For poor Sebastian and all he missed." She drew his head down and kissed him. "I'm afraid of this much happiness," she whispered.

"Don't be. If anything goes wrong, I'll make it right." It no longer seemed a foolish boast. With Judith's love he could do anything. He kissed her deeply, intently, his hands adoring her, as did his lips.

Judith felt every point of contact of their bodies, close, but not close enough. Her knees weakened, and when she began to sag he let her, and fell with her to the floor.

He was on top of her, sweet weight. She was on top of him, and could lose herself in the depth of his eyes as his hands dissolved her gown, freeing flesh to his lips.

She unfastened his waistcoat, pulled at his shirt until she could trace his belly with her tongue, grow drunk on the taste, the smell of his skin. She nipped with her teeth, full of strange hungers, and explored his navel.

What was she doing?

He shrugged out of his jacket and waistcoat. Flung off his shirt. "Judith. My God. We shouldn't . . ." But there was no pause before he brushed her breasts with his lips, and made magic there.

Judith threw back her head and cried out. He smothered it with his hand, laughing. "Oh love! It wasn't going to be like this." But he didn't stop.

She pulled at him. "What is it? What?"

"I'll show you."

He entered. Her body seized him. "Oh criminy. Oh lord. Oh dear. It aches. It's going to make me sick again!"

"Oh, Judith. No. Not this time. Come with me."

"What?"

"Come to heaven."

Judith had a flash of crystal awareness that she was on the library carpet, mostly naked, writhing with Leander, and aching for something so terrible that she feared its achievement could kill her. She didn't care.

His lips captured hers. His hand slid between them.

Sensation swelled, and swelled. She would explode with it! She did, and kept shattering, and shattering until she broke free of everything, let go of everything, and found everything.

Her senses circled down like a top, spiraling slowly to earth, to reality, to Leander smiling at her, heavy on her, sweet heaviness. . . .

"An explosion of pleasure," she said in wonderment.

"I'm the first, aren't I?"

"Oh yes. Oh, poor Sebastian!"

He groaned, but was still smiling. "Why poor?"

"I don't think he ever felt like that." She glanced at him. "Do men . . . ?"

"Oh yes. I just did. I was with you, dearest wife. I will always be with you. In sickness and in health. In heaven or hell. . . ." He rested his head on her shoulder. "All places. All times. . . ."

She stroked his hair softly, eyes unfocused on the painted ceiling. "You are everything to me, too, Leander. I was not truly alive until I met you. . . ."

He looked up and grinned. "I had a most elegant bedding of you planned for tonight, sweet helpmeet. Every step worked out . . ."

She chuckled. "Tonight is yet to come, and I do want to know how to do it properly."

"I doubt we'll ever do it more properly than we just did, love."

Judith's eyes focused on the ceiling. "Leander."

Caught by her tone, he rolled half off her. "What?"

"The ceiling. Your grandfather's up there again."

She instinctively moved to cover herself, and then she started to laugh. "Lord, he looks so shocked!"

Leander laughed with her. "*I* think he's grinning. It's probably the most fun he's had in forty years!"

Some time later, Lord and Lady Charrington decorously joined the rollicking festivities in their hall. Nicholas and Eleanor were fully in the spirit of the decorating, and Arabel was riding on her father's shoulders.

Nicholas looked across the room at them and smiled. It was almost as if he knew what had been going on, though Judith had checked that her dress was neat, and her hair properly pinned. Leander looked as elegant as always. She slid a look at him, and saw the way he was looking at her. Heavens, no wonder Nicholas had guessed.

She wanted to hide her face in her husband's jacket, but instead she tugged him under a kissing bough and kissed him, right there in the hall. There was a mighty cheer. Leander laughed, then beamed about like an old-time country squire. "This is perfect."

Judith, too, surveyed the Temple's perfect hall. It was festooned with greenery and red ribbon. A log fire roared in the huge hall hearth, mixing the tang of wood smoke with that of pine, fir, and rosemary, and the spice of ale and orange peel.

Smiling faces, and happy chatter were the music here.

Children were hurtling about the open space. Even more children than before.

Judith saw that the Charles Knollis family were in here in force. She led Leander over to his aunt. Judith hugged the woman, then Leander followed suit. Judith approved of the encompassing way Aunt Lucy returned the gesture. "I hope you are as happy in your new home as I am in mine, Aunt Lucy."

The woman shook her head and looked around. "I never would have believed it. You're a miracle worker. I wondered if Charles would handle the shock when we walked in, but he seems to like it." She looked to where the haggard man was sitting by the wall with a little one on his knee.

"He's better?" Judith asked.

"Much improved, though his speech is still unclear. Getting out of this place has eased him tremendously. He's better day by day now he no longer has this burden on his shoulders. I came over in case you had need of things, dear, so there's a ham in the kitchen, and a batch of damson pies."

"Thank you, but I hope you don't mind that some of it has gone to the poor. I am determined the Temple will do its duty in the area. Not that we blame you," she said hastily. "I know you have been unable to run things as you would wish."

"That's the truth." Lucy smiled at Judith. "Leander was a lucky man the day he met you, my dear."

Leander's arm snaked around Judith. "Wasn't I? And remarkably prescient when I didn't take no for an answer."

Judith laughed at the memory of that first meeting. "And you the golden-tongued diplomat."

He looked into her eyes. "I've discovered diplomacy is not the key to secrets of the heart."

Judith realized they were neglecting Lucy, though the smiling woman did not seem to mind.

"Thank you for coming," Judith said. "I hope you will all come over as often as you can. Our children should be playmates, and we need regular crowds to bring this place to life."

Lucy chuckled. "I'm sure you two will soon start a crowd of your own."

Judith blushed. Lucy dashed off to corral two of her sons who were heading for the spiced ale.

Judith and Leander went over to his uncle and exchanged Christmas greetings. The older man couldn't speak well, but it was clear he was delighted to see Leander in his home. He gripped Leander's hand. "Welcome. Welcome."

Leander knelt and kissed the hand. His uncle touched his head like a blessing. Judith kissed Charles Knollis's cheek. "Thank you," she said. She knew what it meant to Leander to have a family, and one who loved him.

Bastian and Rosie came running over, full of questions, and Leander explained again what had happened in London. He assured them that Timothy Rossiter was safely on the seas.

Then Judith, Leander, Bastian, and Rosie wandered the hall as a family, greeting and being greeted. More oranges appeared and Bastian and Rosie went off to offer them to the children. Someone started a song, and rough country voices took it up with no pretensions of tunefulness or elegance.

> *Here's health to the master,*
> *And a long time to live.*
> *For he's been so thoughtful*
> *And ready to give.*
> *Wassail, wassail, merry wassail.*

Nasal, gravelly, the chorus swelled up to fill the pristine hall.

> *Here's health to his lady*
> *For her kindly care,*
> *It's but right and proper*
> *That she well do fare,*
> *Wassail, wassail, merry wassail.*

Judith had no hesitation in joining in with the chorus, her imperfect voice lost in the swell. Leander sang, too, rather more tunefully.

> *Here's health to his children,*
> *The lively young sprites,*
> *His line shall be long now*
> *If he has his rights.*
> *Wassail, wassail, merry wassail.*

Rosie and Bastian giggled over this, but they, too, joined in the chorus.

> *And this is a fine house*
> *That noble do stand,*
> *We pray it be blessed*
> *As any in the land.*
> *Wassail, wassail, merry wassail.*

Judith could almost imagine the marble walls absorbing this rough, traditional sound and being transformed into something more true to the good English earth.

Eleanor and Nicholas suddenly appeared at their side, with a wine bottle and four glasses.

"Spiced ale not to your taste?" asked Leander. "Begone. I'm working on being a good Englishman."

Nicholas had a mischievous twinkle in his eyes. "Then this is definitely just what you need." He turned the bottle so the label neatly inscribed *Elderberry 1814* could be seen.

Leander groaned. "Is my love to be put to the test so soon?"

"Ha!" declared Judith. "If I had my way, you would be facing fig juice and vinegar, you wretch!" She took the glass Nicholas had poured and passed it to Leander.

All their eyes were on him as he tasted, and Judith

could see the control he'd clamped upon himself. He sipped cautiously, then relaxed in amazement. "Remarkable. It's very good. It really is." He put his arm around Judith. "Not that I should be surprised. All you touch is good and sound. Will it offend you if I say you truly are my angel bride?"

Judith's smile was radiant. "How could it, for if I have wings and halo, my dearest Rogue, they are assuredly of your providing."

<hr />

More from *New York Times* bestselling author Jo Beverley

• *An Unwilling Bride* • *An Arranged Marriage* •
The Shattered Rose • *Forbidden* • *Tempting Fortune*
• *Dangerous Joy* •

<hr />

The first QRcode will take you to www.jobev.com if you have the app to read it. The second will take you to the page for the Company of Rogues.